April Loves Black Coffee
First Impressions

T.B. Solangel

April Loves Black Coffee
First Impressions

ISBN-10: 1481813129
ISBN-13: 978-1481813129
Volume #1
Reformatted Edition April 2014

The author published an earlier version of this story online with the title(s) "Conversations between Us" and "Conversations between a Gentleman and a Lady" under the pseudonym Solangel between the years of 2003 and 2007.

Cover Design by: Pa Chia Xiong

Book Design by: *CreateSpace*

DEDICATION

To Q.V.,

For all the heart attacks you spoil me with.

ACKNOWLEDGEMENT

A heartwarming thank you to my family for your continuous support of my storytelling endeavors. You are my bright, marvelous, and awe-inspiring guardian angels. The sacrifices, including your enduring perseverance of "making a way out of no way," have made who I am today. I don't know what I would do without your tact and endless love. My heart loves you so much!

To Q.V., your undivided affection gives me more heart attacks than I deserve. You are always by my side–my rock, my pillar–encouraging me to tackle my fears and chase after my dreams. You've brought so much joy, adventure, and love to my life. You mean more to me than you'll ever know. I love you.

To Kelly H.L., thank you for being so supportive and enthusiastic about my first publishing endeavor. Through all the times that we've lost touch and reconnected–all the conversations, laughter, and contemplation–you remain a great and constant friend.

To Pachia Chia Xiong, you swooped in like an Angel and brought to life the emotions and tone of this story with your majestic designs. Thank you for such sincerity and heart for ALBC!

To Con.Template, how do I express my appreciation for your sweet sentiments and splendid advices? It is amazing to have a fellow Soomp! writer's camaraderie and solace. Words will not do my gratitude justice, so I will simply resign with a thank you for all the meaningful messages and amazing counsel. You have been a great pillar of support and guidance.

To my Soomp! readers, I grew up with the simple dream of writing stories and sharing them with those who pursue the joy of reading. You have allowed me not only to achieve my dream, but also take it to greater heights. I could never publish this story without your enduring encouragements, strong and sustaining support, and moving motivations. To put into words and convey my gratitude, thankfulness, and appreciation I would need a bigger heart to contain all the love I have for you all. Thank you, thank you, thank you so much!

And finally, a special thank you to my editors who have dedicated their time, energy, and effort. You are ALBC's guardians!

April Loves Black Coffee
First Impressions

T.B. Solangel

ABOUT THE SERIES

April Loves Black Coffee: First Impressions is the first published novel of the original fiction posted online (between the years of 2003 to 2007) known as "Conversations between Us" and "Conversations between a Gentleman and a Lady." Similar to its original roots, the story follows the narration of Maybelline Lee as she crosses into the treacherous and enthralling worlds of Yoon Jaewon and Choi Sangwoo.

This revised version of the original story reflects the dark undertones, and mature evolution, of not only the characters but the story itself. Dialogues, scenes, plot development, and characters have been rewritten and revamped. Elements of the original fiction have been warped to reflect a more contemporary tone befitting of the story's evolution.

Some important changes to the published version include:

- Maybelline Lee is 21-years-old.
- The character "Feet" is now "Spyder."
- Lina is not only May's best friend, but also cousin.
- The story is written in present tense as opposed to past tense in the online version.
- The reasons for May's involvement with Choi Sangwoo and Yoon Jaewon have been complicated for plot strengthening and background. However, the specifics and original details of their involvement remain unchanged.

The second book in this series is April Loves Black Coffee: *Last Conversations*

April Loves Black Coffee
First Impressions

+

Someone once told me:
First impressions are everything. Conversations are the rest.

"Where my heart still is, I admit I am not too sure.
When the sky starts to cry, I become reminiscent and lonely.
Although I would like to think I've moved on, I can't help but think that
I shouldn't have let go, I should've held on tight.
The beginning was so pure and untainted.
When a person is gone, should you miserably miss him or regrettably
remember him?
If you miss him, do you look back at the old pictures and cry?
If you remember him, do you recall the tone of his voice–the rise and fall of
his laughter?
Do you think back to the conversations between you and him?
Conversations between us?
I need another cup of coffee.

I need him."

April Loves Black Coffee.

PROLOGUE

Maybelline! Service for table twelve!"

I bite my bottom lip in an annoyed fashion when my birth name ricochets off the walls of the restaurant slash bar. Despite the fact that The Trax is trickling with up-tempo music and the cadence of loud chatter, a few customers turn their heads in the Son's direction with natural curiosity. Surely, the waitress with the same name as the makeup brand, Maybelline, will be bounding towards the assistant manager's command any moment now. Maybe she is wearing the everlasting lip color or expert eyeliner or both. Instead, the brand's real life counterpart continues to stand by the bar doing her best to wait out the attention.

"Why does he insist on calling me by my birth name?" I complain in vain under my breath. I lift up a hand to let Son know I hear him. I motion with exaggeration towards the bustling bar, making sure Son can see I am in the middle of an order. Simultaneously, my shoulders sag under an invisible bag of fatigue. I am on the fourth hour of my eight-hour shift. There is never down time or a dull moment at The Trax.

Well, whose idea was it to work here? I keep my head low and look up through my dark eyelashes at the surrounding chaos. I am leaning against the right side of the full bar, blending in with the few customers who are only interested in drinking tonight. A cascade of neon yellow and orange colors, blending and melting from one person to the next, rotates around the venue.

I watch our resident bartender, Tailor Jung, finish the Strawberry Vodka Martini mix ordered by a regular female customer sitting at table nine. I can see she is waiting impatiently despite the fact that I have only been gone two minutes.

"He calls you by your first name because he has a superiority complex," Tailor answers my question with a smirk on his lips. He places the finished Martini in front of me. The pink liquid spills over the top of the crystal glass; the bubbles are settling at the bottom of the drink in a delicious manner. Tailor's dark eyes shine underneath the glaring purple and white lantern lights that stretch above the island of the bar. "And because you let him," Tailor adds.

"I don't let him." I refute it quickly. "Son thinks he owns my name just because he hired me." My little black waitressing order book, bound by its intrepid leather spine and cover, folds neatly into the short apron I am wearing. Now that my hands are free, I pick up the Martini in a steady manner.

"Dare you to correct him then." Tailor throws me one of his signature tip-increase grins before he moves to the other end of the bar. Tailor only uses that specific smile on female customers to draw their attention in and boost his tip scale. Aside from being one of the best bartenders in town, Tailor is also incredibly talented at convincing people to spend more money than they initially plan to. This is what makes Tailor one of The Trax's best assets. I, on the other hand, have a hard time recommending the most basic appetizers. Some people are simply more talented than others.

I concede to our usual bantering by default. It is a tough night at The Trax. I handle table nine's Martini with great care as I veer away from the bar.

Wary of the four-inch heels strap to my feet, I begin my trek down the steps that the bar situates on. I see the brunette customer at table nine sucking in her breath, undoubtedly praying that I will not drop her drink. *It's been a long day for me, so there is no guarantee girl.* My intuition is holding her breath.

It is Saturday night and The Trax is in full swing. Individuals and groups occupy every single table and booth, including bar stools. Most of the people are in the restaurant area, engaged in conversations that range from work to love to stress. In about another hour, the extravagant chandeliers that drape over the maroon ceiling are highlights of multicolored strobe lights and hues. The large restaurant area, complete with its booths and individual tables will be converted to a large dance floor. The plush curtains covering the center stage will be undone to reveal a DJ booth in front of a massive LED screen. In short, The Trax is a restaurant and bar during business hours. After hours, The Trax converts into an underground club with its skewed dance floor, dimmed neon lights, and loud thumping electric dance music.

"Here is your drink." My voice is just below the shouting range when I finally reach table nine. To this very day, I still do not know her name, but everyone at The Trax refers to this regular customer as Number Nine because of her preference for this table. She never answers any personal questions about herself; the only time Number Nine speaks directly to a Trax employee is when she wants to order something. She is that type of customer and not that type of client. Even Tailor, with his wit and charm, has not been able to crack her. It is a running bet among our employees to know something else about Number Nine other than her preferred drink.

Number Nine is engaged in conversation with her friend when I set down her Martini. Her voice is low and rough. She is in crisis mode and her tone is anxious. "He is cheating on me. I just know it. I have to end it with him."

I retract from the table slowly. It really isn't any of my business to listen to her conversation, but I want to tell Number Nine her instincts are right; her boyfriend is cheating on her with a pretty blonde he brings in every Thursday afternoon. A momentary thought flashes in my mind to tell the poor girl that if she comes for Happy Hour Thursdays, she would undoubtedly run into her no-good boyfriend and his new Barbie doll.

I glance at Number Nine. She has her hands against her face now, shaking her head at her friend's words of consolation. Oblivious to the fact that I am still standing next to her, Number Nine reaches for her drink and gulps it down like a goldfish.

It is not my usual nature to meddle in other people's lives, but I am also not a sadist who enjoys knowing the bad news of another person's demise. If there is one staple to be working at The Trax, it is the fortune of being able to peek into other people's lives. Sometimes, it is hard to suppress my internal psychologist from stirring. It is both a blessing and a curse to have this obsessive-compulsive disorder to fine tune injustices that exist in the world. *Girl, you can do better.* My conscience has her red sunglasses on, desperate to give the anonymous tip.

"May, Son is giving you the stink eye. You better hurry to table twelve." A silky voice disrupts my bubble of thoughts. "By the way, one of them looks like a male supermodel," she adds in a husky tone.

Joolie, the only other female waitress at The Trax, taps my right shoulder on her way to the bar. She is all tight, black ensemble and dark, smoky eyes. Joolie flashes a fervent look towards table twelve.

I follow Joolie's gaze, but before it reaches table twelve Son distracts my line of vision. He is standing on the other side of the restaurant on his cell phone. Son has an anxious expression on his face from the result of a strained conversation. Undoubtedly, he is using his assistant manager powers to convince the person on the opposite line to give him what he wants. When we make eye contact, Son points to table twelve and mouths to me, "Get your butt over there. Now!"

I clear my throat and my five-year-old self yearns to stick her tongue at him. Son is overbearingly bossy and takes his job too seriously. It must be the result of his secret desire to rule the restaurant and bar world one day.

"Tell me how it goes!" Joolie orders before she rushes to the bar to fulfill an order.

I let out a low chuckle at Joolie's comment. One can always count on Joolie to notice the good, the bad, and the ugly at The Trax.

I straighten up and walk over to table twelve. I reach into my apron and pull out my trusty order book along with a ballpoint pen. I flip the order book to a new page and approach the table.

"Good evening, gentlemen. My name is May. I will be your waitress tonight. Can I get you started with some drinks?" The smile feels foreign on my face, but I lock it into place. My voice is the required light and airy tone all waitresses are supposed to have.

Oh wow. My intuition sits up in her chair. Of all the times that Joolie's failed to make an impression with her precursors, she certainly hit the head of the nail this time.

Five men are sitting around table twelve; one looking like the exact duplicate of the other as they stake their seats like chess pieces. The men pour over their respective menus as if ordering is a paramount decision. The men are in identical black suits complete with white dress shirts and black ties. They even have the same solemn facial expressions. They appear to form a small company party, although The Trax's usual clientele do not include businessmen.

In fact, The Trax's general demographic is mostly comprised of late adolescents and young adults in their early twenties and thirties with only one motivation in coming here–to have dinner with a date, to find a date, to talk about a date, and the list goes on. Yes, The Trax is that kind of establishment and not that kind of pleasant social environment for anything remotely professional. Everyone who walks into The Trax has their own agenda, and when everyone has just about the same agenda, it becomes quite predictable.

Tonight, however, the game changes.

The men sitting at table twelve do not fit the standard profile of a Trax client. They are not having simple weekend conversations either. In fact, the men are not only older in age but also demeanor and itinerary. It becomes palpable that there exists tension at the table, and it becomes apparent that one man is intimidating the other four.

This naturally draws my attention to him.

Oh my. The stunning creature is already waiting for my attention.

"May, what type of red wine is served here?" He is sitting in the chair directly across from me. His voice is cool and controlled, especially when he addresses me directly. The colors of his eyes are spectacular–a whirlpool of rich brown. I dub him Brown Eyes.

At the present moment, Brown Eyes is taking in the fact that I am wearing the standard black and white uniform all Trax employees are condemned to wear. *Is he checking me out?*

Suddenly, I am conscious of the black makeup I have piled on to hide my true age and the loose ponytail my hair is in. I am a lifetime of insecurities at the very moment. With a small reflex, I reach for my right ear to touch the small earring. I only do this when I am nervous and he notices.

There is a flicker of light shooting across those brown eyes as they follow my movement. He waits for my answer.

"Uh . . . we have the . . . uh . . . standard red wines, sir." I realize I am beginning to stumble over my sentence.

Have we met before? A wave of familiarity washes over me and I endure the feelings of déjà vu and nostalgia. *Well, if I have met Brown Eyes before how can I forget him?* I try to catch the fleeting thoughts in my head.

Before he answers, I peek at Brown Eyes through my eyelashes and an electric jolt courses through my veins again. I catch my breath before it escapes my throat. He is young, approximately late twenties, but the thin beard on his face makes him appear older. A heavy set of eyelashes coat his large brown eyes; and his dark eyebrows are at an angle to complement his prominent looks. His lips are together in a hard, fine line. Unlike his counterparts who are wearing suits, Brown Eyes is wearing a simple white dress shirt with the sleeves rolled up to his elbows. His black slacks make a casual statement, but the shiny sequence of a necklace around his neck signals that there is something remarkable that separates him from the rest.

Brown Eyes is strikingly handsome and breathtakingly . . . *hot,* for the lack of a better term. He sticks out like a sore thumb among the company he is sitting with. In fact, Brown Eyes does not belong in The Trax with the rest of its population. He should be plastered on a movie poster somewhere exotic like Paris or Hollywood–not sitting here waiting for me to get over his intoxicating presence to recite The Trax's wine menu.

"The standards?" His composure causes me to grapple with the fact that I am still lost in a trance. Brown Eyes wants me to elaborate, probably questioning my waitressing intelligence. I fall, hard and fast, back to reality. My intuition stands up, dusting her knees and elbows.

I blink deliberately and look down at my blank order book. I can feel the heat rise in my cheeks as I try to remember wine brands. I try to eliminate the robotic nuances as I begin to recite, "We have the Syrah which goes well with meat like beef and steak. The Malbec complements exotic dishes like Cajun or Indian. The Pinot Noir brings out the flavor in grilled salmon and chicken. And the Merlot is compatible with practically any entrée."

"Which one is your favorite?" Brown Eyes surprises me with his question. Whether he is simply making small talk or genuinely inquisitive, Brown Eyes strikes me as too worldly to care about what a simple waitress like me prefers.

No one, more specifically a customer, has ever asked me for my preference before. But then again, I have only worked here for six months. I keep my voice as steady as I can. "Um, I don't drink wine." *Oh May. Can you be professional and just suggest something? Like this amazingly striking man actually cares about your preferences.* I wish for the ground to swallow me up.

"What do you drink then?" Brown Eyes presses further, giving me the impression that he is trying to help salvage my embarrassment of being so inexperienced.

"Coffee." I find myself whispering. "It keeps me awake for the long shifts."

"Coffee," Brown Eyes echoes after me. For the life of me, I cannot imagine why he cares to carry on this awkward conversation. Swiftly, Brown Eyes nods his head before he changes the subject back to the wine order. "We'll have the Merlot then." A look crosses his face. Maybe he is wondering why I am rambling on. His eyes glow for some reason, leading me to speculation.

I nod my head at Brown Eyes' concise wine order and push for the appetizer and entrées next. "Would you . . . and everyone else . . . like to order right now?"

The other men around the table are staring inquisitively at me. *Did I speak a foreign language?* I look back at them with the same awkwardness. Brown Eyes mumbles incoherently in a foreign tongue that I catch as American English. As though they finally have permission to speak, the men at the table fire off. They make it a point to flip through the menus and gesture toward the entrées.

I keep my composure as I write down their orders. At our monthly staff meetings, Son often holds a waiting contest. I have always placed second to Son when it comes to memorizing and taking down customers' orders. Today, however, I am having some problems for a number of reasons. The most significant and distracting reason is Brown Eyes. He seems to survive without the need to blink. Even when he is telling me his order of the steak, Brown Eyes keeps his gaze steady and unrelenting on me.

"That will be all," Brown Eyes says after the last member of his group orders. His voice is controlled, but it carries with it a beat of breathlessness.

Why is he so good-looking even when he wants to shoo me away? "Thank you. I will put your orders in and be back with your Merlot." I close my black order book and proceed to collect the menus.

Brown Eyes leans back in his chair languidly. He drapes a casual arm against the back of his chair and watches me intently. He doesn't say a word and neither do the other men at the table.

The last menu slips out of my fingers onto the table, and the man to my left helps me. He leans forward and his eyes are soft, almost apologetic. If I can read his mind, he is probably telling me he's sorry that his handsome Boss makes me so clumsy. Maybe Brown Eyes mesmerizes waitresses all the time. The other men around the table are catching on and they are forming identical, amused expressions.

"Thank you," I mumble to Brown Eyes' helpful man. I quickly tuck the menus under my arm and walk away from the table. My heart races and I realize my palms are sweaty. *Don't trip. Don't trip.* When I find balance on the main restaurant floor again, my thoughts continue to dance.

Aish! What is going on? Why did I turn into some kind of silly putty just because an overwhelmingly attractive and enticing customer gazes at me like that? I am usually immune to that kind of attention. A voice on the right side of my shoulder whispers, "Because he's not like the rest. That God-given creature is staring at you!" The other voice, on the left side of my shoulder, hisses, "Just because he asked you what you like to drink doesn't mean he wants to marry you. Get it together May."

I shake my head to chase away the train of thoughts. An electric current is rushing through my veins, waking me up from a long and deep slumber. Suddenly, the night does not seem too long and tedious. I feel as if I can wait tables and serve customers until sunrise.

I try to suppress the giddy schoolgirl inside of me, dying to free herself and somersault all the way back to table twelve. I head through the throng of tables to the kitchen. The chef and his assistants are bustling around the large oval kitchen. As usual, the kitchen staff is attempting to complete the restaurant's orders in an assembly line manner. I place table twelve's order on top of the waiting counter.

"Excuse me," I mutter to a kitchen staff when I am inches away from colliding into him. He is carrying ten dirty dishes in his arms; he nods his head in acknowledgement and continues his gait to the other side of the kitchen.

I head to the small cellar in the back of the kitchen where we keep the wine. The Trax stocks its wine in large, ornate cabinets that line the entire wall. All the wine, including exclusive alcohol bottles, is ordered by date. Since the Merlot is one of our most popular choices, I have no trouble finding its signature dark bottle. I extract the bottle of Merlot from the cabinet and walk to the right side of the closet to pull out five wine glasses.

"How'd it go?" Joolie enters the kitchen with an armful of dirty dishes. Her cheeks flush with color to match the stars in her eyes. "Isn't he gorgeous?" Joolie doesn't need to elaborate on who it is at table twelve.

"Not really." I squeeze by Joolie, hoping she doesn't see the lie on my face. "He's . . . too pretty."

"Pretty? He's drop-dead gorgeous May!" Joolie gives me a desperate and devious smile. "I've never seen him here before. He must be in town for business or something. They're all wearing suits and ties at that table."

"Yeah," I mumble. Before I can stop myself, my mouth runs away from me. "I think I've seen him before." I feel my intuition grimacing at my confession. It is too soon for such a conclusion, but I can't help the nagging feeling brewing at the pit of my stomach.

"You know what," Joolie interjects as her eyes gloss over, "you're right. Me too! He looks like that actor, Song Seung Hun! I watch his dramas all the time."

No. Not that kind of familiar. A wave of disappointment comes over me. I let out at laugh at Joolie's interpretation of my comment. "I have to go. I owe table twelve their drinks."

"You know we've never seen anyone like that before!" Joolie laughs as I exit the kitchen.

I shake my head at Joolie's joke. I continue back to the bustling restaurant. When I near her table, Number Nine waves at me. Her Martini glass is empty and she is undoubtedly requesting a refill. I give her a quick acknowledgement smile.

"The shipment should be arriving in about two hours." The man sitting to the left of Brown Eyes, the one who helped me when I dropped one of the menus earlier, is reporting in a voice that is slightly above an octave of a shrill.

"And all the heads are accounted for?" Brown Eyes questions in that same signature calm and controlled tone.

"Yes," Menu Helper answers. "Boss," he adds anxiously.

The rise and fall of their syllables signal a secret and important conversation. Almost immediately, I feel as though I am brushing against a restless monster living in a foreign world. I know things like danger and violence existing in the world, but to interact and be in the presence of its citizens is new territory for me. A chill comes over me when I catch Brown Eyes' title.

"Here are your drinks." *He's making me feel like I am interrupting something important.* The thought crosses my mind when I set the bottle of Merlot on the table. I keep my eyes low as the heat in my cheek rises yet again. I hope he doesn't think I am eavesdropping on his conversation.

"Thank you." Brown Eyes disquiet voice permeates the air.

"No problem," I mumble as I keep my hands steady. I place the wine glasses at the center of the table. From the depths of my waitress apron, I produce a wine opener. With precision, I wrap it around the tip of the Merlot and twist. I am well aware that I have the undivided attention of all five clients as I open the bottle. I remind myself to breathe when I fill their glasses. After I am done, I gesture with open palms at their glasses of wine.

Whew! I look calm and professional. Inside, I am one impulse away from bolting off the platform table twelve is elevated on.

In unison, the men thank me and I leave. Just as I turn, I make the amateur mistake of glancing at Brown Eyes again. He has his eyes on me, intense and just as provocative as moments ago. I cannot understand his curiosity in me, but I can understand my curiosity for him.

I have seen him before, I tell myself. I just cannot remember from where or when. A face like his is truly unforgettable, but I cannot pinpoint any relevancy. It crosses my mind that maybe he is thinking the same. He remembers me from somewhere too, but cannot pinpoint it either. However, Brown Eyes doesn't strike me as the kind who would struggle with his memory. I do my best to back away from table twelve without tripping on my own two feet.

"Maybelline! Table two!" Son shouts my name from across the room again. He is pointing frantically at the new group of people pouring in. I breathe a sigh of relief. For once, I am glad that Son always has an endless list of responsibilities for me. I turn toward the direction of table two and allow the increasing foot traffic at The Trax to distract me. I take table two's orders and spend more than five minutes helping the clients understand the differences between our popular sauces.

From my peripheral view as the night progresses, I am well aware that Brown Eyes scans the room for me occasionally. Despite the seemingly serious topics at his table, Brown Eyes' gaze catches moments of me throughout the restaurant. His gazes are always brief, but the effect they have on me is long lasting. The dance of I-see-you-looking-at-me goes on even after their entrées.

By the time I deliver the check to table twelve, Brown Eyes picks up the black book with great ease and asks me, "When is your break time?"

Once again, his question takes me back. My next break time is not until another hour, but the latter part of me, the part that believes in happily-ever-after blurts out, "Five more minutes" instead. *What is he going to do now that he knows?*

Brown Eyes hands me back the checkbook with his credit card neatly placed inside. I am nearly transported to a different world when his lips break into a striking smile. He states simply, "I hope you enjoy your break. You've been working very hard," and I try to stop myself from melting into the floor. I keep the smile on my face and take the checkbook from him.

I keep my composure as I walk to the cashier's counter to charge his card.

Did you think someone as handsome, mysterious, intelligent, and beguiling as that man is going to ask you on a brief date on your break? My thoughts scold me. I want to laugh, but the humor buries between embarrassment and desire.

When I return with the checkbook, I drop it off quickly and head over to the next table. I spend no more than a minute chatting with the customers when I notice the activity at table twelve. One-by-one, the men at table twelve leave. They must think I am the waitress utterly smitten with their Boss. Menu Helper nods his head in my direction when he notices I am looking their way. Brown Eyes is on the phone now, his eyebrows coming together to form an expression that should never come across his striking features. He heads the line out of the restaurant. Brown Eyes' stride is confident, inexorable, and ambitious. Brown Eyes doesn't look back at me when he exits the doors with his men in tow.

"It's almost nine!" Son's voice cuts across my silent observation.

I snap out of my daze and pick up a dirty plate from the neighboring table. I make my way back to table twelve to pick up the payment. The black checkbook is shut, but I can visibly see the final receipt sticking from the top. Absentmindedly, I pick up the checkbook. The thin, glossy paper flutters out of the checkbook. I almost let out a gasp when I see the final amount. The Trax, with all its commotion, disappears in the background.

$280 dollars. *$100 tip for May—for her superior customer service.* His writing is elegant, concise, and defined.

CHAPTER ONE

My birth name is Maybelline Lee.

I am not entirely sure if the makeup brand Maybelline was already established when I was born, but my parents decided to add a Western touch to my Korean name Mayi Lee. My father was convinced that his children were destined to relocate to the United States one day. Bless his heart; my father was every bit of a romantic. However, despite the good measure that Maybelline symbolizes all things feminine embedded between the sleek pages of any given magazine, the name was lost in meaning when it rolled down the tongues of evil schoolboys who teased me for its difficult pronunciation. So, I shortened my name to the plain and simple month of May. May reminds me of springtime with colorful flowers and rays of sunshine; Maybelline reminds me of cosmetics on old women's faces trying to be younger, and young girls trying to be older.

In many ways, I am a simple girl in the simple world I work hard to maintain. Contrary to others around my age, I enjoy reading a good book as opposed to going out on a Friday night. My literacy heroines and heroes live in the dark literatures of Edgar Allan Poe, Stephen King, and Anne Rice to name a few. I go jogging, at least once a week, with my cousin because she is a health freak and insists I put my body through the torture. I possess no special talent except for my hospitality and workaholic determination. I am particularly partial to these characteristics.

I currently attend Seoul University as a junior in the noted department of psychology. I am optimistic about studying the malleable human psyche and all of its imperfections–a saying I once read in a prominent psychology book. It sounds great in theory to observe and analyze people, but when it comes to applicability, I am still not brave enough to apply for an internship. In the grand scheme of things, college is the great milestone I wish to conquer. This explains why I am juggling two jobs to save money for college in the fall. With every passing semester, it is increasingly difficult to come up with enough funds for books and tuition.

On top of being a workaholic this summer, I make it a point to remind myself, "This is it, my twenty-first year. It's my time to be an adult."

The first step to being an adult is to stress myself out and divide not only my time, but also body, across my ventures. In order to eliminate idle time and increase the numbers associated with my bank account, I have my schedule filled for seven days a week from morning to night. In the daytime, I work at the local convenience store, *Sansachun*, as a registrar and product maintenance specialist—which is a fancy title for checking off inventory, stocking products on shelves, and keeping the store organized. At night, I work as a waitress at The Trax. The Trax is my last resort for a second income. Although the venue is a lively and somewhat reputable place to work for, The Trax calls the most dangerous part of town home. It is a spinning top because members from different social scales mingle there. Dating, including other unmentionable vices, parades The Trax like a breeding ground.

Mall jobs are hard to come by during the summer season, and I am too young and inexperienced to work at the real clubs. The Trax offers quite an attractive incentive with its pay. Occasionally, I make a substantial amount of tips that would rival any waitress at any high-end restaurant.

Nevertheless, no one has ever tipped me a hundred dollars. Brown Eyes left quite the impression on me.

I end up keeping a copy of the tip receipt inside Nicolas Spark's *The Notebook*, not because Brown Eyes' nice handwriting is on it, but because it is a testament that I actually have a hundred dollar tip to my name. I am not sure if I am fascinated with the flattery, that someone thinks my customer service skills is worth that much, or if it is simply the notion that someone like Brown Eyes thinks I am special enough. I simply reduce it down to the simple fact that such a man fascinates me.

That Saturday night served as a reminder that even the mundane and recycled routines at The Trax can be open-ended. Days after, my usual pattern of work, sleep, and repeat continues. I let go of the glimmer of hope that Brown Eyes will be coming back anytime soon to have another business dinner. Someone of his caliber and importance probably dines at a gazillion restaurants and bars that easily outrank The Trax.

It is next to impossible that someone can consume my thoughts only after meeting him just once. No one man, or person for that matter, has ever made such an impression on me. This could possibly stem from the fact that I am not a social person, and I have not met enough people to refine my social skills, but I am sure that someone like Brown Eyes can rattle even the most experienced social butterflies. On top of that, there exists another unnerving fact that I coyly try to dance around. It is the fact that Brown Eyes strikes me as something familiar to a faded memory. I have met him before, but I cannot track the time or place. The notion that I met him a long time ago makes for a discomforting thought now.

The only time I am distracted from thinking about Brown Eyes is when I am working. I chalk it up to late adolescent fascination about a man I know nothing of, including the dark and captivating world he comes from. Even in my dreams for days to come, Brown Eyes haunts me in a bittersweet way.

IT IS SATURDAY EVENING, SEVEN days since Brown Eyes' appearance in my life. I approach the bus that takes me from Sansachun to The Trax in a bleak mood. My annoyance with Mr. Chun clouds my thoughts about Brown Eyes. Lina and I work at Sansachun with a usual routine that ranges from attending to the few customers who happen to pass by the store to gossiping until Mr. Chun, the owner, starts to wave his favorite broomstick and threaten to fire us if we don't act more productively. Today, Mr. Chun's mean streak outweighed his threats. On his endless list of things to do, Mr. Chun had Lina and me scrubbing every inch of the store from the windows to the cracks underneath the cement. It is not the job requirements that bother me; it is Mr. Chun's crass approach. The negative mood about the minimum wage job rains endlessly on my mood.

By the time the bus finally arrives at The Trax, I am completely drenched in fatigue and short on nerves. My body is aching for some kind of comfortable release, and the thought of having to stand on my feet for the next eight hours makes my insides coil. I yearn for my warm bed and hot cup of coffee. My hectic morning didn't free up any time to stop by the local Starbucks.

I send Lina a text message through my cell phone that I will not be having dinner with her tonight. Warmly, my cousin sends me back an unhappy face with an *aja aja fighting* ninja emoticon. She adds an expletive about Mr. Chun. It brightens up my mood, but not for long.

As it often happens with my luck, Son is on a demanding high kick when I arrive at The Trax.

"Good, you're here. Go over this list." Son hands me a stack of paperwork before he hurries away to the back room. A truck is waiting for his approval to unload the new inventory.

"Hi to you too," I mumble at Son's back. I frown and look down at the documents in my hand. This will take me all night. While my mind groans, my feet are happy to take a rest.

The Trax has one dated computer for paperwork. It is usually my job to check on reservations and inventory when I start the evening shift. Fortunately, I bury myself in work and Son manages to leave me alone when he sees me typing away like a madwoman. I keep myself busy for the first two hours of my shift checking off the new inventory of food, drinks, and other miscellaneous items.

As the night wears on, I try to stay awake when I finally step out onto the restaurant floor and bar. When nine o'clock rolls around, The Trax precisely converts into its club counterpart. I am now officially on edge from a long night of serving inconsiderate and ruthless customers.

We are so busy I barely have time to touch bases with Joolie and Tailor. The venue is crowded with at least a hundred bodies. It is towards the very end of my shift when I finally make my rounds toward the reserved section of The Trax. I am walking with a couple of empty drinks in my hand, through the throngs of people, mumbling the usual "excuse me" and "watch out, coming through" when I spy the lone figure sitting inside one of the reserved booths.

I stop dead in my tracks. *Oh em gee! It's him!* After days of constant speculation, the person who has been haunting my thoughts is now back.

He is sitting alone towards the middle of the booth. Half of his face hides in the shadows, but his distinguished handsome features remain recognizable. Even from afar, his distinctive appearance and dress stands out against the camouflage tone. It isn't very often that The Trax has a lone customer occupying its reserved section. Loneliness and broodingly dark seems to be the MO–modus operandi–of someone like Brown Eyes.

I feel the same familiar chill ripple down my back when I realize that the loner is staring at me. Instinctively, I turn around to see if his gaze line is inadvertently at someone behind me. When I realize his penetrating stare is solely on me, I blush a deep shade of red. Although it is midnight black inside the club, I feel as though he sees my response with his piercing stares.

Brown Eyes.

My heart is doing something similar to somersaults. *He's come back! He's here!* My conscience is singing an entire chorus. It is quite embarrassing to feel this way towards a stranger. I have never felt this type of emotion just by seeing someone that I had only met briefly before. *What is wrong with me? Why do I gravitate towards him?* My intuition frowns, crossing her arms across her chest in a defensive manner. The world stops for a second. All the people disappear, along with the loud tremble of music and flashing lights. For a split second, we lock in a gaze.

"Excuse me! Can I get some service over here?" A screeching sound pierces my ears and effectively slices through the moment.

I am the first one to break eye contact with Brown Eyes.

It feels as though an electric thread collides with my entire body for going against my better instincts. It is as though I am not ready for the moment to escape, to become distinct in such a fervent flash.

A girl, sitting two tables to the left, lets her annoyance show through her hands as she waves me over. I do my best to conceal an attitude when I reluctantly saunter over to her table. "What can I help you with?" After listening to her order, change her order, and order again—five minutes had passed and the moment is gone. When I turn to face Brown Eyes, he has disappeared into the night.

I am busy for the rest of the night, and as though some cosmic force in the universe is against me, I do not cross paths with Brown Eyes. When I try to glance at Brown Eyes, someone is flagging me down for more food and drinks. When I attempt to walk over to his area, someone else is asking me where the bathroom is. Even when I think about making my way back to the reserved section of The Trax, someone is asking me if I can request the resident DJ to play a specific song.

My luck changes when it is closing time. As people clear The Trax at one in the morning, I am free to wander and look at anyone I please without any interruptions. In fact, it is my usual responsibility to gather empty bottles and let the stragglers know the club is closing.

By the time I finally make my way back to the reserved section of The Trax, something similar to a wave of disappointment comes over me. All the booths within the reserved section are currently abandoned and empty. The reality is a mixture of unmet expectations intertwined with anxiousness. I let out a low chuckle beneath my breath. W*hy do I expect Brown Eyes to be here still? But why did he come back? Why was he sitting all by himself? Was he waiting to catch my attention, but decided to leave when he saw how busy I was?*

I retreat to the bar, feeling slightly defeated. Tailor is nowhere in sight behind the usual black granite counter. He is probably taking a break. I contemplate heading in the other direction when someone at the end of the l-shaped bar catches my eye.

A customer is lingering at the edge of the black counter. The left side of his face rests against the counter top while his right index finger circles the beer he is drinking. It isn't uncommon for stragglers to cling to the bar near closing time. Some dread to go home while others are too drunk to move. In this straggler's case, he is a slave to both common reasons.

I approach him just as I would with any customer.

"Excuse me, sir." I tap lightly on the counter top for his attention. "We're closing up."

At the sound of my voice, the straggler lifts his head up.

Brown Eyes. *It's him! It's him!*

Immediately, his face etches itself into my memory. Just as stunning as a week ago, Brown Eyes' striking face greets my own. His large round eyes light up with indifference when he makes eye contact with me. His lips press together in a hard, frustrated line. The emotions that haunt him are apparent in every line on his face. Still, Brown Eyes is remarkable in every sense of the word. Flurries of thoughts flip inside me. Again, Brown Eyes brings with him a sense of familiarity that I am sure is more than just a memory.

He must feel the same way because at the sight of me, Brown Eyes' look glazes over. As though he is expecting me, as though I am a long lost friend, without a second thought he reaches for my hand. "I'm finishing up my beer."

At the touch of his warm hands, the images of his face—from two separate occasions—coalesces and pieces together in my mind. The familiarity of Brown Eyes' presence approaches me like a dark shadow. For the past week, I have been imagining and conjuring up scenarios of what it would be like to see him again. What would I say? How would I appear? Nevertheless, at the moment, to see him so drunk and dishevel, I am at a loss on how to respond. He does not seem like the same calm, controlled, and striking man anymore. In fact, Brown Eyes appears to be another lost soul at the bar. Still, he exudes untouchable confidence. The thought strikes me that this is a complex and dangerous man.

I slowly reach up to disentangle his grip from my wrist. Brown Eyes' hands are soft and warm, but strong and unrelenting. My eyebrows come together in discomfort. "Sir. You're very drunk. You can either empty out your beer or take it with you. We're closing now." *Damn, I am convincing myself. He will never know the effect he has on me.* My intuition nods her head proudly.

"I said I'm finishing up my beer." Brown Eyes stares back at me with intensity. Unlike last week, with alcohol coursing through his system now, Brown Eyes' tone is not reasonable. This time there's a sharp edge of warning. "You don't have to be insensitive. I was here last week, don't you remember me?"

Oh, that has double meaning. My mouth forms into the perfect circle at his reminder. The generous hundred-dollar tip dances in the back of my head. "It's not about insensitivity. It's my job." I feel the need to defend myself. "Of course I remember you . . . table twelve." *I've been thinking about you all week. Why are you back here tonight, all drunk and a hot mess instead of cold and intimidating?*

Brown Eyes narrows his eyes at me and his eyebrows come together in an inquisitive manner. He gives me the feeling that he does not relinquish control often, so now that he is all alcohol Brown Eyes is awkward with a quintessential charm. "Where's that same awarding customer service personality?" he snaps.

What the heck? Is he going to be melodramatic about this? It is my turn to narrow my eyes. "I'm just doing my job. You're obviously very drunk. I have to ask you to finish your beer and leave." He does not say it, but I get the feeling Brown Eyes think he owns me with that hundred-dollar tip. Suddenly I feel cheap, very flea market cheap. I prepare to add a smart remark, complete with all intents and purposes of returning his money to him, when Brown Eyes cuts me off.

"There's more to life than just a job, pretty girl. There's more to life than all of this." Brown Eyes let out a chuckle that indicates he's privy to the secret of life while I am not. Brown Eyes proceeds to bring the beer bottle to his lips again. *He thinks I'm pretty? Is that what you want to be stuck on? He's basically calling you an idiot.* I strike down my conflicting thoughts as fast as I can. Daring myself to take the leap of faith, I peek at Brown Eyes again.

There's a forlorn sadness to him that I cannot quite explain or understand. Maybe I am too young and inexperienced to understand the underlying meaning of Brown Eyes' body language and his sarcastic nuances. But if there is one thing I can identify with, it is the sincerity in his voice. Suddenly, my courage slips away. I find myself speechless at his demeanor. How can someone be so tragic?

"You want to sit down and have a drink with me?" Sensing my hesitation, Brown Eyes offers me the bottle in his hand. "Are you off work?"

His lips curl into the most delicious smile and I feel the blood rushing from my control. One mood swings to the next. *Run May. He's the devil! Or he could just be super drunk.*

"No, thanks," I answer as professionally as possible. "We're closing. You–"

Before I can finish my sentence, Brown Eyes holds up his hand and points an index finger at me. Slowly, deliberately, he stands up from the bar stool he has been sitting on. I stare up at his height of at least six-feet from my five-foot-four frame. He is wearing a crisp white shirt underneath a black blazer today. His signature dark slacks fold over a pair of black dress shoes. Brown Eyes looks as though he is an important businessman stressed from business underpinnings and the turmoil in his personal life.

Nevertheless, there is nothing professional about him now. Brown Eyes points an unsteady index finger at me. "You're a rule follower, aren't you? Any rules or regulations instructed by your Boss, or your co-workers, are absolute authority. You never question the rules, you never bend the rules, and you will never ever–" Brown Eyes leans into me with his half-empty beer bottle and lowers his voice to an alluring whisper, "do something you're not supposed to."

My cheeks blush a zealous shade of red. Brown Eyes is crossing the line. I am not sure what kind of line, but there is a line somewhere. The stench of hard liquor raids my senses.

You don't know me. "No, I don't . . . not always." It is my feeble attempt to appear cool to this stranger.

"Prove it then." Brown Eyes offers me his beer again.

Suddenly, we are in a standoff. A part of me wants to take the bottle from his hand and finish it off, just to prove I am not such a straight edge. The other part of me wants to turn the bottle on him and pour the rest of the content on his nice ensemble. Either way, I want to make a loud statement. The only problem is I don't know if I want to make the good statement or the bad one. Along with the impossible decision, I feel a thrill pulsating through my veins. He is exciting and dangerous, surprising and a complete hot mess.

Eventually, I don't have to make a decision.

"You're just like someone I used to know." Suddenly, Brown Eyes takes the bottle back when he realizes I do not call his bluff. His eyes, once bright and subjective from the alcohol, becomes dark and judgmental as he confesses, "She was stubborn and indecisive too."

I am in a profound state of silent surprise as I watch Brown Eyes slip deeper in his drunken state. He tilts his head back and consumes the rest of his beer in two gulps. Then, without warning, Brown Eyes slams the bottle onto the counter top. Whether he knows his own strength or not, the bottle crushes underneath the pressure of his hand and immediately glass shards disseminate all over the counter.

Drunk Superman power. I flinch when the loud impact reverberates off the surface. A chill slowly, silently, creeps down the spine of my back.

"Hey, man. What are you doing?" From the opposite end of The Trax, the side door opens. Son and Tailor make their hasty entrance to the bar. Evidently, the loud ruckus is noticeable from the other end of the building. Both of my co-workers are wearing confused facial expressions, complete with shock and awe. When bottles break at the bar, it usually involves two people. No one has ever voluntarily broken a bottle at the bar on his own before.

"It's time for you to go buddy." Son reaches us first. He doesn't wait for an explanation. A broken bottle is enough evidence for Son's zero tolerance. Using his assistant manager authority, Son places both hands on Brown Eyes' shoulders to usher him toward the door.

"I'm not your buddy. Don't touch me!" Brown Eyes steps back in a defensive motion. "I'm talking to May." He turns so quickly, so swiftly in a decisive martial arts manner that Son barely jumps out of the way before the left hook claims him.

The familiar chill wracks my body when I hear Brown Eyes mentioning my name. It is all happening too quickly for me to absorb.

"He's drunk. Be careful." Tailor approaches us from the other side of the bar. He gives Son and me a look that doubles as a precaution and warning. We have been through this process before with other drunks. The only difference this time is I happen to discover Brown Eyes alone.

"You know him?" Son asks in a tone that he is willing to relinquish all responsibility to me. He can hardly believe it.

I shake my head halfway, not sure if meeting Brown Eyes last week counts.

"Of course she knows me . . . she doesn't remember . . . but I'm–" Brown Eyes succumbs to the mixture of beer and hard alcohol. He lets out an anguished hiss that accompanies a suppressed belch. "I-I loved her. I loved her so much. Right, Mi–"

"May! Watch out!" Son pushes me out of the way just in time. It happens too quickly for me to realize.

Brown Eyes stumbles forward and heaves. He grips the side of the counter and leans his entire body into it. Most of what comes up and out of his throat is a mixture of the beer, alcohol, and food he ingested previously. The entire vicinity reeks strongly of his stomach acid and the putrid vomit.

"Oh!" Tailor lets out a groan. With his fast reflex and experience as a bartender, Tailor reaches under the bar counter and extracts the infamous blue bucket specifically reserved for such digestive projectiles.

Tailor shoves the bucket towards Brown Eyes and says promptly, "Inside the bucket, man. Inside."

"Poor guy." Son shakes his head.

I take a step back and feel the wetness beneath my shoes. I don't have to look to know that I am stepping into what Brown Eyes is not successfully aiming into the bucket.

"Oh gross," I mumble. I pick up my right foot to see the smear trickling down to the very soles of my shoes. The smell is so strong I have to pinch my nose and breathe out of my mouth.

"You remember me? Don't you?" Brown Eyes gasps. He latches onto my right arm with intense strength.

"No!" I turn my head away from him. I wasn't imagining things; he realizes it too. We have met before. I attempt to disentangle myself from him, but Brown Eyes doesn't budge. *How can someone so drunk still be so strong?*

"What have we come to?" Son whispers. His eyes narrow and there isn't a trace of empathy in his voice. It is as though he realizes something beyond simple admission. "We used to be a cool, upscale place."

"What do you mean?" Tailor refutes immediately. "Since when does The Trax cater to any upscale clients? We're in the part of town where social rejects and dejects roam."

"That's not what I meant," Son retorts quickly. "Even though we get the latter half of the social pyramid, since when do we cater to gangsters?"

I stop fighting Brown Eyes' grip on me. He is on the verge of throwing up his brains at the rate his body is attempting to get rid of the alcohol. Brown Eyes is slipping into a deep subconscious state that most hard drinkers reach.

"Gangsters?" The word burns at the tip of my lips.

"Gangsters," Son restates. He narrows his eyes at Brown Eyes' outfit. "Look at the necklace he has on his neck. It's a diamond-encrusted Cross. He's a Crist member."

CHAPTER TWO

I have always been taught to help other my whole life, but allowing a super attractive male to throw up on me is not how the good Samaritan act often plays out in my mind. If there is a lesson to learn from this incident, it is the fact that the heroine does not choose the situation but it is the situation that makes the heroine. *It is your fate working at a bar. You're lucky it's only vomit.* My intuition is always looking for a fight with my better judgment.

Brown Eyes continues to heave into Tailor's reliable alcohol bucket with one hand on my wrist. Son and Tailor do little to help me; they figure it is better for Brown Eyes to hold onto me as a crutch than to throw up on the bar's floor. So I take one for the team, as the saying goes. During the last couple of seconds, I realize Brown Eyes is not just a pretty face; he has the distinctive presence and personality to match, including the indomitable strength. He is also a very sad soul who fills the heavy void with tangible pain and hard alcohol.

After Brown Eyes finishes with a throaty cough, Son and Tailor take him outside of The Trax. I try to convince them otherwise, but my co-workers refuse to hear my opinion.

"He's too dangerous!" Son hisses.

I feel guilt raiding my body and consciousness when I watch them. I know that Brown Eyes is alone, and in his drunken state, I am not sure he can get home safe. I grab a spray bottle filled to the brink with bleach solution. I don't know what else to do but to keep my hands busy. I am still in the midst of wiping down the bar when Son and Tailor return with identical sunken expressions. They appear shaken up, as though they had dealt with something dangerous and unworldly.

"What did you do with him?" I ask them. *Why do you care so much?* My intuition rolls her eyes.

"We took him outside," Tailor replies quickly and disappears behind the bar.

"You left him in the cold?" I ask Son; he is spraying the counter with bleach solution now. Son is cleaning what I just cleaned.

"It doesn't matter May. We had to get him out of here fast. He's affiliated with Crist. I don't want to make any phone calls that I'll regret later." Son's voice is stressed and non-negotiable.

"I think you're overreacting. Just because he's a gangster doesn't mean we just throw him out like that. He's alone and unconscious. What if he gets killed?" An unsettling feeling permeates my body. I am cold and shaky for some reason.

Son stops cleaning the counter and shakes his head at me. "You don't know anything about people like him, do you May? He is a member of a social section that we're better off leaving out in the cold than in here with us. We don't want any of his associates or affiliates coming in here, blaming us for purposely getting him drunk or trying to take advantage of him. Even worse, we don't want any of his enemies to come in here and take advantage of him while he's drunk. He's a gangster May. They rob, cheat, steal, and kill. If we feel sorry for him, then who is going to feel sorry for us?"

Enough of a reason for you to leave this alone? My intuition throws a dark notion. Son is right. I don't know anything about someone like Brown Eyes. All I know about gangsters is from Lina's preconceived stories and notions, along with cinematic depictions of guys in baggy pants and bandanas as they tote guns. I have never come across gangsters like Brown Eyes who seem to be selected by their ridiculously good looks, impeccable personalities, and overwhelming strength. More specifically, hierarchical *money-driven* gangsters. There is nothing cheap about Brown Eyes from head-to-toe.

"Any more doubts about my decision?" Son lifts up an eyebrow. He is all assistant manager on me now.

"No," I mumble and return to wiping the bar.

"Good," Son replies shortly. He glances at me again, takes pity, and adds, "I'm doing this for the security of our jobs, May. I'm not being an ass for no reason. Stay far away from gangsters like him. It's not a warning. It's a life lesson."

I frown at Son's wise advice. I try not to laugh, but the corners of my mouth simply lift into a smile. Son ends up letting out a chuckle too. We have been working together for six months now, so Son knows that I take his comments with a grain of salt. We have been able to build one of those working relationships where he lectures and I laugh. Today is no different, although the undertone is completely different from the usual.

It takes us another ten minutes to wipe down the bar and sanitize the entire area. Son is in charge of closing the entire venue down, so he dismisses me to go home first. When it comes down to it, Son often takes on the brunt of the work. He prefers it that way.

I head for the bathroom to clean myself up. I am looking forward to some peace and quiet, but that is not happening when Joolie comes stalking into the bathroom. She is fresh off the gossip train and wants to talk.

"I cannot believe Super-Gorgeous-Sexy is a Crist member! I knew there was more to him than just a handsome face!"

I lean over the white porcelain sink to splash a pool of cool water over my face. The water trickles down the sides of my arms and eventually end at my elbows. I gather the courage to lift my head up and look in the bathroom mirror. The glaring fluorescent lighting highlights the tired lines and dark spots on my face. I look beyond dead tired and feel it to the hilt.

Joolie is still in the background going on about the unbelievably beautiful gangster. Joolie's pining over the fact that she missed all the action.

Joolie is a co-worker completely immersed in her job. Joolie is the first one to formulate opinions and churn out rapid suggestions about everything and anything that happens in and around The Trax. Joolie grew up very poor with only a single father and five siblings. Her mother died when she was young, so Joolie has been self-sufficient for most of her life. Joolie holds down two jobs with only a high school diploma. Despite her credentials, Joolie is actually very intelligent and calculating. Her grand goal in life is to own venues like The Trax. Essentially, Joolie's motivation for knowledge derives from sound reasons. It's Joolie's way of going about it that makes it difficult to empathize with.

"Are you listening, May?" Joolie often questions my attention span to her ramblings. Tonight is no different. She is standing a sink away from me, tying her hair into a large mound at the top of her head. She repeats again with, "God, he's so beautiful . . . he's like a tragic, beautiful soul."

"Yes," I agree absentmindedly to her comment.

"I wonder why he picked The Trax of all spots." Joolie has a faraway look on her face. "He looks like he could go to the classier places like the Prosper Room or Ekco. Maybe he likes our cheap drinks. He can't be here for the girls. God no. You and I are probably the most attractive girls here. Oh! Maybe he came back here for one of us! I did notice him sitting in the reserved section earlier."

Joolie has such an elaborate imagination. Dreams can feed off her for life. "Umm hmm," I mumble again. I grab some towels from the dispenser to run under the sink. When they are wet enough, I lift my right leg and wipe my shoes clean of Brown Eyes' vomit.

"But I can't believe he's a Crist member." Joolie stops fixing her hair and lowers her voice. A look of secrecy and fixation crosses her face.

Joolie leans against the sink and watches me clean my shoes. "A Crist member. Have you heard of them?"

"No," I answer shortly. I continue running my hands up and down the soles of my shoes. "What does it matter, anyway?" *Son and Joolie have the same look in their eyes when they talk about Crist members.*

"Hah!" Joolie lets out a scoff as though she can't believe my ignorance. "A Crist member visited The Trax, May. Even if you don't know, you should at least understand that we are going to be getting a little more popular. Think of it as a celebrity going to eat at an unknown restaurant. Pretty soon, everyone will want to eat at that restaurant too!"

I stop wiping my shoes to look at Joolie. I am not oblivious to the world around me, but brushing up with a gang member sounds like bad news. Joolie sees it from a publicity perspective while I regard it as a bad omen. "Son kicked him out. It's a bad omen to have him here."

"What the hell does Son know?" Joolie snaps adamantly. "You can't keep a Crist member from going anywhere he wants! No. Super-Gorgeous-Sexy has his reasons for coming here twice in two weeks. He's planning something."

Hmm. Is Joolie onto something? "I think he just came back tonight to have a drink. He seemed upset over something. He probably got drunk to forget what he really needs to deal with," I reply with what I believe is an insightful comment.

"Uh huh." Joolie nods her head for a moment, but then changes her mind as she shakes her head in the opposite direction. "Nah. He has an ulterior motive for coming here. Probably wants protection money from the club."

"Well, whatever he is here for has nothing to do with you or me." I throw the dirty towels in the trash can and wash my hands again.

Joolie's cell phone lights up in her bag at the same moment, playing an upbeat electronic dance music anthem. Joolie gives me a playful push as she heads out the bathroom with her cell phone in hand. "You might think I'm crazy, but there's a reason why he was here last week and again tonight. Good night May. Sweet Dreams. Don't let the gangster bite!"

Before she exits, Joolie marks her right hand across her upper body to create the symbol of a Cross.

Did she really just do that? "Good night Joolie." I feel incredulous from her exit display. Joolie knows how to rile things up.

I do my best to ban my thoughts about the night and Brown Eyes. I spend another five minutes in the bathroom cleaning myself up. When I finally decide there is nothing more I can do, I head straight to the employee's room. I change into my regular clothes. I end up wrapping my work uniform in a plastic bag. Ever the light traveler, I tie the plastic bag around the strap of my worn-out tote bag.

Most of my co-workers are already gone when I head out of the front door. There is only one way in and one way out for Trax employees and customers. It is some sort of policy implemented for this kind of establishment. Son told me once that it is easier for police to keep track of people coming in and out with only one front door. Again, this is just one of the stringent staples that comes with working at a place like The Trax.

"Good night May!"

"Get home safe!"

"Good night!" I wave to a couple of co-workers who are still lingering around.

The cool summer air greets me as soon as I exit The Trax. The Trax is at basement level; grand steps lead up to street level. These steps are usually not a problem, but after tonight, my legs threaten to give in with every step I take.

I take in a deep breath and inhale sweet, fresh air once I reach street level. I pull the strap of my tote bag higher on my shoulders and begin my trek towards the nearest bus stop. I am off-work mode, daydreaming about my warm bed and maybe a glass of milk before sleep. Coffee is a long, lost dream at this point.

I am barely three feet away from The Trax when I stop in my tracks.

"Suni . . . ," a soft, distinctive voice calls out to me.

Although I have no recollection or familiarity with the name, I follow the voice emanating from the darkness. A distill sense of silence clouds my judgment for a second. Streetlights are rare around this area of The Trax; the dim lighting from the street rarely marks its presence here. People do not usually linger around these shadows. Whether they are tourists or locals, people typically disappear quickly into the accompanying shops or bars when they enter this part of town. I am the only one who is lingering for a stranger.

"Hello?" I muster enough courage to call out. *Don't get yourself killed*, my conscience taunts.

"Suni . . . ," the voice calls again.

Almost instantly, from the rise and fall of his voice and the repetition, I know it is Brown Eyes. My mind immediately calculates the time frame. He was kicked out of The Trax forty-five minutes ago. *He's still here? I was right. He has no one to take him home.*

Strings tug at my heart. Against my better judgment and Son's warning, I follow the sound of Brown Eyes' voice with caution. The dark shadows looming over the side of the large building are the perfect hiding spots for Brown Eyes. His silhouette attaches to the gloom created by the orange moon and black sky. Brown Eyes sticks out like a sore thumb against the background of the area. He does not belong here. Broken sorrow looks like this.

"Suni . . . ," he calls wistfully.

"Hey, are you okay?" I inch closer.

"Suni . . . ," he whispers the same hauntingly sad name.

I realize the closer I move to him, the more I am reducing my chances of walking away. As a matter of fact, I am involved the moment I decide not to go home and find out what is wrong with him. But I cannot leave him. My conscience doesn't let me. She's got a tissue box out already.

Brown Eyes looks pitiful as he sprawls against the side of the building with the residue of vomit drying on the front of his shirt. He is someone's son, someone's brother, someone's friend, someone's lover, someone's everything. And yet, at his saddest moment, Brown Eyes is alone and miserable.

"I'm going to turn you over on your side ok?" I grab his shoulders and move him to the side so I can reach into his pockets for his wallet. He doesn't attempt to fight me. In fact, even in his drunken state, Brown Eyes is staring at me with an unreadable expression. *God, he's so beautiful . . . he's like a tragic, beautiful soul.* Joolie's voice swims in my mind.

I break eye contact with him and try not to let my personal opinion influence what needs to be done. When I finally find Brown Eyes' wallet, I open it eagerly and peer in. A flood of information, I am sure, is waiting for me in every single pocket.

I am sorely disappointed. There is nothing of record inside his leather wallet. No ID. No money. No credit card. But, there is a small picture of a smiling couple. It is too dark for me to make any sense of it. I place everything back into his pocket, and then ask Brown Eyes in clear syllables, "Do. You. Have. A. Cell phone?"

Brown Eyes doesn't respond as he slips below consciousness.

"Hey, try to stay awake. Do you have a cell phone? Someone I can call to help you?" I ask him again.

When Brown Eyes doesn't answer, I place a hand around his chin and lift his head up. I realize his temperature is abnormal. I press my right palm against his forehead and my left palm on my own forehead.

His temperature must be a few points beyond the healthy ninety-eight degrees Fahrenheit. I drop both hands and grab his right wrist. With two right fingers, I press them against the vein on his right hand. Brown Eyes' heart rate is rapid, indicating an irregular body rhythm due to alcohol or illness.

"What am I going to do with you?" I whisper to the darkness.

I let go of Brown Eyes' hand and slump back against the side of the building with him. A million thoughts run through my mind. I can call the police to help, but they will probably cite Brown Eyes for violating public intoxication laws. He could end up in even more trouble than if he sleeps off the alcohol somewhere else. I can't bring him back inside The Trax nor rent out a room in a motel for him. I don't have that kind of money to spare.

He's a gangster. Joolie's voice reverberates in my mind as I think about the police again. *Look at the necklace he has on his neck. It's a diamond-encrusted Cross. He's a Crist member.* Son's voice raids my mind next. *He's a gangster . . . they rob, cheat, steal, and kill.*

Without thinking, I turn to Brown Eyes and look down at his shirt. The diamond necklace is between the right flap of his white collar and his black blazer. Even under the poor night lighting, it is still clear that the diamonds are comprised of carats beyond my mathematical concepts. There is no mistaking the sign of the Cross. A chill wracks my body. Gangsters. What do I know about gangsters?

"Hold on a second." An idea strikes my mind. I reach inside my tote bag for my cell phone.

On the home screen of my cell phone, I have missed two calls from my stepmother and a text message from Lina. Usually after work at The Trax, I check in with my mother and Lina to let them know I am off work.

I will text them back later. I exit the message screen and press down on the camera function until it turns on. Then, I angle the camera away from Brown Eyes' face and press for the picture. The flash lights up and in less than a second, it is all done. He is committed to memory with the aid of a device.

Brown Eyes doesn't even move an inch.

"Come on." I reach for his left arm to wrap around my neck.

"Suni?" Brown Eyes opens his eyes half-heartedly. He repeats the endearing name again.

"Suni." I nod my head. "We're going to go find Suni for you."

It is bad to lie and make promises to a drunken person, but I am willing to do whatever it takes to get Brown Eyes up. Slowly and carefully,

I help him balance on my side. Brown Eyes must be extremely motivated to find this Suni of his because he musters up some gross motor control to walk. But Brown Eyes remains a challenge to hold up. Because he is taller than me, Brown Eyes' chin continues to collide with my head. *Ow. Ouch. Ow.* I wince with every step we take.

Brown Eyes and I begin our walk down the street. The bright lights of the city fade into the background. Looming dark buildings, combined with ribbons and streaks of color, follow us all the way out to the main street. There is still a decent amount of traffic on the road. Cars hum and zoom by at a steady speed. The last bus has left for the night. My only resort now is a taxi.

When I see a taxi crawling up the street, I use one of Brown Eyes' arms to flag it down. It is clear to see the taxi driver hesitating behind his car's windshield. Evidently, business must be slow for him because he pulls over.

"Is he drunk?" The taxi driver is an old man in his early sixties. The lines on his face crease together when he asks the question. He rolls his windows down halfway, weary of our company.

"A little bit." I put on my best smile. "But he's fine. He's just sleepy. He won't throw up in your car."

"I hope not," the taxi driver states shortly. He glances at Brown Eyes and then back at me again. "Get in."

"Thank you," I breathe. If he didn't let us in, I don't know what I would do.

I make my way around the left side of the taxi swiftly. With Brown Eyes still leaning on me, I move him around and place him inside the taxi first. Immediately, he slumps over in the seat. I have to go around the other side to get into the car.

"Where are you two headed?" From his tone of voice, the taxi driver is making clear judgments.

"East Point apartment complexes, please," I answer. I nervously touch the strap of my tote bag.

"Uh huh," is the taxi driver's snappy remark.

I sit to the far right in the back seat for the duration of the ride to my apartment complex. I don't want to take any chances of Brown Eyes going for his second win if his stomach starts to act up. But I don't need to worry. He is fast asleep. Now and then, the taxi driver glances in the rearview mirror at us. I have a smile on my face, putting on a show that everything is fine. Little does he know I am on edge about this situation. I am anxious about what to do.

When we finally arrive at the familiar iron white gates, I do my best to wake Brown Eyes up and guide him out of the car. I pay the taxi driver ten dollars. He mumbles something that sounds like "good luck" before speeding off.

The walk to my apartment complex feels as though it stretches on for miles. *Why do I have to live on the sixth floor with no elevator?* I mentally curse my luck. East Point apartment complexes are home to families who are in the bottom income tax brackets. Each complex is sectioned off into different compass points. I live in the southeastern region of East Point at the village most residents refer to as sun and moon. Each East Point apartment is no bigger than a thousand square feet with amenities included in the monthly rent. It is a practical place to live, so many residents remain at East Point for most of their lives.

My stepmother, Eunhye, and I have been living at East Point for a couple of years now. The location of the apartment, along with its affordable monthly expenses, is exactly what our household of two needs. Since moving in, we live a quiet life. Tonight is the one and only exception.

When Brown Eyes and I finally reach my apartment landing, I am completely out of breath. A cool sheet of sweat coats my back. I lean Brown Eyes against the apartment front door. Lina would label this stage of drunkenness as 'blackout.' Speaking of my cousin, maybe I should call her for help. Did I make such a rash decision in bringing Brown Eyes home?

I don't have time to contemplate my decision. Brown Eyes is shivering from the cold air. I rummage through my tote bag for my keys. When I get the apartment door open, I muster one last drop of strength to pick up Brown Eyes again. "Come on. You can collapse inside." He does little to struggle against me.

The apartment is completely dark except for the light illuminating from the empty fish tank. I used to have two gold fishes, but when the first one died of old age the second one died soon after of a broken heart. Since then I have not had the heart to buy new fishes to replace them or to throw out the fish tank. So now, we have an empty fish tank with the sole purpose of providing a night light. I convinced Eunhye that it goes well with the layout of our apartment; a large living room that connects to a vast kitchen complete with its own amenities.

"You can sleep here–" I stop before I complete my sentence.

I realize I am about to let Brown Eyes sleep on our white couch completely exposed in the living room. When Eunhye comes home from her graveyard shift at the hospital as an emergency nurse, she would have a panic attack. The only man to ever step foot inside this apartment was my father and even then he surprised us.

After careful deliberation, I decide to take Brown Eyes to my bedroom. It is the only alternative.

As soon as I open the door, Brown Eyes goes straight for my bed. He is incredibly intelligent for an unconscious drunk.

"Oh no, you don't!" I grab the back of his shirt and pull him down on the floor.

Brown Eyes stumbles and fall onto the hard carpet, but he doesn't seem to feel the pain. Immediately, he curls up on the floor and falls back into sleep.

I ransack through my closet for a clean pillow and blanket. After I find them, untouched after two years, I place the pillow under Brown Eyes' head and cover him with a blanket. I stand over him for a couple of minutes to watch the rise and fall of his chest as he sleeps. His handsomely defined features have a story to them. The same sense of familiarity comes over me, but I do my best to ignore it. It is difficult to imagine that we have before and decided to forget one another. There is no point in assuming there is a past if it doesn't exist in the present.

I hover over Brown Eyes for a couple more minutes. When I am finally convinced he is dead as a rock, I grab my bathroom bag and a clean pair of pajamas.

I make my way down the hall to the bathroom with a heavy feeling of tiredness, anxiousness, and anticipation. Everything in the apartment feels foreign because of Brown Eyes' presence. I am used to existing by myself with only the few people I allow in my life. Yet, here I am tonight, giving full access of my life to a stranger. Granted, he is beyond intoxicated to take advantage of the situation. It looks as though misery left him to die.

When I reach the bathroom, I turn on the light and lock the door behind me. I nearly drown myself underneath the rainfall showerhead. I take my time shampooing my hair and scrubbing myself with body wash. Afterwards, I dry my hair with the wall fan by the mirror and clean my ears out with fresh cotton swabs.

Eventually, I run out of things to do in the bathroom. Now, I have no choice but to go back to my room. Sleeping on the couch would raise suspicion when Eunhye comes home. My elaborate plan is to have Brown Eyes leave the apartment while Eunhye sleeps off her graveyard tiredness.

I take a detour into the kitchen to grab a fresh cloth. I run it through some warm water and enter my bedroom quietly. I am sure that if I scream at the top of my lungs and bang on the walls, Brown Eyes will still be sleeping like a baby. I tiptoe to him and place the folded cloth over his head. His forehead is still hot. The fever is taking hold of his bodily functions. I watch him for a couple more seconds hardly believing that this beautiful creature is sleeping like a child in my bedroom.

Brown Eyes is in a deep state of sleep. At least in sleep, he is able to forget the pain he is experiencing.

Before I crawl into bed, I make my way to the closet and pull out a softball bat. It is a Pro Maple, approximately thirty-four inches long and six inches thick, made out of authentic African wood. I remember begging my mother for it when I was in high school, believing that my calling in life was to join a softball team. Evidently, it didn't work out that way, but at least I am able to put it to good use. Granted, this is probably not how Eunhye would have dreamed of me using it.

With the baseball safely underneath my right arm, I climb into my warm bed. I lay on my right side with the bat against my body and pull the blanket up to my chin. I chase away as many thoughts as I can sleep. I have work tomorrow as well as some errands to fit in.

From the other side of the room, I can hear the soft rise and fall of the Brown Eyes' breathing.

"Good night Brown Eyes," I whisper into the darkness. *Beautiful, tragic, and bittersweet soul. Or in Joolie's words Super-Gorgeous-Sexy.*

Then, slowly and peacefully, I drift off to a deep sleep. My body aches, especially my arms and legs. The heaviness on my eyelids feels relieved from the pressure. I lose sense of time and physical being. *Hmm. My bed is warm.*

THE NEXT THING I AM conscious of is a soft breeze against my skin. The morning sunlight casts several rays into my bedroom, lighting up the walls with orange shadows. I shiver slightly from the cool air and pull my blanket over my shoulders. At the same time, my baseball bat falls onto the ground. The unmistakable thud on the carpet reminds me why I have it in my bed in the first place.

I immediately sit up in bed and look down at the floor where Brown Eyes is supposed to be sleeping. Now, it is just the usual empty spot in my room. "Oh no," I mumble. I throw the blanket off as fast I can and run out of bed. *Where is he? Where is he?* I am frantic and afraid. *See what happens when you let strangers in?* My intuition wakes, stretching and yawning.

As soon as I reach my bedroom door, I can hear the voices in the kitchen. I pray that Eunhye is on the phone and Brown Eyes is long gone. Instead, I find the both of them leaning against the kitchen.

"Well, I do enjoy getting up and going to work. But, it can get quite tedious," Eunhye is saying. She holds her favorite tea mug as she laughs.

"It's really admirable though," Brown Eyes replies to my stepmother. "You save a lot of lives."

This is all wrong, all out of sorts. He doesn't belong here in my drab and normal kitchen. In fact, he doesn't earn any right to hold a full conversation with my Eunhye. Now that he is conscious and sober, Brown Eyes is back to his strikingly handsome and charismatic self. He looks presentable despite the fact that he is still wearing clothes from last night, sans the black blazer. In the light, it is easier to gather the features of his face. With dark hair cascading over his features, Brown Eyes' bright complexion makes his face appear more open. It is evident Brown Eyes doesn't belong to our world. Everything about him, including his demeanor and attitude, is not from mainstream society. Brown Eyes belongs to a much deeper and darker world than mine.

"Oh, look who's awake. Good morning."

I am too busy staring at Brown Eyes and Eunhye to realize that they see me looking at them.

My stepmother's face softens at the sight of me. I normally call her mother, but Eunhye is actually my stepmother. My biological mother died when I was younger, so my father ended up integrating me into his primary family. From the beginning, Eunhye treated me as if I am her biological daughter. She makes it easy to like her and over time, I began to love her like my biological mother. The stereotypical myth of stepmother and stepchild drama was never applicable to us. Of course we have our differences, but what mother-daughter pairing doesn't? Eunhye never misses an opportunity to teach me a lesson, however.

At the moment, Eunhye has her relaxed and entertained face on. She is the prettiest Korean woman I know with her bright eyes and full smile. My stepmother always has her hair piled on the top of her head to display her favorite gold earrings. She is only five feet tall and about a hundred pounds, but her personality makes her comparable to a stick of dynamite.

Brown Eyes must have already worked some kind of special magic on her because Eunhye doesn't seem upset that he's in the apartment. In fact, she is standing there with an expectant expression on her face.

"Good morning," Eunhye repeats again.

"Good morning," I mumble under my breath. "I see you met—"

"Your friend, Choi Sangwoo?" She completes my sentence shortly. "We've been chatting for the past half an hour, sleepyhead. You want a cup of tea?"

Choi Sangwoo. Sangwoo Choi. I like the name I gave him better. Choi Sangwoo sounds too regal and elite, dangerous and obsolete. But I have to admit the name is befitting of him. It embodies him from head-to-toe. I am not sure if I will ever find out just how much, but I am willing to bet on it. Now that Eunhye and I know his official name, Brown Eyes is moving from stranger to acquaintance quickly.

"No tea," I answer Eunhye finally.

I turn my attention to Choi Sangwoo. I am still mentally testing out his name. *The face does match the name.* My intuition gapes at him.

"Good morning May," he says as soon as we make eye contact. Sangwoo is holding my usual coffee mug in his hand.

"Good morning," I reply shortly. *Who does he think he is, looking so gorgeous after such a drunken escapade, standing in my kitchen buttering up my mother?* I know it is easy for him. Choi Sangwoo probably has the charms and wit that only experience conjures.

Fortunately, Eunhye doesn't catch the awkwardness between us. "You never told me about Choi Sangwoo." She turns back to look at him. "He's very handsome."

Sangwoo lets out a chuckle, but doesn't look shy. *A little bit conceited huh?* It is too much of a boyish response for someone like him to pull off.

"There's not much to tell . . . about Sangwoo," I reply to Eunhye. My mind is ransacking all the lies I need to come up with on the spot. I am well aware that Sangwoo has his undivided attention on me now. "We've been friends for—"

"Ever since I started working at The Trax," Sangwoo cuts me off. He gives me a nod as if to say he can handle this. Sangwoo turns back to my mother and continues with unfathomable confidence. "As I explained earlier, we had a promotional campaign for the club last night. I had too much to drink with a few customers. I wouldn't have been able to make it home. May was nice enough to help and let me crash on her floor. I hope you understand."

"Oh. Of course!" Eunhye replies quickly. She lifts up a hand to touch Sangwoo's right shoulder softly. It is a clear indication that she likes him. "I would rather you stay here and sober up than get in trouble on the way home."

The situation is too precarious for me to interrupt, so I keep my silence and let Sangwoo tell my mother the fabricated details. Apparently, he is a master at stringing the lies without any detection of false play.

"Well, I'm glad May is putting herself out there and making more friends. She's quite the loner, you know. I tell her all the time to make more friends. She's consistently working two jobs and putting her social life aside. She doesn't let too many people into her life, so I welcome the ones that she does." Just when I think she isn't going to embarrass me, there is the classic remark mothers tend to make. I suppose a mother's worse nightmare could go either way when it comes to her daughter having too many friends or none at all.

I don't miss Choi Sangwoo glancing curiously at me after hearing that piece of information. There is a clear delight in his brown eyes.

". . . Your phone is ringing mom," I announce abruptly.

She thinks I am making a smart excuse, but Eunhye's smile subsides when the familiar ring emits from her bedroom. "It must be the hospital calling." Eunhye clutches her mug with alertness. The classical conditioning has her wired.

My mother doesn't forget her manners. Eunhye pats Sangwoo's shoulder with endearment before leaving the kitchen. "Come by when you're free. We can have dinner together. I'd love to get to know you better."

What? You're inviting him to dinner already? My intuition shifts uncomfortably on her meditation mat.

"I definitely will. It was nice meeting you Mrs. Lee." He bows respectfully in return.

Eunhye gives me a smile before she leaves; it's her we-need-to-talk-later smile. My heart sinks a little.

"Thank you for what you did last night." Choi Sangwoo waits until Eunhye is in her room before he addresses me.

Heart stop. I find the words jumbling in my throat. I should feel violated. He took advantage of my Samaritan act too far by introducing himself to my mother without my presence. But when Brown Eyes addresses me with the whole package of alluring tone of voice, sultry look, and commanding presence I am silly putty again.

"You're welcome," I answer in a submissive whisper. *Who are you?* my intuition hisses at me with condemned betrayal.

"I hope you don't mind. I introduced myself to your mother. I woke up thirsty, so I went out to the kitchen to get some water. Your mother was making tea and she looked very surprised and . . . hurt that I was here. You're a good girl. You don't usually bring strange men home, do you?"

Of course not! I'm not a slush—Lina's term for a slut. "No, I don't." My tone of voice is unwavering. I narrow my eyes at Sangwoo to let him know I take offense.

Sangwoo smiles without teeth. He is clearly joking with me. "So I had to conjure up a story about how we work together," Sangwoo continues to elaborate calmly, but his facial expression is hard to read.

"You could have woken me up," is all I can respond. My conscience is shaking her head, not impressed by how I am handling the situation.

Sangwoo's eyes appear delighted that he has me eating out of his hands. "You were sleeping so peacefully with your baseball bat."

I have no reply to the truth. My cheeks heat up at the look in his eyes. *Well, a girl's got to protect herself.*

Sangwoo brings the mug he is holding back up to his lips. *How many girls would give anything to be that mug right now?* My face increases with heat as the bad thought crosses my mind. Choi Sangwoo's body language is the same as the previous night. Only this time he isn't drinking alcohol, but instead fresh green jasmine tea—one of Eunhye's favorite concoctions for a hangover.

"But thank you, though, for your hospitality." Sangwoo's eyes glow. "You and your mother remind me that there's still humility, innocence, and peace in the world."

I am careful not to let the confusion show on my face. When I realize why he is describing us like that, I remember the necklace on his neck. As my eyes move to his collar, Sangwoo's hand nonchalantly tucks the diamond-encrusted chain inside his shirt.

In that instant, he knows that I know.

I lift my eyes up to look straight into his. "Why did you come back to The Trax last night?"

Sangwoo pauses at my blunt question as though he hadn't anticipated for me to be so straight forward. He places the mug back on the counter. Then, he deliberately turns the sink faucet on and washes his hands. The seconds tick by in awkwardness with a tint of tension. When he finishes, Sangwoo rinses his hands on one of the sink towels. *How can someone make washing their hands look so sexy?* My conscience is staring at him with her undivided attention; this creature confounds her.

Finally Brown Eyes, Choi Sangwoo, turns to face me and answers my question with, "You can say I'm in town for business."

Illegal business? My intuition lifts up an eyebrow. "Why The Trax?" I question further.

"That is a matter of personal record, Maybelline." Just like that, he stops me in my tracks. Sangwoo narrows his eyes at me, and all of a sudden, the warnings from my co-workers about gangsters inundate my mind. *I should never forget his career choice. And he called me by my complete name. Eunhye gave me up!*

"I'm sorry." I peer up at him. *Crap. My big mouth always gives me away.*

Sangwoo never breaks eye contact with me. A thought crosses his mind, and Sangwoo's lips part in a seductive manner. "Are you afraid of me?" Sangwoo's question comes with a forceful tone. He waits for my response with parted lips and smoky eyes.

"N-no." I deny immediately as a defense mechanism. "If I am afraid of you, I wouldn't have helped you out last night." *One point for me.*

"You should be afraid of me." There is a signature of cockiness in his voice. *Two points for Brown Eyes.* "Why did you help me last night?" Sangwoo is proving to be intelligent and cunning.

"You wouldn't understand," I reply shortly. A nerve of mine pinches. I am rising to the challenge of speaking to this intimidating man.

"Why wouldn't I?" Sangwoo raises an eyebrow at my statement. Evidently, he doesn't like responses that undermine his ability to comprehend. "Because someone of my means couldn't possibly understand the world of goodness you come from?"

It is apparent and decided. We are not going to get along at the rate of this push and pull. "I didn't mean that. I just don't feel the need to justify and explain why I helped. I don't usually—"

"Associate with my kind. So now that I have exhausted my quota of help from you, I need to leave," he completes my sentence with haste. Slowly, Sangwoo's lips part into a smile that reveal the whitest set of teeth I have ever seen. "Don't worry May. I already have a car coming for me. I'll be out of your life soon."

Wait! Let me dust off my debate book! I feel the wave of guilt hover me when Sangwoo finishes his sentence. "Can I be honest?" I ask.

Sangwoo stares with amusement. I expect another snappy comment from him, but he surprises me instead. "Please do," he says softly.

I lick my lips in anticipation as my heart rate picks up. "Have we met before? Aside from last week, have we met before somewhere?" There, I did it. I jumped off the cliff and am now dangling in the air. I wait for his answer expectantly.

As though Choi Sangwoo has been anticipating this question, this mysterious man doesn't shed a clue that my question rattles him. "Do you feel like we've met before?" Sangwoo's brown eyes ask me. He is in control, not giving anything away freely.

"Yes," I answer shortly. My conscience stares at me with her jaw on the floor. "But I can't remember," I confess softly. *Why don't you tell him you have been dreaming about him for the past week too?* my intuition snaps.

The seconds tick by. Our eyes lock in a stare off.

"No, May. I don't believe we've met before." Sangwoo drops our eye contact. The heavy air dispels between us.

I feel the heaviness of my heart on my feet. I glance down at my toes for a second and mentally paint them a fuchsia color. I expel silent air out of my lungs. At least I asked.

"So, this is why you helped me last night? Because you thought we've met before?" Sangwoo questions. He frowns slightly, possibly on the border of frustration that I am still withholding the reason. *He really, truly does want to know.*

"Not just because I think I know you from somewhere before," I tell Sangwoo as sincerely as possible. I want him to know that I really do believe we have met before. But I am not going to dwell on something he so easily denies.

Choi Sangwoo's calm and collected facial expression remains undisturbed.

"It's because you just looked so sad. I don't know much about why people choose to drink, other than because they're really emotional about something or they just want to get drunk. I've seen plenty of sad people who get drunk beyond consciousness at The Trax. But you were just miserable. You didn't have a cell phone or any information in your wallet. There was no one else around. I was going to call the police to help you, but I figured that wouldn't be a good idea since . . . I just wanted to help you, that's all." I feel uncomfortable explaining my good deed.

"So if it wasn't me last night, would you still have helped a random drunk person?" His follow up question isn't what I am expecting. I get the feeling that Sangwoo is assessing the type of person I am.

"Yes," I answer without hesitation. "But I have never done it before. You're the first one." We just cleared the air that I am not a slut and that we don't know each other from somewhere before. What more does he want from me?

"And I am the last one you will help," Sangwoo commands as if he has the right to. "Don't help others like that again. Be smart. I could have turned out to be a serial killer or a rapist."

Hey! "That's not a very nice way to thank someone for carrying you all the way from The Trax to her apartment. It's also not appreciative of the person who let you sleep in her room." I am not about to be lectured by someone who does nothing but break laws for a living. Before I can help myself, I add, "And because of the hundred dollar tip you left me last week. I felt like I owe you a favor."

A pretentious look crosses his face. My sharp tongue surprises Sangwoo. "The tip wasn't meant to be a favor."

The loud voice inside me quiets down at his calm remark. "What was it then?"

Sangwoo stares at me, but chooses not to answer. He continues, "I already expressed my thankfulness for last night."

"Feels like you're taking it back," I retort.

"No. I think you are misunderstanding. I'm just saying your good heart could have gotten you in trouble."

"So, if I were to ever help anyone again, I have to make sure it's you?"

"Yes. Only me."

I feel an instant thrill from our double negative banter.

Sangwoo quietly observes me. I expect another barrage of comments, but he surprises me instead. "I like how straightforward you are."

"Really?" A tinge of fascination ruminates inside of me from his compliment.

Sangwoo leans against the kitchen counter. His expression is on guard despite his disclosure. "I spend most of my time with men who refuse to apologize and clarify. It is always their way or no way. It's actually refreshing to meet people like you and your mother. No questions. No qualms. You just help without wanting anything in return." Sangwoo's voice, the familiar calm and collected tenor, intensifies the praise.

"That's how my mother and I are," I mutter with a slight fixation of pride.

"But then again, it makes you an easy victim. People pretend to be helpless and then hurt their rescuers all the time." Sangwoo has a special craft as a realist.

"Is that how it works in your world?" I can't help myself with the ridicule.

Sangwoo's eyes land squarely into the pockets of my gaze. "Very much so. It's a cut throat industry."

"You speak of it like you're doing a business." I am fascinated with his style of juxtaposition.

"It is," Sangwoo agrees with contention. "It is a business. It has a social and hierarchical structure just like any other institution. But, what separates one person from the other is climbing technique on the food chain."

I can feel myself drowning under the wealth of information. I am way out of my element here. So far, this is debunking all the misconceptions and stereotypes I have about the underground world. I feel a bit foolish for judging him so quickly. *So gangsters wearing baggy jeans and listening to rap music are not members of his? What kind of underground world and hierarchical structure is he talking about?*

A loud car horn breaks through the bubble Sangwoo and I have apparently created. A large part of me is not prepared for our conversation to be over so soon, but the other part knows that this encounter has to end at some point.

At the sound of the horn, Sangwoo pushes up his left shirtsleeve to reveal an expensive silver watch. *Oh, I didn't notice that last night. This man is adorned in jewelry. Expensive jewelry.*

Sangwoo's eyebrows come together in concern when he observes the time. I am not sure if his ride is on time or late, but it is apparent that our conversation is over.

"My car's here. I have to go," Sangwoo announces. Without waiting for a response, Sangwoo walks to the living room where his black blazer is hanging from one of the coat hooks on the wall. I don't remember doing that for him last night.

"Ok . . . bye," I say faintly, not sure how this farewell should go. I am certain there isn't a correct protocol for saying goodbye to a high-up gangster.

Choi Sangwoo tucks his blazer underneath his arm and then faces me. "Again, thank you for what you've done. I don't get ever get to that point, but last night was the only exception. I know it wasn't easy for you to take me back here and let me stay. But I'm really glad you did. I hope that despite what we just talked about . . . we can be friends?"

Sangwoo extends a hand to me. *Friendly gangster May. He's a friendly one.* My intuition folds her arms across her chest; she is letting me make the call on this one.

I am not sure if his definition of a friend is the same as mine. But, denying anyone's good intentions, especially if there is no opportunity gained or lost from it, would be an insult to what my parents have always taught me.

"Yes, sure. Friends." I take Sangwoo's hand in mine.

As we touch, Sangwoo's smile fades. His brown eyes narrow minutely and focus on my features. I feel the immediate assessment. A million of thoughts spark.

I wasn't born exceptionally beautiful, but my father always did tell me I have very stark features. Of course, all parents think their children are beautiful. I am average in height at five-feet-four inches with long, layered black hair. My eyes, my biological mother's gift, are round with thick lashes outlining the outer rims. My nose evens out my features, accentuating my round baby face and plump lips. When asked to describe me, most people will probably choose to say, "She's a very quiet girl when she doesn't have an opinion" rather than describe my physical attributes.

I wonder if Choi Sangwoo is thinking the same things when his eyes linger on my face. He ends up surprising me when he states, "You . . . you look like this girl I used to know. Much younger. Much more passive. But the same life in you."

A chill ripples down my spine. I stare back at him, unsure of what to say. This is the second time Sangwoo's mentioning how similar I am to the girl he once knew. However, his comment is not supposed to elicit a response from me. It is a simple observation, a quick comparison, a rhetorical statement.

"Bye May. Thank you for everything." With those last words, Sangwoo opens the apartment door and turns away.

"You're welcome," I answer. Slightly mesmerized, I stand against the door and watch him.

Sangwoo walks with ease out into the bright sun, but with every step he takes, it is evident that he is a creature of the night. He moves quickly down the apartment steps to a black, unmarked car that is waiting for him. Its engine is still running; the emblem on the front of the car belongs to a foreign brand. When Sangwoo nears the rear of the car, the passenger door opens.

A man, wearing a trademark black suit, steps out with haste. He bows respectfully to Sangwoo. They exchange a few words before he steps back to let Sangwoo in the front passenger seat. He ends up in the back seat. As soon as the doors are closed, the intimidating car makes a perfect roundabout circle out of the apartment complex.

This all takes place under a minute.

Just like how he entered my life last week, Choi Sangwoo quickly vanishes with the black car as it disappears from sight. I stand there for a couple more minutes. Thoughts run through my mind, replaying our conversation repeatedly. I wanted to ask Sangwoo about his presence at The Trax last night, but I accept the fact that I will probably never see him again. He says he doesn't know me from anywhere before. But from those brown eyes are hiding something from me. *But why?*

I understand I have encountered someone significant, someone belonging to a different world than mine. To have had him so close, so relatable, despite the different paths of our lives is unnerving. He wants something that normal people take for granted. Choi Sangwoo wants to be friends. More specifically, he wants to be friends with me. *Did he ask for your number though? No he didn't, so snap out of it. He was just being nice.* My intuition begins the long process of picking up my daydreams off the floor.

"What a charming guy."

"Mom!"

My hands fly to my chest in surprise. Eunhye has successfully scared me with her phantom appearance. Now, she is standing on her tiptoes trying to see over my shoulder.

"He left already?" She is completely oblivious to the fact that I am in the midst of a heart attack.

"Yes." I step back inside the apartment and make it a point to close the door loudly behind me. "I have to get ready for work."

"How come you've never told me about this Sangwoo? How long has he been working at The Trax?" Eunhye follows my heels all the way into my room. She is the motherly type on energy pills. Eunhye's parenting skills have always been a little unorthodox. It might be because Eunhye's line of work keeps her attentive and youthful.

"A few months," I answer shortly. I keep my expressions steady, hoping to be discreet. I don't want Eunhye to misunderstand the situation or exacerbate it.

"I trust you, honey. But next time, if any of your co-workers get too hammered to go home, just call me ok?" Eunhye asks. "I know you're twenty-one, but there are things you still need to run by me."

Surprised, I turn to face her. *Oh no. She's mad.* "I thought you were fine with me letting him crash here last night. You said it is better than him getting in trouble on the way home." My eyes search for forgiveness.

"Of course I have to say that," Eunhye remarks immediately. I know she forgives me when she smiles. "It's done. I can't turn back time. Besides, there's no point in lecturing you in front of him. Sweetheart, at the end of the day, you're a girl and he's a boy. Thankfully, nothing happened and he turned out to be a very good person."

I bite my tongue on what I really want to reply. "I'm sorry mom. I'll use better judgment next time," I say instead.

My mother's face expands into a large smile. "I wouldn't mind if you date him. Not only is he one of those rare handsome ones, but he's also very intelligent."

"Hmm." I make my way over to my closet and start rummaging through for clothes. This is my cue to get occupied; this is also the part in the conversation where I revert to my adolescent ways. Eunhye knows I don't do the boyfriend thing because I haven't found anyone interesting in all of my twenty-one years. All the boys my age are only interested in money, sex, and drugs—which isn't a far cry from the rest of the male population, I have heard through the grapevine. Besides, Choi Sangwoo is way out of my league and I am too a lifetime-of-insecurities to think otherwise.

Meanwhile, Eunhye is rambling on in the background. She's on a mission. "We had a very great conversation. I would actually approve of him if you two became an item. Don't you think it's about time you find yourself a boyfriend? Someone to share your life with?"

I stop looking through my closet. "Mom, he's just a friend. Besides, I'm not interested in a relationship right now. I have other goals in my life."

Eunhye proceeds to narrow her eyes at me. "Maybelline Lee. I was a teen once you know? Before I got this old and wise, I was your age once."

I let out a laugh. Eunhye knows how to lighten up a situation. "Mom, you were a teen when bingo night meant a great date."

"Ouch!" She playfully pinches the underside of my left arm. "That was the best thing in the world! Don't make fun of me."

I shake my head and continue ransacking through my closet. "Our generation is doomed, mother."

"Does he do anything else besides The Trax?" Eunhye presses on, diverting the conversation back to Choi Sangwoo.

I pause shortly, fighting the urge to laugh. "Not that I know of."

"That's a shame. He could really use those brains and looks of his to go far. He's a gem May. Mark my words. He'll do something big with his life. This won't be the last time you hear from him." Leaving me to mull on that, Eunhye walks out of my room with a dreamy sigh.

I want to laugh at Eunhye's premature prediction, but when my eyes land on the spot where Sangwoo slept last night, I spy the shiny object. I make my way over to the area without any mental registration. As soon as my hands touch the object, I realize what it is quickly. It is the same diamond-encrusted necklace with a Cross on it.

Thoughts floor my mind. Why is it here in my room? Didn't Choi Sangwoo tuck his necklace back inside his shirt just moments ago? I saw him do it in the kitchen. I spin the necklace up to the light. *It's so beautiful. It must be a fortune.* The diamonds–tiny sliver studs embedded in-between the crust of the design–glisten as the symbol of the Cross swings like a pendulum in my grip.

My cell phone rings in the corner of my room. I am still staring at the magnificent piece of jewelry when I answer it.

"Hey, you didn't text me back last night!" Lina's voice engulfs my ears.

Just like that, I'm thrust back into reality. Choi Sangwoo and all the mysteries that shroud him will have to wait.

CHAPTER THREE

Life as I know it continues in the same mundane routine. Meeting Choi Sangwoo is unequivocally in my top five most-noted life events. Another seven days goes by and as I expect, there is no word or sign of Choi Sangwoo's existence. It is as though he doesn't exist, as though he is just a figment of my imagination from working two jobs and long hours. An abhorrent illusion. He is like a phantom, appearing and disappearing at his will and leisure. Choi Sangwoo is verified to be real only when Joolie or Tailor mentions him. They mostly refer to him as the lonely gangster and anticipate his return to The Trax. Many theories circulate the area without any reliability or validity. Most of the gossip starts with Joolie and often ends with Joolie when she becomes disinterested.

Only when I look at the Cross necklace am I reminded that Choi Sangwoo is real. He existed in my apartment at one point. And now, he is just a symbol left behind in my sock drawer. I can hardly bear the thought of throwing away something that costs as much as a house, so I keep his necklace next to the tip receipt. I realize I am starting to collect remnants of his being.

By the end of the week, I turn my focus on time management to forget him. I throw my time and energy into work. Every day after work I go home mentally, emotionally, and physically tired. The mundane patterns of work, sleep, eat, and repeat continues. I try to add some variation to my week; every couple of days, I take up my cousin's invitations to jog with her. I also spend more time rereading my favorite books and college recommended literature.

But when Sunday arrives to wrap up the revolving week, I lose my battle with time management. I wake up in the morning covered in a sheet of sweat from a nightmare I can't quite remember. By the time I convince myself that my past is long gone and the people who used to hurt me are no longer around, I miss my first bus.

I am fifteen minutes late when I arrive at Sansachun, fresh out of breath from running.

"Good morning."

Lina, my cousin and best friend, is standing at her usual place behind the glass counter. Lina's mother is my father's sister; we are first cousins and share the dominant genes of the Lee family. Although Lina has her father's last name, Kim, she still desires to change her name to a Lee someday.

Lina and I both work the morning to mid-afternoon shift at Sansachun, the smallest convenience store on the busiest street in Seoul. The irony is hardly anyone shops here. We have other major conveniences and liquor stores around the block to compete with. Mr. Chun refuses to lower any of the prices on his products or develop better marketing schemes. He believes in running with the competition.

Because of Mr. Chun's business approach and the inconsistency of foot traffic at the store, Lina and I mostly spend our shift waiting around. It is hard to do our job when the main component, such as customers, is close to non-existent some days. There are days when the store has a decent flow of customers. Then, there are some days, like today where Lina and I can hear each other breathe from the lack of activity.

"I missed my bus," I start explaining to Lina why I am late.

"That sucks . . . . Watch this." Lina ignores me without regard. Lina's glued to the tiny TV mounted on the wall above the cash register. Lina has her elbows prop on the glass case that contains various products, including cigarettes and calling cards. Lina's eyebrows form a nervous frown as she watches the TV. My cousin's intense interest in the news is contagious.

I follow Lina's gaze. The usual morning news is running its popular feature. I glance at the timer at the bottom of the TV screen; it is supposed to be weather hour. However, a somber male anchor is currently replacing the weather woman. His military hair matches the blue vest suit he is wearing. His eyebrows run flat against his face, giving him the expression of restlessness. His dark skin tone and demeanor reflect the news story he is covering.

"Last night, around ten-thirty, in the unmarked turnpikes of Busan, two rival gangs were embroiled in a massive street war. It was reported that an internal disagreement between the notorious Mayhem and violent Crist—a play on words of The Holy Christ—is what sparked this unusual public event. Although these two sophisticated rivals have never orchestrated reckless encounters like other street gangs, last night was an exception to their rising hostility against one another. Surprisingly, police were unable to apprehend any of the gang members from either side. Multiple cars stolen, properties vandalized, and stray shells accounted for civilian casualties. The local authorities ask that if anyone has any information on Crist or Mayhem members to call the hotline. Both gangs are known to operate mainly in Japan, but in recent months have been increasingly active in South Korea. The National Safety-Against-Gangs, the NSAG, warns civilians to report any suspicious activities and to notify the police when a gang member is identified."

At the end of his sentence, the anchor picks up the stack of papers on his desk. He looks uncomfortable, possibly afraid of the backlash that reporting about gangs might bring him.

Meanwhile, I feel a chill run down my spine. The Crist gang. Choi Sangwoo's face flashes in my mind. Did he participate in the fight last night? I can't imagine him engaged in a hostile fight. Common media portrayals of gang fights rotate in my mind—guys wielding bats, sticks, and guns chasing after one another. Some fight while others are on the wet, dark ground bleeding to death. In the background, their respective leaders are screaming out commands.

"It's so crazy the police can't even do anything about it." Lina's comment brings me back to reality.

My thought bubbles pop and fade away. My intuition is eating grapes and shrugging her shoulders. She has no idea what to do with the news no more than my conscience. I snap out of my daze to focus on Lina. My cousin's eyebrows furrow together in concern.

Lina hates gangs, gang members, and gang-affiliated anything. Apparently, her uncle from her father's side was associated with a gang in his younger years and was double-crossed by someone he thought a friend. Long story short, Lina's uncle got shot in the back. Lina was really close to him as a child, so she grew up renouncing all social groups. Convinced that it was better to have one-on-one relationships than to be associated with a clique, Lina conducts her friendships in linear lines. None of her friendships run in circles. I am her only close, best friend.

In many ways, Lina is a lot like me in personality. She is blunt, straightforward, and a natural loner. But, unlike me, Lina lives with both of her parents. My aunt and uncle raised Lina under strict religious rules. Lina often cites her natural family composition to be the reason why she rebels in life.

Lina has a natural beauty to her that's overshadowed by her rebellious streak. In middle school, we used to look like twins with the same dark hair and height. Then, high school rolled around and Lina developed a health conscious mindset. She began drinking milk every day and practiced yoga religiously. Now, she is two inches taller with platinum blonde hair.

It was during junior year in high school when Lina announced she is going to bypass the academic route to discovering life. True to her sense of humor, Lina proclaimed that her life goal is to find a rich husband and live happily ever after. Lina thought she was one-step closer when she met her boyfriend, Spyder, a year ago at a party.

When I first met Spyder, I was sure that his money couldn't possibly be his. Spyder had *shady* written all over his face. But Lina is convinced that he can take care of her. She is only working at Sansachun because I am. In fact, Lina is the one who recommended me this part-time position. I am supposed to be her replacement, but Mr. Chun ended up keeping us both.

Lina has relentless thoughts and strong opinions about the world. While I prefer to be an observer, Lina is the more proactive one. So, the news obviously doesn't sit well with her. I haven't told Lina that I've met a Crist member, and he is not at all how social media tends to portray gang members. But I am not ready to defend or agree with Lina's comments about Choi Sangwoo. In fact, I'm not even sure how I feel about the incredibly mysterious, fascinating, and intimidating gangster.

At the present moment, Lina's face is in a permanent frown. The more I observe her, the more convinced I am that her reaction to the news isn't just at the superficial level. It is one of the perks of knowing someone for so long.

"Are you okay?" I ask Lina with a nudge. "You don't seem too happy about the news."

"I'm fine," Lina mumbles. She looks away from the TV.

I glance back up at the TV. Now, the anchor is reporting about pipe problems in Seoul's main business district. From gang fights to pipelines. Our world is never consistent.

"Why were you late this morning?" Lina changes the subject.

I try to gauge Lina's facial expression. Is something there or is it my imagination? But Lina only stares back at me, waiting for an answer.

"I had a nightmare last night." I finally give in. "I couldn't sleep all night, just kept tossing and turning. When I finally did sleep, I woke up from a bad dream. You know, the kind you don't really remember in the morning? I think it's because I've been working late. I'm trying to manage my time a little better."

"Nightmares?" Lina is sympathetic towards my issues. Because she is family, my cousin is privy to my past. "The same ones?"

I nod my head slowly. Not wanting to give too much away, I state softly, "It's not a big deal. You know how it comes and goes."

Lina surveys my face shortly. I can tell she is deciding if I am up to talking about it. Something in my face makes Lina decide it is better to leave me alone for now.

A small smile graces her lips instead. "You know what we should do after work?" Lina wraps an arm around my shoulders. "Let's go shopping and get some milk tea. Girl time."

"What about Spyder?" I ask. If I am not taking up Lina's time, her boyfriend does.

"You come first to me, baby." Lina places her head against my shoulder.

"Uh huh!" I laugh. My mood brightens from Lina's humor. "Sure."

Lina breaks out into fits of giggles. My endearing cousin always knows how to lift me up.

At the very same moment, a couple wanders into Sansachun. The husband wants to find motion sickness medication while the wife peruses the aisle for generic allergy pills. From then on, the foot traffic at Sansachun increases fivefold. A few more customers step into the store, interested in items ranging from beverages to household products.

It turns out to be one of those fast-paced and productive days. Neither Lina nor I could have predicted that Sansachun is going to have another successful day. Mr. Chun's business hunch is turning out to be right. If he keeps his prices firm and doesn't give into the competition next door, he can still generate income and keep the customer's interests. The tour-de-force of good luck that is blowing through the store keeps Lina and me busy until the end of our shift. While Lina works at the cashier, I help the customers roam the aisles.

BY THE TIME THE LAST customer exits the store, Lina and I are so tired we decide to close up and wait for our co-worker Bae to release us for the night shift. We only know Bae by his first name, and the only personal information he has ever told us is he has a family with a wife and two kids. During the day, he works as a mechanic and at night, he works at Sansachun for Mr. Chun. He is a good soul, and treats Lina and me as though we are his kids. Every other day, he would bring us a snack.

Today, Lina and I opt to have our things ready to leave by the time Bae comes in.

"I'll go get our bags," Lina says. She volunteers to go to the back room while I wait out front.

I am in the middle of stacking the remaining products in an orderly fashion on the glass counter when the store's door chimes open. I turn, expecting to see Bae and the dark blue uniform he always wears. Instead,

I face an unfamiliar customer.

A male, in his late twenties, comes striding into the store with purpose. His hair is in the style of a Mohawk; one strip of black hair rules down the middle of his head. He is wearing a black dress shirt, with the top two buttons exposed to reveal the shadow of his chest, over dark jeans. The dark sneakers he is wearing ruins his otherwise professional outfit.

Immediately, a red flag flashes in front of my eyes. *Get the phone.* My intuition scrambles up from her nap cot.

"Hi, welcome to Sansachun. How may I help you?" I force myself to state the usual greeting. Above all, I want to make sure Lina hears me.

I must blend into the shelves behind me because Mohawk's body language changes when he finally sees me. He reminds me of a tiger when he moves, the slow and calculated movements of a feline stalking its prey. When he approaches the counter, and I can see his face clearer, I realize more than ever that my instincts are right. Mohawk is not here to buy anything that Sansachun offers. He is here with a different agenda entirely other than shopping.

"Hello." His voice is whimsical with a dangerous undertone. Mohawk leans across the glass counter and smiles without teeth.

"How can I help you?" I repeat again. Part of me wants to call for Lina, but the other part is too perplexed to move.

"I'm looking for someone . . . I wonder if you can help me." Mohawk's sharp facial structure is home to a broken nose, slightly bruised cheekbones, and a small cut on his upper lip. Whether these are fresh battle scars or not, the three foreign symbols tattooed on the right side of his face indicates the jurisdiction for it.

"Well, sir, all stores have a privacy policy in which we are not allowed to reveal our customers and—" I start explaining at a rapid pace.

"No," Mohawk cuts me off quickly, conveying a rapid sense of impatience. "I'm not looking for a customer. I'm looking for your co-worker."

I feel the chill down my spine, but something is clearly stuck in my throat. A new type of fear washes over me. Before I can respond, Lina returns from the back room.

"Ok. Let's go. Did Bae come in yet?" She has a fresh smile on her face, excited to leave work. Lina has her bag swinging from her left hand and her right hand clutching her cell phone. But everything comes to a stop for Lina when she sees the figure standing on the opposite side of the counter.

Immediately, the smile disappears from my cousin's face. I feel as though the bottom of my stomach drops too. Lina and I wear our emotions on our sleeves. If we are happy, mad, or sad anyone and everyone can read it from our expressions and body language. When I see the look of surprise changing to fear on her face, I know my cousin has gotten herself into irreversible trouble.

Lina knows this all too well. Yet, at the present moment, she is speechless and immobilized at the sight of Mohawk.

"Hi Lina." Mohawk stands from the counter at the sight of her. He smiles at her as though they are longtime friends. Whomever Mohawk represents requires him to be professional, patient, and particular.

"Hi," Lina's reply is barely above a whisper. She walks slowly over to my side. "You're here at my work . . . ."

"I am," Mohawk agrees without hesitation. "I was beginning to worry about you and Spyder. Maybe you two got into a horrific accident, I thought. That would be the only reason why you both have been ignoring my phone calls for the past week. But, look at you standing here healthy and alive! Not a care in the world."

My eyebrows come together in confusion. I don't have to wait long to understand the topic of conversation.

"I-I'll pay you back. Spyder and I will pay you back. It's just been rough this past month. We weren't avoiding you. We were just trying to gather the money–"Lina's words are long-winded bursts.

"Shut up." His playful demeanor subsides at Lina's pleas. Without warning of an emotional outburst, Mohawk slams his right fist onto the glass counter.

Lina and I both jump back, convinced that the glass counter would shatter under his force.

"What is he doing?!" I can't help myself. "What's going on Lina?" I ask my cousin with haste.

My cousin simply shakes her head as the colors of fear change on her face. She desperately wants me to shut up and for the situation to be a dream.

"I didn't hunt you down to hear your excuses." Mohawk's voice lowers with menace. "My Boss is currently on his way to Spyder's house as we speak. He required that you be at the meeting as well."

The realization of Mohawk's threat drains the remaining blood from Lina's face.

"Spyder's house? Your Boss?" Lina blinks furiously as the tears form in her eyes. "P-please! I beg you. There's no need to involve your Boss.

We'll pay you back. Just give us an extension."

Boss? Extension? Pay you back? What the hell is Lina talking about? My heart is pounding in my ribcage from the tides of confusion and surprise.

"I didn't come here to negotiate terms. My job is to make sure you attend the meeting." Mohawk steps back from the glass counter. His face becomes hard and cold as stone. "So you can decide to come by yourself or I can help you."

"Please . . . ," Lina mutters. By now, the tears are free falling from her eyes. Lina hastily wipes them away with her shirtsleeve.

I have never seen my cousin cry with such fear before. I reach out to her. I'm so baffled my head starts gathering the necessary chemicals for a migraine. "Lina, what's going on?" My voice sounds like I am squeaking.

"I owe them money," Lina sobs into my arm. "They're after me now."

Shit. I do my best not to gasp aloud. My conscience peeks over her glasses. *Choi Sangwoo*, my conscience whispers. I cover her quickly with a sheer blanket.

Meanwhile, Mohawk stands as a motionless statue. I suppose in his field of business he is used to the tears, sweat, and even blood of others. I want to give my cousin a hug and console her, but I decide against any sudden movements with Mohawk standing in such close proximity.

"I'll go," Lina states when she faces Mohawk again. She wipes her nose one last time. "I'll go to the meeting."

"I'll come too," I volunteer immediately. "I'm her cousin. Maybe I can help and settle a deal with your Boss. I'll help Lina pay back what she owes," I add before Mohawk opposes me.

"No May," Lina protests. She grabs onto my arm tightly. As if there is a fourth wall between us, she says, "Stay out of this. I'll call you after."

"No," I retort. Lina must be crazy if she thinks I am going to let her go with Mohawk alone. "I'm going with you. I'm not going to leave you, Lina."

Mohawk narrows his eyes at my suggestion, but his lips curve into an entertained smile. "What a loyal cousin you have, Lina. It isn't a bad idea for a third person to co-sign your hefty loan. It might save your head."

Lina gives him a resentful look. When she turns to me, Lina's eyes are full of defeat and remorse. "I'm sorry May. I don't want to get you involved."

I can only give her arm a small squeeze. It is my way of telling Lina that I am going to be here for her, regardless of how bad the situation turns out to be. I am still in shock, but I do my best to compose my surprise. *You think you have enough credibility to deal with loan sharks after your brush with the gangster?* My intuition purses her lips at me and shakes her head.

"My Boss does not like to wait ladies." Mohawk takes a couple of steps back from the counter, a clear indication that we are supposed to follow him now.

Lina holds onto my arm as we follow Mohawk out of the store. The feeling of leaving Sansachun without a choice is terrifying. Lina and I could not have predicted our great day would take a turn for the worse. There are so many questions I want to ask her, but I know this isn't the time or place. With a heavy heart, I walk with Lina and follow Mohawk out of the store. The silence is hard for me to bear when the questions are dancing on the tip of my tongue.

It becomes apparent that the red carpet treatment allows Mohawk to be here. A large, black sport utility vehicle is waiting for us outside of Sansachun. Its engine is still running at a steady beat. Mohawk stops when he reaches the driver's side of the car. He waits for Lina to close up the store. Lina's hands are shaking uncontrollably as she locks up the front door of Sansachun. I offer to help her, but Mohawk makes it clear he wants her to feel the torment of anxiety and fear. *Asshole.*

After Lina extracts the key out of the lock, Mohawk motions for Lina to get into the back seat of the car first. I follow shortly behind her. Once I am in the car, Mohawk closes the door behind us and walks around to the front passenger's side.

Inside, the car is total darkness. There is a solid black partition separating the back seat from the front. It is halfway down, revealing a driver who has one hand on the steering wheel and the other on the gearshift. The driver is wearing black sunglasses that cover more than half of his face.

When Mohawk gets into the passenger seat, he simply nods to the driver. The car's automatic locks switch on as it pulls away from Sansachun's curb.

The late afternoon sunlight is as bright as ever. However, inside the car, the light is a mute dark blue color. The streets are bustling with the spontaneous commotion of cars and people. It all seems worlds away from where Lina and I are heading.

Occasionally, I catch my cousin's concerned face. Thoughts run through my mind at a rapid pace as I try to find some logical and rational meaning to the situation. Then, I remember Spyder and his money issues. To the naked eye, Spyder has plenty of money, but a closer introspection would probably cite an unreliable income source. After all this time, I am about to find the truth to my suspicions. It is just too terrible that Lina has to be involved in something as reckless as this.

"Is Boss on his way?"

From the front passenger seat, Mohawk's left hand flashes to his ear. He is holding an unidentifiable cell phone. At the same time, the car's partition rolls up. Mohawk and the driver disappear out of sight shortly. Apparently, the partition is not only vision proof, but sound proof as well.

"Who are they?" I immediately turn to Lina. "We need to call the police!"

Lina's eyebrows came together in worry. She looks at the partition to gauge if it is safe to talk. "We can't call the police May. It'll be worse for us if we do. They're loan sharks. I'm sorry May."

A feeling of dread comes over me. "How long has this been going on?" Somehow, I feel betrayed.

Lina gives me such a sad look that she almost appears to be a different person. Apparently, she has been hiding this fact from me for quite some time. "About two weeks now. Last time, we asked them for an extension and today's the last day."

"We?" I have been under the impression this is Spyder's sole doing.

"Spyder and I have some financial problems. I borrowed ten grand to help my parents. Spyder borrowed an additional ten grand for his own personal reasons," Lina whispers as rapidly as she can. Her eyebrows come together in defeat. Lina's shoulders sag as her tone of agitation increases.

"Why didn't you tell me?" I know it is an impractical question to ask, but I can't understand why Lina kept such an important problem from me.

". . . Because I thought I could handle it. It's embarrassing to have such financial problems." Lina makes a sour facial expression. The regret is also evident.

"Everybody has financial issues," I remark and attempt to conjure up something that would brighten up the situation. But a dark thought crosses my mind instead. "How deep are you in this?"

"Enough," Lina mutters in reply. "Hopefully, I can ask the Boss for an extension."

"You–" I start to reply when the partition lowers with a soft hum.

Evidently, Mohawk is done with his private phone conversation.

"Talking about us?" Mohawk rests the left side of his head against his chair's headrest. When Lina and I don't answer him, Mohawk lets out a feigned sigh. "That's right . . . not everyone gets to have a meeting with my Boss. We're not the type of business where you can schedule an appointment with us when it is convenient for you. We are also not the type of business where apologies and pleas can earn you extensions and forbearances. You're lucky my Boss is taking time out of his day to entertain your sorries. I would choose my words wisely if I were you."

Who do you think you are?! My conscience is shoving a closed knuckle at his head. I bite my lower lip at Mohawk's rude diction. I want to disagree, but Lina touches my hand softly. She shakes her head feverishly, adamantly advising me to let it go. Fortunately, I don't have to put with him any longer.

The car makes a sharp turn around the familiar bend of the dreary road. Spyder's house is on steep hills that lead to a shabby neighborhood. His is the only house on top of the highest plateau with skewed black gates. Every single window is tinted a dark shade of black, and the front door is constructed entirely out of shutters. At the moment, however, the most fascinating thing about Spyder's house is not its unusual design. It is the fact that the uninvited vehicles line the front like flies attracted to a particular light.

Four unmarked sports utility vehicles, identical to the one we are sitting in, park in front of Spyder's house. From the headlights down to the grill of each tire, the cars make an intimidating convoy. The SUV Lina and I are in round out the end of the group. It comes to a slow and calculated stop right in front of Spyder's gates.

"Let's go." Mohawk is out of the car before the driver can turn off the engine.

"I can't do this, May." Lina turns to me with abrupt panic. Fear, anxiety, and nervousness splay themselves on her expression.

"Stay calm." I try to comfort my best friend and cousin. "It'll be ok. Take a deep breath." *Are you convincing yourself too?* My intuition is gulping down her Red Bull with a lets-do-this sticker around her forearm.

Lina inhales tentatively and then exhales again.

"Let's go!" From the outside, Mohawk pounds on the car door.

"Come on. He's getting on my nerves." The irritation free flows through me now.

I open the door and get out of the car first. Lina clasps both hands around my left wrist to pull herself out. I don't want to let it show, but a sinking feeling develops at the bottom of my stomach. I survey Spyder's house and the area. The quiet neighborhood is oblivious about the house on top of the hill. Many of the houses on the block are empty; their owners are still a long way from home at this time in the afternoon.

"This way." Mohawk leads the way into Spyder's house.

Lina and I make our way towards the black gates behind him. The gate groans when Mohawk moves through them. The steps leading up to the front door has various cracks and breaks in them. At the top of the very last step, the front door is left ajar.

Mohawk pushes the door open with only one hand. The door swings open without a sound, revealing its hollow appearance. The house's modest furnishing includes two small chairs, a coffee table, and a large wooden bookcase against the wall. It is a shocking contrast to only two months ago, when I was last here for Spyder's birthday party, where miscellaneous furniture and items claimed the entire area. Now, the only sign of life in the room is the natural mid-afternoon sunlight; it is the only source of lighting from the front window.

Mohawk's footsteps pick up speed as he leads us around the house. I am familiar with the layout enough to know that Mohawk is leading us to the dining room.

The house has an old rusty smell to it. The floorboards creak with every step that Lina and I take. Spyder's dining room is set to the very back of his house. Its threshold is of a large oval shape. Inside, a glass table for six is front and center behind a large window. The walls are redwood, dated and ancient. The dining room is housing the company of more than ten people today.

"Don't try anything funny," Mohawk instructs under his breath as we near the dining room. He nods to two men who are guarding opposite ends of the dining room's entrance. Without another pause, Mohawk heads straight in with us in tow. Then, he steps to the side wall and stands guard. Just like that, Mohawk recedes into the background.

No one can truly prepare themselves for a meeting with citizens of the underground world. This isn't a typical meeting in which the most precious thing at stake is failing to impress the potential employer or lacking the correct qualifications. This also isn't the type of meeting in which being prepared for questions and the pressures of intimidation are tools for resolution. This is the type of meeting where ignorance is bliss, and giving in to another person's rules is not a sign of weakness but rather survival.

The scenario in the dining room is already chaotic. There are four figures surrounding the dining room table, but none sitting. All clues suggest that a physical confrontation occurred prior to our appearance. Strange faces occupy the dining room, except for Spyder who is the present victim. Each individual gang member is dressed in the same stylish suit as Mohawk with the same silver diamond watch on their left wrists. The face of the watch yields a serpent wrapped around the bold letter *M*.

"Please stop!" Spyder is begging. The imminent distress in his voice permeates the walls of the dining room.

This no-good-son-of-a-bitch! my intuition hisses. She has her boxing gloves on at the sight of Spyder. I can't say he doesn't deserve the pain that is raining on him. I have my reasons for disliking Spyder and this moment proves my intuition right.

"Shut up!" One of the suits extends a right fist to the bottom of Spyder's throat. The impact of his closed knuckles and the exoskeleton of Spyder's throat collide at a painful speed.

Oh, this can't be good. I mentally die. This is not a simple conversational meeting after all. I actually feel pain for Spyder. Even though I don't like him, he doesn't deserve to be treated like a dog.

"Stop! Please!" At the sight of her boyfriend's assault, Lina breaks away from me and runs to Spyder.

At the sight of us, the gang member assaulting Spyder steps back to watch Lina rush toward Spyder. He is hardly breathing; it doesn't take a lot of energy out of him to hurt Spyder. "Look who's finally here." His face is bright and welcoming, but the tone of his greet laces with dangerous sarcasm.

He is menacing in every sense of the word. His black hair is slicked back from his face, revealing a widow's peak hairline and large brown eyes under overarching eyebrows. His sculpted facial structure rounds out hollow cheekbones and thin, hard lips. From the way he carries himself, it is easy to see that his position was earned and not given.

"Are you okay?!" Lina ignores him to address Spyder. She wraps her arms around Spyder who has apologies written all over his sorry facial expression.

"I'm sorry baby." Spyder buries his head into her arms.

Are you? My thoughts are salacious. I bite down on my bottom lip. I haven't decided where I stand on this.

Sang Junjin is his birth name. But in many ways, Spyder epitomizes the nickname given to him by people who have interacted with him over time. He is tall with a potbelly, but at the same time wiry with curly hair that gives him the impression of wearing a mop. Spyder is always spinning webs of lies and deceit to trick people into doing what he wants them to do. But his web of lies is going to fail him. This is not the first time Spyder's dragging Lina down with him. But there is no point in bringing up the past when the present is uncertain.

"Danny, I thought Boss says there's no need for physical violence." From behind us, Mohawk's demure voice addresses Spyder's attacker.

Danny, as his name turns out to be, points at Spyder and Lina on the floor. "They need to learn that they need to uphold the terms of the loan!" The look he gives Mohawk is unnerving. "I'm just doing my job unless you have better ideas to make them pay."

I glance around the room and realize the actual Boss of this group is not here. Should I be relieved the Boss isn't here yet? Could it get any more violent than this?

"Suit yourself." At Danny's outburst Mohawk steps back to the corner of the dining room.

"Aish!" Danny wipes the corners of his mouth as though this is not worth his time. "Get up," he tells Spyder and Lina. When they are too slow to heed his order, Danny extends a black heel and kicks Spyder's side.

Spyder groans in pain as he doubles over.

What the heck?! A surge of courage liquidates my veins. *Ok. I'm all for kicking Spyder, but this is inhumane.*

"Ok! Ok!" Lina shouts at Danny. With great effort, she pulls Spyder into a dining room chair. Tears are cascading down the side of her face. "Is this really necessary? Do you really have to beat him up like this?!"

"Is it necessary for you to borrow money from us and pretend you don't need to pay it back?" Danny retorts with swiftness. "We made multiple attempts to reach you. You not only ignored us, but also hid from us. Is that necessary?"

Spyder and Lina cringe at Danny's outburst. Spyder is clutching onto his nose; the blood is cascading in a linear line. Lina is inhaling and exhaling in rapid breaths; her body starts to shake.

"Look, Lina. We've been reasonable." Danny's lips curl into a cruel smirk. "As we were discussing with your disgusting boyfriend, before he opened his mouth and made me punch him, we don't enjoy taking drastic measures such as this. Not only is it time consuming for us, but also incredibly . . . demeaning . . . for us to deal with situations like this. It's embarrassing, Lina. We're not some average street gang that you can just borrow from and then ignore our attempts to contact you. It went from a business transaction to some street transaction. How did it get so bad?"

Lina shifts uncomfortably in her seat. "We understand that. We understand it all. But please believe me, Spyder and I are doing everything that we can to gather the money and pay you back. We don't want it to get to this point. We're trying very hard, Danny." Lina's eyes become big and soft as she looks up at him. Lina nudges her boyfriend to come to her rescue. "Tell them, Spyder."

"I did. I've been telling them," Spyder speaks up at Lina's encouragement. He shakes his head, conveying the notion that he has exhausted his pleas prior to our appearance. That is when I notice the purple bruise on Spyder's right cheek.

"Uh huh." Danny nods his head; he has heard it all before. "Yes, you've been trying to pay us back for the last two months. Extension after extension. I don't want to hear it anymore. Either you come up with the money or we will take it, including everything you love, from you. I don't want to hear the bullshit anymore."

"It's not bullshit," Lina argues with Danny. There is a fire of justice dancing in her eyes. "We honestly and sincerely mean it! After the last extension, we asked for a grace period. It's not the end of the month yet. Twenty thousand dollars, including interest, is not a feasible amount for Spyder and me right now. Please understand."

Twenty thousand dollars?! I do my best to remain calm from Lina's words. Can Spyder even spell twenty thousand dollars? Slapping her forehead, my intuition is spellbound by the event.

Danny begins rubbing the temple of his forehead as though he is overcoming a major headache. "Shut up," he states simply.

The other men around the room remain motionless.

"You're being unreasonable!" Lina lashes at him. My cousin's temperament is working against her. "You're not listening to us. How can we get twenty thousand dollars within such a short deadline?"

"I said I don't want to hear the bullshit anymore!" Without considering the fact that she is a girl, Danny raises his hands to her.

Oh hell no, he is not about to hit her. "Stop!" I shout before Danny does anything more drastic. *Why does my voice sound like a child?*

He lowers his hands at the sound of my cry. Danny turns to me with deliberation. He glances at the other members in the room, who are all standing as still as stone. Apparently, Mohawk is the only person who dares to challenge him. The rest remains as still as statues without command.

As though he sees me for the first time, Danny's question comes out in a quick and bored snarl, "And who are you?"

". . . May," I answer him as calmly as I could.

"May, what?" he asks with sarcastic diction.

"May Lee." I am not comfortable with the thought of introducing my full name to this stranger. But the look in his eyes stops me from thinking twice.

"Hmm." Danny looks over at Lina. A smirk expands on his lips. "Maybe we can use your friend as collateral?"

I can feel the blood rise in my veins at the threat. "Don't hurt them."

"Why shouldn't I?" In a calculated manner, Danny makes his way over to me. Now that he is inches away from me, the blood in my veins races with fear.

"I'm associated with Crist. I can help them pay the debt." The words tumble out of my mouth before I can stop myself. The ticking noise inside my brain causes my logical reasoning to malfunction. This often occurs when I lie beyond reasonable means.

From the corner of my eyes, I can see the shock and surprise hitting Spyder and then Lina the hardest.

"Ha!" Danny tosses his head back as he laughs in a mocking tone.

For the first time, the other men in the room let out low chuckles at my revelation. Even Mohawk shakes his head at me as if I am making a mistake.

Without warning, Danny's hand snakes up to the base of my throat. I hear Lina shouting something at him in the background, but my heart is in my ears at this point. With great force, Danny pins me against the wall. My back presses against the cold and hard structure. The weight of his body encloses my much smaller frame. I do not have time to register what is happening. *Shit, what have you done?* Shaking underneath her bed covers, my intuition has her eyes closed and her hands over her ears as she chants, *See no evil, hear no evil, speak no evil.*

"Judging from your weak reflex you're only using Crist as a crutch, but you need to be taught a lesson for lying." Danny narrows his eyes at me. The light in them dances gleefully. *Sadist!*

"Stop!" I reach up and attempt to disarm his grip from my neck, but it is useless. His fingers are not budging from their grip.

"Let her go!" Lina jumps up from her place, but one of Danny's men get to her first. My cousin lets out a loud yelp when he presses on her shoulders.

"Don't touch her!" I can hear Spyder coming to Lina's defense, but another gang member has him helpless on the ground.

"Get off me!" Meanwhile, I am trying to break away from Danny as fast I can. But he doesn't budge. Now, he has both hands around me against the side of the wall. He blocks my view effectively so I cannot see what is happening with Spyder and my cousin.

"Stop, stop, stop!"

I can hear Lina and Spyder suffering on the ground a distance away from me. This is beyond anyone's imagination. As I look into Danny's eyes, he makes me realize why the news story this morning affected Lina to the extent that it did. Lina and Spyder have gotten involved with gang members; the kind of gangs that are not written about in stories or immortalized through movies. These are the kind of gangs that the FBI and CIA keep behind interrogation rooms and shut away in confidential files. These are the gangs that news and media warn and caution its citizens about; gangs, that when shrouded in mystery, become stronger and powerful, dangerous and violent. Gangs that chase after their goals and pursuits without mercy, apologies, and regrets.

"Please stop!"

"Stop!"

"Don't do this!"

There is a flurry of activity going on at the same time. I can hear Spyder yelping in agony when one of the gang members elbows him in the stomach. The other member has Lina on the floor when she tries to help Spyder; my cousin screams as he steps on her open palm.

"Get off!"

Meanwhile, I shove at Danny's chest as hard as I can. That only angers Danny more and he grabs my left arm. I feel as though the bone, along with its ligaments, is going to snap off any moment now. The fight response in me screeches like a siren.

"Please, stop!" I wail in pain. *He can't do this. This is illegal!*

"Prove you're a member of Crist!" Danny growls into my ear. He jerks my arm so hard that I know any second now he is going to break it. Danny maneuvers me against the wall and his masculine frame overpowers me.

"You can't do this!" I shout at him through gritted teeth.

"But I am sweetheart. You're just like those lowlife friends of yours! You use Crist to scare Mayhem? They beg on their hands and knees when they see us!" Danny grinds the words into my ears.

I shut my eyes, praying for some type of release and miracle. I was not built for this; my only experience with violence stems from childhood and even then I always lost.

"I guess the meeting started without me."

A voice, steep and firm, overpowers the chaos and commotion in the dining room. With only one sentence, he is able to put a stop to the tyrannical occurrence. The newcomer is able to stop time and cause all motion to stop. Is this person the answer to my prayers?

Danny drops his hands, immediately releasing me. He takes several cautious steps back. The gang member looks over his shoulder with his eyes releasing the strength burning inside them.

The two gang members terrorizing Spyder and Lina do the same. They let my cousin and her boyfriend go. In unison, the gang members assemble into a distinct line structure with hands behind their backs.

"Boss."

"Mayhem."

Mayhem . . . where have I heard that name before? Thoughts and memories roll through my mind like the domino effect, one fact setting a chain of reaction to the other. Then, my throat tightens and the palms of my hands gather sweat. The news this morning about the notorious gangs Mayhem and Crist grip my memory. As the realization sweeps over me, I do my best to settle my emotions. Lina and Spyder have not only borrowed money from loan sharks, but the very same loan sharks are a division of the infamous Mayhem gang.

Despite the throbbing pain that is shooting up and down my entire body, I focus all of my attention on their leader. His presence has managed to silence not only mouths, but also behaviors. Now that he is here, the other faces recede into the background while he moves through them like an electric ripple.

The Boss scans the room before his eyes fall on Danny. "I thought you graduated from violence to negotiation skills Danny. What's going on?" His cold voice permeates the room. There are command and strength in Mayhem's tone.

"I tried with them." Danny's voice comes out tight and unforgiving. "The two rascals don't want to pay and their friend makes a claim for them."

"It doesn't look like you were trying hard enough," Mayhem argues with limited interest. "Kicking, punching, screaming, cursing. We look every part like the average street gang right now. It's embarrassing Danny."

"I am just trying to–" Danny starts to explain himself, but is immediately cut off by his Boss.

"I'll take over for now if that's alright with you." The command and authority in Mayhem's voice makes it clear he would deal with his second-in-command later.

Danny retreats into the shadows of the dining room. His eyes flick towards me with a pronounced expression of anguish. *This is not over*, his eyes are saying.

I can take you! My intuition is doing air kicks at Danny while my conscience is holding her back.

"Sit down, all of you," Mayhem commands for the rest of us, along with the rest of his men, to sit at the dining table. Mayhem takes the seat to the right of the table instead of at the head.

Four of his men, including Danny, take their respective seats. They are completely quiet and resemble something similar to robots. Even Mohawk is standing like a statue in his corner. If I didn't know any better, I'd think he enjoys seeing Danny get served.

Lina sniffles loudly as she helps Spyder up. He grimaces with pain. Despite the fact that they are in pain, Lina and Spyder actually appear relieved that the Boss is here. Lina helps Spyder sit down in the dining chair nearest to him.

"Are you okay?" Lina walks over to me next. She takes my hand and guides me to a chair that is coincidentally straight across for Mayhem. Lina sits down in the neighboring seat with my hand still in hers.

How can someone who is threatening us bring such peace at the same time? My heart picks up speed.

Now that I am across from Mayhem, I can study the Boss in plain sight. Mayhem sits back against his chair, his arms fold across his chest and his legs cross neatly under the glass table. His dark brown eyes are staring at me with unbridled attention and intensity. His black hair is long and styled in an upwards fashion, revealing an Adonis facial structure that embraces high cheek bones and lips that enhance a strong nose. He is attractive—super attractive; the kind of intimidating attractiveness that makes it hard to talk to him and not regard him as a Godly figure. Dare I say it, but Mayhem is even more handsome than the striking Choi Sangwoo. In fact, his distinctive looks rival Sangwoo's. Why are these men gangsters? They should be models or celebrities, particularly Mayhem who looks as though he should be sitting in front of photographers rather than in Spyder's miserable dining room.

But there is a danger to him that is clearly apparent. Simply from his stare and silent demeanor, it is easy to see that Mayhem's beauty is the mask of a hunter who does anything to capture his prey. I feel powerless in the seconds that we make eye contact. A feeling rumbles from the depth of my soul at the way he looks at me; I am fearful of him as well as curious. *Gawd, why are all these men so intimidating and good-looking?*

I am the first one to break eye contact and pay the price for it. I realize I have been holding my breath. My chest constricts when I finally exhale. All the blood rushes to my cheeks and I face an unfamiliar sensation of dizziness.

I turn back to Lina who is doing her best to garner some sympathy from these men.

"We understand that time is up and we need to pay back the money," Lina is saying. She wipes the remaining tears on her cheeks.

"Please." It is Spyder's turn to try now. "We know and understand our responsibilities to you, to Mayhem. All we ask is for more time."

"No, you don't."

His voice is clear and crisp, commanding and authoritative.

If Spyder can sink deeper into his chair, he would try. A remarkable stretch of fear dawns on his face, and eventually on Lina's too.

"You don't know and understand your responsibilities to me," Mayhem continues with marked dominance. His voice is deep and dark, tantalizing and hypnotic. His effect is similar to being drawn in by something so beautiful and majestic that you don't feel the pain until it is too late. "You don't understand anything that has to do with Mayhem," Mayhem adds with conviction.

"Boss," Danny interrupts, but Mayhem silences him with a hand.

At the moment, my existence at the table is similar to a mere fly on the wall. I am an intruder and trespasser on this society and its calculating ways.

Mayhem focuses on Spyder and Lina, evidently unsatisfied with how Danny conducted the meeting. Mayhem sits up in his seat and clasps his hands together. With a tentative demeanor to him, Mayhem's undivided attention on Spyder and Lina causes his men to stir in their seats. It is becoming more apparent that their participation in the room is not to be his entourage, but to be his advisors. Danny, his most outspoken one, remains silent beyond reprieve.

"Mayhem." Lina's voice is soft and apologetic. She inclines her head towards him, a respectful gesture. It's clearly Lina's first time meeting him and she is a nervous bumblebee. "With all due respect, we're not trying to pull a fast one on you. In no shape or form are we planning to rip you off, take your money and run. We knew when we borrowed from you that we would have to pay in full. The problem is time. We just need more time. Please understand."

"No, I don't understand," he retorts simply. Mayhem glances at Spyder; a look of disgust draws across his face. "You're going to sit there and let your girlfriend plead with me while you hang your head in shame?"

Confusion crosses Lina's face. "What, Spyder?" she asks him.

Spyder lowers his face, staring at the glass surface in front of him. Guilt wracks his entire body as his secrets become imminent.

I knew it! I want to shout. Spyder has a hidden agenda that is screwing everyone over. *Where there is smoke there is always fire,* my intuition hisses.

"It's not twenty thousand." Mayhem turns to Lina. His dark, attractive eyes are guarded. "I figured he didn't tell you. Danny has his reasons to resort to physical violence. Spyder asked for an additional ten thousand dollars three weeks ago. Emergency money, he called it. Then, he laundered it out to another rival of mine. So, your total, including interest is not twenty thousand dollars. It is thirty thousand dollars and collateral. It is thirty thousand and my reputation. It is thirty thousand and my pride."

"What?" At first, Mayhem's news doesn't register with Lina. She looks at Spyder who is avoiding her eyes. "How did it go from twenty to thirty, including collateral now? Spyder?"

". . . I'm sorry," is all he says.

"What do you mean you're sorry?!" The blood drains from Lina's face as she turns to her boyfriend. "Why is he saying we owe him thirty thousand and collateral?! Why is he saying that?! What have you done?!" Absentmindedly, Lina pushes Spyder's shoulder.

"Don't you dare disregard my Boss like that?!" Danny shouts across the table at Lina.

She doesn't even wince. A minute ago she was protecting Spyder from getting hurt, but now Lina slaps him clean across the face.

You go girl! I root for my cousin. Inside, I am boiling at Spyder's confession. He deserves it all.

At the same moment, I see the replay of Lina and Spyder's relationship in front of my eyes. They were so in love and enamored with one another when they first met. You didn't see Lina without Spyder, and you couldn't hang out with Spyder without Lina. They laughed, played, and loved harder than any other couple I have ever seen. They fought, hurt, and caused one another pain more times over than I can ever imagine. When they are good, they are really good. But when they are bad not even the Bible can save them.

"I'm sorry!" is Spyder's weak defense.

Tears are running down Lina's face once again.

"How could you do that behind my back? No wonder why Danny's trying to kill us! You borrowed an extra ten thousand dollars! And you cheated it behind Mayhem's back?! Look at them! Look around us, Spyder! We're dead! We're fucking dead!" The tears are streaking down Lina's face as she cries. Lina's voice is deafening in the room.

"I don't have time for this," Mayhem speaks up. His majestic voice is like ice descending on fire. He looks at Lina and tells her steadily, "Calm down."

Lina's chest rises up and down in anger. Her lips pinch in a tight, fine line. Apparently, she is on a rampage. "How can I calm down? You, of all people, should know how hard it is making a living in society. You, of all people, should know how difficult it is making a decent living with the government breathing down your neck with every paycheck that you make. You, of all people, should know that everyone has financial problems and asks for help. You should know all of this because that's why you allowed us to borrow from you, a notorious gang known for black market and underground money. We're not your only account, so why are you terrorizing us?!"

The dining table stops in its entirety. Hearing a pin drop in a silent room doesn't hold a candle to the present tension. I don't know who is more shocked at Lina's outbursts, Spider and me or Mayhem and his men. But the only person who seems to find humor in her rant is Mayhem himself. The corners of his mouth curve into a distinctive, dangerous smile at the same moment Danny stands up from his seat.

Evidently, my feet think for themselves. I stand and extend my arms protectively in front of my cousin when Danny reaches our end of the table. For a moment in time, I see Danny's hand slip into the breast of his suit. Mayhem holds up a hand to stop Danny from retrieving the object. A chill wracks my body when I realize Danny has every intention to pull a gun on us.

Danny lets out a scoff when he reaches me. "Are you going to pull the Crist card again and hope it'll scare me, little girl?"

At the mention of his rival's name, Mayhem turns his full attention on me. It is unsettling the effect this particular gang lord has on me. No man has ever affected me this way, not even my father or Choi Sangwoo. This is a different type of effect on a level that is beyond my league.

"The Crist card?" Mayhem addresses Danny. He keeps his gaze steady.

"Yes." Danny turns to his boss. His voice is full of excitement; he is eager to tell him the news. "This little girl told me earlier she is associated with Crist, and that she would pay us back on behalf of her friends."

"Really?" To have Mayhem's undivided attention and gaze upon me is unnerving. Now, I understand why Spyder and Lina are having the nerves twisted out of them. Mayhem is intimidating in every sense of the word itself. With one look, one glance, he makes my heart tighten and throat constricts. I can only compare the feeling to meeting someone like the President or a feared figure in children's stories–the unsettling attractive version, of course.

There is no going back now that I have lied. I can see Lina shaking with absolute fear behind me while Spyder is on the verge of bleeding internally. I can't take my word back now. I know that the consequences are going to be far greater than I bargain for, but for the sake of my cousin and my life, I have to see this lie to the very end.

"I am," I reply calmly. I force the words out as strong as I can. I am desperate to say something that would deter the impending violent conclusion. "I am associated with Crist." My conscience is holding a shovel and digging in the dark, deep dirt.

"So, you know Choi Sangwoo personally?" Mayhem asks simply. The electric interest shines in his eyes.

"Yes," I answer with unwavering fear. "So, I'll help my cousin pay her debt." My voice has a slight tremble to them. I do my best to control the tenor of my vocal cords to convey my promise.

Lina trembles behind me. ". . . May."

"I'll help you." I turn to her momentarily. *I got this Lina. Please don't freak out or I'll fall apart too.* "It's ok. We don't need to get violent. Right?"

"You're right." Mayhem's eyes level and sweep over my body. A shock runs through me with the understanding that he is checking me out. "We don't need to be violent."

"That's right." I can hardly get the words of agreement out. *Stay strong May. Don't let the attractive looks shake you.* My intuition is shaking in her boots. *You're in deep shit now.*

"So prove you're associated with Crist." Mayhem sits back languidly in his chair.

"Humph." Danny's disbelieving scoff sounds in my ear.

I look around the room, weary of the intense attention and scrutiny. The bottom of my throat feels as if it is going to drop. Every Mayhem member, including Mayhem himself, is waiting for me. They are all waiting for me to slip up and falter. It is similar to swimming in the ocean with sharks. They are circling me, waiting for the right moment to strike because they can smell blood in the water now.

I have no other choice but to see my lie to the very end. My hands shake as I reach into the back pocket of my jeans.

After looking at the diamond-encrusted necklace this morning, I inadvertently took it with me. I have developed the embarrassing habit of carrying it on my body every Saturday since I met Choi Sangwoo. Never in my wildest dreams have I imagined the necklace would come in handy this way.

"Is this proof enough?" I place the necklace on the dining table.

Danny's eyes narrow as the necklace transfers from my hands to the table. Almost immediately, as though it is a contaminated object, Danny steps away from Lina and retreats to Mayhem's side.

That's right. Run back to your Boss! My conscience is doing an early victory dance.

Mayhem is looking at the face of the necklace. He doesn't touch it, but Mayhem's reserved facial expression acknowledges the necklace's authenticity. The diamond-encrusted necklace is the only type of jewelry that Choi Sangwoo wears on his body.

"What is your name?" Mayhem's eyes roll back up to my face. The muscles on his jaw clench together. If possible, his face becomes more unapproachable.

Shit. What have I gotten myself into? "May," I answer. *Why am I whispering?* I am sure I am not the only one Mayhem makes whisper. The thought stops me in my tracks. *I should have said my name is Slicer or Blood. May doesn't scare anyone.*

"Crist doesn't have any members, associates, or affiliates with such a name," Mayhem retorts quickly. He narrows his eyes at me. There is something guarded behind those eyes. Mayhem is all business and he doesn't take any bullshit from anyone. I see something in him that I do not find in Choi Sangwoo. This gang lord is much more relentless and every bit of a control freak.

"Where did you get this necklace?" Mayhem demands again.

"I told you, I'm associated with him," I reply, every single lie drips from my tongue. I have to stand my ground. I am a bit brave after seeing the expressions change on every single Mayhem member.

"Watch your tone little girl," Danny growls with a low threat. "This necklace doesn't protect you from us."

"Then why haven't you killed me?" It is a bold statement, but I am beyond angered by the acts of unreasonable violence. "If you don't care that I'm associated with Crist, why haven't you made something of your empty threats?"

"You bitch!" Danny spits as he advances toward me.

"Danny," Mayhem calls his name. It stops Danny in his tracks. He reminds me of an impulsive child who consistently needs reminding. Far from a father figure, however, Mayhem awards Danny with a cautionary look. Then the gang lord addresses me in a crass tone. Mayhem states clearly, "The reason why we are hesitating to do away with you is because we're conducting business. You must think every gang and division is the same. But we're not aggressive pack dogs that go in for the kill for reputation. We're aggressive pack dogs to run a society far greater than your understanding."

I swallow a thread of fear lodged in my throat. Mayhem's explanation sounds like the echoes of Sangwoo's words.

I expect more questions about Crist, but Mayhem gestures toward the necklace. "Put it away. You don't want to lose it if you run into another rival of Choi Sangwoo's."

Slowly, I pick up the necklace and place it inside my pocket. Lina nudges me to sit down.

"So, how do you suppose you will help them pay back their debt, my reputation, and my pride?" Mayhem's hands clasp together as though he finds this amusing. "Within the next week?"

"It doesn't matter how, just as long as I do. Right?" Now that I have the couple of seconds to gather myself together and overcome the shock of speaking to him, I ask the question with greater purpose. "Within the next week, I can get you thirty thousand dollars. As for your reputation and your pride, I'll think of something, but I can't guarantee anything intangible like that. Money can't buy that."

For a high-intensity period, Mayhem stares at me. He is gauging me, determining whether my words are promises or bluffs. Stealthily, Mayhem leans forward in his seat with unexpected grace. "Who are you?"

Dumbfounded, I can only stare back at him with a blank expression. I don't know whether I should tell him my whole life's story or give him the reader's digest. I end up giving him the most intelligent answer I can muster. "I'm May. I'm Lina's cousin."

"And you would do this for your . . . cousin?" Mayhem questions with an even tone. "You would sign your life away to pay off a debt that your cousin is responsible for? You would sign yourself away to save your cousin who was foolish enough to borrow from me?"

"Wouldn't you?" I ask in return, proving to be more than weak sauce. "If your friends," I pause to gesture towards the group of men surrounding him, "needed your help, I'm sure you would the same."

"Actually, I wouldn't," Mayhem disagrees vehemently. "These men are not my friends." He gestures toward them. "That's the difference between you and me. So I would advise you to stop making assumptions about me, or anyone else that you meet for that matter."

My tongue sticks to the roof of my mouth. *Jeez, I take it back. You're a jerk. A good-looking jerk.*

Mayhem surveys my facial expression as he waits for another response from me. Noting my silence, Mayhem keeps his eyes on me as he motions for Danny. "Fair enough. I'll let you play superwoman and help your friends. I would be a fool to say no to someone who wants to pay me back my money."

I step back as Danny picks up the piece of paper in front of Spyder. He transfers it over to my side of the table. I've been too focused on Mayhem and the entire situation to notice its frailty on the glass table. Now that the paper is front of me, the magnitude of what I have promised begins sinking in.

"Sign and date." Mayhem gestures toward the piece of paper. "By signing, you agree to co-sign for the thirty thousand. Since you are the third party, you are collateral at the end of the week if the terms of the contract are incomplete. I would advise you to read the terms and conditions carefully before you sign, but seeing that you are a member of Crist you should have no qualms. Thirty thousand is really nothing at all, but it is the principle you see."

I stare at him, out of breath and at a loss for words. *Gang lord and rich snob.* But my intuition is too busy ogling at him to make a decision yet.

"Saturday night, at approximately seven o'clock, you will have the money for me. The location will be determined later. A black vehicle will pick you up to transfer the money to my personal accountant. Thirty thousand dollars cash," Mayhem adds with a harsh tone.

"Sign." At the end of Mayhem's words, Danny extracts a ballpoint pen from inside his vest pocket. Danny makes sure my eyes are following the pen when he places it on top of the paper.

"May." Lina tugs at my arm.

"It's fine, Lina. I'll help you." I try my best to reassure my cousin. The brave face I am putting on is faltering as the seconds tick by. I can kick and fight like my cousin or I can figure a way out of this. I am in too deep to back out now. There is no way Mayhem and his men will let us leave without a guarantee.

Spyder keeps quiet in the corner of the room. Lina is chewing on her bottom lip. I avoid Mayhem's piercing gaze.

Just get it over with. I pick up the pen and compose my signature on the contract. My eyes scan it, but nothing stands out except for Lina and Spyder's name with the amount of money they owe. Their signatures, along with dark blotches are already on the paper. The contract is professionally articulate; the amount of legal jargon and context parades the entire piece of paper. It will take a day to read all of it, but the main stipulations are there.

Just as I finish the last letter on my signature, Danny's quick hand takes the paper from me. Then, with speed that rivals lightening, Danny extracts the pen from my hand and a small blade juts out. It is too fast for me to see, but Danny nearly slices my right index finger with the point. A droplet of blood falls onto the piece of paper.

"Ow!" I jerk my hand back in pain. *Son-of-a-bitch! He cut me!*

"Thank you for your cooperation." Danny flicks the pen into the air, catches it, and then proceeds to tuck into his suit.

Without another word, in a simultaneous manner, the chairs around the dining room table groan as their occupants leave. Mayhem is the first one to stand from his seat. At his height of what must have been at least six-feet, he states simply, "I hope you are better at paying debts than your cousin."

I can really get violent right now. I press my thumb against my palm. The pain is throbbing. I bite my lower lip to prevent myself from crying aloud. The look in my eyes must surprise Mayhem because a cool look crosses his face.

"You people are so cruel," I mutter. All the pent up tension and anguish unleashes. "Do you enjoy serving people death sentences?"

Mayhem raises an eyebrow at me. *Shit. Don't piss the attractive gang lord off.* My conscience is not on my side at the moment. Behind Mayhem's devastatingly handsome face is a force to be reckoned with.

"Your innocence is humbling." Mayhem surprises me with his answer. His eyes are burning with such intensity that I naturally shy from the heat.

What does that mean? I find my tongue in knots again. This man is the complete opposite of the way he looks. How can such a contrast be probable? There's no ounce of sweetness or willingness to compromise.

"Just focus on the debt. You have no idea exactly how much I revel in other people's miseries. You have seven days." Without lingering, Mayhem proceeds out of the dining room. His men follow in a line with complete unison. Then, he pauses at the threshold of the dining room.

Mayhem looks over his shoulders at me. His stunning profile contrasts his sarcastic nuance. "Please give Choi Sangwoo my regards."

Then, he is gone.

"See you!" Danny approaches Spyder on his way out. Before anyone can stop him, Danny draws the same pen straight across the right side of Spyder's cheek. The sharp blade marks Spyder's skin.

"Ow!" Spyder howls in pain as the cut nearly splits his cheek open.

"No! Stop!" Lina pushes Danny away. But the damage is done.

Danny steps back with an amused expression on his face. He watches Lina's reaction with an indescribable expression his face. "Isn't love amazing? Even after all the shit he's putting you through, you still care." He tucks the pen inside his suit and moves away from Lina and Spyder. Mohawk follows Danny out with a fiendish grin.

"See you next week little girl. You better have the money or I'll cut both sides of your cheek like little Spyder over there." Danny winks at me as Mohawk's laughter trails behind him.

A loud commotion erupts as they destroy furniture in their wake.

"Are you okay?" Lina sobs as she unties Spyder from his chair.

"I'm sorry baby. I'm so sorry!" Spyder weeps in her arms.

I stand frozen in time by my chair, essentially ignoring Lina and Spyder's reunion. I stare at Mayhem's vacant seat. An indescribable feeling comes over me. I don't have money anywhere near the amount of thirty thousand dollars. Did I just make the biggest mistake of my life? As though the answer is right in front of me, I stare down at the prickling sensation of where Danny extracted blood from my hand. My finger continues to bleed, the pool of blood drips from one end to the other.

Without thinking, I run from the dining room. *Impulsive!* my conscience hisses.

"May! Where are you going?!" Lina shouts behind me.

I have no idea what I am doing. I don't know what I am going to say when I catch up to him, but I have to speak with Mayhem. I can't stomach the idea of what he stands for and the kind of power he exerts over us. I have to make Mayhem understand that I am not playing the hero for my cousin and her boyfriend. I am going to help them out of the goodness of my heart because I am a genuinely good person. Since I am the third party, I need more time than a week to get the money. I need Mayhem to understand that.

A burst of desperation comes over me as I pick up my pace and run out of the dining room, through the shallow hallway, and to the front door.

"Wait!" By the time I reach the front door, Mayhem and his men are descending the front steps of Spyder's house.

An unforgettable sense of dread and unfamiliar fear grips me. Just as I gather one last drop of courage to go after him, the sound of a ferocious engine raids the entire neighborhood. In unison, Mayhem's men flank his side in a protective manner. Mayhem, however, doesn't move an inch as his eyes narrow at the incoming car. He's not affected by sudden disruptions and surprises.

The incoming car is a black Mercedes, the one with the identification of GL Amg SUV. If my father weren't such a vehicle enthusiast when I was younger, the hefty car would mean nothing to me. It also helps that these types of cars are extremely rare on the road, especially since this particular one has a yellow tail.

The distinctive vehicle climbs the slope to Spyder's house in a steady manner. The car comes to a complete stop in front of the gate. The door to the driver's side opens with a soft click. The driver steps out of the car and leans against its hood. He touches the dark sunglasses at the tip of his nose; his distinctive black hair glints underneath the late evening sun. The visitor adorns a familiar smile as he surveys Mayhem.

"No," I whisper when I realize who the driver is. "It can't be." *I told you so!* My intuition is doing a victory dance complete with a hula skirt. Life continues despite my airtight, frozen response.

"What are you doing here?" Mayhem's tone is punitive. His demeanor inside Spyder's house was less hostile and aggressive than at the moment. Mayhem turns his head slightly, giving his opponent the notion he is only half-interested.

"You're a hard man to track down, Jaewon," the driver replies with conviction. He pays no attention to the fact that Mayhem's men have formed a human barrier around him. More Mayhem members step out of the awaiting SUV.

Jaewon . . . is that Mayhem's real name? *Hmm, he does look like a Jaewon.* My intuition purses her lips together as she gives the attractive gang lord another look over.

"All you have to do is call me, Sangwoo," Mayhem remarks with contrived sarcasm. "You don't have to chase me all over town. But it is flattering that you took the time out of your busy schedule to catch me at a meeting."

Choi Sangwoo.

Thoughts and questions fire inside my mind like uncontrollable fireworks. Choi Sangwoo, the Crist member who sporadically entered my life last week, is now standing only a few feet away challenging a rival gang leader. The contrast of the poor man, who tried drinking away his emotional pain for someone and the confident rugged appearance now, juxtaposes a black and white canvas. All this time, I thought Sangwoo was a gang member. Never would I have been able to fathom, without the help of reality, that Choi Sangwoo is *actually* the leader of Crist. There goes another gang myth debunked.

"Don't play games with me Jaewon." Now, Sangwoo is shaking his head at Mayhem. The tone in his voice marks dark humor. "You and I both know that if I don't track you down, you would never come to me. Then, we'd go on to one violent stand off to the next. You enjoy promoting the hostility and propaganda. What happened last night in Busan is a prime example. It's all over the news, Jaewon. It's unbearably embarrassing."

"Well then, the solution is simple, isn't it? Why don't you tell your minions not to provoke my members when they are out and about?" Mayhem replies with a stern emphasis. He remains relentless and unstoppable. "My members have every right to defend themselves last night. You and I are both in the leader seats, we always choose our men above anyone else. This is protocol, nothing personal, you understand?"

The tint of dark humor slips from Choi Sangwoo's demeanor. His eyes grow murky at Mayhem's lack of participation. While Mayhem is a leader who enjoys striking fear in others, Sangwoo appears more forgiving and willing to negotiate. However, Sangwoo's willingness to make conversation with Mayhem dwindles like quick sand. The more Mayhem struggles, the more Sangwoo's patience thins.

"Last warning, Yoon Jaewon, stay out of my territory. Busan is mine. You want to poison your men with thoughts about me and what I stand for, that's fine. But if you think you, or any of the ingrates you have groveling at your feet, can touch a Crist member one more time you will pay in full. This time, it won't just be national news. It will be in the international press. I am sure the Boss will be happy about that. And we both know who he favors." At the end of Sangwoo's threat, he points at Danny is watching with silent aggression. "Point that gun at me and you will answer to Crist."

"The Bible banned me a long time ago Sangwoo," Danny snaps back. "You were one of the first demons God kicked off the clouds, so I suggest you stop with the threats."

I expect a violent blowout to follow Danny's threatening remark. Instead, Sangwoo remains poised and refined. He doesn't dignify Danny's jab. Instead, Sangwoo makes it point to look at Mayhem expectantly. Clearly, Danny is Mayhem's responsibility.

"Like kids fighting over candy, Sangwoo. Fine. We stay out of Busan. You scamper out of Seoul. We'll call it a deal," Mayhem consents with reserved contention. The look in his eyes is dark and dangerous, similar to lightning and thunder.

Without waiting for Sangwoo to answer, Mayhem moves toward his awaiting SUV. He makes a motion for his men to step aside. Evidently, Mayhem doesn't feel the need to be protected from Sangwoo. Most of Mayhem's members, as aggressive as they are, walk around Choi Sangwoo to their accompanying vehicles. Only Danny and Mohawk have no qualms walking through Sangwoo.

"By the way, I had the pleasure of meeting one of your associates in the house. I hope to see her more often." Mayhem holds up a hand in the air before he disappears into his awaiting vehicle. Like a phantom of the night, Mayhem marks his exit with his brigade of dark vehicles.

Sangwoo remains in his place. He doesn't move an inch as Mayhem's parade of cars peel out of the neighborhood.

I have been so mesmerized in watching that I don't see Lina and Spyder standing behind me.

"They finally left?" Lina is helping Spyder hold a handful of napkins to his bleeding cheek.

"Lina, shhh." I try to signal to my cousin, but it is too late.

From the bottom of the steps, Choi Sangwoo sees me. "May?" he calls out in absolute surprise. Shades of revelation color his facial expression. I am the last person Sangwoo expects to see here. Frankly, it is the other way around; he is the last person I want to see right now.

With no other choice, I face Sangwoo. Fortunately, the sun is setting and he can't see how red my face is. My conscience is fanning herself. I should run back inside the house. Seeing Sangwoo evokes such a surreal feeling. The domino effect of everything happening all at once is increasingly difficult for me to internalize. "Hi," is all I can manage to say to him.

"May, you're bleeding a lot." Sangwoo invites himself through Spyder's gates and up the steps. When he reaches the final landing where I am standing, Sangwoo reaches for my finger. "Are you okay?"

"I'm okay." I blink furiously, trying to gather my thoughts together. *He has my finger in his hand.* I attempt to take my finger back. I can't stand the electric underpinning that travels from his hands to mine. "It's just a small cut. It's nothing."

"Hi." The traces of the vividly upset and tense expressions are gone. Instead, a smile spreads across Sangwoo's face. Sangwoo's overall complexion is healthier today. "I meet you under some of the worst circumstances, don't I?"

"Depending on how you define it," my reply is above a whisper. I am well aware that Lina and Spyder are staring at us curiously. I only have a matter of seconds before they intervene.

"You're the leader of Crist?" Before I can stop myself, I blurt out.

"Yes," Sangwoo replies shortly. An understanding comes over us.

It has been approximately a week ago since I have seen him— seven days, one-hundred and sixty-eight hours, and fourteen seconds. But who is keeping count now that Sangwoo's here as though he's never left.

Sangwoo's lingering eyes yield to a more concerned look. "What are you doing here? Were you inside when Mayhem was here?" He is catching on to Mayhem's comment about an associate.

Fortunately, I don't have to answer. My cousin, acting like my guardian angel, interrupts our short reunion with, "How do you know Mayhem?" With dry tears on her cheeks, Lina's eyes are large and alert as she surveys Sangwoo.

Sangwoo draws his attention away from me to look at my cousin. His gaze moves from Lina to Spyder in a simultaneous manner. Sangwoo chooses not to answer Lina's question. "I'm Sangwoo. I'm a friend of May's," Sangwoo introduces himself shortly,

"Friend?" Lina's eyebrows come together as she looks at me. I can read Lina's mind without her having to ask me verbally. She wants to know why I haven't mentioned him before. Boy, am I going to get the investigation later.

Sangwoo waits expectantly for me to add, so I muster something weak. "Yes. He's my friend." I quickly divert the conversation to Spyder's cheek. "Spyder, are you okay?"

Sensing my discomfort, Sangwoo joins me in the diversion. "Are you okay? That wound on your cheek is going to get infected and bleed out if you don't get to a hospital soon."

Spyder has his hands against his bleeding cheek. He nods with tears brimming in his eyes. I still can't say he doesn't deserve the pain. But right now, I am too engrossed in the fact that Choi Sangwoo has magically appeared in my life yet again.

"Come on. I'll take you all." Without waiting for us to agree, Sangwoo reaches for my left hand. His quick and rapid touch makes my heart race. *Whoa, he's super forward.* My intuition winces; she has no experience with good-looking gang lords.

I had the best intentions to turn back inside the house before Choi Sangwoo could recognize me. I know after meeting Mayhem and observing the encounter with Sangwoo that my world and theirs should never collide.

CHAPTER FOUR

P lease. Order anything you would like to eat."
The restaurant is bustling with commotion. People are sitting in a number of groups, chattering and laughing at their respective tables. Dishes, plates, and silverware clink and clash into one another. The servers move through the sea of chaos to seat customers and ring up orders.

Although Chopsticks is one of the trendiest restaurants in Seoul, the food speaks for itself. With a varied menu that serves dishes ranging from sushi to kimchi to pizza, the restaurant has no trouble bringing in the locals as well as tourists. Choi Sangwoo chooses a sleek, granite table near the back of the restaurant with a beautiful view of the city. The evening sunlight casts a hue of orange, yellow, and purple streaks in the sky. It should be a fun and relaxing setting, but under the current circumstances, it is a safe haven more than anything–especially for Spyder and Lina who are sitting across from Sangwoo and me.

As I watch Lina rag on Spyder about his idiocy, I allow myself to peek at Choi Sangwoo. My thoughts travel back to when Sangwoo offered to take us to the hospital for Spyder's injury and the bloody cut on my finger. Initially I refused, but Lina convinced me for Spyder's sake. Sangwoo insisted that he wanted to return the favor last week. When he put that charm of his to convincing, I couldn't find any grounds to rebuff Sangwoo's good intentions.

"I KNOW A DOCTOR HERE." As soon as we get to the hospital, the mysterious gang leader takes charge and directs help to us. Sangwoo arranges it so that Lina and Spyder are taken care at the hospital wing for external injuries. Spyder ends up with six stitches on his cheek and a generous dose of morphine in his system. Lina gets an antiseptic for her abrasions and bruises.

My fate is on the other side of the hospital wing for minor cuts. My finger is throbbing like a severe paper cut. The sensation is similar to having a hundred ants biting in one concentrated area. When we are in the examination room waiting for a doctor, Sangwoo asks me the one question I have been trying to avoid. I am not ready to tell him the truth about my lie to save Lina, Spyder, and myself from Mayhem's wrath.

"Are you the associate Mayhem mentioned?" Sangwoo observes me with intense scrutiny. I cannot tell if he finds it funny or not. "What happened inside that house?"

I look up at him with a guilty expression on my face. I can't help it; I wear my emotions on my sleeves. "Can I tell you later? I'm trying to digest everything still. It doesn't help my finger is bleeding." I hold up my index finger for him to see that the blood continues to seep through the emergency gauze. *Weak sauce!* My conscience taunts me.

Sangwoo tries to cover his laugh at my childish gesture. Before he can retort, the good doctor knocks on the door and enters the room. He turns out to be an older man with kind eyes behind green spectacles.

When the doctor tells me, "This isn't going to hurt much. You'll feel a bit of pressure. There's blood embedded underneath the cut itself. Once I relieve the pressure, the pain will subside and it can heal," I close my eyes tightly and breathe out of my mouth.

"Don't laugh at me," I mumble to Sangwoo who is chuckling at my childlike response. "Can you do it quickly, doctor, please."

"I will try," the doctor responds.

I glance back at Choi Sangwoo again. He looks like he would enjoy a bag of popcorn and soda to go along with this scene.

"Are you still laughing at me?"

"No, I'm not."

"Yes, you are. You're smiling."

"I can't smile?"

"No, this is serious. My finger is bleeding," I reason with him.

"You're right. This is life and death. No smiling." Sangwoo shakes his head, taking the chance to turn away and let out another wide grin. Deep down, I appreciate his humor. Gangsters do have a sense of humor. *But he's not a gangster. He's a gang leader!* my intuition hisses. I want to lock her away and close the door. I don't need any more wayward thoughts to make the situation worse. I am in too much pain.

From outside of the room, any random passerby can hear my long and drawn out, "ouchhhhh doctor oucchhh!" Sangwoo's soft and entertained laughter quickly follows my bouts of self-expression.

After treatment of our wounds, as though we are his longtime friends, Sangwoo offers to take Lina, Spyder, and me to dinner. Sangwoo's generosity appears to have no bounds. The situation should have been awkward, but it is next to impossible to be awkward when the leader of a notorious gang is orchestrating the entire situation.

Sangwoo has quite the charm to him. He is completely different from the drunken straggler last Saturday. Now that he's sober and focused, it is easy to gauge his true personality. Sangwoo has a way of making the people he engages with feel as though they have his undivided attention, care, and understanding. He has that special tendency of moving people as if they are under water with him. It becomes apparent that Sangwoo is a natural social butterfly and conversationalist; he makes everyone who encounters him feel as though they have known him for a long time. I don't know what to do with this larger-than-life presence. In all honesty, I am beyond intimidated. Most of all, I swear I know him from somewhere.

NOW THAT I AM SITTING next to Choi Sangwoo, it is hard to dwell on what happened earlier, especially since Lina has taken a special liking to him already. Even Spyder, who has a large band around his right cheek now, expresses no emotional doubts about going to dinner with my new friend. Even the confrontation with Mayhem seems worlds away at the moment.

"So, how do you know May?" Lina has the menu prop open against her chest when she starts bombarding Choi Sangwoo with questions.

I try to signal to Lina that her staring is borderline rude, but my cousin appears completely oblivious. It is hard to deem her as the same Lina who cried, begged, and thrown a fit in front Mayhem a couple of hours ago. Now, Lina is tearless and full of questions for Sangwoo, who I introduced as a co-worker at The Trax. My cousin wants to hear it from his own mouth; she is not entirely convinced about Sangwoo's origins yet.

"At The Trax. I just recently started working," Sangwoo answers Lina's question with the same ease he had with my mother last week. "May doesn't talk about me, I'm guessing."

I wonder if Sangwoo's statement is an implied assumption that I haven't told anyone in my life about his true identity either.

"No, she hasn't at all." Lina flashes me an unforgiving look. "I've met all of May's co-workers at The Trax. I have to say, you're the best looking one."

Really? Are you going to be that embarrassing family member? I want to face palm at Lina's blunt responses. If only my cousin is aware she's having a conversation with the gang leader of Crist. Choi Sangwoo, on the other hand, takes her compliment with greater ease than I deem for someone of his caliber. Perhaps in his line of work Sangwoo is used to the comments and critiques. Even Spyder, who is still riding out his pain, doesn't seem to mind Lina's straightforward comment.

"Lina," I mumble as a feeble attempt to control her inquisition.

She turns to me momentarily. "I'm already in a relationship, so I can say he's handsome. Handsome enough for you, I mean."

The corners of Sangwoo's mouth lift into a smile and it triggers the heat in my cheeks. I yearn to reach under the table and pinch Lina's leg for her inability to censor her thoughts.

"The waiter's here."

For the sake of social balance, at the same moment, our waiter returns with a harried expression on his face. The hustle and bustle of the restaurant is evident in the dark purple bags under his eyes. His long, shaggy hair hangs over a white name tag with the word *Nam* etched on it. "Are you ready to order?" He extracts a fashionable blue notepad from the left side of his slacks.

Sangwoo turns to me first. "Order first, May." A kind smile appears on Sangwoo's face as he encourages me.

"Uh, well." I immediately become flustered at his attention. *Keep it together, May.* Bored, my intuition is taping her feet. "I'll have the autumn salad with the chicken. Dressing on the side please."

I have never felt such thrill in successfully ordering food before. Sangwoo nods his head inconspicuously as though he agrees. Then, he motions for Lina to order next.

Lina beams at him for being such a gentleman. "I'll have the teriyaki chicken noodle bowl." Then, Lina turns to Spyder who has his hands under his chin. "Maybe you can share some with me?"

Spyder can only nod his head in reply.

"The doctor ordered him to not have any food," Sangwoo reminds Lina gently.

"Oh yeah," Lina mutters as the memories of what happened to Spyder's cheek come back to her. "Maybe just a glass of water for now."

Spyder looks less than happy with the idea of nursing a glass of water while we eat solid food. But when he winces at the throbbing pain in his cheek, Spyder's facial expression subsides to subtle agreement. I want to roll my eyes at his feigned act. The cut on his cheek holds Spyder back from being his usual overbearing and overzealous personality.

"And I'll have the tour of Japan," Sangwoo states when he turns back to the waiter. "Thank you, Nam."

Although the waiter is furiously writing down our orders, Nam looks up from his notepad with a quick smile on his lips. Perhaps being recognized by his name reminds Nam that he isn't just an expendable employee, but also a human being who deserves to be commended. I empathize with Nam. Choi Sangwoo had the same effect on me when I waited on his table two weeks ago. I begin to question if there isn't anything or anyone that Choi Sangwoo doesn't affect. The only other person who always told me to be mindful of others, especially with social manners is Eunhye. I suppose Sangwoo is more proficient at certain social scripts I cannot imagine.

When Nam finishes jotting down on his notepad, he finalizes the orders by sending out another round of water.

"So, you live around here?" Lina's inquisitive voice draws me back to reality. She's adamant about more information.

Sangwoo nods his head lightly. His brown eyes remain passive. It is hard to tell if he is enjoying this twenty-one questions game with Lina. "Actually, I split my time between Seoul and Busan."

At the same time, I glance at Spyder to see that he is staring at me intently. I am quiet by choice while he is quiet because of pain. He has a lot to say behind those sad eyes of his, but I know that his deepened silence is the direct result of his earlier traumatic experience. Otherwise, Spyder would probably have no problem asking how Sangwoo and I really met. I don't like Spyder and he knows it. When I first met him, my intuition warned Lina about his shady ways. Now, the warnings are coming to fruition.

Meanwhile, my cousin and Sangwoo are carrying on with their conversation.

"Wow. Homes in Seoul and Busan. Are you working somewhere else besides The Trax?" Lina marvels at Sangwoo's revelation. She is all eyes and ears now that he has real estate.

"I'm also in sales as a customer service representative for a company," Sangwoo replies without hesitation. "The Trax is just a night job."

I clear my throat and pretend to look at the silverware in front of me. From my peripheral view, I can see the small smile on Sangwoo's lips. He inclines his head towards me as though we are privy to an inside joke.

Wow. I am breathless underneath his gaze. *Will I ever be immune to this man?* My intuition shakes her head and then changes her mind to lackluster nods. The pattern continues.

"Wow," Lina states with wonder. "How old are you?" Lina obviously doesn't have a stop button on her train of questions.

"I'll be turning twenty-nine soon." Both Lina and I are surprised at Sangwoo's disclosure.

Sangwoo is seven years older than me, I make a mental note. How can someone only seven years older than me be so refined and successful in his own terms? *That's because he's a gangster, and you are a lowly college student.* My conscience has a dull look on her face.

"But enough about me. What about you two?" Sangwoo changes the subject easily and steers it back to Lina and Spyder.

"Us?" Lina looks at Spyder and then back at me. "Well, May and I are cousins. My mom is her dad's sister. May's been working her little butt off this summer to prepare for college in the fall. She has one more year to go before she graduates. College isn't for me, so I opted out."

Sangwoo leans with interest towards me. "College?"

Why is Lina only talking about me? I feel slightly insulted by the surprised tone in Sangwoo's voice. "Yes, college."

"Do you think spending your time in classrooms will help you achieve what you want in life? Not just a job or a career, that's a given. But, what you really want in life?" Sangwoo asks with such candor that it is challenging to not only interpret, but answer. His dark eyes are as penetrating as ever.

Whoa. Where did the philosophical questions come from? Why is he so interested in what I choose to do with my life? I suppress the impulse to stick my tongue out at him.

"I'm going to college to become a person with a goal," I answer, feeling the ardor to answer this selective question correctly. "People chose different pathways to live. Some people are good at navigating the world and achieving the goals they set out for themselves without having to go further in school. Lina and Spyder know what they want to do, even though it's a bumpy ride for them. I'm the other percentage of the statistic. I want to learn, see, and do more."

That's right! I can articulate myself. I mentally pat myself on the back.

"You can learn, see, and do more just the same in the real world." Sangwoo's voice is soft and genuine. There is a bemused smile on his lips.

Lina agrees wholeheartedly. My cousin jumps onto the college-isn't-that-great bandwagon. "That's exactly how I feel! Spyder and I are doing things our own way. We're not going to let four years of our lives go by while we can jumpstart our future now."

It must be difficult for Sangwoo to break eye contact with me, but he does. Casually, he steers the subject to the elephant sitting on the table. "And how does Mayhem fit into your future?"

A dark look dawns upon Lina's face. It is better to let Lina go on with her spiel than to remind her about reality. Sangwoo knows perfectly well who Mayhem is, but he doesn't know the reason for Mayhem's presence at Spyder's house. The way Sangwoo proposes the question makes it clear he is more than interested in the reason for Mayhem's involvement with Spyder and Lina. Sangwoo has been lenient with the questions. Now that he has us sitting with undivided attention, the true intentions of what this dinner is about starts to show its roots.

"Mayhem doesn't fit into our future. He's just a terrorizing gang leader," Lina confesses to Sangwoo finally. She glances at the surrounding tables to gauge eavesdroppers. My cousin lowers her voice and divulges, "Gangs have no mercy and no sense of justice."

I glance at Sangwoo for a particular reaction, but his facial expression remains in the same stunningly cool manner. The lines on his face are still uninterrupted and smooth. "They can be unreasonable," is all he states.

Lina shakes her head at his comment. The passionate response about Mayhem boils inside her. "You don't understand. They're not only unreasonable, but also vindictive. They're like vampires. They will suck the life out of you and leave you to dry for the scavengers!" Lina hisses.

Sangwoo has an innocent look on his face; it is almost comical. "Vampires? I've never thought of them that way."

"You never see them orchestrating their evil deeds during the day, do you?" Lina retorts. My cousin does have a rational point.

"Lina," I interject before I can stop myself.

"So what exactly did you do for a gang to suck the life out of you and leave you to dry for the scavengers?" Sangwoo disregards my interjection carefully.

At this point in the conversation, Lina glances at Spyder. "It's all my fault," Spyder manages to say. He looks at Lisa with a wistful expression. For a person under morphine, Spyder's pain is still evident in his dry and hoarse voice.

Sangwoo watches the exchange between them with an indescribable expression.

"It's our fault." Lina's voice softens. She forgives Spyder too easily. "We shouldn't have gotten involved with them." Lina is not ready to divulge to Sangwoo the true reason for Mayhem's visit. Instinctively, I wonder why.

"It must have been serious enough for them to actually come to your house." Sangwoo splits his attention between Lina and Spyder. It is his subtle way of pushing for more answers.

"It is," Lina replies somberly. "But it doesn't justify the fact that they could hurt us and treat us like garbage."

"They just don't care." Spyder winces as his cheek moves painfully. "Especially that Mayhem. He's completely ruthless. No wonder why his rivals would do anything to squander him."

Sangwoo listens with intense concentration, but he doesn't push the subject any further than what Lina and Spyder want to talk about. His lips remain in a hard, fine line.

"Let's talk about something else," I interject again. I can't bear the conversation dwelling on Mayhem any longer. I pick up my glass of water and chug it down in large gulps. Incidentally, the mentioning of Mayhem makes me remember his intensely beautiful expression, especially those smoldering dark eyes that watched me sign the loan repayment contract. *They never even gave me a copy.* I scowl inside.

He is sensitive to the tone of my voice. Sangwoo reaches for the bottle of white wine to the side of the table. The cork is already open, so Sangwoo conveniently pours the wine into our glasses. Lina, Spyder, and I watch Sangwoo disseminate our drinks with silent participation. When he is done, Sangwoo picks up his own glass and holds it at arm's length to the center of the table. He states simply, "Let's toast."

In a simultaneous manner Lina, Spyder, and I reach for our glasses and raise it to Sangwoo's. Since Spyder can't drink, he picks up his own glass of water with a pleased expression on his face. Even Lina looks content despite her troubles.

Sangwoo smiles at us and says with that distinctive charm of his, "To new friendships and staying away from vampires."

Lina lets out a surprised laugh while Spyder does his best to keep from splitting the stitches on his cheek open. I stifle a laugh. *What the hell. If a gang leader asks you to raise a glass, you do it even if his speech has a dangerous undertone to it.*

Together, we bring our glasses to the center of the table. Sangwoo and Lina are the only ones who finish theirs in one gulp. Even white wine is difficult for me to hold down. Spyder barely takes a sip of his of water.

"It's nice to have an older friend who can get us drinks," Lina jokes. My cousin wipes the corner of her mouth. She definitely cares what Choi Sangwoo thinks of her. He has the same effect on Lina too. Maybe everything I am imagining about him is exactly that—imagination.

"Oh, this is only a one-time thing," Sangwoo corrects Lina with the same humor.

The topic of conversation eventually transitions from the gloom of Mayhem to reviewing our food when it's served. The rough patch of the conversation gets covered by topics that are more general. By the time dinner is over, two hours later, we are all in a different mood and mindset. Sangwoo and I fight over the bill until Lina suggests that I pay next time. My cousin gives me a sly smile when Sangwoo agrees. It is apparent that Lina and Spyder like Sangwoo. Sangwoo, on the other hand, is a bit more difficult to read. He has such a calm air to him that it is challenging to gauge if the feelings are mutual.

After dinner, Sangwoo leads the way out of the restaurant with the three of us in tow. I don't miss the fact that more than half a dozen females look up from their dinner at Sangwoo. He appears completely oblivious to the attention and exits the restaurant in a disquiet manner. I realize then that Choi Sangwoo has an intense air of privacy to him. His eyes scan a room before he walks into it, but Sangwoo never makes eye contact with a stranger. His mannerisms are more deliberate than casual. This is a man full of mystery and calculated movements.

When we step outside of the restaurant, the Mercedes is already waiting for us. Sangwoo coolly slips the valet a bill and motions for me to get into the front seat. Lina squeals silently behind me.

SANGWOO **ENDS UP DRIVING SPYDER** and Lina back to her house. The car ride is comfortable and relaxing, especially after the amount of food we have consumed. By the time we arrive at Lina's house, unique for its red bricks and slanted roof, Spyder is in a deep sleep. Lina has to wake him up and he does nothing more than stagger out of the car in his sleep coma.

When Lina leaves the car, she pulls me along with her. My cousin gives me a tight hug and whispers in my ear, "Thanks so much May. We'll talk more tomorrow. I can't believe you never told me about him! Thank you for everything, cousin. I love you. Good night."

Yeah, we definitely need to talk! My conscience is glaring at Lina. I cannot agree more. I need some alone time with her as soon as possible. For the time being, all I can do is return Lina's hug. While she marches over to Sangwoo's side of the car, I pull Spyder to the side. He regards me with a passive facial expression.

"How can you be so irresponsible?" I hiss under my breath.

APRIL LOVES BLACK COFFEE: FIRST IMPRESSIONS

"Borrowing money from gangsters and taking my cousin down with you?" I am taking advantage of the free moment to scold him. I have been holding the frustration inside for too long.

Even though he is handicapped, Spyder narrows his eyes at me, "Not the time or place, May. You think I don't know who that guy is?"

Irresponsible son-of-a-bitch. A fusion of emotions rises in my throat. I shake my head disapprovingly at Spyder. His black eyes harden and that unforgivable charm of his permeates the air. I can longer stand it.

"He's my friend. He helped you today!"

"He's not your friend. What are you doing with a Crist member?"

I swallow hard and step back from Spyder. All this time, I thought he bought the story, but it turns out Spyder knows. I cannot do this with him now. Lina is running out of ways to thank Choi Sangwoo and will be returning soon. Without saying another word to him, I stalk back to Sangwoo's awaiting car.

Lina is still saying goodbye to Sangwoo on behalf of Spyder too. "Bye Sangwoo. It was nice meeting you. Thank you for all your help today. We really appreciate it."

"It was nice meeting you too." Sangwoo returns the goodbye. He's still in the driver seat; the engine continues running.

"Bye Lina." I touch my cousin's arm lightly.

She observes the look on my face and turns to Spyder. Lina immediately puts two-and-two together. My cousin simply nods her head and steps back from the curb.

"Everything ok?" Sangwoo asks me. He recognizes the upset expression on my face.

"Yes," I whisper. I strap on the seat belt and face forward.

Sangwoo nods to Lina one more time before he shifts the car into gear. Instantaneously, the car pulls away from the curb and treks down the darkly lit street. Blurbs and circles of colors roam silently outside the window. The quiet hum of the car is soothing. Sangwoo drives with only his left hand while his right hand folds over the gear shift.

How can Spyder be so stupid? My head is still stuck on his statement. He doesn't even have the courtesy to tell me thank-you for saving him. I'm going to tell Lina everything on my mind tomorrow. I owe her that.

A small flash of light emits from the far left side pocket of the car. It startles me. I turn just in time to see Sangwoo press a button his steering wheel. Suddenly, static frequency invades the silent car.

"Ren," Sangwoo answers calmly. He inclines his head towards me as though to apologize for the surprise.

"Boss. The packages arrived." A male voice permeates the car. His young voice combines professionalism with a tint of reserved fear.

"And the reapers?" Sangwoo asks shortly. He looks in the rearview mirror before switching over to the next lane.

"All counted for. The Gods are going to accompany our shipment," Ren reports with consideration. "The Council just issued the approval an hour ago."

"Take some more of our men with you. This could get messy and I don't want to risk any of the constraints," Sangwoo commands with authority. "Anything else?"

There is a short moment of hesitation on the other end of the phone line. "And Mayhem, Boss?"

I peer at Sangwoo through my eyelashes. My hands go numb at the mentioning of his rival. Sangwoo, on the other hand, is cool as a cucumber.

"The same. Anything else?" he answers with a controlled tone.

"No," Ren concedes lightly. "Good night Boss."

Sangwoo hangs up without a reply. The muscles in his jaw tighten. *Is he mad?* I can't gauge this man. I have forgotten that in his world, Sangwoo is a much sought after person. His time is often auctioned, bought, and sold. *Then why the hell is he here with you?* Doubt is nipping at my conscience while she tries to fight him off.

Sangwoo glances at me with an arched eyebrow. He's caught me staring at him.

Guilty. "Thank you for today," I tell him in order to redeem myself for the intrusive staring.

"You're welcome." Sangwoo gives me a breathy reply and I feel an electric buzz through my veins. I don't know how many times my stomach can continue to drop every time he looks at me like that. Why does he have such an effect on me? *Because he's so different from anyone you've ever known. Plus, you're still stuck on the idea that you've met him before silly.*

"I guess we're even now," I joke. "I helped you last Saturday and you helped me this Saturday."

"If you put it that way, we're never going to be really even if you think about it," Sangwoo replies with quick wit. "Now that we've helped one another, it might be favors next."

"You think so?" I do my best to hide the slight fascination I reserve for this man.

"I know so," Sangwoo replies with the same cadence in his voice. He concentrates on the road ahead, but it is easy to see he knows the streets as though he is retrieving a personalized road map in his head. "Your cousin is a very strong character."

"She is." I am quick to agree. I begin to play with the strap on my tote bag. It is a nervous habit. "I'm still warming up to Spyder, to be honest." I feel the need to vent about Spyder's outlandish behaviors.

"Why?" Sangwoo leaves no room for assumption.

"Because he—" I cut myself off before I allow emotion to determine how much I want to divulge to Sangwoo. Part of me wants to tell him that Spyder is dragging Lina down with him while the other part of me is still trying to absorb the situation today.

Sangwoo senses my hesitation. "Is it because of his involvement with Mayhem?"

He hits the nail on the head with that one. I feel the avalanche of truth tumbling down. "Look, I'm going to be honest with you. I saw your confrontation with Mayhem." Here I go.

Sangwoo keeps his eyes on the road. His lips press together in the same tight, fine line manner. His jaw muscles clench together, giving off the impression that he is considering what he is willing to disclose. "Mayhem and I . . . do business together, occasionally. Sometimes we get along, sometimes we don't. That is just the unruly way it is in our business."

A chill ripples through the back of my neck at Sangwoo's disclosure. "Judging from your confrontation, Mayhem hasn't been very compliant. Is that why you came to Spyder's house today?" All the questions I want to ask march out of my mouth.

"Something like that," Sangwoo answers shortly. He pursues the question again. "What happened today between Mayhem and you? Did you tell him you were an associate of mine?"

Shit. Does he think I'm some kind of user? I fiddle tightly with the strap of my tote bag again. My mind is trying to formulate the best possible answer without giving up all the details, but I realize there is no way I can dance around the truth. I look down at the large gauze around my index finger, and the memory of what happened earlier comes flooding back like a reoccurring nightmare. Contrary to what I know will produce the better outcome, I find myself willing to confess to Sangwoo that I have been putting up a front. The truth involves the fact that I have to come up with thirty thousand dollars in a week. That is not humanly possible at the rate I am going. Besides, I don't want to tell Sangwoo how stupid I am for agreeing to pay Lina and Spyder's debt. I am out of my league with Mayhem, but I dug my own grave.

Slowly, I reach inside my tote bag for the necklace. I inadvertently tucked it inside my bag before we left the hospital. In the darkness, I am still able to find its distinctive bearing against my skin.

"You left this at my house last week." In a smooth motion, I extract the necklace for Sangwoo to see. "I don't know what I was thinking. I was just so scared when Danny was hurting my cousin. The look in Mayhem's eyes scared the living life out of me too. So, I took out this necklace and told them I am associated with you. It gave me credibility and saved us."

Sangwoo is silent as he listens to me. His eyes do not leave mine to look the necklace. Fortunately, we are at a red light. For some unknown reason, Sangwoo's quiet demeanor gives me the courage to continue.

"Spyder and Lina borrowed money from Mayhem," I confess. My voice comes out small and shaken. Even speaking about it takes quite some composure on my part. "They borrowed twenty thousand in the beginning, but apparently Spyder laundered some money out to a rival of Mayhem's. So now, Mayhem doesn't just want to add another thousand to the total but also collateral."

The relief of confessing the truth feels similar to a breath of fresh air.

"And you're collateral. You associated yourself with me so that you could help Spyder and Lina pay him off." As though I am an open book and an indefinite easy read, Sangwoo offers the final details. He turns to look at me momentarily.

Anxiously I answer, "Yes."

Sangwoo faces the road again as he shakes his head disapprovingly. "Let me guess, they pricked your finger to sign a blood contract to pay back the loan."

I shouldn't be surprised that Sangwoo knows the details to a dangerous fault. After all, Choi Sangwoo probably handles similar business transactions the same way. What is the difference between one gang and the next anyway? My emotions climb a steep hill, so I bite my bottom lip from replying to Sangwoo's comment.

"Are you upset?" He senses it in my rigid body language and tense silence.

"No, why would I be?" I lie with a clear intonation.

"You have every right to be upset," Sangwoo states. He's poised to let me know. "Your cousin and her boyfriend have you involved with one of the most notorious gangs known for extortion, blackmail, and money laundering."

I keep my eyes focused on the road, taking note of the fact that Sangwoo is driving through an unknown shortcut that leads to my apartment complex. I didn't think about asking Sangwoo if he remembered where I lived, but Sangwoo is having no trouble navigating. I focus on the amount of traffic ahead of us.

"I can help you." Sangwoo's offer sounds more like a decision.

My eyebrows come together in question. "Thank you, but I didn't tell you the truth or lied about my association with you so that you can help. I just wanted to confess." I want to be clear that I am not about to involve him in this mess.

"Well, because you've associated yourself with me, I'm involved whether I want to be or not. That is a fact," Sangwoo states with diction. "You do know that, don't you?"

I nearly bite my bottom lip off at his stringent point.

My disheartened silence causes Sangwoo to turn his full attention from the road to me. His eyes deepen and the same intensity lashes out. Sangwoo continues to drive with a magic peripheral view. "You remind me a lot of this girl I used to know . . . that same passive-aggressive reaction," he states passively.

"I know," I retort too quickly. "You called for her when you were drunk last Saturday." *For a guy who claims that we've never met before, he sure likes to compare me to a girl he once knew.* My intuition has her shady sunglasses on.

Sangwoo's lips curl into a small, indefinite smile. He faces the road again. Sangwoo's warning chills my spine. "You know, May, there's nothing to be embarrassed about if you need to ask for help. Thirty thousand and Mayhem's pride is not going to be easy to pay him back. They don't call him Mayhem just because the syllables roll down the tongue easily. He is chaos and disorder as well as pandemonium and bedlam. He is also childish when he doesn't get his way and will be manifest many things that the Bible warns against."

I sit very still as I listen to Sangwoo's rendition of Mayhem, including the colorful adjectives that describe the tantalizing gang leader. I am well aware that Sangwoo is trying to reach a point, but the other part of me has trouble with the idiom of the pot calling the kettle black in this situation.

"And what about you? If Mayhem means to destroy, then what is Crist?" I question. Far from trying to be smart with him, I really want to unearth the mysteries of these gang lords.

Sangwoo lets out an amused chuckle at my question. Deep humor cascades the features of his face. At the same moment, the car rounds down the familiar street. Sangwoo's Mercedes comes to a slow stop in front East Point. He parks the car indiscreetly.

The leather seat gives in as Sangwoo faces me with undivided attention. In the darkness of the car, with only a dim street lamp as the only source of lighting, Sangwoo's face is strikingly handsome. The more I look at Sangwoo, the more I am aware that his world and mine will never easily merge.

"I am different than the rest," Sangwoo states with such confidence that it is difficult to object. "I am not your typical street gangbanger and neither is Mayhem. But what separates me from the rest of my cohort, including Mayhem, is my business strategies are anti-competitive and product driven. We sit on top of the average street gangs, but we are still under the palms of the mafia, the mob, and a private Council. This may be unnecessary information for you, but I highly recommend that you stand behind a wolf to deal with a snake."

I feel as though my head is spinning from the influx of information. Apparently, I have hit a nerve with Choi Sangwoo and he is doing everything in his verbal power to drive home the situation.

"I'm sorry," I apologize with dejection. "I didn't mean to question you like that. Obviously, you're different than Mayhem. Otherwise, you wouldn't have helped me today. I just have a lot of preconceived notions about gangs and things like that."

"I didn't tell you all that for an apology, May," Sangwoo repeats the same rebuttal structure I used on him earlier. "And if you stick around long enough, every single myth and stereotype you've heard about gangs will be debunked. I'm telling you all that to let you know I can help. You've inadvertently involved me now." Sangwoo has a boyish smile on his face.

I glance down at my finger again. The gauze feels tight around my fingers. I am still holding his necklace in my left palm. Thirty thousand dollars is more than I can ever dream of. I have never imagined such money to fall into my hands much less be faced with the reality of having to pay it forward.

"I'm pretty dumb, huh?" I mumble. "I sign a contract to pay back money I don't even have. I used your necklace and claimed I'm a Crist member. I don't know what I was thinking." *Yeah, what the hell were you thinking?* My conscience wakes up from her nap.

"No. You're not dumb," Sangwoo answers quietly. "You let your heart decide. It was very brave."

At his kind words, I want to ask Sangwoo if he is an angel sent from above to alleviate mortal matters of mine.

"Are you always this nice to everyone you meet?" I can't help the curiosity biting at my tongue.

"No," Sangwoo answers deliberately. "I'm only nice to you."

"Why?" My heart picks up a few more beats.

"Because you helped me last Saturday. If you haven't taken me home, someone could have killed me if they spotted me alone and unconscious." Sangwoo's answer is so logical it makes the doubts disseminate. "Mayhem isn't the only person after me," he continues.

How can he sound so happy about that? "So your life is worth thirty thousand dollars?" I break into a small smile, anticipating Sangwoo's comeback.

"It's worth more than thirty thousand, but I can spare some for you," Sangwoo retorts with good humor.

We both laugh at our banter.

At the same moment, the familiar flash of Sangwoo's cell phone lights up the dark car. Because the phone faces the side pocket of the car, its bright white light causes an eerie shadow. The frustrated look on Sangwoo's face intensifies when he looks at the screen.

I take it as my cue to leave. I remove my seat belt when Sangwoo places his cell phone back into the car's side pocket. He chooses to ignore it.

"Here." I extend my left palm to give his necklace back. "I'm surprised you haven't realized it's missing."

Sangwoo reaches up to his neck, drawing my attention along with it. There is another sliver chain under the collar of his shirt. "I have another one. Keep this one."

"I couldn't."

"Since you're associated with me, you should."

I try to suppress how pleased I am at Sangwoo's gesture.

"I'll walk you out," Sangwoo offers with great sincerity.

"It's ok, you don't have to. My apartment is on the other side," I tell him. Again, my voice is above a whisper. *Why is he so forward?*

"I don't mind," Sangwoo answers with a nonnegotiable tone.

"Ok," I mumble in response.

We get out of the car from our respective sides. I pull the strap of my tote bag over my right shoulder and walk over to meet Sangwoo at the head of the car. He motions for me to lead the way.

The walkway through East Point is similar to an elaborate labyrinth. Overgrown trees, weeds, and tall grass surround each complex. The only sources of lighting emit from the recessed outdoor lights. Usually, it takes me two minutes to reach my apartment complex from the front gates. Today, however, I decide to take my time because Choi Sangwoo seems content on walking at a snail's pace. He is busy observing the surrounding area, giving off the impression that he's fascinated by where I live. I imagine Sangwoo living in a mansion with tall, white gates and his own swimming pool.

"You carried me through all this last Saturday?" Sangwoo asks with surprise. His question dissolves my reverie.

Now I understand why Sangwoo is marveling at the area. I cannot get over how tall he is and how he moves with ease and agility. Even Mayhem, who rivals Sangwoo's height, possesses the same grace. Where do they breed these gang lords?

"Yes I did," I answer Sangwoo's question. I inhale a deep breath of the cool night air. "Amazed?"

"Absolutely," Sangwoo remarks. "Now that I'm fully conscious, I can appreciate it."

I laugh at Sangwoo's comment as I steal a glance at him.

"What do you want to study in college?" Sangwoo surprises me as he brings the question back to what we discussed at dinner.

"I don't know if I should tell you," I tease him lightly, testing the boundaries. "Since you critiqued my choice of going to college."

"Hey, I went to college." Sangwoo surprises me again. He looks over his shoulder and says, "I'm serious. I went for four years and studied business management."

Business management? How apt. I am not sure they have a course on how to be a gang leader, unless this is a special college designed for gang lords.

"What are you studying?" Sangwoo brings me out of my thoughts again.

"Psychology," I answer with a smile. We are nearing my apartment complex now. I point to Sangwoo towards the stairs. "I want to be a psychologist."

The playful smile on his face fades slightly, but Sangwoo overcomes it quickly. "A psychologist? Why?"

I am reveling in the fact that I surprised Sangwoo. He gives me the impression that very little will take him back. "I think it's an interesting profession. I can help others figure things out."

"You know there's more to it than just helping others right?" Sangwoo inquires. There is humor in his voice.

At the same time, we are climbing the stairs to the sixth floor of my apartment. I lead the way with Sangwoo only a step beside me.

"I know that," I agree with him. "But like I said, I like helping people."

"But you don't like to be helped," Sangwoo corrects me.

"Are you out of breath yet?" I deflect the conversation, surprised that he is able to keep up with me. I look back to see Sangwoo with a fresh grin on his face.

"You'd be surprised by my physical stamina," Sangwoo replies quickly.

Oh wow. "I'm sure." I turn around and continue up the stairs. I am not sure if it is the stairs or Sangwoo's comment that makes my face deepen another shade of color. Fortunately, it is too dark for him to see. *Girl, you are out of your element!* my conscience barks at me under her stunner shades.

"You don't believe me? I can show you sometimes."

"Do all gang leaders have big egos?"

"Ha ha."

When we finally descend the sixth floor, and my apartment door is just a couple of steps away, I face Sangwoo. Once again, he sticks out like a sore thumb underneath the dreary lighting of the apartment hallway. Sangwoo's mouth stretches into that charming smile of his, and there is a tint of playfulness in his eyes now.

"Have a good night," I tell him shortly.

"You're not going to invite me in? That's a little rude." It's a joke, but there is a notion of truthfulness to it. The playful light in Sangwoo's eyes dims when I stare at him, slightly gaping.

"I'm sure you have work. I can't stay long either," Sangwoo recovers with a soft tone.

"I took tonight off from The Trax, so I'm working double shifts tomorrow," I tell him. This handsome, mysterious, dangerous, and intimidating man wants to come into my dreary apartment to talk to me? I will probably have a heart attack if I am alone with him tonight.

"You really do work seven days a week," Sangwoo notes. He crosses his arms over his chest. "You're a workaholic like me."

"I'm not a workaholic." I feel the immediate need to defend myself. "I just . . . work every day."

"Why are you afraid of idle time?" Sangwoo asks poignantly.

No one has ever come out and ask me this question so bluntly–at least not anyone besides Lina. I get the feeling that Choi Sangwoo has an insatiable thirst to obtain as much information about me as he can.

"I'm not afraid of idle time. I just work hard to save up money for college," I remind him again. "I have goals I want to reach."

"I know you do," Sangwoo replies with calm. "I just wonder if it's your schedule or you who can't stand to sit still."

"What about you? You chose a job that requires you to work twenty-four seven." I take the liberty of reminding him.

"Yes, it does. But I choose to take breaks," Sangwoo replies with contention.

"I take breaks." I make it clear that I don't want to explain why my schedule is packed. "Good night Sangwoo."

"Will you think about my offer?" he asks with haste. It is the first time I hear the impatience and speed in his question. "About helping you with Mayhem?"

I can read it in Sangwoo's face that he isn't just offering to help me because it is a money issue. Sangwoo is offering to help because he fears the consequences if he doesn't.

"Help me?" I repeat again.

"Within professional grounds," Sangwoo adds. "We will draw up an official contract, including clauses and stipulations."

A contract? What kind of contract and details will I have to adhere to? My instinct kicks at my heart who is struggling to breathe.

"A contract?" I repeat like a minion again. *You really are incompetent*, snaps my conscience.

Sangwoo stares at me as though he is wondering about my intelligence too. "Yes. So, it doesn't mean I am just giving you money. You will be providing a service to me as well." His eyes burn with intensity, as though he is afraid of my rejection.

"What kind of service?" I want to pick at this longer.

"Why are you alarmed?" Sangwoo ignores my question.

"Why are you so nice to me?" There, the burning question finally slips out. "Two weeks ago, I didn't even know you existed. And now, you want to help me." *Just admit that you know me from somewhere before,* my intuition growls impatiently.

"Because I was you once. I was helpless because of circumstances. And because I want us to be friends." Sangwoo's reasons are all over the place.

"So, a contract is the answer?"

"A contract will help you get comfortable with the idea I want to help you," Sangwoo remarks. "We can talk about the details tomorrow night."

Just like that, he stops me in my tracks. I want to talk to Lina first before I agree to anything else. If only Sangwoo knows that I want to take up his offer so badly my throat is hurting from rejecting it. "Ok. We can talk about it tomorrow night." Finally, I muster up the response.

When he gets his way, Sangwoo's eyes sparkle with agreement. He is still hard to read, but he appears more youthful now. "Good night May." My name hangs in the air.

"Good night," I reply breathlessly.

All of a sudden, I see the sadden expression return to Sangwoo's face. Last Saturday was the first time I saw that facial expression— when he was drunk beyond consciousness.

Tonight, it returns. Sangwoo calls to me as though he can no longer control his impulse. "Can I ask you for something?"

"What is it?" My voice is barely a whisper.

"Can I have a goodbye hug?" Sangwoo's gaze reaches my face with a definitive pull.

What? My insides curl up and the butterflies are expanding in my stomach. *He wants a hug?* My conscience scrambles to pick her jaw off the ground.

Before I can answer or think, Choi Sangwoo makes his way over to me. He reaches out in a precise manner and wraps his arms around my back, enclosing me against his body. It isn't the type of hug in which he wants to prolong the night with me, and it isn't even a hug that is meant to be romantically affectionate. It is a heart-wrenching hug, a metaphysical hold. The difference, I know, is in his words from last Saturday night. And I know, as I am locked in Sangwoo's embrace, it has to do with the girl he says I remind him of. I feel the pain still living and growing inside of him like a virus. The powerful memories, along with tears of happiness and pain, is in the strength of his clutch.

I feel myself swept away in Sangwoo's warm embrace. He has a distinctive smell to him, not the typical kind easily assessed at the mall or store. It is the scent of someone from his world, dangerous and vibrant. I am not sure what I am doing, but I wrap my arms around him in return. I attempt to share his pain as if I know an ounce of it.

"It's getting late. You should go in now."

In a matter of seconds, it is all over. Sangwoo releases his hold and I am free from him. Sangwoo steps back from me as if he cannot stand the pain of touching me anymore. It is a rare moment of weakness.

My heart starts racing and the more I want to speak, the harder it is to hold the tears back. *You silly putty.* My intuition is dabbing her cheeks with a tissue.

"You know, you remind me of someone from my past." Sangwoo's voice is soft and heartbroken.

"You were calling for her the night you threw up," I tell him. A faint image of Dead Girl haunts me again. "Is that why you were so drunk?"

Sangwoo looks up at the sky as if the answers are up there. "Yes."

"Because you wanted to forget her?" I ask him.

Sangwoo's face hardens suddenly. "You can't forget someone who doesn't want to be forgotten."

My eyebrows come together in confusion, but the right words fail me.

"Good night May." Without another word, Sangwoo retreats. Just like that, the moment is gone.

The feeling of having someone in such close proximity walking away calls for sensations like abandonment and rejection. I watch as Sangwoo makes his way down the apartment stairs with the same dejected feeling in my stomach.

"Sangwoo," I call to him. I finally find my voice, but it is too late.

He is already gone.

I stand listening to his footsteps retreating until the echoes disappear altogether. When Sangwoo is indefinitely gone, I head inside my dark and desolate apartment with bouts of emotions riding on me. The weight of confusion and uncertainty falls upon my shoulders when I press my back against the door. I stare at the darkness stretching ahead of me. My heart is pounding. My ears are throbbing. My soul is aching.

His necklace remains inside the palm of my hand.

CHAPTER FIVE

Nightmares torture me that night. I toss and turn into the wee hours of the morning before exhaustion finally hits like a ton of bricks. Like a zombie, I feel lifeless and neurotic. No matter how hard I try, I cannot fall back asleep and I find myself staring at the gloomy reflections of the sky peeking through my window. Choi Sangwoo's face continues to permeate my mind. My thoughts dwell on his offer and the eerie, provoking encounter with Mayhem.

Memories and thoughts run through my mind like a script, scrawling and scrolling in red letters. In just one day, my entire world is no longer in equilibrium. One thing led to another and now not only do I owe Mayhem thirty thousand dollars, but I am also associated with Crist. I am not sure if this is final destination or I am the center of a cosmic joke.

When I can no longer stand it, I get out of bed and sit down at my desk. My pride and joy, a Sony Vaio laptop, sit on top of my desk waiting with silent speculation. Abandoned since last semester, the keyboard has collected dust. I try to stay away from social media and technology because I consider them white noise. However, at the present moment, I gather all the tech savvy skills I have. I am silly and gullible, but my fingers are itching to get information.

"Here we go," I mumble. I switch on the laptop's power button and sit back. For the first time, I'm excited to see the window's screen flash on with its familiar chorus.

The trusty Google search engine pops up, welcoming me to the wealth of knowledge waiting for digestion. I feel giddy as I type the simple word *gangster*. Immediately, Google directs me to more than twenty million results.

"A gangster is a member of an organized crime group. There exist a variety of gangs differentiated by prerogative, objective, and success. The categorization of a gangster depends on his membership in the type of organization. Street, prison, city, and nation gangs vary in degrees of organization and location from low to high. The Japanese Yakuza and the Italian Mafia are two of the most highly organized nation gangs while street and prison gangs are less organized local gangs. Gangs organized around motorcycles and cars are based upon modes of transportation. Street gangs claim neighborhoods while drug gangs traffic illegal substances. A street gangster's cause is different from an entrepreneurial gangster's objective. Small street gangs engage in low-level crime; well-structured gangs such as the Triads, Mafia, and Drug Cartels orchestrate complex crime . . . ." I read slowly and carefully. My eyes feel heavy from the amount of information; they burn from the raw black and white print on screen.

I click out of the link and type in *gang leader*. Another link expands to display a plethora of information. I read to myself. "Highly structured gangs operate formally with leadership falling to the individual or individuals who take control, much like a business or corporation. Such entrepreneurial gangs are intensely private in their illegal, underground transactions. A gang leader, or gang lord, is responsible for the recruitment, management, and orchestration of criminal activities." I scroll down the screen, over the Mob and Mafia—the Italians and Sicilians. I stop at South Korean gangs. "Gangs in such countries are often highly-organized and entrepreneurial operating with distinctive formal proceedings. In order to join such high-level gangs, potential members undergo initiation ceremonies that may include brutal beatings, killing a police officer, committing theft/larceny, and engaging in sex with members of the gang and so on. Very few members are invited in or blessed-in—family members who are already in the gang . . . ."

Had enough? My conscience looks over her dark glasses, narrowing her eyes at me. The amount of information is beguiling at the same time it is disturbing. Boldly, I continue with my investigation and type in *Crist gang*. Despite the amount of general information about gangs, the search for the specific gang yields weak results. There is one recent news article about their brawl with Mayhem, but nothing beyond what the news anchor stated yesterday. As I continue my search, nothing of significance comes up about Choi Sangwoo. The lack of information doesn't surprise me. Sangwoo doesn't seem like the type who would allow such information about him to float freely online. There are articles, however, of a family-owned business—Choi International Incorporated. The company has investments and ties with the national banking system, along with travel and commerce industries. There is no history about the company's origins or the current CEO. In fact, CII is a private company with only one CEO and no board. It seems as though any adverse or negative reports no longer exist.

Testing my luck again, I type in *Mayhem gang* and the search results are scarcer. There is no gang listed or associated with the name Mayhem. No single business entity has the name Jaewon attached to it either. It appears as though this second gang lord is even more mysterious and intensely private than Choi Sangwoo.

I slump in my chair. The amount of information dances in front of my eyes. I am not sure what to think now that I have informally educated myself about this underground society. If anything, I am more apprehensive about the gang lords. Everything they do is above, below, or behind the law; they do not uphold the law. As I continue searching, more research articles about violent gang crimes trickle through the links. Some gangsters die never knowing who their Boss is; others kill, maim, steal, and cheat as Son warned me about. I can no longer handle the heaviness of the research. I decide it is better to switch the screen off and forget it.

AFTER A THIRTY MINUTE SHOWER, I finally emerge with an aching index finger. I take off the gauze to reveal a deep, linear cut right down my index finger. Fortunately, the doctor told me that as long as I keep the cut clean, it isn't going to scar or be infected.

I wash the cut thoroughly and replace a new Band-Aid on my finger. When my mind wanders back to Choi Sangwoo, I do my best to shun the thoughts. I follow my usual morning routine and make my way back to my room for my cell phone. Just as I expected, Lina has left me a message that she wants to meet at Mula. I am not due at The Trax until later in the afternoon, so I reply a quick yes to my cousin.

"May! Breakfast!"

From the depths of the kitchen, I hear Eunhye's morning call.

"You're up early," I greet her when I enter the brightly lit kitchen. I sit on a stool at the small island counter.

Eunhye is dressed in her multi-colored scrubs. She is bustling between the stove and sink, putting away utensils and cooling off the freshly cooked toast. Eunhye's hair sweeps out of her face in an elaborate bun, but her tired eyes can't hide the exhaustion of working fifty hours a week.

"I'm leaving for work soon. The hospital called and they need me as soon as possible." She places a plate of toast, complete with scrambled eggs and salad in front of me. "Eat. Do you have work today?"

I stare at my mother with a wave of emotion. Not only does she work hard, but my mother is also one of the most giving people in the world. Just watching her in the frantic state of preparing breakfast before heading off to work makes my problems feel insignificant. Life continues despite the cracks and potholes that I seem to encounter lately.

"I have work today. Thanks mom," I tell her when I reach for the coffee maker at the end of the counter. *I need some coffee.* My intuition rubs her hands together in anticipation. I pour myself a cup of coffee, enjoying the pungent smell.

"At Sansachun or The Trax?" Eunhye glances at her wristwatch before she sits down at the other end of the kitchen counter. Her plate of food is stacked with eggs and salad. It is her favorite breakfast.

"The Trax," I answer. I take a sip of the black coffee and cringe at its potent taste.

"What happened to your finger?" Before I can stop her, Eunhye has my finger under her control. Fortunately, I have taken the gauze out. Eunhye will never let me live it down if she knows I went to a hospital that wasn't hers.

"I cut myself yesterday." I make the decision to lie to her. I don't make eye contact with my mother, afraid that she will be able to read my façade. I pretend to pick at my plate with the fork.

"Why didn't you go to my hospital? I could have taken a look at it." Eunhye lets go of my finger. She observes the rest of my hands before her eyes move back to my face. "Did it happen at work?" My mother raises an eyebrow. I already know where she is going with her questions. This is the perfect opportunity for Eunhye to provide yet another reason why I should quit The Trax. Eunhye has been actively trying ever since I started; she has been against The Trax since day one.

"No." I am starting to feel worse as the conversation goes on. "At Lina's. We were cooking at her house and I cut my finger."

Eunhye gives me a weary look as she snaps, "The two of you together is always trouble." She ends it at that and doesn't pursue the topic any further.

I am pleasantly pleased with Eunhye's reaction and try to hide my smile the best way I know how. I pick up the cup of coffee and take another sip. The hot moisture along with the caffeine rush soothes my mind. "Mom," I call to her, "maybe next week you and I can take a day off and go do something together."

Eunhye's eyebrows come together in immediate surprise. "What brought this on?"

I don't expect her to agree right away, but I also don't expect the astonishment on her face. "We work seven days a week mom. I was just thinking we could take a day off to relax and have fun."

"Oh honey." Eunhye gets up from her stool and begins cleaning her area. She has devoured her breakfast throughout the course of our conversation. "You know I would love to take time off from the hospital, but it's not a good time right now. If I'm not taking care of patients, I have paperwork to do. The list never ends."

Something similar to disappointment comes over me. I know she has to work, but I feel sad by the circumstances. I keep my eyes focused on my teal green coffee mug. "I understand. I was just suggesting."

"Hey." Eunhye wraps her arms around me. "I will still try ok? You and I are both working hard towards improving our lives. I promise you, we will get to spend some time together soon."

I look up at my mother's kind eyes and feel guilty. If only she knows what I am going through.

"I know mom," is all I can say to her.

"Ok. Be good." Eunhye plants a kiss on my forehead. She glances at her watch again and makes a face. "I better go. I'm going to be late. Can you clean up before you go to work?"

"Yes," I answer simply. I take another swig of the coffee, hold it in my mouth for a few seconds longer, and then swallow. The black coffee is still hot. It burns all the way down my esophagus and into my stomach. There is nothing like this feeling in the world.

"Oh, I forgot to ask you," Eunhye starts, "have you seen Choi Sangwoo since last weekend?"

My head snaps up faster than it should at her question. "Why?"

Eunhye scrunches up her nose. "I thought I saw him last night when I came home. It must have been close to midnight, but I saw a very fancy car parked at the front entrance of the apartment complex. Granted the car windows were too dark for me to see, but I would recognize those facial features anywhere."

Did Sangwoo sit in his car hours after we said our goodbye? Curiosity and flattery strike me. My conscience is twirling in the middle of the room on her tiptoes.

"I don't think that's him." I am doing well with all the lies today. "Why would Choi Sangwoo sit in his car until the early hours of the morning?" I add a scoff to make it seem even more ridiculous.

Eunhye purses her lips together momentarily; she only does that when she scours for answers that are not obvious. "I don't know. I just thought it was him. He hasn't contacted you?"

"No." I keep my answer as concisely as possible.

"Hmm, I bet money he will contact you. He obviously liked you very much." Eunhye makes another silly face.

"And how can you tell that by meeting him only one time?" I

entertain the notion with her.

"Because I am old and wise, my child." Eunhye spreads her arms in an exaggerated manner. "Besides, I saw the way he looked at you. It was the way your father used to look at me."

"Mom, trust me, Choi Sangwoo does not like me."

"Maybe you're not ready to like him back."

"I don't think so, mom."

"You do like him, don't you?"

"I hardly know him."

"Don't deny. Remember, in therapy we—"

The conversation has fallen into an automatic mode of talking without censorship. When the mentioning of therapy slips from her tongue, Eunhye stops speaking. For a brief moment, we hold our breaths—afraid of one another's response. The silence we vowed to keep about our broken family history exposes itself. The simple slip-up brings back painful memories for us.

I look away from Eunhye at the same time she lowers her eyes. The emotions grapple inside me. Why is Eunhye so careless to bring the subject up? Didn't we promise never to mention it again, and pretend that it is only the two of us in this family composition?

At the same moment, the familiar ring of Eunhye's cell phone breaks through my thick fog of thoughts.

'That's my phone." Eunhye turns toward the living room for her bag.

I'm glued to my stool with only two sips away from finishing my coffee. I am lost in a trail of thoughts as I listen to Eunhye's muffled voice. When she returns, it is as though the restart button activates.

"I'm heading to work now. Afterwards, I'm going to play poker at Dongwan's house. If you get home before I do, turn off the light in the fish tank ok? You've been forgetful about that." Eunhye begins packing her items. Ordinary day, ordinary conversation. Just like that, we sweep everything under the rug once again.

"Ok mom. Have a good day," is all I can I say.

Im Dongwan is Eunhye's best friend from childhood. Mr. Im doesn't have any children and lives alone in a house not far from here. Ever since I can remember, Mr. Im and Eunhye have been very close. They spend most of their time watching dramas, playing cards, eating, telling stories, and acting like the teenagers they once were. Together, they have been through a lot. Eunhye appreciates Mr. Im very much because he was there when she really needed him, when our family was going through the problems. At least once a month, Mr. Im holds a poker game at his house and Eunhye always makes it a point to support him.

As though she read my thoughts, Eunhye gives me one last smile before she leaves the apartment. I stay rooted with my cup of coffee. I hear the distinct ringing of my cell phone from my bedroom. I have to snap out of it quickly. Time is ticking.

I clean up my area and prepare to leave.

LINA WANTS TO MEET AT Mula, a local milk teahouse we frequent since middle school. Its distinct interior of blue and yellow colors attracts many teenagers as well as college students. Mula has private booths and partitions for study sessions and confidential conversations. It is close to the perfect meeting place for Lina and me given the circumstances.

Mula is only two blocks away from my apartment so I end up walking there. When I enter the bustling store, I scan the area for my cousin. There are five people standing in line waiting to order. Others fill the open tables, including the seating area by the window. Even the cushioned sofas near the exterior walls are unavailable.

I decide to round the main area towards the partitions.

I find my cousin sitting at the last booth. She is wearing a black baseball hat to match her black leggings and droopy black T-shirt. Lina twitches lightly when I round the partition. When she sees me, Lina relaxes.

"Thank God. I thought you were a vampire," she says with a nervous glance behind me. Her reference to gangsters doesn't escape me. Lina's voice is a mixture of apprehension and breathlessness. "Did anyone follow you?"

I look around Mula. Nothing seems amiss. "Not that I know of." My intuition has her brown detective coat on.

"Sit down. I got you a drink." Lina pushes the original honey milk tea towards me. The liquid at the bottom makes a clear streak on the wooden brown tabletop.

I notice that Lina's halfway done with hers. I am slightly alarmed at my cousin's need to stay inconspicuous. I'm not as nearly prepared as she is. Compared to my cousin, I am too casual for someone who owes a dangerous gang lord an obscene amount of money.

"Thanks for meeting me." Lina strums her fingers on the table. Her anxiousness and apprehension is contagious.

"Are you okay?" I ask her, taking note of the fact that my cousin is on the verge of falling to pieces.

"I'm not." Lina shakes her head. "I couldn't sleep last night. I couldn't stop thinking about what happened. I'm feeling mad, sad, guilty, and everything in-between. I wanted to call you a million times, but I knew you needed to rest too."

I listen to my cousin's confession with a heavy heart. "What about Spyder?"

"He's staying at my house for now. I told my parents he got hurt and there's no one at his house to take care of him, especially with his parents gone. So my mom let him stay in the guest room. He's still sleeping. He's in a lot of pain," Lina recounts softly. She makes a frustrated face. "I can't wait until he gets better so I can kill him the right way."

I shake my head. I want to ask Lina how my aunt and uncle are responding to Spyder sleeping over, but refrain against it.

"You and me both," is my remark. My eyebrows burrow together in frustration. "Lina, why did it get so bad?"

Lina remains silent. She doesn't want to talk about her poor decision in a partner. From the very beginning, Lina's been Spyder's first line of defense. I don't expect my cousin to let her guard down when it comes to her no-good boyfriend, but I don't want her to make excuses for him.

"Why did you guys borrow money from Mayhem, Lina?" I ask instead.

Lina's eyes flick in a rapid blinking pattern, giving the impression that negative thoughts are tugging at her tear ducts. Lina begins her confession at a rapid pace. "My parents are underwater with their bills. The hardware store is not doing so well. I'm not making enough money and I couldn't rely on Spyder. We heard through his friends that Mayhem's loan shark division is one of the wealthiest to borrow from. Their interest and turnaround rate was supposed to be low and slow. We really thought we could pay the twenty thousand back within the given time frame. But I didn't know Spyder was going to go behind my back and launder out the money to Mayhem's rivals. To be honest, I don't even know why he did that."

"Breathe Lina." I reach across to touch her shoulders softly. "It's going to be okay."

My cousin nods her head, but her brave face does little to hide her impending tears. "I'm sorry I got you involved in this. Before the end of this week, Spyder and I might be able to scrounge up about ten grand. We still need twenty more."

I am hesitant to speak up next, but I know I cannot have an honest conversation with Lina without telling her the truth. I know now is not the time to introduce another complex issue, but I am willing to reduce my cousin's pain. "I asked Choi Sangwoo for help. He's the leader of Crist," I disclose with conviction.

Lina lifts her head up, revealing her misty eyes underneath the worn baseball hat. "What?" It is clear she's beyond surprised.

"Sangwoo, from yesterday, is actually the leader of Crist. He says he'll help," I repeat with a low tone.

If Lina's eyes can pop out of their sockets, they probably will. "I knew it!" she exclaims with a whispered gasp. "How did you meet him? No wonder why you told Mayhem you were an associate of Crist. How did he know to come to Spyder's house yesterday?"

I take a deep breath before I tell Lina the truth–from how I met Sangwoo last week to him leaving his necklace behind in my apartment to how we said goodbye last night. I tell Lina the facts, but keep my emotions out of it. By the time I am done, my cousin is dizzy with the amount of information.

"Wait a minute, so he's willing to give you thirty thousand to pay off your debt to Mayhem under the condition of a contract? What is the contract made of?" Lina remains flabbergasted when I end my recount.

"It's not like that, Lina. I don't know what contract he's going to propose." My voice is barely a whisper. "We're supposed to have dinner tonight after I get off work."

"You're having dinner with the leader of Crist?!" Lina gasps too loudly.

I motion for Lina to lower her voice. Swinging my head around, I make sure no one is listening. "I'm thinking of canceling." The thought of being alone with him scares me beyond reprieve. I don't want to tell Lina about my Google history. She will definitely be upside down about the situation.

"Canceling?" Lina gives me a winded look. "You are not going to cancel dinner with the Crist leader. Give him a chance May. You can't go through life exiling yourself from new people and new experiences."

I feel drained now that I have divulged to my cousin the truth. "But he's from a different world than ours. He's a gangster. Regardless of the fact that he's a high-end gangster, he's still involved in illegal and volatile businesses. You saw how Mayhem dealt with us yesterday."

"Yes, but that's Mayhem. Choi Sangwoo was incredibly nice yesterday. He helped us. He took us to the hospital and took care of everything. He's offering to draw up a contract to lend you money. Who does that? He clearly likes you." Lina chucks reason after reason at me.

My cousin is on a mission to help me see the light.

I am aware that I am gaping at her bold statement. "He doesn't like me Lina. It's not like that." *Eunhye and Lina are both seeing something you're so blind to.* With one eyebrow lifted, my conscience sticks her head into my business again.

Lina shrugs and simultaneously takes another sip of her milk tea. "You're very naïve May. Men are very simple. Men only want one thing in this world . . . and that's a woman. Everything they do, create, make, and maintain is always for a girl or woman. Everything that they do would mean nothing without a woman or a girl, as James Brown would say." Lina's penchant for music proves itself useful.

"Why would he be interested in me?" I am definitely not his type. I am not very interesting or exceptional beautiful. I know nothing about his world. All I know is work and school. I'm not especially talented at anything, and I have a marred childhood.

Lina narrows her eyes at me. "Hey, what's wrong with you? You're smart, ambitious, motivated, and pretty. He's the one who's lucky. You're a Lee, May. Where's your self-confidence?"

They always say no one loves you like family does.

"But if you're really uncomfortable with the idea, then don't worry. Spyder and I will still find a way to pay Mayhem back," Lina concedes softly. A dark look crosses Lina's face and I know she is thinking about her debt. Although it is entertaining to Lina that Choi Sangwoo can help us, my cousin will support my choice.

I reach for her hand. "I'll help you."

"Ah hell May, don't worry." Lina tries to take her hand back but I don't let go. "Besides, one dinner and talking about a possible contract won't kill you."

"Are you sure?" I mean for it to be funny, but I know the truth is all too real.

"Choi Sangwoo might be a gang leader, but he doesn't seem scary or intimidating. You can tell he has a good heart. He didn't flip out when you told him you lied about being associated with him. He actually wants to help you. I don't think you should judge him yet, especially since he was sincere in helping us yesterday. He took us to the hospital and then dinner," Lina reminds me.

When I don't answer her, Lina grows anxious.

"I'm not defending him or even advocating for you to like him." Lina throws her hands in surrender.

"Oh god, Lina." I place a hand against my forehead and sit back in the booth. "I just wish you told me all of this earlier instead of putting me through all this shock in less than forty-eight hours."

"I'm sorry. I didn't plan it like this. I wasn't going to involve you. I didn't know Mayhem would send one of his guys out for me like that." Sorrow clouds her gaze. Lina's regretful tone is difficult to bear as her family member.

"I'll figure it out with Sangwoo." I am determined. *Damn it Lina! You've been getting us into trouble since we were young. Thought this crap was over with!* My intuition puts on red boxing gloves. "I'll help you as much as I can, but you have to promise me you're never going to borrow from another gangster again."

"I'll be homeless if I have to." Lina holds two fingers to her heart. "You don't know how much this means to me."

Now that I can share with Lina my worries, I feel better. Just when I think I can manage the stress, a shrill voice breaks through our quiet meeting.

"Lina? Is that you? Is my brother with you?"

"Oh crap," I mumble when I recognize the voice.

"I swear I didn't know he was going to be here." Lina gives me an apologetic look. She squirms in her seat.

"May? Is that you, May?" He approaches the end of our booth with such eagerness that I have to brace for the worse.

"Hi Bryan." My tone marks the dark clouds spilling over a sunny day.

Sang Baean, who often goes by his American name, Bryan frowns at my lackluster greeting. "May, where have you been? I missed you!"

"Busy," I mumble as I stare at him in disbelief. I have forgotten the fabulous Bryan.

Bryan is Spyder's younger brother at the fresh age of eighteen-years-old. Even though he and Spyder are biological brothers, one would never know it because they look nothing alike. Bryan is shorter in stature with a lean and muscular body to accompany a childish face. On the outside, Bryan appears quite average. It's the inside that has severe issues. Ever since Lina started dating Spyder, Bryan attached himself to me like a lost puppy in love. When I first met Bryan he was normal, but over time he's developed an intense crush on me. It isn't a serious crush, but it is serious enough where Bryan is convinced I will be his wife one day. I don't like to talk about Bryan for the same embarrassing reasons why some people are simply uncomfortable discussing their bowel movements.

"I called you, texted you, left you messages, and you never got back to me." Bryan takes it upon himself to sit down next to me. He wraps an arm around my shoulders.

I close my eyes as I listen to Lina's soft laughter. I choose not to answer Bryan's comment. It's true that he blew up my phone last week, but I ignored it out of habit. Bryan is entitled to the hope that one day I will return his phone calls and text messages.

"Bryan, take your arm off me please. You smell like old cologne," I mumble. "Come on!" I do my best to remove his arm.

"Did you know when you hit and yell at someone, it's an expression of love?" Bryan asks as he refuses to move his hold around me. His affections have always been suffocating to say the least.

"Bryan, this is so not the day." I toss my head back against the booth. *I have bigger fishes to fry!* Amused, my conscience gives Bryan an adoring smile. She has a soft spot for him—much like adoring an orphaned puppy.

"Aww, what's wrong May?" Bryan examines my face. "Can I help you with anything?"

"Yes, go away," I tell him bitterly.

"Bryan, leave her alone for once." Lina finally intervenes with a grin. My cousin finds our relationship hilarious and often does little to prevent Bryan from crawling under my skin. "What are you doing here anyway?"

"Looking for my brother," Bryan answers her. He starts running his hand up and down my hair. I dig my fingernails into his arm. Bryan pulls away quickly and says, "You want me don't you May?"

"Yes Bryan," I say lazily, placing a finger on my temple to keep my head from exploding. "I want you just as much as I want to open a freshly delivered pizza box to find maggots inside. I want you just like I want a good sunburn that will leave me with skin cancer. I want you just as much I want to squeeze lemons onto a cut."

"Oh god." Bryan withdraws from me. I think for a second my comment has finally put him off, but he reaches for my right finger instead. "What happened to your finger?"

This is where I drew the line. "Nothing." I pull my finger away from him. I don't want to explain or disclose any information.

"Leave her alone Bryan." Lina slaps him on the forehead finally. "Your brother's at my house."

Bryan looks back at Lina with suspicion. "Because he tore ours apart?"

"We'll be by later today to clean it up," is all Lina says.

Evidently, we are not going to tell Bryan what is going on. The less Bryan knows about the incident last night the better. It is difficult for him to keep anything a secret, especially since he has gotten in with the wrong crowd lately. Bryan used to be a sweet and nerdy teenager, but now he's into hard styles and harsh words.

I glance at my watch and realize noon is rapidly approaching. "I got to go to work. I'm going to be late."

"I'll take you to work." Bryan reaches for my wrist again.

I shake him off me. "Bryan, do me a favor and get yourself a real girlfriend."

"I'm dating May. I'm dating to forget you, but I haven't met anyone with your *it* factor," Bryan replies as though this is all truth coming from the depths of his soul.

Girl! This kid is hilarious! My conscience is grinning with all her teeth showing.

"Sometimes I wonder if you really do like me or you just like to annoy the living life out of me, Bryan." I pull away from him indefinitely. "I don't have time for this. I'll talk to you later, Lina. Call me."

"Bye May." Lina is suppressing laughter at the sour look on Bryan's face. "Call me after your dinner tonight."

"I will," I answer my cousin. My heart beats a little faster at the reminder.

"Dinner?" Bryan makes a face. He leaves nothing to the imagination. "With who, May?"

I give him a brisk wave before leaving. If he thinks I am going to tell him, Bryan seriously needs me to set him straight one day.

"She's just playing hard to get." I hear Bryan's statement behind my back.

"I don't think that's playing hard to get Bryan, it's more like a plain rejection," is Lina's snappy remark.

I suppress a laugh at Bryan's childish ways. I realized long ago that Bryan continues to tease me because I put up with it. If I return his supposed feelings, Bryan will be the one hiding from me. Bryan makes it hard to take him seriously because his antics are so outrageous.

I END UP LEAVING MULA feeling lighter. Now that I have worked out the kinks with Lina, I do my best to keep my mind off the impending dinner with Choi Sangwoo tonight. I allow myself only a moment to think about how he is going to call me; I never gave Sangwoo my number, so how are we going to meet tonight? Something tells me that predictability and organized scheduling is not Choi Sangwoo's style. Now, I am on a different tangent thinking about how I want to discuss the money-borrowing ordeal with him. I have never borrowed money from anyone, much less thirty thousand dollars. Mayhem must be affluent to have thirty thousand lying around for someone as average as Spyder to borrow. *Well, Mayhem's going after it so that proves he doesn't regard money lightly.* My intuition's whiny voice shatters my peaceful flight.

I arrive twenty minutes later at The Trax no longer refreshed. Instead, I am on edge and wired. The Trax is in its full restaurant mode. The foot traffic increases by mid-afternoon and all staff members are wholly busy, so break schedules shift to an hour after the usual time.

By the time my break comes around, I find myself sitting at the end of the bar. Tailor mixes me a refreshing drink before fulfilling his bartender duties with a group of executives at the other end of the bar. I am in the middle of stirring the ice cubes against the bluish green drink when the stool next to me groans.

Son plops heavily down next to me. "God, it's hot!" He wipes a sheet of sweat off his forehead. Without waiting for Tailor, Son reaches over the counter and grabs a bottle of water.

"I thought Joolie is taking her break," I comment. I look around for my other co-worker and find her taking orders from a table near the window.

"We switched," Son answers with a hoarse throat. He opens his water bottle and chugs it down like a fish. When he finishes, Son wipes the corners of his mouth. "Are you okay?"

Uh Oh. Can he see it on my face too? I glower inside, hating the fact that I am such an open book.

He may not show it often, but Son does care about the people he works with. Although Son takes his job seriously, he's mindful of the people associated. As of the moment, Son is looking at me with sincere concern.

"Of course I'm okay. Why wouldn't I be?" I let out a feigned laugh and do my best to hide it by taking another sip of my drink. *Remember that Crist member Son? He's helping me pay off a thirty thousand debt my cousin and her loser boyfriend racked up.* My conscience sits down on the talk show chair.

"You just seem kind of out of it lately," Son remarks. He cocks his head to the side and eyes me warily. "Like you have a lot on your mind."

"Really?" I ask nonchalantly. "Maybe working two jobs is getting to me. I'm almost always on the brink of exhaustion."

Son nods his head at the familiar sentiments. "That makes sense."

I tap the side of my glass twice as a thought permeates my mind. "Can I ask you something?"

"What?" Son asks. He takes another swig of his water bottle.

"Remember that night when that Crist member was here?" I start slowly, not wanting to sound too eager for the information.

"Yeah, and he threw up everywhere on this counter?" Son makes a face.

"Oh yeah." I withdraw my elbow from the surface. "How did you hear about gangs like Crist?"

Son's eyebrows come together. He has a faraway look in his eyes. "You live under a rock May?"

"Come on. All I know is work and school."

"How long are you going to use that excuse for?"

"It's not an excuse!" I laugh at Son's aggressive tackle on my ignorance.

I expect him to laugh with me, but Son's smile slowly fades from his lips when he answers my question. "My cousin was a Crist member."

My eyes grow big at Son's revelation. *Oops. This is not what I was expecting.*

"They're more prevalent than you'd think May. You just have to know how to identify them." Son narrows his eyes in an obtrusive manner. "People have preconceived notions that gangsters wear saggy pants, oversized shirts, designer shoes, and stand on street corners. Those are the lower street gangsters. Crist members are higher up in the food chain. There are social rankings and a complex hierarchical system in organized gangs. There are the street soldiers, the carriers and runners, the recruiters, the underbosses, the bosses. There is a lot more that I am not too familiar with. I only know from when my cousin was active."

"When he was active?" I repeat after Son. There's a queasy feeling in my stomach.

Son gives me a lost look. A sad expression strikes his face. "That's how it usually ends when you're in a gang, May. The only way out is death."

I suck in a deep breath. Electricity charges through me. "Was his Boss nice to him?" I imagine Son's cousin working under Choi Sangwoo.

Son lets out a deep chuckle that rumbles from the bottom of his throat. "Yeah, his boss was nice to him. Nice enough to green light my cousin's execution."

Shock electrocutes me. I nearly drop my drink from Son's comment. "What else do they do?" My voice is barely above a whisper.

Son doesn't answer me. Instead, his eyes focus towards the front entrance of The Trax. I follow his gaze to see two figures entering the restaurant. The woman is walking briskly with the man following her heels closely. The two are dressed business casual. The man is wearing khaki pants with a dark blazer while the woman is wearing black slacks and a white blouse. Even at a distance, I see her red nails curling over a dark manila folder. Her dark eyes are scanning the room. When her keen eyes land on Son, the blood drains from his face. I can almost see the hairs stand on his arms.

Son stands abruptly from the bar and mumbles, "What are they doing here?"

"Who are they?" I ask.

"The Bosses." Son leaves without clarifying if I had heard him right.

I'm alarmed by his abrupt departure. I have never seen Son react this way. In fact, I have never seen even one Boss much less two of them. There is something unsettling about them. A couple of co-workers stop in the middle of their tasks, shell shocked at the sight of Son scampering after the two unfamiliar figures. When Son reaches them, the woman gestures toward the long hallway as though to indicate why she is here.

"She doesn't look like a health inspector." His breathless voice breaks my concentration.

I jump slightly at Tailor's phantom appearance. He is in full bartender gear, complete with the Fedora hat. Tailor's usual grin is not apparent on his face. He looks worried, reflecting how I feel inside.

"Son says they're the Bosses," I mumble, well aware that I am lighting a fire under the gossip log.

"Bosses?" Tailor lifts up an eyebrow. "I've never even met one Boss. I've worked here for three years."

Right? I feel another chill ripple down my spine. "I'm going to the bathroom."

I get up from the barstool and head into the bathroom to wash my face. Thoughts of my conversation with Son travels back to my consciousness. The thought of Choi Sangwoo green lighting someone's execution traumatizes me. I don't know what to think about all the rumors. It seems as though the more I try to figure out these gang lords, the more rumors and tainted truths I am coming across. There are too many grapes marching through the grapevine.

At some point between running the cold water under my fingers and thinking, I decide to give up. There is no use dwelling on something I cannot settle on. I will probably never get to the bottom of the truth. The only conclusion I am sure of is Choi Sangwoo, and his dangerous counterpart Mayhem, will remain in shrouded mystery. People who dedicate their entire lives to investigating gangs may never obtain the type of information I am asking for. Who am I, a nobody, to be pursuing such truth?

Talk about positive thinking, May. My conscience is all sarcasm when I leave the bathroom.

I go back to work with a buffer mindset. I put the rest of my efforts into a happy appearance and customer service mannerisms. Fortunately, time speeds by and before I know it, The Trax is nearing its closing time. Because Sunday nights are never much at The Trax, the venue closes two hours earlier than its usual time.

Son is still missing in action. A couple of the co-workers start to whisper that Son is in trouble for his management executions while others speculate he is getting an award for his czar-like pursuits.

As the remaining customers trickle out of The Trax, I head to the bar to drop off some empty glasses. Tailor is in the middle of stacking bottles back on the shelves when he greets me. "Staff meeting," he states. He motions towards the hallway where a couple of co-workers are heading.

"Staff meeting?" I don't even disguise the surprise in my voice. Our staff meetings are usually at the beginning of the month.

Tailor shrugs his shoulder in an I-don't-know fashion. Seeing Tailor's worried facial expression concerns me. He leads the way to the back room where the meeting is taking place. I follow with a heavy heart. I don't know if I can take any more surprises.

There is only one meeting room at The Trax. It is behind the kitchen, tucked away from wandering eyes. There is a wooden plaque on the door that says *Meeting Room* in dishevel marks. Tailor reaches the door first, and I can hear voices rumbling inside when I approach it next.

Tailor knocks on the door and the voices inside die down.

"Come in," a curt female voice answers.

Tailor glances at me briefly before he opens the door. I take a deep breath and follow him in. The meeting room is hot, stuffy, and small in the claustrophobic sense. There are wall-to-wall paintings of nightlife depictions that range from an artistic replica of a bar to photographs of city lights. The brown furnishings, coupled with the beige walls, convey a gloomy room. In the middle of the room is the large, oval table. Son is sitting at one end of the wooden table next to Joolie. Son has a dreadful look on his face; Joolie gives me a small smile when we make eye contact. Three other co-workers are already sitting around the table. The chef and his assistant sit across from Son and Joolie, looking equally disturbed.

The Bosses are sitting at the front end of the table. Their eyes are unrelenting when they focus on Tailor and me. There are two empty seats next to them, seemingly reserved for us.

I can feel the hair on my arms standing up. These people are definitely not here to give any raises.

"Have a seat." The female extends a long manicured hand. Her red nail polish dance in front of my eyes again. *Like a viper.* She reminds me of Medusa, if Medusa is hauntingly beautiful with long spiraling red hair and lacquered black eyes.

The male sitting next to Nailpolish reminds me of a vampire with his pale white skin and long, flowing hair framing his face. His facial expression remains emotionless as he watches Tailor sit down next to him. I take the seat next to Tailor.

"Now that everyone is here, we thank you for attending this meeting on such a short notice." Nailpolish's dark eyes flick from one Trax employee to the next. "We are the owners of The Trax. The sole proprietors. My name is Naili and this is my partner."

Naili only introduces herself.

Oh, this can't be good. My intuition digs in her secret stash to count how much money she's saved. I fidget in my seat as several co-workers do the same. Son is looking down at the wooden table. He already knows what this meeting is about, so he is trying to hide the emotions associated to it. Joolie is the only one who cannot contain her emotions. Disbelief colors her face as she gives me a look. I want to shrug my shoulders at her.

"We have been running things behind the scenes. The Trax is not the only venue that we own," Naili continues as though she is explaining some known fact. She looks at each of us. When Naili's eyes land on me, her gaze lingers.

Quit imagining things May. She doesn't even know you. I bite my bottom lip in a nervous manner. I break eye contact with Naili and look down at my hands.

"With that said," Naili continues. "The Trax has been active for three years now. Business has been good, but not great. We have been calculating, adjusting, maintaining, and striving to improve. But I am afraid the time has come for us to move on. We are closing in a week."

A ripple of shock and surprise travels throughout the table. Son finally looks up and makes eye contact with me. His eyes are dark and brewing with emotions. Joolie has her hand covering her mouth; a horrified expression wanes on her face. Tailor is sitting as still as a stone, carved indefinitely in some ancient substance. The chef and his assistant look as though Nailpolish just ran them over with her car. The other three co-workers are murmuring under their breaths.

"Closing in a week?" Joolie finally speaks up. She lowers the hand covering her mouth. Leave it to Joolie to speak up first. "So this means we're all getting laid off?

"We're letting you all go, yes," Naili repeats with a frown crossing her delicate facial expression. It is as though Naili is assessing whether Joolie is mentally competent.

"But everything is going great." Joolie does her best to save The Trax. "Shouldn't you give a two-week's notice? One week is hardly any time to turn around."

"No. We are an LLC." Naili narrows her eyes at Joolie in a fashion that send chills down our backs. "What that means," she adds with impatience, "is we're a limited liability company. We're a flexible enterprise, which also means we are not a public company, but rather a private entity. We are allowed to exercise sole rights, especially since there was no contract when you signed to work with us."

Joolie is giving Naili a look that says, "Who are you people and what gives you the right to fire us? You're going to hear from my lawyer!"

"You may be upset enough to garner a second opinion, an attorney perhaps. But let me give you some advice. By the time you succeed in bringing us to court, you are better off saving that time, money, and energy into finding another job. Just because our appearance at The Trax has been . . . limited . . . doesn't mean that we are fools. Behind every enigma is the force that creates it."

She knows her shit. But she's also threatening us! My conscience is shaking her head over the newspaper she is reading, scouring for another job already.

"So what will become of this place?" My voice is a whisper.

Naili turns her attention to me. There is light dancing in her eyes. It is quite alarming to have such a remarkable woman look at me like that. "The new owner will see fit it to his liking."

"It's been bought over?" This is news to Son. He speaks up for the first time. The concern is apparent in his face. "Who is buying it?"

Naili gives Son a look that signals he is crossing the line by asking. "That is a matter of private records."

"We have a right to know," Son refutes. He looks around the table at all of us. "It's like we're getting hit by a bus."

Naili nods her head, but there's no sympathy bone she is willing to toss at us. "That is why we are giving you a week's notice in advance. The new owner has taken it upon himself to release severance checks as well."

Tailor whistles under his breath.

Who will be the new owner? Why is he paying us a severance check to kick us out? My scalp prickles. The onset of a migraine is coming on.

"We will be handing out written notices tomorrow. Any further questions or comments may be conducted with us in a more personal form." Naili ends the brief meeting. She scans the room at our blank and disquiet demeanors. "You are all excused." As if we're errant children, Naili dismisses us quickly from her sight. The man by her side watches us with a lazy and almost bored expression.

Slowly, I get up from the table with Tailor. My knees feel like noodles and my head feels like a puddle. Son and the chef remain seated, undoubtedly wanting to discuss this matter in further personal detail with Naili and her quiet vampire. Joolie is the first one out of the door with us following in her wake.

"It's gangsters!" are the first word out of Joolie's mouth when we travel down the hallway. She turns to us with eyes too bright.

"Gangsters?" Tailor asks with an unconvinced tone.

"Remember that Crist member?" Joolie takes the liberty of reminding us.

I am never going to escape Choi Sangwoo, am I? *Nope!* My intuition grins passively. *There is something seriously shady about him.*

"You think Crist bought this shit hole?" Tailor asks. I have never heard him curse. Tailor's eyes are scorching from the news, mirroring Joolie's upset expression.

"He probably bought The Trax. I warned you guys about this!" Joolie hisses. "He came here twice on two separate occasions. He is probably getting revenge on us throwing him out when he was drunk!"

Not true! I took him home and took care of him! My conscience shakes her head in defense. There is something inside of me that wants to negate the idea altogether. Sangwoo doesn't seem like the type to do petty revenge. It is not his style.

"He can't possibly have enough money or power to do this. Besides, if he's a true gangster, he'll be too busy to do something like this," Tailor refutes. "Besides —"

"Shhh!" Joolie's shush comes just in time as the door to the meeting room opens again.

Son exits with an angry look on his face. "Finish closing up. Why are you guys gossiping?" Son snaps at us.

Joolie shakes her head at him. "If I didn't know better, I'd think you were in on this too." She points an accusing finger at him.

"How am I in cahoots with this when I'm losing my job like you all?" Son shoots back at Joolie. "I'm just as surprised. But, there's no point standing here and talking about it. Transfer your gossiping energy to finding another job." He shoulders past the three of us and disappears down the hallway.

"Why does he always have a stick up his ass?" Joolie snaps at Son's retreating back. "He definitely knows something!"

Tailor lets out an agitated sigh. "This was definitely not how I thought my day would end up like. Maybe we can talk more about this when we're all clear headed. I'm leaving." Tailor holds up a hand before he saunters down the hallway.

Joolie shakes her head at Tailor's goodbye. Joolie turns her fervent energy on me. "Come on May, don't tell me you don't see anything fishy about this. Our Bosses, who we've never met before, are telling us we have a week before the place closes down because it's been bought over. Everyone knows that The Trax is in no way, shape, or form a good investment. I smell underground and black market money all over this."

What are we supposed to do Joolie? Pick up sticks and boycott? I don't have the mindset or the energy to go through this with her. I simply shrug. "Things happen for a reason Joolie. Maybe it's time to move on."

"Move on?" Joolie scoffs. "Naili will hear from my lawyers." She emphasizes lawyers with a finger gesture.

With her usual dramatic exit, Joolie disappears briskly down the hall. Whether or not Joolie can truly afford a lawyer to fight this, her can-do attitude fascinates me.

Laid off. The words swim in my head. I am feeling defeated and exhausted, first Sansachun in the morning and now The Trax. My life is taking unpredictable turns at every corner. I am not sure I can take much more before I cave in. I just wish for my warm bed and some time to absorb all this. Tailor is right, we can discuss this when we're all levelheaded again. Everyone is riding on high emotions right now. We need to get off it.

I **LEAVE THE TRAX FEELING** empty and dark. The Trax resembles a ghost town now that most of my co-workers have left in a hurry and anger. The entire building is dark, except for the bar and main dance floor. Soft, neon yellow and purple lights roam the designated areas. I stop by the meeting room on my way out. Naili and her vampire are gone, leaving in their wake the void their troubling news created. It is fascinating how one person is able to change the course of others' lives.

My shoes make a soft noise when I push open the entrance door. The cool summer air greets me as soon as I am outside. As I climb the steps that lead to street level, I look for my cell phone in my tote bag. The dim street light isn't much help as I ransack my bag for my cell phone. I want to call Lina and talk to her. I want to call Eunhye and cry. I feel like a child who is in desperate need of attention, love, and care.

My phone lights up and I realize I am staring at an incoming call. I don't recognize the phone number when I answer.

"Hello." My voice is scratchy and unfamiliar.

"Hi." His tone is clear and precise, but all at once commanding.

A wave of emotion comes over me. *Shit.* I am too sensitive from all the events today. My memory runs like a rolling train and reminds me that I, Maybelline Lee, have a dinner date with the underground gang lord tonight. Well, to my credit, I was busy getting fired.

"How did you get my number?" I swallow hard. *Very cool May.*

The trademark smile is in his voice. "I have all the information I need to know about you May."

Stalker . . . and somewhat flattering. Stalker because he probably knows what I ate for breakfast this morning; flattering because someone as mystifying, striking, and contagious as Sangwoo is interested in me. I feel like a walking poster for advocating how dangerous romanticism can be sexy. I need to snap out of this.

"Are you off work?" Sangwoo asks, ultimately breaking the silent void between my rampant thoughts and us.

"Yes," I breathe into the phone.

"Good. Are you ready to go?" Sangwoo presses on.

I am partial to his voice. I sink into the slow and deep sand. For some undemanding reason, I lift my head up. My footsteps come to a full stop when I see a white, gleaming Mercedes SLS550 parked at the end of the dark tunnel that divides The Trax from the rest of the world.

Choi Sangwoo is standing near the driver's side. He is dressed down in a black dress shirt that showcases the muscles spanning over his broad chest; the sleeves are rolled up to the creases of his elbows, showcasing developed arms with healthy muscle bars that wrap and twist from disciplined workout sessions. A pair of aviator sunglasses folds into the crest of his front shirt. Sangwoo completes his look with black jeans—

casual and camouflage in the night. He is darkly handsome with his tousled hair styled away from his face. He is everything that gang leaders should not be and definitely should not look like.

What should I say to him? All thoughts dispel from my mind. I slowly hang up my phone while he mirrors my movement from only a distance away.

Choi Sangwoo, leader of the dark underground world, is picking me up in a flashy car. Oh my. This is going to take some time to digest. I am more nervous now than if I had never seen him throw up. It is funny how memories can fade when current reality is overbearing.

Sangwoo looks at me with speculation. "Hi," he says again when I approach him slowly. "I decided to pick you up from work since we never got to work out the details about tonight, last night."

How does he make complex thoughts flow so simply? *Say something May.* My intuition is gaping at him with her mouth formed into a perfect circle. He makes her task very tough. "Uh . . . you didn't have to." I feel as though the balloon above my head deflates in disappointment.

Sangwoo's brown eyes briefly survey me before he motions with his head towards the car. "It's not a problem. I want to. Come," he states with a commanding tenor.

I clutch my tote bag and look at him, rocking from the current of curiosity and hesitation. A sudden bout of awareness comes over me like never before. I know that the moment I step inside Choi Sangwoo's car, and go wherever he is going to take me, I am indefinitely never going back to my boring and mundane life. There is nothing ordinary about this man, and the world that he lives in is chaos and possibly immoral.

His brown eyes are speculative and encroaching. The gang leader comes out through his courteous offer. "I prefer to follow up with our discussion from last night in a less public place, Maybelline."

Oh damn. He said my full name. For some reason, I don't find it annoying when the syllables of my name hang in the air like that. The music rises invisibly above me as I clutch my tote bag and walk to the beast of a car. I am going to be lost in his world, falling perpetually somewhere in the current.

"Where are we going?" I do owe him a dinner.

"The Aston House at the W Seoul Walkerhill Hotel." Sangwoo already has the passenger door open for me by the time I step into the air that surrounds him.

The what at the where? The Aston House at the W Seoul Walkerhill Hotel. That doesn't sound like anything I can afford. Does the whole world bend for this man?

One look into those brown eyes of his and I know the answer.

CHAPTER SIX

T here is electricity in the air. It is rocking and rolling, permeating to fill every nook and cranny. I am well aware of the soft music playing in the background of Choi Sangwoo's remarkable vehicle. It is a classical piece that I am not aware of; the tone and cadence are foreign in both melodic diction and harmonic rise. On the screen of the car's instrument panel, I see the song's artist. *Thievery Corporation*. How appropriate.

The Mercedes SLS550 travels down the road with ease and command. Colors and the existence of life fade behind its darkly tinted windows. The leather seats still emit the distinctive new smell to it. The entire matte black interior panel appears to be untouched. In the short time that I have known him, Choi Sangwoo has two cars to his name.

Just as I am daydreaming about how many other cars he must own, Sangwoo's phone lights up and a female voice replaces the music. "Boss. The package is traveling northbound at fifty-five."

Her announcement is a shock to the peace circulating in the car.

"Good. And Ren?" Sangwoo's short reply is all business.

"He is in touch," the female reports.

"Make sure the rest of the cargo is intact. I want the data retained and generated before the night is over. Send him to me when it is ready," Sangwoo states precisely. He hangs up without waiting for a reply from her or a goodbye. "Sorry. I'm trying to tie up some loose ends for work," Sangwoo remarks briskly.

I am mesmerized and perplexed by this man. "It's ok," is all I can manage. Why do I feel so perpetually shy around him?

"Is something wrong?" Sangwoo is aware of my silence.

Nothing. Except for the fact that you bought the place I work at and now I am going to be jobless soon. My intuition stops gaping at him long enough to throw her accusations. I bite my tongue.

"I had a long day at work," I hint.

I expect his facial expression to change emotions or some colors to flourish, but it is not Choi Sangwoo's style. He keeps his face forward, and although he is driving carefully, Sangwoo weaves in and out of traffic. The other cars on the road are just merely moving roadblocks to him.

We are traveling through the city of Seoul to the more affluent part of the town, to the area where the stable roads give way to slopes and slants.

The glitz and glamour of the area are apparent. Buildings, structures, and evidence of city life recede to make way for large alpine-like trees and condensed cement. The skies darken and intensify as the Mercedes pushes the city limits.

"Have you ever been to the W Seoul Walkerhill Hotel?" Sangwoo asks, giving me the impression that he is trying to keep the conversation light.

I have only been to one hotel in my life, and it was only two stars. This W Seoul Walkerhill Hotel sounds like it is in the five-star range and ghastly expensive. More and more my stereotypes of gangsters are being debunked. Not only do gangsters look good, but they also drive expensive cars and live a very affluent lifestyle. *Why hasn't anyone corrected Hollywood and the drama world?* Once again, I am way out of my league here.

"No," I answer Sangwoo once my thoughts die down. "I don't go to hotels often."

Sangwoo glances over his shoulder at me. He keeps his left hand on the steering wheel and his right hand on the stick shift. It is a habit, I conclude. "It must be nice to have a home to go to at night." His voice is reminiscent.

"You don't have a home to go to?" The question darts out of my mouth. Another fact Sangwoo is choosing to reveal about himself.

Even in the dark evening light, Sangwoo's brown eyes smolder as they glance at me briefly. The hint of a smile approaches his lips, but is not welcomed. "I travel frequently, so hotels are my home. In my line of business, it is not wise to stay in one place too long."

I'm reminded, once again, of what his profession is. Some people have jobs like me, others have careers, and then there are the select few who have professions like Choi Sangwoo and Mayhem. *I wonder what the other gorgeous gang lord does on a typical night.* My intuition kicks in with her inappropriate thought.

"It must be exciting though." I try to lift the dense mood. "You get to travel and experience the world."

Sangwoo contains his facial expression. "It can get rather lonely."

I gasp silently. It is an unexpected comment from him. A hardcore gang leader with emotions and feelings of loneliness? Heaven forbid. Sangwoo is completely different from the portrayals of the Godfather and all the other gangster movies I have seen. He doesn't fit the cookie cutter definitions that Google described this morning.

Sangwoo's cell phone buzzes again. This time, he doesn't answer. He presses a button on the Mercedes' steering wheel and his cell phone quiets down. The Mercedes turns smoothly to the right of the road as the pathway narrows. The headlights of the car sharpen as the ground hitches to a slope. Suddenly, we are traveling to greater heights. My back presses against the smooth leather seat. The sports car curves the lengthened slope, following a marked pathway.

The view of the luxurious hotel stuns me. Pale and bright yellow, incandescent lights lead to the hotel's entrance. The grand area, where the cars come to a standstill, displays an elaborate entrance. It dawns on me that we are at the Aston House itself. The main hotel, the W Sheraton, is another mile from this private structure; at least that is what the elegant sign on pearl gates indicates.

The SLS550 comes to a slow and unnerving stop. The valet, dressed in a crimson red suit, appears out of thin air.

"Come." Sangwoo leaves the car running as he steps out.

I follow his suit. *Jeez. I am completely out of my element here! This type of wealth is intimidating.*

"Sir." The valet bows to Sangwoo. He looks petrified and makes no eye contact.

Sangwoo coolly slips him a bill and then turns to me.

The smoldering look in his eyes stuns me. It is a mixture of intimidation and something else.

"We're going to eat at the restaurant first," Sangwoo tells me. It dawns on me without conjecture; he knows the effect he has on me. "Are you hungry?" The smile in his voice is meant to ease my anxiety. If only he knows I am trembling like a leaf inside.

I nod my head. "Yes." I don't really have a choice, do I?

Sangwoo leads the way into the Aston House. He walks in front of me, keeping a conscious space between us, but his gait is relaxed.

I am about to have dinner with Choi Sangwoo, the leader of Crist. Isn't he one of society's most wanted men? Yet here he is, casually strolling through a reputable hotel.

"The Aston House is a mansion that is built on top of a very lavish hill at the W Sheraton Hotel. It is an exclusive location with a panoramic view of Seoul and the Han River. It's named after the 17th century Jacobean-style mansion in Aston, Birmingham, England. It is often converted into the ideal venue for corporate events, birthdays, and even weddings." A large, ornate painting displays the history of the elaborate mansion we are walking through. The font is professional and grand, giving off the impression that even those with limited sight can still read it.

The entire Aston House is a contrast of white and gold. Even the customer service desk, an oval structure that wraps around the entire floor, embeds in elaborate gold. There is an old man and young brunette standing at the customer service counter. When he sees us, the old man abruptly leaves his place.

"Mr. Choi." *Joo* is on the name tag of the manager's shirt. His eager eyes flick from his high-paying customer to me. A look comes across Mr. Joo's face as though he is afraid to make any assumptions that his valued client is with someone as ordinary as me.

I square my shoulders as a feeble attempt to look like I belong. I am vaguely aware that I'm still wearing my work uniform. The black pencil skirt with the white blouse makes me look as though I work here too.

Choi Sangwoo, on the other hand, seems oblivious to the comparison all the personnel at the Aston House are making. Abruptly, he surprises me. Sangwoo reaches down and casually, with his right hand, grabs for mine. The electric current rushes through me and I freeze.

Choi Sangwoo is holding my hand. What the hot fudge on a Sunday? My conscience is fanning herself.

Mr. Joo's eyes travel faster than lightening. The look on his face softens now that hands are holding and the no-contact space reduces. Mr. Joo clears his throat and immediately snaps out of his surprise. "Your reservation, sir. This way." He extends a wiry hand and motions for us to follow him.

I am well aware that Sangwoo does not let go of my hand. Sangwoo's facial expression remains unreadable as he follows Mr. Joo. We walk down a corridor of the Aston House, past the ornate and elaborate elevators, to an open threshold. The entrance to the private restaurant is a cascade of plush curtains. It's dim inside with a wave of blue and white colors. Half-walls and drapes section each seating area.

Mr. Joo leads us to the very back of the room and gestures with a prickly hand towards the reserved table.

Sangwoo lets go of my hand and motions for me to take the seat across from him. *Even the chair is fancy*, I take notice. I fist my hand together. The sensation of his palm is still against mine.

As soon as we are situated, Sangwoo orders without the menu. "The usual, Mr. Joo." Sangwoo explains briefly to me, "I always get the best Aston has to offer."

Control freak much? I think you should start running. My intuition composes herself and throws out orders. Part of me is glad that I don't have to decide, but the other part is weary of Sangwoo's hasty decision-making.

Mr. Joo does another customary bow before retreating.

Sangwoo places his hands on the table and unleashes the power of his gaze on me. "So, tell me. What's bothering you?"

Gangster and a mind reader too? I feel my heart thudding in my chest. Suddenly, I feel like a child again. *Oh, what the hell. I should just tell him the truth.*

"I got fired today," I tell him. How is Sangwoo able to get me to commit information so easily?

Sangwoo's eyes narrow. "Fired . . . from Sansachun or The Trax?"

First of all, how does he know I work at Sansachun? And secondly, if he fired me, Sangwoo should know. Instead, he is looking at me with an unreadable expression on his face.

"The Trax," I answer finally. He probably knows how much is in my bank account too. I am not sure how I want to tackle this man who is passively stalking me. These are all assumptions, however. Sangwoo could have asked around about me. I'm sure his sources are more reliable than my Google searches.

"Who fired you? Naili?" Sangwoo asks, bringing me back to the grounds of reality. For confirmation, he adds, "She has long hair like Medusa and stark nail polish."

How does he know Medusa's name? He knows exactly what she looks like too. Sangwoo really is the new owner. My intuition is jumping up and down, pointing at him with fervor.

"Yes," I confirm with a braver tone. "I have never seen her before and she came in today, laying off everyone from the assistant manager to the chef to the servers. How do you know her?"

"My world runs in circles," Sangwoo offers a simple explanation.

"Naili's a gang member too?" I ask with shock.

"No." Sangwoo shakes his head, letting out a low chuckle. "In my world, we tend to know who owns what."

I am more confused than when we first started out. I should just let this go.

Sangwoo's gaze on me is unrelenting. "I'm sorry," he says simply. "Perhaps it is a blessing in disguise."

I look at him under my eyelashes. A tinge of shock travels down my body. "Blessing in disguise?"

"It's a dangerous place to work May." Sangwoo's voice is soft and calculating. "Especially for a young girl like you."

A burst of emotions rushes through me. "I don't think it's a blessing in disguise," I refute his opinion. "For someone like me, a second income is very important."

If Sangwoo is surprised at the fact that I am standing up for myself, he doesn't show it. He hangs his head in an intrigued manner. "You think I don't understand the predicament you're in."

How can you? You drive a Mercedes that is equivalent to an average person's three-year income. You dine at restaurants that cost hundreds of dollars. You have people waiting on you, eager to fill your half-full glass.

"I don't think you do," is all I can say to the face of intimidation.

"You'd be surprised at much I know about the struggles only one income can produce," Sangwoo states. "But doesn't your safety matter more than money?" A dark look crosses Sangwoo's face as he challenges me.

He cares. He cares about me, but in what way? I cannot understand this man. Does he have a hand in my unemployment or not?

I pick up my glass of water and drink it. My throat is thirsty and scratchy. "Of course it does. Are you the one who bought The Trax?" *Very casual May.* My intuition slaps her forehead.

A smile touches Sangwoo's lips, but not his eyes. "So the truth comes out. It makes sense now why you were distant in the car."

He's only known me for a short period of time. How can he be so versed in my behavioral cues? "You did buy The Trax, didn't you?" I am eager, very eager to know the truth.

Sangwoo's eyes smolder. Perhaps he's thinking I overstepped our invisible boundaries. "I am a responsible businessman May. I usually make acquisitions based on projected capital gains, not emotions. So, the answer is no. I did not buy The Trax." He gives me a look that lets me know jumping to conclusions can be socially costly.

Don't I feel like a jerk? "I'm sorry," I mumble. "I just thought you might have since you've been around The Trax a lot lately." *Way to go with the unwarranted explanations May.* I mentally kick myself for always jumping the gun. *There's still something shady about him.* My intuition doesn't wait long to chime in with her red warning sign.

Sangwoo acknowledges me with a fleeting look. "You don't need to apologize. I can assure you. I am not the type to invest in bars and clubs. No true, reputable gang lord will be foolish enough to take part in such nonsense breeding ground. It is something our lower counterparts, the street gangs, take part of. They need the protection money."

Sangwoo is talking in his gang jargon again and his diction

mesmerizes me.

Before I can continue our conversation, two waiters approach our table. They are carrying a plethora of mouthwatering entrées. One-by-one they set the plates in a specific formation in front of us.

Choi Sangwoo is completely oblivious to the fact that I am gaping at the food. He picks up a plate with a mixture of Asia on it. The plate's full of fried rice, freshly cooked shrimp and chicken, grilled pieces of sausages, celery, and foreign spices.

"This is a western dish known as the Jambalaya. It originated in Louisiana with Spanish and French influence. Try it." Sangwoo's worldly knowledge of food doesn't surprise me. His food source is probably only limited to the world's best restaurants.

"Thank you," I mumble. I am completely in over my head and out of my element here. Even the food is more regal than I am.

Sangwoo picks up a knife to his right and selects a plate with a steak, prawns, scallops, and concisely cut vegetables. In his element, Sangwoo appears comfortable and at ease.

"You know you can always come to work for me." Sangwoo begins slicing into his steak with a knife in one hand and a fork with the other.

I nearly drop my fork at his offer. What can I possibly do in Choi Sangwoo's line of business? "Work for you?" It is an incredible accomplishment for me to remain in my seat.

Sangwoo narrows those trademark brown eyes at me. "Do you have a problem coming to work for me?"

". . . What would I be doing?" I am still trying to absorb his offer. Is this a prelude to the contract?

Sangwoo gives me a mysterious smirk. "Does that mean you accept?"

"Well-no . . . I–" The colors are increasing on my cheeks. *Come on May, get it together.*

"Do you know anything about what I do?" Sangwoo's eyebrows come together. When I don't answer, he says simply, "I figured you don't. If you do, you would have probably never taken me to your apartment when I was drunk and unconscious. And you most certainly wouldn't be sitting here right now."

There is a sad tone to Sangwoo's voice, as though he is afraid that I will run when I find out who he is. If only Sangwoo knows how curious I am. *They always say curiosity kills the cat, May.* The thought horrifies me. I do my best to shut down my intuition before she gets me into trouble.

"Who are you then?" I finally ask the question I have been dwelling over for the past two weeks. *I even Googled you and I couldn't find any information.*

Obviously, Choi Sangwoo is a gang leader, but there's something unnerving about him. What does he want with me? Choi Sangwoo is from an underground world where the shadows scamper from light, from the bleak and mainstream world that I live in. I am not expecting someone of his caliber to spill his entire heart and soul to me, but I want something I can believe in.

"I . . . ." Sangwoo's lost look is interestingly sorrowful. A tint of hesitation crosses his lips and his tone of voice softens. "I have been searching for someone like you for quite a long time now."

I gulp on the invisible air bubble traveling in my throat. Brown Eyes has been searching for someone like me? A reminder of Dead Girl billows into my mind. I do my best to pop each bubble of thought to protect my emotions.

"When I first walked into The Trax, two weeks ago, I couldn't believe it." His voice is like chocolate melting into my ears. "After all this time, I've found you."

I listen to Sangwoo with undivided attention and speechlessness. His words and emotional expressiveness suck me in. This is definitely difficult to take in. He's been searching for me, but for what and why? I am silently relishing the thought.

"What do you mean you have been looking for me?" The chills are fresh now that I am repeating his statement. I am beyond curious by his cryptic messages. "Why have you been looking for me?"

Sangwoo is at a standstill in his fluid movements. He is waiting for something, waiting for me to give something up. It is a dance we are doing. "Someone *like* you," he corrects my statement.

"Someone like me," I repeat under the tone of a whisper.

"I believe we can greatly benefit from each other," Sangwoo states instead of answering my question. It becomes apparent that he is not ready to explain the full extent to me. "Through our contract, of course."

"Contract." *Right.* I squirm in my seat, finally realizing that I am hunched forward, lapping up his every word.

"We can talk about that after dinner." Sangwoo is back to being enigmatic and disconcerting. Sangwoo bites into his steak to indicate the end of the discussion for now.

I mirror his sentiments and eat my food; I allow the hunger to take over. I continue to eat, savoring the exotic taste and flavor. Just when I think he is going to disregard me, Sangwoo's looking at me again with those intense brown eyes.

"Do you only live with your mother?" His food is forgotten momentarily as he asks me a question I am not prepared for. It is casual enough, but I am weary of the consequences that will result from confiding in this man.

I swallow the half-chewed shrimp in my mouth. Surprise taints my facial expression. "Yes." Why does he want to know so much about me?

"Do you have any other relatives besides Lina?" Sangwoo presses on. His interest is piqued and directed at my family composition.

"No. Lina is my only cousin from my dad's side," I reply.

Sangwoo stares at me, unleashing the full intensity of his gaze. He steadies his breath for a couple of seconds. "No other relatives?"

"No," I answer shortly. The soft rhythms in my heart pick up speed. "What about you?"

Sangwoo drops his gaze when the question directs back to him. "I had a brother," Sangwoo replies curtly. "That's all."

I stare at him, waiting for more, but Sangwoo adds, "I'm not going to be a very good friend to you May. I'm far too private and the questions are going to be often one-sided. I prefer it that way."

That's not very fair. *Shady!* my intuition sings. But then again, Choi Sangwoo will probably always have some type of leverage over me. The fact that he had a brother doesn't escape me. I want to ask Sangwoo what happened to his brother, but his forewarning disarms my curiosity. All I can manage to flagship my thoughts is, "You seem to know a lot about me and I don't know anything about you, except that . . . you're some sort of celebrity in the nation."

Sangwoo's brown eyes narrow. Suddenly, I feel like a schoolgirl again. "Not many people would think of me as a celebrity, May. I'm more of your 'most wanted' guy."

Flashes of the TV report cross my mind. "Most wanted?"

"You haven't noticed that I tend to disappear from one box to the next? From one building to the other, from one car to the next, never staying longer than ten minutes?" Sangwoo pitches a question I am not sure how to answer.

Now that he's bringing it up, I am weary of it. Just the mentioning of his name garners unwanted attention. Here, at this grand hotel, just one flick of his finger and Sangwoo has the management scurrying after him. This type of power is unnerving and difficult to digest. There are probably people who will trade their left arm to be sitting from across from him. He's probably wanted for a number of reasons.

"Like a recluse," I state. "Can I ask, by choice or because of circumstances?"

Sangwoo shrugs; the question doesn't bother him. "Both."

"Are all gang leaders shrouded in mystery?" Suddenly, Mayhem's strikingly handsome and enigmatic face invades my mind's eye. I am momentarily crippled by the unwelcome thought of the more rambunctious and dangerous gang leader.

"Some more than others," Sangwoo replies. Keeping his brown eyes steady, Sangwoo picks up his glass of wine. "There are some leaders that the world will never see or hear of. Then, there are those that the world will fear well beyond the legacy he chooses to leave behind."

I am getting a verbal, guided tour of this world. My scalp tingles at the amount of information. "How does one . . . become a gang leader?"

Sangwoo gives me the opportunity to contribute to this theory building. "How do you think?"

I fidget in my seat. My cheeks are on fire from his gaze. Should I give him the Google version? I decide against it for the sake of not wanting to look like a fool. "Well, you mentioned that it is just like any other business. So, I guess you would first become a gang member and then work your way up."

Sangwoo nods his head with those unwavering eyes. "Yes. That is one way." He takes another sip of his wine. Then, he proceeds to run an index finger around the side of the crystal glass when he adds, "Or, you could be born into it."

A chill ripples down the middle of my body. *Blessed-in,* my intuition hisses. Although Sangwoo said it casually, the impact of his statement creates a ripple effect the same way a rock does when it expertly skips above water. "Were you born into it?" I dare myself to ask.

There's an edge to Sangwoo voice. "I am an heir. Yes." Sangwoo gauges my reaction; his undivided attention is on every line of my face.

"Is Mayhem an heir?" I do my best to relax every surprised line on my face.

"No. In our world, royalty is scarce. Mayhem worked his way up. That is why his methods are a bit more unorthodox, brutal, and blatant." Sangwoo makes a face as though an unwelcome thought crosses his mind.

Wow. This is more complicated than I can imagine. One gang leader was born and groomed to be one while the other, the more ruthless leader, became one of his accord. It is just my luck to owe the scarier one thirty thousand dollars. I make a mental note to draw up my own contract with Lina.

"Why are you asking about him?" Sangwoo's voice is back to its cold tenor.

Shit. Why is he looking at me like that? I feel like I am in trouble. "Just exactly how over my head am I?" I ask Sangwoo with rendered control. "Be honest."

Choi Sangwoo dips his head and lets out a low chuckle. He finds humor in my question and is beyond amused. "Becoming friends with one gang leader who comes from a long line of organized crime leadership, and making enemies with another brutal gang leader doesn't mean you are in way over your head. It just means you are drowning without a life jacket or boat to save you, Maybelline Lee."

I try to contain the small gasp that threatens to leave my throat.

Sangwoo picks up his glass of wine again. He swirls the last remaining drops before finishing it in one take. "That is why I am going to help you. As long as you are associated with me, Mayhem will think twice before he does anything."

"Think twice?" I ask. There is a glimmer of hope for me.

Sangwoo breaks our eye contact briefly when he answers, "He'll think twice, but it won't stop him from doing what he wants done."

"Which is what?" I press on. Is there nothing that will stop Mayhem?

"Not many people borrow money from Mayhem. At least, not the ones who are smart enough." Sangwoo pauses as though to remind me of my cousin's poor decision making. "Yoon Jaewon is probably the second richest gang lord in all of Asia. At face value, his loans' interest rates are low and his return rates have suitable grace periods. But he will chase his loans to the world's end. I have seen countless people maimed and massacred because of his money. Your cousin chose the crème de la crème of loan sharks–of unforgiving gangs." Sangwoo's voice is steady and calm, as if the story he is telling derives from children's literacy.

"Do you lend people money?" A mental comparison chart chalks up in my mind.

Sangwoo's brown eyes flick to pin my gaze to his. "I do. But the difference is I only loan my money to groups, companies, and organizations. I refrain from loaning to small businesses or individuals. We're not all out for blood, May."

I remain silent with a mixture of trepidation and awe. I pick up my glass of water and nervously drink it. My throat feels like the desert and rough sand. I am aware that Choi Sangwoo is watching me with that same unreadable facial expression. Maybe he expects me to run for the hills. I think about Lina and the hot shit she is in with Mayhem's money. I can attempt to escape from all this drama, but I am reminded with a prickling sensation that I have my blood marked somewhere on a piece of paper. That damned Danny guy. *Your life just got a little more exciting,* my intuition taunts. She's done with dinner and wants to get out of here as quickly as possible.

"Are you afraid of me?" Suddenly, Sangwoo asks with a passive-aggressive tone. Unexpectedly, I transport back to my kitchen on that Sunday morning when he first asked me the very same question. At the time my answer was a precise, "No" but now I have mixed feelings.

I try not to spit out the water I have in my mouth. "No. Yes. A little bit." I am all words of contradiction.

"You should be," Sangwoo says, deadpan. Then, he relaxes his facial muscles and gives me a brief smile. "You really want to know who I am?

Don't answer, it's a trick question. Somehow, I find myself nodding my head. I know it is all for the wrong reasons, but I am intrigued by this man and his world.

Sangwoo places both hands on top of the table. For a second, it looks as though he is preparing to clasp his hands into a prayer. "I don't do this often, but I wish for a more private place to speak with you." His tone is hushed and inviting, mysterious and soothing.

My appetite disappears as Sangwoo's spoken words end. "This isn't private enough?"

There is no one else sitting in this vast restaurant except for us. It is as though Sangwoo had the entire restaurant on reserve. The soft trickling of classical music is spinning above our table, emitting from invisible speakers.

"I am staying in the penthouse here. There is more privacy up there." Sangwoo removes his hands from the table. His brown eyes lower and his lips appear as though they are waiting for me expectantly.

"Penthouse?" I ask, slightly dumbfounded. Of course he would be staying at the penthouse. The thought of Choi Sangwoo staying at anything less grand just doesn't go hand-in-hand.

Sangwoo nods his head. There is a burning infusion deep in his brown eyes. "You can choose to come with me," he pauses and then adds, "or not. It is your choice."

"I am getting the impression that not many girls, or people, would turn you down." I am all tongue and cheek. Although I am enamored, I haven't completely lost my mind.

"I don't invite many people, or many girls, to where I am staying." Sangwoo's eyebrows come together with slight irritation as if I have offended him by implying that he is a manwhore. His brown eyes are telling it all.

Damn. Can his eyes burn a more intensely stare? I need time to think about this. I am all nerves. "I need to use the bathroom," I tell him softly.

Sangwoo gives me another smoldering look, but holds his tongue. "I will wait for you here."

I force my legs to stand up.

Mr. Joo appears, as though he has been watching, and promptly directs me to the back of the restaurant. I incline my head to thank him and I am on my way. The bathroom hides behind another set of plush curtains. It turns out to be just as upscale. It smells like a meadow of strawberries and blossoms. There is a red sofa to the right of the interior along with gleaming sky-high mirrors.

I retrieve my cell phone from my bag and hold it up to the light. I have only one bar of signal in here. My eyebrows come together in question when I see five missed calls from Lina. I decide to check my text message inbox. Lina's text message comes in clear*: Call me when you can, please.*

Oh no. What's going on? I redial Lina's number, but the call goes straight to her voicemail box. I check her call times and they are sporadic with half an hour time scales. I can't believe I neglected my phone for so long. I quickly send Lina a text message: *I tried calling. Is everything okay?*

I wait for another minute and my phone remains silent. The hovering shape inside the mirror calls for me. I am pale as a ghost; my eyes too big for my face and cheeks too gaunt for my complexion. I turn on the water to wash my face. When I am done, I dry my hands and return to the restaurant.

Choi Sangwoo is still sitting at the table. His cell phone is next to him on the surface. He looks up when I return. His brown eyes are inquisitive, but hooded.

"I would like to discuss the contract with you," I tell him. I wonder if he knows all along that I will give in.

"Good." The anxious look in Sangwoo's eyes recedes. Apparently, he isn't able to read me completely. Slowly, he rises from his place. Sangwoo tucks his cell phone into the pocket of his dress pants with great ease. Sangwoo motions for me to follow him out of the restaurant.

WHAT AM I DOING HERE? I mentally kick myself as I follow Sangwoo's heels out of the extravagant restaurant. Lina's text message swims in my head. I am all but a sheet of sweat this point. If Mayhem is turning up the heat and threatening Lina's family, what's to say that he won't do the same to my Eunhye? The thought sends my heart racing as I imagine the shock and fear that will grip my stepmother.

What if he turns out to be some sort of serial killer or a rapist? I am putting too much trust in someone I barely know. *Why can't I triumph my curiosity and not follow him?* I am too weak for my own good. My intuition is angry at me and refuses to discuss my foolishness.

I do my best to focus on Sangwoo's back as he leads me to the lobby of the hotel. We arrive in front of the baroque elevators.

When the elevators open, Sangwoo and I step inside. The elevator is quiet and whisks us to the very top. The tension and expectations are palpable within the four walls of the elevator. I hold my breath as though I am waiting for the moment to implode. Just when I think I cannot take it any longer, the golden doors part to reveal a lavish lobby. Sangwoo steps out first; his body language tells me to keep a close distance. Two men are sitting outside of his door. They spring to their feet immediately. Ignoring them, Sangwoo extracts a card from the sleeve of his shirt. After Sangwoo swipes the card through the cardholder, it lights green and the doors open.

I suck in my breath.

"Come in." Sangwoo leads the way into the beautiful penthouse suite. The décor is white and royal blue. The furnishing is simple and concise, a sofa here and a coffee table there. In the middle of the room, before the grand windows, is a state-of-the art fireplace.

Sangwoo strides over to the open kitchen area complete with a dark granite island. He opens one of the hanging cabinets and extracts a bottle of wine. "Would you like a drink? This is very light in alcoholic content. You won't get drunk."

Well, hell. If I am going to sign another contract with a gang lord, I might as well have something. "Yes, please."

A look crosses Sangwoo's face as though he enjoys my agreement very much. He is probably taking delight in the fact that he is slowly corrupting me. *But then again, he can't corrupt you, or seduce you, if you don't want to be corrupted or seduced.* I shoot down my intuition and hold her hostage.

Sangwoo takes out two glasses of wine from the hanging rack. I am still standing awkwardly by his white leather couch when Sangwoo approaches. He holds the bottle of wine and glasses with great ease.

"Have a seat." Sangwoo hands me a wine glass.

I sit, placing my tote bag on the floor next to my feet.

Sangwoo takes the seat across from me. The skyline view of the city is a kaleidoscope of colors behind him. The beautiful view is distracting, but not enough to take my partial attention away from this man.

"Thank you for agreeing to talk." Sangwoo holds up his glass of wine as a form of a toast.

We press our glasses together. I take a sip of the wine. Surprisingly, it has a sweet and sour tone to it. I find myself grateful for the liquid courage. I drink a bit more and set my half-full glass on the table. I am feeling warm and lightheaded.

"The contract that I want to offer you will be stated first in verbal. Like with any other contract, there are three steps. The first is the offer. Next, it is an acceptance of that offer. And lastly, the consideration. Consideration is the bargained-for exchange point." Sangwoo sets his glass of wine down on top of the pristine coffee table. He sits back on the sofa, folding his legs together at the ankles. Completely in his element, Sangwoo is all business and the eagerness that he applies to his business transactions unfold.

I can feel my heart pulsating in my veins. Is this really happening? Never in my wildest daydreams would I imagine sitting here with Sangwoo when he first walked into The Trax. Now that this is reality, I am mentally kicking myself to make sure I am fully conscious.

"I can help you with thirty thousand dollars in exchange for your service and companionship," Sangwoo continues on. The lost expression on my face makes it easier for him. "In other words, work for me." He is giving me bits and pieces of the contract, gauging my reaction and responses.

"Companionship?" I do my best to keep my facial expression neutral. I know I am failing because my cheeks are heating up and my tongue is a syllable away from stuttering. "Like a love contract?" I've never been asked out by a boy before, and Bryan does not count. Frankly, I don't even know how people ask one another to date nowadays. But I do know this is definitely unorthodox. I have seen too many movies and read countless books not to see the good humor in the current situation. This is every bit of the cliché and corny notions that capture romantics' attention while being shunned by the skeptics.

More than anything, this seems like a joke—a plight sense of humor that is not only overused but also overdone. How can someone, of his world and caliber, want to carry out a contract with someone like me? Granted Sangwoo is not going to give thirty thousand dollars away freely, but this hardly seems rational.

Choi Sangwoo remains deadpan and watches me carefully. The look in his eyes tells me that I am better off not mocking his words, intentions, or meaning. "Service and companionship," he corrects me. "This is not a love contract. I don't want to date you. This is a six-month, legal binding contract where your service and companionship is exchanged for thirty thousand dollars. Of course, you are worth more than that, but that amount seems to be our situation."

At his compliment, I squirm in my seat. "And what exactly entails service and companionship?" I am trying the idea out although the pieces of the information confuse to me. He doesn't want to date me, but he wants my time and company. Potato *potato*.

"Service means I may have you carry out, participate in, and conduct some work-related things for me. One day we may be in Seoul and the next day we may be in the United States. Companionship means that you may be required to accompany me to certain functions, including parties, dinners, or a movie. Technically, you will be at my disposal on the weekends for the next six months. Far from a love contract, it is more about recruiting another member to the team who is required to wear many hats. You will be working with me directly."

Disposal? Basically work for him and be with him. I gape at Sangwoo unnaturally. This is under some impossible constituents. There is no way this man can be in his right mind. Now that I am reassessing it, Choi Sangwoo must have some insane streak in him. After all, his profession relies on dominating and overpowering other people. Sometimes, it requires being violent and taking people by force. This man has deeper and darker secrets than I can imagine.

Taking my silence for shock, Sangwoo presses his lips into a tight line. His eyes are now hooded and extremely guarded. "Nothing is legally penned yet, so you have every right to refuse. But I do wish for you to be aware that if you do refuse, I cannot protect you from Mayhem."

The blood flows twice as rough in my veins now. Suddenly Choi Sangwoo's brown eyes are no longer sensual and endearing, but intimidating and calculating. Taking someone at face value can be consequential in the end.

I clear my throat, feeling my equilibrium return after the influx of thoughts. "You can have anyone you want. Why me?" I am sure he knows individuals who are more qualified.

Sangwoo rocks his head to the side as he scans me. Casually, he leans forward to pick up his glass of wine again. "You don't know why or you don't remember?"

I shut down his question the best way I know how. "I don't know what you are talking about."

He watches me carefully, waiting for me to say something more. We are deep in a game, a game of I-know-the-truth-but-I-will-deny-until-you-give-in-first.

Sangwoo's brown eyes flare once more before he concedes to our silent stare-off. "I live my life not knowing if I am going to make it through tomorrow." He waves a long fingered hand to his surroundings to convey the notion of relative emptiness. "I have everything I need, except one thing. I need someone I can trust. You're young and inexperienced, but also intelligent and shrewd. I need someone like you on my team. I need someone like you by my side."

"Have you been looking to recruit more people?" I question further. Is he actually hiring?

"No," Sangwoo answers shortly. He offers no other explanation.

All of a sudden, I am brave and courageous. It is completely the wine's doing. "I am sure in your world, with your accessibility to wealth, materials, and incentives you can buy trust. I'm sure you have more viable options," I offer with conviction. I refuse to let Sangwoo's flattery make me eat from the palms of his hands. There is more to this gang leader and I have to look through the fog.

Sangwoo eyebrows come together. He looks offended that I am implying again. "May, I am not asking you anything beyond your service and companionship in the next six months. I want to make this clear. It is you who I want to work with, to attend functions with, and to dine with. We will not do anything physical . . . holding hands, kissing, or sex if you do not consent to it. This is not a dating contract. Let me rephrase, it is also not hiring-you-as-my-assistant contract."

Oh shit. That passive-aggressive streak of his is quite remarkable. His blatant mentioning of intimacy flusters me. In a twisted way, Sangwoo is confessing that he is attracted to me, but at the same time he is not.

"Then what is it?" I ask. Sangwoo is playing mind games with me. But why? If it barks, it's a dog. Why won't Choi Sangwoo call it like it is? Maybe he wants to avoid the semantics and make me think there are less ropes tightening the situation.

"It is an initiation contract," Sangwoo replies, disarming me.

An initiation. My thoughts travel back to what Google told me this morning about joining gangs. New members must complete an initiation ceremony, passage, or act. I remember reading the brutal beatings, self-sacrificing, and not to mention other terrifying blood-in requirements.

"You want to initiate me into your gang?" I do my best to clarify. *Girl, walk away now. You are no gangster. This is a cosmic joke.* With a bullhorn in her hand, my intuition persists in her boycott of Operation Lina.

"I want you in my gang," Sangwoo states with confidence now that the cat is out of the bag.

I hold my breath. My heart thuds behind my ribcage. A gang member? Me? This really is some sort of cosmic joke. Isn't there a place out there where gang members are bred? Google found social media depictions of potential gang members in broken down neighborhoods where the potential recruits are in dire need of protection, money, belongingness, and a way out. In the documentary world, potential members dwell in the more dangerous parts of the world like South America and Africa where political heists and war are imminent. In societies that I am living in, gang members engage in extortion, drug trafficking, and a myriad of other violent measures. If there is a requirement, I am sure I do not even meet the bare minimum. How can Choi Sangwoo see me as a facet to his gang?

Evidently, he can read the confusion.

"As much as I refuse to allow the terminology to apply to me, I am a gang leader and my money is washed through the black market machine. I will need your consent, loyalty, and dedication to Crist before or after thirty thousand slips from my fingers." Sangwoo studies my facial expression carefully. "I need to learn more about you. I need to know every detail of your past, your present, and your projected future. I need to know that my investment is worth it. You will not only be associated with me, but also what my gang stands for and represents. Six months will be your trial period."

It is all becoming clear. He said service and companionship to distract me. In the end, it all boils down to me joining Sangwoo's gang for the money. He doesn't want to use or date me. He wants to hire someone who can be under the radar to carry out underground activities without detection. The skewed picture frame is starting to align.

"What's to say you won't take advantage of me?" I challenge him. The wine's definitely giving me the courage to ask such a bold question.

"I don't take advantage of anyone unless they want to be taken advantage of." Sangwoo takes another drink of his wine. His eyebrows come up as though he is wondering why I am making hasty assumptions.

Don't back down, May. My cheeks flare of heat. I swallow hard. "I don't know anything about your world. Speaking from a business standpoint, your investment in someone like me is not a very wise one. I can't intimidate anyone. I can't hurt anyone. I certainly can't be a gang member." Even saying it aloud sounds ridiculous.

"That is why I chose you." Sangwoo sets his glass of wine back down on the coffee table. He intertwines his fingers together. "I will teach you. I will teach you what I want you to know. You will do what I ask without any questions or second thoughts."

What if it's to kill someone? I want to ask, but from the look in Sangwoo's eyes I already know his answer is I'm not qualified for that type of dark business yet. I will probably be doing easy errand runs, something that keeps me busy and he entertained.

"Will I receive a list of responsibilities?" I ask with curiosity. What would the job description as a gang member look like?

"We tend to avoid a list of responsibilities for our employees for survival reasons." There is a hint of a smirk on his lips. Sangwoo finds my naïve questions entertaining. Alternatively, he could be laughing at the fact that I call his members' employees.

"So there are no traces or evidence." The thought strikes me as terrifying. There's no record to keep even if death occurs.

Sangwoo nods his head vaguely. "Lina is perceptive . . . for someone like her."

I frown slightly. Where is he going with this?

Sangwoo continues, "In my world, we are like phantoms, ghosts, and vampires. We don't leave clues, hints, or trails. We obtain tangible, materialistic things through invisible means."

I am afraid to ask him at what emotional price does all this wealth and opulence cost?

Sangwoo notices the thoughts brewing in my mind, but he rides on my silence. "You will reserve three days a week for me. This may include mornings, afternoons, and nights. I will let you know in advance, but for now we can designate the days of the week as Thursdays, Fridays, and Saturdays. This will give us enough time to work and tend to our individual needs before coming together."

"And what would a typical day be like?" I am beyond curious now.

"Whatever I have on schedule and whatever I am in the mood for, whatever I please." The gang leader complex comes into full light.

"Ah." The word falls off my tongue as though it is too hot to handle. I look down at my fingers. My head is swimming with too many thoughts. I think back to Lina's text message. Like an ominous thrill, Mayhem's striking face invades my consciousness again. *Mayhem probably has more binding contracts, if you want to look at the flip side.* My conscience finally speaks up, but runs back into the shadows at the glare of my intuition.

Sangwoo reaches for the drawer to the right of him. It's a large, white dome; a baby blue antique lamp perches on top of it. The dim light underneath the lamp's cover touches Sangwoo's profile when he extracts a cell phone from the first drawer. It is a brand new pristine iPhone. The number five elegantly sketches on its side.

Casually, without any emphasis, Sangwoo slides the phone on the glass coffee table. "This will make it easier for us to keep in touch."

I stare at the phone thinking about my old slide phone inside my tote bag. *Wow. I would have to work for a solid year before I can afford this type of phone.* I look up at Sangwoo with the best of my abilities not to gape at him.

"I will take care of everything for you during the six months. If you need money, other than the thirty thousand I mean, I can assist you with your rent and bills. I also noticed that you don't have a car, but I can provide you one. Should you need any medical, dental, or vision services I can set you up with the nation's best. When our contract is up, you will get to keep everything that I have given you during our contract. We can re-negotiate. You have my word." In every sense of the literal meaning, Choi Sangwoo is speaking like he is a God. A God who can move mountains, control time, and manifest materialistic objects. There is no sense of mortality in his words and offer. This kind of world only exists for immortals. Who did he have to sell his soul to?

I swallow hard. My heart is in my ears. I don't miss the fact that Sangwoo has omitted the mentioning of me walking away freely after six months. He only mentioned re-negotiation. My thoughts wrestle with one another if I should mention it now, even before I agree to sign any contract.

"I can take care of you May. Everything you want, anything you need. I can have the contract drawn up by tomorrow. After you sign it, I will provide you with a briefcase for Mayhem and I will accompany you personally to hand it to him," Sangwoo continues and freezes my thoughts.

Oh my. My thoughts swirl on a different axis now. I am reminded of the anxiety on Lina's face and her recent text message. Most of all, I am reminded of Mayhem's lethal threats. If Danny can carve out Spyder's cheek in such a quick move, what would he do to me? If I agree to this impossible contract with Choi Sangwoo, I just might be able to save everything.

"I would say to take all the time you need, but seeing that Mayhem has handed you a personal timer I hope you are aware of the time crunch." Sangwoo is taking advantage of my silence to push the envelope further. His eyes are guarded. I am making the gang lord hesitant because of my shock.

"I need time to think," I tell him honestly. There is a slight tremble to my voice now that I am speaking again. I am well aware I have less than a week at this point to come up with thirty thousand dollars for Mayhem. I would be a fool not to consider Sangwoo's offer, but the decision I make not only impacts my life for the next six months but for the rest of my life. I have a hard time believing that signing my life away to a gang leader will end peacefully if Sangwoo doesn't wish it to.

Sangwoo's brown eyes are careful to shield his true thoughts. His facial expression remains passive, but his body language is tense. It dawns on me that Sangwoo hopes I agree quickly so we can start the process. Sangwoo withdraws as though he doesn't know what to do with my indecisiveness.

"I can't accept the phone from you."

"Why not?"

"Maybe we should wait until I decide to sign the contract."

"If that is what you wish."

My tongue's at the very tip of my mouth. Sangwoo wants to give me things. I'm not used to these notions, especially from someone like him. His pursuits know no bounds, and his methods are unreasonable. I'm not the first person he showered materialistic things with. Does he buy people so easily?

A knock at the front door breaks the slight tension between us. The rhythmic pounding sends waves through the vast penthouse suite. For a moment, I was lost in the sea that is Choi Sangwoo.

Sangwoo does not break eye contact with me when he states, "Come in, Ren."

The door to the penthouse suite swings open.

The first thing that stands out about Ren is the fact that he looks like the modern day Grim Reaper with his black bomber jacket, black dress shirt, and black leather pants. What makes Ren go against the grain is the fact that the entire left side of his face has dark ink running in lines, resembling intricate embroideries, displaying a distinct tattoo.

Ren's dark eyes bounce from his Boss to me. When he makes eye contact with me, Ren's steps slow and he inclines his head in acknowledgement. He looks at me with a mixture of surprise, recognition, and almost shock folding in layers. I mirror Ren's movement and realize he is Menu Helper. I can hardly believe I didn't notice Ren's facial tattoo the first time I met him. *Well, you were too busy ogling at Choi Sangwoo that Saturday night*. My intuition yawns lazily.

"The reports?" Sangwoo rises from the sofa, slightly towering over Ren. A protective and almost feral response expresses in Sangwoo's stance, as though he's uncomfortable with the fact that Ren's staring at me without blinking in a frozen, almost intrusive state.

"Ren," Sangwoo's call is stern and forceful. A dark look crosses his face and it is reminiscent of an owner reminding a trained wild animal of its classical conditioning.

Ren finally turns to his Boss. The color drains from his face, a clear sign of apology. Ren becomes all thumbs and fingers as he struggles to extract a black manila folder from the right side of his bomber jacket. He bows before handing it over to Sangwoo. "Data is compiled and generated. Everything is set for the end of the week."

Sangwoo opens the mouth of the folder and thumbs through the documents inside. "Anything new?"

Ren shakes his head. "Silent and passive."

A look passes between them based upon their cryptic exchange. Sangwoo cuts it short and states, "I will be leaving in five minutes. Get the 320i ready."

Ren nods his head. "Yes Boss." He steps back from Sangwoo and turns to me again. This time Ren's better at hiding his fascination with me. He inclines his head once more before retreating from the room.

I look back at Sangwoo to see his intense gaze. His lips press firmly together. He is scrutinizing Ren's fervent attention. It really wasn't just my skewed imagination.

"It's getting late. I will take you home." Contrary to his hard facial expression, Sangwoo's brown eyes soften when he offers. He places the black manila folder on the coffee table and straightens up.

Sangwoo releases the urgency of my agreement to his initiation contract. He does not mention or attempt to coerce me into thinking about it any further.

"I can get a taxi," I offer. I don't want to take up his time anymore. I feel as though I have intruded on his world enough.

A look comes across Sangwoo's face as though I have offended him. "I'm not going to let you take a taxi home, May."

I want to tell him I have been walking, taking taxis, riding buses, and sometimes biking home my entire life. Why does it all have to change now that he is in my life? I look down at the chain hanging from Sangwoo's neck.

A deep wave of familiarity rolls over me again.

I feel it in my bones that I have met Choi Sangwoo before. I have seen those eyes and heard that voice before. There was a reason why he disappeared from my life. Now, I am afraid of the reason why he is back.

Memories are very hard to find, especially if they don't wish to be found.

I look back up and catch the smoldering, intense, and slightly dangerous look in those brown eyes.

"Let's head out," Sangwoo says in a quiet tone.

I find my feet following his orders, even though my heart shakes.

CHAPTER SEVEN

T he 320i turns out to be a 2013 BMW coupe in the color of a dreamy midnight blue. The entire interior is a contrast of black, white, and blue lights outlining the daunting texture of the car. The entire coupe is blackout; the darkness encases its occupants in a manner that is borderline suffocating. Even the leather seats reflect the madness of what an obscene amount of money can buy.

Aside from wondering what kind of superhuman power Choi Sangwoo has, I marvel at the fact this is car number three since his appearance in my life.

He insists on taking me home. I want to argue, but when Sangwoo unleashes his street gaze on me, I relent. The only argument I can come up with–regarding the power Sangwoo has over me–is it's all imaginary. I am giving into him because I am curious, but the reserved apprehension I have is real.

During the car ride to my apartment, Sangwoo keeps the conversation light. He wants to know how I ended up working two jobs, what I want to do with a psychology degree, and why I choose to be a loner. Sangwoo appears to be especially interested in my answers as if he's filling in the gaps that a background report missed. We end up discussing superficial things among trivial matters, never mentioning the initiation contract he previously proposed. I find myself thankful for Sangwoo's natural ability to cause a mental diversion. I don't think my head can handle the amount of information I am now responsible for.

He's giving you time and space to let it sink in; it's all part of his master plan! My intuition takes off her glasses and boxing gloves.

"Do you always drive different cars in a day?"

We are walking through East Point to my apartment. The cool summer breeze distracts the heat boiling inside me. Just like last night, Sangwoo is walking a step behind me, always letting me lead the way around my territory. He has a contemplative look on his face.

"Yes," Sangwoo answers shortly. "Mainly for safety reasons."

"Safety reasons," I echo with contemplation.

"From those who are hunting me." Sangwoo's facial expression is set, almost expectant that I should already be aware of this aspect.

All I can muster up is a weak, "Oh." That explains a lot. Or a little. I frown at my inability to garner a clear response from him. It's always so vague and cryptic. I suppose all gang leaders suffer from this silence-is-golden syndrome.

As we near my apartment door, thoughts of Sangwoo hugging me last night creep into my mind. I do my best to strike down the alarming memory. I gather the courage and glance at Sangwoo, wondering with slight indifference if he's thinking the same.

Apparently, his thoughts attend to facts that are more important. Sangwoo is not looking at me at all. Instead, his gaze is straight ahead. His eyebrows furrow together. Abruptly, Sangwoo extends a hand and stops me in my tracks. I follow his fixated gaze toward my apartment door and see what has Sangwoo wary.

A lone figure leans against the side of my apartment door.

I blink deliberately to focus in the darkness.

"Don't move." Sangwoo's voice is barely above a whisper. His right hand moves towards the left side of his blazer. Long, extended fingers disappear into his blazer.

I realize with a start that Sangwoo carries a weapon. *Of course he carries a weapon. He's a gang leader. What do you expect?* My intuition rolls her eyes; she's not impressed.

"Wait." I make a feeble attempt to stop Sangwoo from jumping the gun, literally. Placing my hand softly on his arm, I feel Sangwoo stiffen.

In the middle of my panicked state—believing that the stranger standing in front of my apartment door is an assassin sent by Mayhem to kill me, and disbelief that Choi Sangwoo has a weapon to kill the supposed assassin—it takes me a few more seconds to recognize the familiar outline of the figure.

She is petite and my height; a thick black hood covers her hair and face. The heavy sweatshirt she's wearing engulfs her black leggings.

"Lina?" Her name catches wind in my throat.

"May?" My cousin responds. She stands up from her folded position by the door.

A deep sigh of relief escapes me.

Sangwoo's hand immediately retracts from his blazer. It's eerie how quickly he is able to resume his casual stance. However, I don't miss the fact that his eyes are guarded as ever. Sangwoo stands back at an arm's length when I move towards Lina.

Why is she here in the middle of the night dressed like the Death Angel?

"What's wrong?" I grab my cousin's hands and almost yell out in surprise from how cold they are. Lina was fine this morning when I left her. Now, one look into her eyes and I know that something is terribly wrong. The tears on Lina's cheeks make the matter even worse. Memories of her missed calls and cryptic text message run quickly through me.

Now that she is in front of me, Lina doesn't answer my question right away. She is staring at the statuesque figure of Choi Sangwoo. "Hi," she mumbles with embarrassment in her voice. Lina quickly wipes her cheeks.

"Hello," Sangwoo replies with such softness it is hard to believe that only seconds ago he was about to withdraw a weapon on her. *What did he have? A gun? A knife? What kind of concealed weapon does a gang leader carry with him anyway?*

"Are you okay?" I am in Lina's face again.

Her brooding eyes switch back to make eye contact. She shakes her head slightly, wary and conscious of Sangwoo watching our exchange.

Before I fight through the contemplation of how to say goodbye, with his smooth mannerism, Sangwoo saves me with his usual proficiency.

"I'm glad you were able to join me for dinner tonight." The sparkle returns to those brown eyes. "I enjoyed talking to you very much. And I really do hope you consider everything that we discussed. I will be waiting for your answer."

"Thank you for inviting me," is as formal as I can answer. "I'll call you. That is your number, right? From when you called me at The Trax?"

"Yes. I will be waiting," Sangwoo states. He gives Lina a small smile. "Good night."

"Good night." For a few seconds, Lina forgets every inch of her problems.

Sangwoo stalls slightly as he looks at me again. I give him a small smile and realize that Sangwoo is thinking of the last time he left me on my doorstep. The heat rises to my face again and it takes everything in my power not to react.

"Good night May." My name hangs in the air as Sangwoo turns and strides down the apartment complex. He disappears into the night.

"He's too good to be true," Lina mumbles. "What is he talking about hoping that you consider everything and let him know your answer?"

"Nothing really." Immediately my defenses go up. I do not want to discuss the possibility of the contract with Lina yet.

I fish for the keys inside my trusty tote bag. Acting busy is always a monumental distraction.

"It doesn't sound like nothing." Assumptions run rampant in Lina's tone of voice, but there is distraction and emotional turmoil in her pitch.

"Come in." I reach for my cousin's arm and usher her inside the dark apartment. The only source of light comes from the lonely fish tank in the corner.

Eunhye is still at the hospital carrying out her graveyard shift. I close the apartment door behind Lina and make sure to lock all three notches. Next, I unravel my tote bag and set it near the door. In one convenient swipe, I turn on the light switch by the coat rack. The warm lights flood the dark apartment.

Meanwhile, Lina makes her way to the couch and collapses on it. Her facial expression is somber and she doesn't pursue the matter of Sangwoo and me anymore. Silent tears roll down Lina's already tear-stained cheeks. My cousin places her face into her hands.

"Gee, Lina. What's wrong?" It's been a while since I'd seen my cousin in such an emotional uproar.

I fold down next to Lina and study her strained facial expression.

"Spyder and I got into a fight. He left me and went back home." Lina sniffles and wipes her nose with the back of her hand. The orange and yellow light in the living room outlines every line on her face, showering my cousin with an older appearance.

I grab a tissue from the Kleenex box and hand it to Lina. Another fight. Stress can cause a couple to argue, fight, and even break up sometimes. This is not the first time Lina and Spyder have argued to the point of walking away from each other.

"Is it about the money and Mayhem?" I guess with a here-we-go-again attitude. Suddenly, I am reminded of the reasons why I don't like Spyder. He is all wrong for my cousin, but her bad boy complex just keeps increasing over time.

Lina shakes her head, stunning me with surprise. "You're going to hate me," she whispers.

All traces of wit leave me. "What is it Lina?"

She blinks at me and another set of tears splatter on her cheeks. Lina begins to bite her nails—an alarming habit that only occurs when she's in distress.

"Lina," I say again. My eyes narrow and I am suddenly warm all over. "What's going on?" First Lina borrows money from loan sharks—and a dangerous and perhaps murderous gang lord—and now she is going to drop another piece of information that I am not sure I can handle.

"I hate him," Lina whispers again with large watery eyes. She is biting her index finger to the point where I can see blood seeping from the skin.

I grab Lina's finger. "What's going on?"

Lina swallows hard and the confession slips from her lips, "He hit me."

Oh hell no! my conscience barks. "That son-of-a-bitch." Immediately I know it's not the reaction Lina expects out of me. She starts her hopeless silent bawling again, and I reel with anger. In my heart, I knew this day would come. Spyder, by nature, is only violent with people he's familiar with. He would never pull the same stunt on someone his own size.

Lina sniffles, shaking her head fervently. "I fought back, but he was too strong," Lina grumbles. She narrows her eye at the unpleasant memory.

My lips press into a hard, fine line. How can one person cause the other such pain? "That bastard. I'll take care of him." The hostility I have for Spyder unleashes.

"No." Lina shakes her head. "I don't ever want to see him again. First, he drives me into debt with Mayhem and now he abandons me when I need him the most. I don't want to see him ever again. I'm done with him May. I'm completely done with him!"

"Oh Lina–" I begin. "He hit you!"

"I hit him too."

"Lina, you know what I mean!"

"This is all my fault." The tears continue to free fall from Lina's face. "Please don't tell anyone about this yet. Especially my parents. Not yet. My mom will just tell me she was right all along. I'm wrong. I'm wrong May. I messed up. I messed everything up. Everyone was right from the beginning about Spyder, but I refused to listen. Now, I have to pay the price for it."

I wrap my arms around Lina as the sobs spiral out of control. "Shh. It'll be ok."

"I messed up May. I messed it all up." Lina clings onto me. She buries her head into my shoulder and cries soaring tears.

"It's ok, Lina."

"I should have listened to you. I thought I could change him. I'm so wrong. I hate him so much May!"

I don't know what to say to my cousin. It's been a couple of years since I became emotionally stunted. Part of me wants to console Lina by letting her cry it all out, but the other part wishes for her strength and proclivity in letting go of Spyder. It is bad enough that Lina is having money problems, but to engage in a physical altercation with Spyder is the final nail in the coffin. I can only imagine the amount of hurt and pain Lina has for him. The weight of Lina's situation crashes around the two of us.

"I don't know what to do May. I just don't." Lina has my neck in a tight hold as she continues to weep.

Find Spyder and kill him. I wrap both arms around my crushed cousin and curl closer to her. My thoughts freeze in hard fragments. I don't know how long I sit with Lina and listen to her muffled sobs.

Thirty minutes. One hour. Two hours.

Aside from Eunhye, Lina is the one person in my life who has cared for me unconditionally. Together, Eunhye and Lina have been my pillars of strength. But for the first time since we were young, Lina is showing her vulnerable side. I have never seen this part of her—the damaged, broken, and pained side. She's always been the strong one. Now, the tables are turning and I find this role to be quite challenging.

Lina's emotions sweep me off the ground too.

"I believed in fairy tales. I fell so hard and fast for him and his promises. I didn't know that promises can become lies and that his 'I love you' really stood for however long he wanted to love me," Lina continues with anguish. "When we first met, he was such the gentleman. Now, he can't even show me an ounce of mercy."

I listen as Lina relives the memories. Through her tears and wails, Lina tells me of how she met Spyder, what he did to make her fall in love with him, where they made plans to be together forever, and why it is all coming apart only a year later.

Now, it is just her in constant pain.

Sometimes, just listening is the best way to comfort someone. I learned this a long time ago. I keep my arms around Lina and let my cousin grapple with the darkness that is taking over her. She is consistent and then incoherent. I suggest we go out for drinks, and then we can burn everything that is Spyder-related. Lina entertains the idea, but decides against it. She's too exhausted. So we spend the rest of the night in.

When the warm, late night weather gives into a chilly morning air, Lina finally falls asleep.

In exhaustion, I fall asleep too. My thoughts tangle with concern. I sleep dreaming about leaving The Trax, giving Choi Sangwoo an answer to his contract proposal, and helping Lina with her situation. Slowly, my molehill of problems is turning into mountains.

BY **THE TIME I WAKE** up, it is already early afternoon and I am restless with a slight headache. My body aches from sleeping on the couch with little leg space. I leave Lina resting on the couch for my tote bag by the door. As quietly as I can, I head for my bedroom to call Eunhye. I have errands to run before work at The Trax, but I need to take care of an issue first.

Eunhye is still not home. I call my mother and she answers with haste. "Hi honey. Is everything okay?"

"Hi mom. Everything's fine. Just calling to see how you're doing. Are you doing double shifts at the hospital?" I wander to my closet for a pair of jeans and a gray sweatshirt.

"Yes. We are backed up here. A lot of traumatic injuries related to summer sports activities." The fatigue is easy to decipher in her voice. I can imagine my mother tapping her left hand against a solid surface on the other side of the phone line.

"Oh. I take it you slept at the hospital?"

"I did. Six hours of sleep. I'll be home later on tonight though. Maybe we can have dinner before you go to work? I've been meaning to invite aunt Yuna, uncle Dom, and Lina out for the last week."

"That sounds good mom."

"Great. I'll see you later honey. I love you."

"I love you too mom."

I hang up the phone wondering if Lina will be up for dinner tonight with the family. She probably wants nothing to do with the adults as of the moment. I will have to deal with that issue later. I have matters that are more pressing at the moment.

I scroll back to the home screen on my phone and scan for my contacts book. Bryan, filed under *Spyder's Brother*, is located at the bottom of my lackluster contact list.

I mentally prepare myself before I press the call button.

"Baby." He picks up on the second ring. Bryan's voice is smooth and desperate as usual.

"Hi Bryan," I stress his name. "Question. Where would I find your brother on a Monday afternoon?"

"May, baby, if you want to talk to me you don't have to use my brother as an excuse. I'll be back in Seoul in an hour. We can go for ice cream and a movie?" Bryan is deadpan even in his tone of voice.

"Bryan, I'm not calling you for a date. You know better than that. I need to talk to your brother. It's important. I need to know where he is." I hold my ground. *Come on, I can overpower an eighteen-year-old.*

Bryan hesitates with that quick tongue of his. Perhaps hearing the dire tone of my voice changes the impending wisecrack he has lined up.

"He's probably at the pool place he always goes to," Bryan divulges with nonchalance. "Why do you need to talk to him for? Isn't Lina with him?"

"Thanks Bryan," is all I say. I have to cut him off before he withdraws further detail.

"Alright. Well, if you're up for a date afterwards, call me back," is his goodbye. "It's nice to hear your voice May. I miss—"

"Bye Bryan." I hang up the phone quickly before he can harass me.

With the location of Spyder's whereabouts, I quickly change into the jeans and sweatshirt. On my way out of my bedroom, I grab a small blanket for Lina; she is still in a deep sleep. My cousin looks helpless, like a small child who is resting after a run-in with her bully. *Don't worry Lina. I'll set that no-good-ex-boyfriend of yours straight!*

The morning sunlight greets me when I step out of the apartment. The summer chill surprises me, increasing my appreciation for the gray sweatshirt. My ensemble gives me extra protection at the place I am heading to, but the weather is also in favor of it.

I head down the apartment complex to the center square of the neighborhood. The perks of living near downtown Seoul is any destination is always a five-minute walk. A slew of people are out-and-about; some are going to work while others are hurrying to their next forsaken destinations. I am invisible, ducking in and out of the crowd with diligence.

The billiards place Bryan refers to is not the one that is often populated by older gentlemen who prefer another pastime beside chess. The billiards place that Spyder, along with other social degenerates, frequents is at the edge of downtown Seoul tucked in a crowded alley. Miscellaneous stores, along with unmarked businesses, tower together in a horde.

8-Ball Pool is notorious for its underground affiliations and unwarranted social schemes. It is open twenty-four-seven and operates in absolute darkness. It is a place where vampires, ghosts, and phantoms dwell in. Mainly social degenerates, rebels, and troublemakers keep this particular place alive.

I have only been to 8-Ball once and planned to never go back. Today, however, I am breaking one of my many rules for the infamous Spyder.

When I enter 8-Ball, clouds of smoke hanging in the air with varying degrees greet me. Here, the implied dress code is all black. Everyone blends into the shadows and melts with the walls. There exists a dark undertone to the entire place. It is a one-story building; there's a lonely bar to the far right of the billiards place. A number of pool tables scatter throughout the entire vicinity.

"Can I help you?" Fake Blonde at the front cashier is in my face. Her platinum hair spirals from her face. Her dark eye makeup makes her cheekbones and lips protrude. Fake Blonde is two inches taller than I am with a no-nonsense attitude.

"I'm looking for someone." I scan the room and it takes me all but five seconds to see Spyder's wiry body against the back of the room. Obviously, he's not in enough pain if he can play pool.

"Fifteen dollar cover." Fake Blonde holds out her hand. The bubble gum she is chewing cycles in her mouth.

"Fifteen dollars?" I can barely contain the horror in my voice. Who are they trying to rip-off? *Do I have rich tattooed on my forehead?* My intuition sighs, shaking her head fervently.

Before I can refuse, I look behind Fake Blonde to see a beefy security guard approaching. The dark suit he's wearing gives off the impression of gangster. I wonder briefly if he belongs to a lower gang, as Choi Sangwoo would refer to them. Oh no, even my mindset of thinking about other people is rapidly changing.

"Is there a problem here?" he demands. The security guard is fabulously bald and heavyset. *Baldy*, my conscience names him.

"Nothing," I grumble. I reach into my bag and pull out three five-dollar bills. I slap them into Fake Blonde's hand and she steps back to let me through.

Baldy eyes me as I cross the threshold.

Shit. I have to make this quick. I curse Spyder to hell.

I walk through the dark cloud of smoke and bodies that are moving around me. They remind me of shadows in nightmares, lurking and waiting for the right moment to strike.

"Spyder," I call out his name when I approach his table.

Spyder's holding a pool stick and doesn't notice me. The Band-Aid on the left side of his face is still there. Spyder is currently playing with four other men, one looking like the miniature replica of the other. Don't these people work?

"Spyder," I call again.

He finally turns at my voice and surprise coats his eyes. "May, what are you doing here?"

"We need to talk," I tell him sternly.

"Shit, May. We have nothing to talk about. Go home." Spyder brushes me off quickly, doing his best to remove me from the situation as soon as possible. This is the Spyder I know underneath the fake one.

I am boiling with anger at his blatant disregard. "You think you can just hit my cousin and leave her?"

"Shit May. You're going to put me on blast like this? Get the hell out of here. Whatever is going on with Lina and me is our problem," Spyder snaps at me.

All four of his friends freeze at their posts around the pool table. Spyder glances at them and deciphers the curiosity bouncing off each one. Evidently, Spyder hasn't updated them on what is going on with his relationship.

"Well, you made it my problem when you abandoned her you bastard. It's bad enough that you're walking away when she needs you the most, but you're also forgetting you owe Mayhem a shitload of money, so no you don't get to get off so easily with me!" I retort with contention.

"Shit Spyder. You owe Mayhem money?" One of his friends looks like he swallowed something foul.

Suddenly, the entire billiards area is quiet. I glance around and can see the fear tripling from one person to the next at the mention of the gang lord's name. Is he really such an infamous enigma?

"Fuck." Spyder drops his pool stick and grabs my right arm.

"Let go of me!" I hiss. I struggle in his grip. For a tall, wiry guy he sure is strong.

"Let's talk outside!" Spyder pulls me to the nearest exit. I am now aware of 8-Ball's second exit. Only someone who haunts this place frequently would know of its existence.

"Let go of me!" I am normally not a violent person, but I manage to jerk my arm from Spyder's hold with brisk force.

Spyder lets me go and slams the back door of 8-Ball open. We spill out into the back alley bustling with people taking the shortcut to the main street. Some of them pause to watch the commotion we are causing.

Spyder corners me near the door and leans in close. He lowers his voice in a menacing manner. I had forgotten the cruel features on Spyder's face; the way his lips turn into a malicious sneer and the malevolent glare in his eyes send my stomach hurling.

"Are you stupid?" Spyder growls at me. "Why the hell are you going around screaming that I owe Mayhem money? Don't you know anything? You do not speak of Mayhem's name! His name is a death wish, a death threat, and a death sentence."

"You coward," I rebuke him the best way I know how. "You're only afraid of him because you're powerless at repaying him back. You have to resort to your girlfriend and me to pay him back. What kind of a man are you anyway? I should have let that Danny beat the shit out of you! You deserve it."

"Don't talk to me like that May. Watch what you're saying to me." Spyder's attempt at threatening me doesn't sit well.

"I knew you were no good from the beginning. We all saw through you. Now you want to abandon my cousin? If you ever touch my cousin again, I will kill you. Then, I'll let you figure out how to pay Mayhem back thirty thousand dollars!" I threaten him.

"Oh really?" Spyder narrows his eyes at me. "And you think I'm the only one they will come after? Lina had part in that money too. So it won't just be me that they're coming after, but Lina *and* you. Did you forget you're associated with Crist?"

And the true demon inside Spyder rears its ugly head.

"Wow, Spyder." I take a step back from him. The shock radiates from me.

A couple strolls past us, glancing at Spyder and then at me. The girl tugs on her boyfriend's shirt. He shakes his head and they continue walking. They must think we are arguing over mundane problems.

"So you're going to be like this. You're really going to do this to Lina. After an entire year with her, you're going to do this to her–the one person who put up with your bullshit and even managed to love you?" The revelation is clear in my eyes. "You're even worse than what I thought. I told my cousin that you were bad news when I first met you, but I supported her when she told me there's good in you."

Spyder glares at me. "Stay out of this May. Just get the money to Mayhem like you promised."

"So you can run away from Lina and the debt as free as a bird?" I ask him in disbelief. "I'm not asking you to be reasonable. I know I can't. But how is this fair for me to take the brunt of your mistakes? You better make things right with Lina or I won't pay Mayhem back, and let him do away with you whatever he wants to. Lina and I will be protected by Crist."

"You will pay Mayhem." Without warning, Spyder's hands grip my right arm. He thrusts me back against the wall of the building. "And you will stay out of what is going on between Lina and me. You don't even know half of the story. Your cousin is not completely innocent in all this."

"Let go of me!" I hiss. I attempt to escape from his hold, but Spyder has me in a death grip. "Stop it!"

"You listen to me!" Spyder snarls in my ear.

"She said let her go."

A cool, mild voice interrupts our heated confrontation.

Spyder relaxes his grip on my arm from fear of social judgment. When he sees who it is, Spyder releases me. Fear and anxiety replace the violent look on his face.

I am still reeling from the shock and trepidation. My eyes slowly travel to my savior, and I feel the revelation trickle from the top of my head down to my toes.

It appears as though he is in the middle of exiting the adjacent, unmarked building. The dark aviator sunglasses he is wearing covers more than half of his face, but that distinctive jaw line is hard to miss. His black, tousled hair is styled back from his face, revealing the stunning model-like facial structure. He's incredible looking in the morning sunlight, despite the fact that his rugged biker ensemble–complete with black pants, black T-shirt, and white bomber jacket–negates the purpose of the summer season.

Mayhem. My intuition is clapping feverishly at his dramatic entrance.

I feel my heart stop and the great precipice of anger I am on with Spyder crumbles beneath my feet. What are the odds of us running into him here? Has he been watching us? How can I forget? I am probably walking on gangster's paradise right now.

"Mayhem," Spyder breathes in shock. "What-what are you doing here?" Surprise colors the bastard's face; this is the last person he wants to see right now. Rational thoughts escape Spyder.

Even behind those dark midnight sunglasses, it is apparent that Mayhem's narrowing his distinctive eyes at Spyder. Mayhem doesn't entertain Spyder's question with an answer. I see his face lift back up towards me. The gesture lets me know Mayhem is scanning me now. A thrill shoots through me. *Deadly attraction.* My intuition holds her breath.

"Boss."

From the adjacent building, three Mayhem members emerge. Apparently, they had some business to attend to in there. When Mayhem's members see their gang lord looking at Spyder and me, they step forward in a protective manner.

"Please escort Junjin back inside the billiards. Check his pockets for extra cash that can be considered payable towards the interest of his loan," Mayhem's command comes out smooth and controlled, almost bored and surmised.

Mayhem's men step forward at his orders. Spyder throws his hands out in protest. "No. Please. I don't have any extra money. I'm playing pool with my friends so I can rack up some money to pay you back. Please Mayhem! We will pay your loan back soon!"

Like the true coward that he is, Spyder begins to beg. He folds in front of the gang lord. Mayhem stands in complete silence as three of his men escort Spyder back inside 8-Ball. Spyder is kicking and begging, but does not fight the gang members. They drag him back inside the building.

The back door slams shut behind them, leaving Mayhem and me in the deserted alley.

"You seem to have a lot of family problems," Mayhem states coolly. He towers over me, displaying worldly characteristics of darkness, danger, and magnetism. "What are you doing here, arguing with that arthropod in public?"

Mayhem's cunning reference to Spyder doesn't escape me. The dark humor simmers in his voice. Now that I have obtained more information about Mayhem, and gangs in general, I am little more apprehensive about talking to him. But I will not back down to this bully.

"You're the reason why I'm having family problems," I tell him with great courage. With Spyder's help, I am beyond the point of censorship.

"Is that so?" Mayhem asks calmly. Too calmly. "You're saying that I stuffed thirty thousand dollars down your cousin and her useless boyfriend's mouth?"

"Pretty much," I reply stubbornly. His lips press together in that signature style of his. It is quite impressive what an overwhelming and unforgettable presence he is. Suddenly, I remember the fear and menace people feel just hearing his name.

"I was under the impression that Choi Sangwoo trains his associates and members with better mannerisms." Mayhem saunters towards me slowly.

Oh shit. He's so freaking tall. I am not as tough as I think now that he is standing in front of me. I can smell his distinctive cologne; an exotic mixture evokes the notions of danger, dark magic, and temptation. *Oh my, what am I doing?*

"Are you working hard at getting me my money?" Mayhem leans in close.

The gang lord's nose is almost touching mine. I can see my reflection in his dark glasses. My heart is in my ears and I am straining to hear him speak. Slowly, Mayhem takes off his glasses and those dark eyes that haunt me since our first meeting are staring at me now. Mayhem unleashes the full power of his gaze, and I feel like heavy rocks moving against the current of water. The milky look in his eyes, his light complexion, and chiseled features are unnerving.

I look at Mayhem, attempting to tell him telepathically that I do.

"Do you?" Mayhem asks again.

"I will," I force the words out of my mouth. "The end of this week."

"Saturday night, at approximately seven o'clock, you will have the money for me. You will wait outside of your apartment complex and a black vehicle will pick you up to transfer the money to my accountant. Thirty thousand dollars, cash." Mayhem's voice is a thick velvet material of threats. "It doesn't matter to me that you're an associate with Crist. A debt is a debt, and you must pay in full. Even Choi Sangwoo is reasonable enough to understand that rudimentary rule."

I gasp slightly as Mayhem withdraws from my space. *Breathe May, breathe.* My intuition swoons at him.

I stand rooted to my spot as Mayhem retreats. He puts his sunglasses back on, and I can no longer see his face. As if on cue, three of his men exit 8-ball. One-by-one they shuffle out of the back door. The tall one with black ear gauges reports, "It's all taken care of Boss."

"Good," Mayhem states simply. "Let's go."

The men head in the opposite direction to some parked motorbikes.

Mayhem turns back to me. His lips curl into a charmed smile. *He knows the effect he has on me, bastard.* "Stay away from that nuisance," he says, inclining his head towards 8-ball, clearly referring to Spyder. "He'll pay for what he did. Karma doesn't forget."

Surprise glosses my eyes. This is the last thing I expect out of him. Why does he care what goes on with Spyder and me? I would never peg Mayhem to be so philosophical. He's even more complicated than Choi Sangwoo.

Without another word, Mayhem heads to his awaiting gang.

I want to tell him to mind his own business, but I am speechless as I watch Mayhem slip onto a sleek black motorcycle. The bike is an exotic style, harnessed for only experienced riders. Mayhem starts up the engine seamlessly and it roars to life. Within a matter of seconds, Mayhem speeds out of the alleyway with three of his men in tow. Mayhem's masculine physique leans with the motorcycle as he maneuvers it onto the streets. *He's not wearing a helmet,* my conscience whines. *He doesn't have to.* My intuition has her hands on her heart.

The motor difference between Crist and Mayhem? While Crist prefers the shelter of hooded and armored cars, Mayhem fully exposes himself on a motorcycle bike thundering down the streets.

The skin on the back of my head prickles. I don't know how long I stand rooted to my spot, staring at the now vacant space. When I finally convince myself it is time to go, I attempt to get back into 8-Ball. The back door doesn't open anymore. Cursing underneath my breath, I round the building and enter from the front again.

I'm not done with Spyder yet. Determined to finish the conversation with him, I enter 8-Ball again.

Fake Blonde looks up at me. "You again," she states.

I peer through the darkness, trying to see Spyder and his group. "I need to get back in."

"Fifteen dollars," Fake Blonde states without blinking. Her ridiculously long eyelashes threaten to overpower her eyes.

"I was just here fifteen minutes ago," I remind Fake Blonde. "I have to pay again for coming back?"

"I don't make the rules." She gives me the nonsensical shoulder shrug.

"That's ridiculous! I just want to talk to someone really quick," I tell her. The frustration must be transparent in my voice because Fake Blonde softens her eyes.

"Are you looking for that Spyder guy?" she asks with a tone of empathy in her voice.

"Yes." Her willingness to disclose information without any monetary gains surprises me.

"Didn't you see Mayhem's men kick him out? He and his friends are long gone. No one stays at a location if Mayhem doesn't want them to," Fake Blonde tells me.

I gape at her. The ripple effect of his power is never going to stop amazing me. "Thanks," I mumble under my breath and exit 8-ball.

Even though the sun is flying over the blue skies, a dark cloud descends on me. I walk down the street through the people and the noise. A million thoughts run through my mind and I am still reeling from the confrontation with Spyder and Mayhem.

From the pockets of my gray sweatshirt, I extract my cell phone and scroll through the recent calls list. Taking a deep breath, I press the call button.

"May," he answers on the second ring. His voice is a cool, breezy air that floats from the other line to my ear.

I bite my lip, closing my eyes. "Hi Sangwoo."

"I have been waiting for your phone call."

"Yes."

"Yes?"

"I'm in."

CHAPTER EIGHT

He takes my acceptance with ease and minimal surprise. Perhaps the gang leader is used to having every offer of his taken. Whatever the case may be, I feel an incredible mixture of anxiousness, fear, and dare I say it—excitement when I hang up the phone with Choi Sangwoo. His instructions echo in my mind long after our phone conversation ends. Sangwoo wants me to meet him first thing tomorrow morning at his work. He promises to text message me the address of the building, and requests that I dress in an all-black ensemble.

I walk home in a state of limbo and jumbled thoughts. My heart races a mile a minute as I contemplate the magnitude of what I have done. I will be joining a gang, and not just a simple street gang that the media often depicts to be senseless troublemakers and territorial minions. I will be joining a prestigious gang that belongs to a hierarchy beyond average comprehension. I may not know what the next six months of my life will be like, but I am sure I will be at the epicenter of it all—if I am going to work with Choi Sangwoo.

Deep down, I know it's childish to believe that this will work out in a favorable manner. I have no special skills to offer someone of Choi Sangwoo's caliber. I entertain the thought so there will be reasonable cause for the money I am asking of him. My thoughts are weary and dreadful, strife with apprehension. Questions about what I will be doing with him, along with other possible complications such as hiding it from Eunhye and explaining it to Lina, bombard my mind.

But at the present moment, thoughts jostle out of the way as soon as I enter my apartment.

The sound of Lina vomiting in the bathroom permeates the dead silence.

"Lina?" I call for her.

When I reach the bathroom, my cousin has her arms around the pristine toilet. Lina's lengthy hair hangs in a halo around her neck and back. *Hair tie,* my conscience grumbles.

"Where have you been?" Lina manages to ask me in the middle of gagging. Her eyes are red and puffy from crying too much.

"I went for a jog," I lie. I sit down behind her and grab a fistful of Lina's hair. I watch my cousin lurch forward to dry heave. The contents inside the toilet are clear. "Are you sick?" I ask in a subdued tone.

"I don't know," Lina groans. "If I keep feeling like this, I need to go to the doctor Saturday."

"Saturday," I mumble as Mayhem's words float back to me. I remember the way his eyes lingered on me. My stomach feels the fresh batch of butterflies setting in. I do not see the malice and violent Mayhem everyone talks about. Perhaps I can only see the charisma and dangerous allure. But then again, the violent spark that he's infamous for resonates in his entire being. I shouldn't forget what he's capable of. Maybe he finds my stupidity about his world adorable. He's only entertaining me until he devours me for not paying him back.

Stop thinking May. Just stop. My conscience shakes her head.

I rub Lina's back. "We have to pay Mayhem back on Saturday," I remind her gently.

"Shit," Lina groans at the uncomfortable thought. "There's no way I can get even half of thirty thousand dollars at this point."

"That's why I'm going to help you," I tell Lina. "I'm going to meet with Choi Sangwoo at his office tomorrow and hopefully work something out."

Lina is shaking and trembling. "What do you mean?"

Before I can help myself, I disclose the details of the impending contract to my cousin. After explaining to her what happened last night, I am breathless at the end.

"Join his gang?" Lina asks me with disbelief shining in her eyes. "What are you going to do for him? You don't have a mean bone in your body May. How are you going to be a gangster?" When Lina says it aloud, it sounds even more ridiculous.

I shake my head. "I don't know. He's adamant about making me part of the team. I don't have any skills that are even remotely gangster."

That brings a smile to Lina's face. "He likes you."

The thought strikes me as foreign. "No, he doesn't."

"Why else would he forge a new job position and want to be near you for the next six months?" Lina questions.

"I don't know," I tell her quietly. I do my best to hide my true emotions. I don't want Lina to know that I am thinking about Sangwoo's Dead Girl. It'll bring everything too close to home and full circle.

Suddenly, the front door to the apartment opens. I can hear Eunhye's voice calling for me. "May? I'm home. Where are you?"

Crap. I look at the clock above the bathroom mirror. It is already five o'clock.

Horror flashes across Lina's face. She spits into the toilet and flushes the clear contents down.

I jump and motion for Lina to close the bathroom door behind me. I am out of the bathroom and into the living room in a matter of seconds.

Eunhye is still in her scrubs, but she's holding a handful of groceries. True to her word of having a family dinner tonight, my mother looks like she bought the whole grocery store. Eunhye smiles at the sight of me, but then a questionable look crosses her face. "Everything okay?"

"Lina's not feeling well," I tell her the partial truth.

"Oh? Lina's here?" Eunhye makes her way over to the kitchen counter and drops off the grocery bags. She washes her hands at the sink and then proceeds to the bathroom.

"Don't worry mom, it's ok. She'll come out when she's ready." I walk around the counter to become a human obstacle. "How are you? How was work?"

Eunhye glances at the bathroom with a worried expression, but addresses my question before mentioning Lina again. "Stressful. If it's not the patients, it's the paperwork. What is she sick with?"

I start taking the ingredients out of the grocery bags, wary that if I make myself busy Eunhye will join me. She bought mostly vegetables and fruits along with the main dish. "Oh, I love salmon. Are we grilling or frying it tonight?" I pick at the first slab of salmon in its package.

"Frying." Momentarily, Eunhye forgets about Lina and heads over to the cupboard for a pan. She rinses the pan under the sink first. "I was thinking something healthy and less heavy on the stomach tonight. Besides, Yuna loves salmon."

"I guess I'll start chopping the carrots and the bell peppers," I offer. I wander over to the kitchen's hanging rack for the chopping board. Then, I retrieve a knife from our kitchen tool cabinet. I'm hopefully that cooking will be busy enough to distract my thoughts.

"So what is Lina sick with?" Eunhye steers the conversation back. She props the cooking pan onto the stove. Next, Eunhye expertly tosses in some cooking oil to prepare the pan for the salmon.

Just as I am preparing to dish out another lie, Lina enters the kitchen with a guarded look on her face.

"Hi aunt Eunhye. I think I have the flu," Lina sniffles deliberately. Lina has her hands on her stomach, and the pale colors of her cheeks do the rest of the convincing.

"Hi honey." Eunhye approaches Lina with her arms out. She grabs Lina into a big bear hug. "I was just talking to your mother today. She didn't mention you were sick."

"It just hit me this morning. May and I were going for a jog and I doubled over." Lina has always been the better liar. She gives me a look over my mother's shoulders.

I focus on cutting the carrots. I place the small orange pieces in a line and bring the knife down in a simultaneous manner. For some reason, I am on a mission of cutting the carrots in a precise manner.

"Can I help with anything?" Lina offers. She looks around the kitchen with an uninterested facial expression. It is a matter of social and familial respect for her to ask, but we both know it is not in Lina's heart right now to help with dinner.

"No, no. You just sit down. Tell me what's going on." Eunhye motions for Lina to take the nearest bar stool. Eunhye returns to her place by the stove and places the first slab of salmon into the sizzling pan.

Lina looks at me and I shake my head slightly. It's an indication that I have not disclosed any information to Eunhye. It is better to go with the flow and avoid any signs of suspicion.

"Are you planning to attend college in the fall?" Eunhye launches into the usual topic with Lina.

A balloon of relief expels from Lina's concerned face. She produces the same, unchanged answer about college not being for her. Not much has changed since high school graduation when it comes to Lina's answers about her college decision.

Eunhye listens with sympathy, but offers advice on vocational schools. As per usual, Lina shoots them down one-by-one; she would rather invest her early years in gaining experience than flipping through textbooks. Her stubborn justifications run for the duration of my vegetable prepping and Eunhye's salmon frying.

Eventually, Eunhye ends the aunt-niece banter with, "I wish I could go back to your age when life was what you made of it. No one is pushing you to be a doctor or lawyer Lina. But a college education can go a long way when you're older."

Lina shrugs and apologizes to Eunhye for being the black sheep in the family. Eunhye laughs and the two of them exchange an inside joke that even I am not aware of. Soon, the conversation shifts onto lighter topics. Eunhye is both interested and entertained when we start talking about Sansachun and Mr. Chun. When she finally asks about The Trax, I tell my mother it is closing in a week.

Eunhye is ecstatic at the news and nearly burns the fourth slab of salmon. "I'm sorry May, but I am glad that place is closing up. It's definitely going to lessen my worries and anxieties about you going to work every night."

Lina lets out a small chuckle. She starts setting up our small kitchen table with plates, napkins, and utensils.

"It's not that bad mom," is my half-hearted reply. I start to feel the different shades of defense coloring my voice. "Nothing's ever happened to me."

"Thank goodness!" Eunhye lets out a disbelieving comment. "Maybe I can get you a position at the hospital. I think we need a candy striper in the geriatrics department. You'd be working with the older generation, and it's nothing but humbling." Eunhye gives me a look that tells me she thinks I need some grounding.

If only I can tell her I already have another job lined up. *Yeah mom, I'm going to be a gangster soon!* My intuition is rolling on the floor, clutching her stomach as she laughs with hiccups.

I look up to see Lina flash me a secretive look. My partner-in-crime finds my mother as humorous as I do.

Fortunately, the doorbell saves me from having to continue this conversation.

"I'll get it." Lina bounds towards the front door.

"Hello!"

Aunt Yuna is the first one through the door with uncle Dom shuffling behind her. Yuna is holding a bottle of wine in one hand and fruit tart platter in the other. In many ways, my only aunt from my father's side is a lot like him. Yuna has the same brown eyes and soft nose on a delicate face structure. She stands three inches taller than the rest of the other female family members. Yuna is a blunt personality with specific habits and believes that the world should operate accordingly.

My uncle Dom, on the other hand, looks like a typical retired wrestler. He sports a short haircut and signature black belt. Since his retirement from the wrestling world, Dom's passionate about business since he owns a small hardware store at the center of town.

At the sight of a pale Lina, Yuna scolds her only daughter. "Where have you been? I called you ten times today. Why are you so pale?"

"I've been here all day mom." Lina reaches up to take Yuna's hand off her forehead. Lina makes a face at her anxious mother.

"You know the rules Lina. One phone call is all it takes," Dom chimes in.

"It's my fault uncle Dom. I kept her busy today with errands." I offer a small smile to diffuse the attention.

Lina mutters a, "thank you" behind me as Yuna and Dom direct their attention to them.

"Hi May. How are you?" Dom gathers me up into a hug, wrestler style.

"I'm good. It's nice to see you." I return Dom's hug just as Yuna joins the latter half of our lackluster group hug.

"Oh, you lost weight." Yuna always makes it a point to comment on my current physique. She kisses the right side of my cheek. "It's good to see you honey."

"It's good to see you too." I return her hug before she abandons me for Eunhye.

"I smell salmon!" Yuna and Dom make their way over to the stove where Eunhye is waiting with open arms.

More hugs exchange between the adults. We are a big hugging family. Dom and Yuna have always been particularly fond of Eunhye, my father's first and only wife. Despite the bad decisions that my father made Yuna was there when everything in the immediate family crumbled, and even voted in favor of Eunhye over her own brother. Aunt Yuna usually bases her judgment on the events that happen rather than familial ties.

I am very blessed to have such forgiving family members.

"Alright, let's have some dinner." Eunhye shuts off the stove and begins dishing pieces of the salmon onto plates.

"Let me help you." Dom is already by my mother's side.

Suddenly, the kitchen is bustling with movement. Lina finishes setting up the kitchen table while Yuna scolds her for not watching her health. I open the wine bottle and pour each adult a glass. Lina and I resign to drinking water. We have to be on our best behavior.

By the time we all sit down, the small kitchen table is overflowing with plates of food. Yuna sits next to Dom while Lina and I sit at the edge of the table. Eunhye is at the head of the table; her eyes are glossy and a content smile comes across her lips when she surveys the food and her company.

"I want to thank you for taking the time to come over for dinner. I know we've all been so busy," Eunhye addresses her gratefulness first. She reaches for Yuna's hand who flashes her megawatt smile.

"Of course Eunhye." Dom smiles kindly at my mother.

Eunhye swells with emotions as she points to the feast in front of us. "Please, let's eat."

Lina begins piling food into her plate, undoubtedly hungry from being sick all afternoon. Yuna serves some rice onto her plate, glancing at my cousin's passive facial expression.

"How are things going for you May? Are you taking summer school?" Oblivious to the exchange going on between his wife and daughter, Dom is picking at his piece of salmon, dragging it across his plate towards the marinated sauce.

"No. Not this summer. I've been working to save up for college in the fall," I answer him, thankful for the easy question. I take my first bite into the salmon. "This is delicious mom."

"It is Eunhye. I always tell you your talents are going to waste at a hospital. You should open a restaurant. People would be standing outside in a line." Yuna is inspecting the salmon before popping a piece into her mouth.

"Ah, I miss having family around." Eunhye smiles in response to the compliment. She checks on Lina, who is awfully silent. "Everything ok Lina?"

Lina is chewing away at her food. A closer introspection reveals that my cousin is chewing her bottom lip more than her salmon. "Yes. The food is delicious."

Eunhye beams as she hands Lina the plate of vegetables. "You definitely need to eat more of this then. By the way, where is that boyfriend of yours? Spyder?"

A dark look flashes across her face. "He's busy tonight," Lina replies shortly.

Yuna watches Lina with apprehension. "He spent the last couple of days at our house. His entire cheek was nearly sliced open."

Eunhye's eyes widen in response. "What happened?"

"He won't tell us, but it's definitely those hoodlums that he hangs around with." Dom casts a dark look at Lina. "And of course she doesn't know what happened to him."

I force myself to continue eating. From Yuna to Dom's facial expression, I know that my aunt and uncle know something is wrong. Lina is skating on thin ice with them.

"So where is he now?" Eunhye pursues the topic further.

"He went home yesterday," Yuna answers. She looks at Lina. "Did you two get into another argument?"

"No," Lina answers shortly. As though she is a seasoned actress, Lina takes a gulp of her water and says, "He has his own life to live. We're not attached at the hip."

Dom narrows his eyes at his only daughter, but doesn't say anything. Yuna shakes her head in response.

"Oh you two," Eunhye laughs. "Adolescent romance is very fleeting. One day you're happy and the next day you want to break up. You make up to do it all again."

"I wish you would break up with him Lina. He really is bad news," Yuna comments. The disdain laces in her tone of voice. "He doesn't have a real job and he is always hanging out with people who have no names and no reputable profession."

"And who would those be?" Eunhye leans forward in her seat.

I can feel my scalp prickling before the answer is stated.

"Gangsters, degenerates, the likes," Dom hisses his disapproval.

I glance at Lina. She has gone from passive to frustration. "Can we please talk about something else besides my love life? I've heard your opinions about Spyder a million times."

"So why don't you do something about it?" Yuna rebukes her daughter. "Lina, we love you. You know that. We want what's best for you."

Lina narrows her eyes at her mother. The hurt is easy to see in them.

Eunhye clears her throat. "Yuna," she says softly. "I'm sure Lina knows. She'll figure out her own way. I've been telling May the same thing. I keep telling her to slow down her work days, but she's quite the workaholic nowadays."

"I'm not a workaholic." Taking the point from my mother to help change the subject and reduce the tension around the table, I chime in quickly.

"You missed our last family dinner because of your second job." Dom takes the liberty of reminding me. He winks at me, letting me know that he is on board with changing the subject.

"Speaking of which, that god awful place is finally getting shut down." Eunhye's voice animates with interest.

"Really?" Dom puts down his fork. "What happened?"

Now, I have the attention of everyone at the table. Even Lina stares at me with surprise. I haven't had the chance to tell my cousin the news.

"A new owner is taking over," I answer to the three pairs of eyes watching me. "That's as far as I know. We're closing by the end of the upcoming week."

"Tsk, tsk." Yuna shakes her head. She picks up her glass of wine and looks over it with a weary facial expression. "In this type of economy, people are still buying and selling."

Eunhye finds this statement poignant. "The rich will always be able to buy and sell whatever they want. It's a mystery that us little people can never understand."

"Well, I'd rather be poor and have my morals than those who kill and maim for their money," Yuna scoffs in a disapproving manner. "Gangsters swarm that area anyway."

"Gah." Lina chokes on her piece of salmon. She looks up from the table and mumbles, "Bone."

I carefully kick Lina's right ankle beneath the table. She scrunches up her nose. Fortunately, the adults are engaged in their conversation about capitalism and work.

Eunhye gives us the run down on what is going on at the hospital. Two new doctors have just transferred in, and the mortality rate has held steady for the past two months. When Eunhye asks about them, Dom volunteers that the small hardware shop he owns with Yuna is underwater.

"People aren't fixer-uppers or do-it-yourself anymore. Everything is technological now. Help is now a phone call away. Shopping can be done online." There is stress running through Dom's voice. He shrugs his shoulders to convey the notions are lost with him.

I glance briefly at Lina to see her guarded eyes. She shakes her head lightly at me, indicating there's no purpose for us to chime in. Now, the true reason for Lina's debt surfaces clearly. My heart sinks a little deeper at the depth of my cousin's problems.

"If you need anything, let us know," Eunhye offers quickly. She takes Yuna's hand into her own. "We don't have much, but we can help. We know the store is your sweat and tears."

"We'll be fine Eunhye," Yuna answers quietly. She steals a glance at Dom who remains tight-lipped.

Dinner ends on quite the somber note. We finish out the fruit tart for dessert, and Yuna helps my mother with the dishes while Dom begins the inquisition about The Trax. He is naturally interested in businesses, including their development and demise. When the last dish hangs on the drying rack, Yuna bids Eunhye goodbye.

"Have you heard from Hyun?" Yuna asks suddenly, setting everything into a standstill.

The mentioning of my father's name sends chills down my back.

"Yuna," Dom scolds her passively.

"It's ok," Eunhye answers like a professional. "No. We haven't heard from him since the last time we met at the therapy session."

"I'm sorry," Yuna apologizes when she glances at me. "I don't mean to bring it up like this. I've just been wondering where my brother is. I'm sorry, May."

"It's ok," I tell her softly.

Lina is looking at me with an apologetic face. She glares at her mother. "Mom, can you please be more sensitive?"

Yuna's face reddens. "I didn't mean it like that. It's been a while since we've heard from him. I'm worrying if he's still alive at this point."

The dark thought, at the start of its inception, travels from Eunhye to me. I refuse to think that my absent father is deceased. But I also refuse to think about his existence.

"We understand Yuna." Eunhye's face softens. The sadness and sorrow are still apparent in her eyes.

"Let's go." Dom places a hand on Yuna's shoulders as a gentle reminder.

"If you hear anything, please let me know." Yuna gives Eunhye an encouraging look. She grabs Eunhye for a departing hug.

My mother returns the hug. Eunhye closes her eyes tightly.

"Bye May." Yuna turns to me next.

"Bye." I hug Yuna first and then find myself sandwiched between her and Dom.

Lina hugs me next and whispers in my ears, "My mom can be so insensitive sometimes. I'm sorry. I will talk to you tomorrow."

"Bye. Text me if you need anything," I whisper back.

The look on Lina's face does little to hide her broken heart. She gives me a final squeeze before receding into the background with her parents. Yuna and Dom fire rapid goodbyes at us when they step away from the door's threshold. Eunhye and I wave goodbye to our relatives until they disappear out of sight.

"It was nice to have the family over." Eunhye closes the apartment door behind her. She lets out a heavy, exhausted sigh. The lines on her face press together in exhaustion. She doesn't want to bring up what Yuna mentioned. I join Eunhye in sweeping our crap underneath the worn-out rug.

"It was nice having them over," I add shortly to my mother's sentiment.

"I'm exhausted honey." Eunhye gives me a brief kiss on my right cheek. "Everything ok with you?"

In her arms, I want to spill everything. I feel like a little child who wishes for her mother's unconditional advice and comfort. Still reeling from Yuna's reminder of my father, I also want to divulge to Eunhye the imminent issues I am tackling. I want Eunhye to hold my hands and guide me through this, but I know better. I should never involve the only parent in my life. I am afraid of Eunhye's parental mindset and behavior. She will never allow me to pay back a gang lord by agreeing to join hands with another one. Eunhye will probably work triple shifts at the hospital to help pay back the loan rather than let me take matters into my own hands. I can't bear the thought of the woman, who raised me as her own daughter and opened her heart unconditionally, doing so.

I bite my tongue lightly and resign. "I'm just a little disappointed about The Trax," I tell Eunhye the partial truth. "I know you don't like it, but the job was helpful with money."

"Honey, there's no need for you to stress about losing this job. When I said I'm happy the place is closing, I mean it. It's dangerous working in that part of town. The last thing I ever want is for you to come across certain individuals." Eunhye hits the nail on the head with her mother's intuition. "Like I said, I can help you find something else. I know you want to save up money for college, but I'm here to help you. Don't you ever forget that. You're too independent for your own good."

"I know mom," I tell her softly. Feeling as though I might just blurt out the truth any second now, I lower my eyes from her gaze.

Eunhye examines me at arm's length. It's clear Eunhye wants to probe more, but the expression on my face disarms her somehow.

"Yuna means well when she asked about your father today."

Almost immediately, the walls rise and cover my inner thoughts. "Please," is all I can say.

Eunhye's eyebrows come together in question. "I know you don't like to talk about him, but it's ok to acknowledge him May. He will come home one day, baby."

"Please mom. I don't want to talk about it." I feel the vile building in my throat. I don't want to choke on the emotions that surround my absent father.

Eunhye looks as though I am cutting her off emotionally. She reaches up to smooth the right side of my hair. "Ok," she says softly.

"I'll figure something out about work." I attempt to reassure her, quickly changing the subject. "You should go to bed. I know you're really tired."

Eunhye looks torn, but she relents. "You're right. Have a good night honey."

I force a tight smile on my lips as my mother turns down the hallway to her room.

"Good night mom," I call after her.

When Eunhye's door closes behind her, I resign to sitting on the couch. The thought of banishing myself to my dark room, when sleep is clearly a million miles away, is a difficult decision. I turn on the TV and the bright screen flashes on. I begin my routine of flipping through the channels, desperately trying to find something to distract myself with.

My mind is too heavy to sleep. The thoughts of my random meeting with Mayhem ignite in my mind. His conditions and terms of the loan repayment exude socially immoral things. On top of that, I will be meeting with Choi Sangwoo tomorrow. How did my life go from zero to a hundred miles per hour?

IT **IS DARK AND HOT**. The sensation is foreign. I am standing on a spinning plate. The darkness cloaks me, cascading in layers. I walk forward into the vast darkness, not sure of where I am going. All I know is I am desperate to escape this dark labyrinth. A shadow approaches me and my throat tightens. I reach out for him.

Sangwoo. I want to say. He reaches out and his warm hands are on my cheeks. The lights flare behind us and I am lost in his embrace. Warm and tantalizing. I melt into his arms. Then, his lips are on my lips. They are soft and caressing. I open my eyes, looking into his eyes.

My heart stops.

It is Mayhem.

I **WAKE WITH A START.** A warm blanket drapes around my shoulders, courtesy of Eunhye sometime in the night. I do my best to catch my breath. My eyes are blinking at a rapid pace to match my chaotic thoughts. Embarrassment colors the undertone of my thoughts. Why am I dreaming about Mayhem? I was lost in his warm, comforting embrace. I can almost taste the tones of his lips on mine.

I wait for a couple more seconds to calm down before I drag myself off the couch and down the hallway to my bedroom. There is no time to dwell on my overwhelming dream. I have a meeting to get to. My knees feel like wet noodles. I grab my bathroom bag and disappear into the shower. I shower quickly and dress in an all-black ensemble—black shirt, black pants, and black shoes.

Eunhye is still sleeping when I leave the apartment. On my way to the nearest bus stop, I check my cell phone and see Sangwoo's distinctive text message in the inbox. The message is simple with the address to a business building located in the metropolitan part of town.

I send Lina a good morning text message and she texts me back within seconds. Lina wasn't able to sleep last night, and she agrees to tell Mr. Chun I am sick today. Lina promises to keep me posted on what happens at Sansachun. I call Mr. Chun next and leave him a voice message anyway, afraid that he might fire me. However, if I work for Choi Sangwoo I wouldn't need to work two jobs to support myself. My thoughts run off tangent. Choi Sangwoo really is not an average employer if he wants to hire me on. There is no gangster bone in my body, blood, or skeleton. *You're just something to keep him entertained*, my intuition taunts.

As the bus continues en route to the elusive building, the anxiety and apprehension build up inside of me. When the bus finally stops at the nearest stop, I walk one more block. I expect the private building to be behind towering public ones, but to my pleasant surprise Choi International Inc., is a glossy building with baby blue and white tones. It is a long rectangular building with glass and marble encasing. It towers above its adjacent neighbors. I take notice that the neighboring buildings range from a national bank to an insurance group.

Everything about the building is large and intimidating. I walk through the revolving glass doors. The large lobby bathes in the morning sunlight. High windows enclose the entire structure. Above the revolving door is a large magnetic shield; it buzzes slightly when I walk through. The thought that it is a state-of-the-art metal detector flashes through my mind.

The building itself bustles with light foot traffic. Men and women wear professional attire, black on white. It looks just like a scene out of the movies where people are rushing off with manila folders while others are slowly trickling through the building with coffee in their hands.

In the middle of the large lobby is a l-shaped counter. An attractive receptionist is standing behind it. Her hair twists in an elegant hairstyle out of her pale face in modern Audrey Hepburn style. She's wearing a crisp white pencil skirt with the tail of her pink blouse tucked inside. The diamond studs in her ears match her expensive wristwatch. She stares at me as I approach the counter. Her lips press into a fine line as she asks, "Hello. How may I help you?" Her tone's professional and clipped.

"Yes. Hello. I have an appointment with Cr-Mr. Choi Sangwoo," I stutter.

The receptionist's eyes light up as though she realizes who I am. "Oh, are you Miss Maybelline Lee?"

I cringe at my full name. "Yes." I suppose Choi Sangwoo has already prompted her.

"Yes. His eight o'clock appointment. Follow me please." She steps out from behind the counter and extends a hand to me. "Nice to meet you. My name is Yoojin."

"Nice to meet you too." Awkwardly, I take her hand in mine.

Yoojin has a strong handshake, making me feel as though I underestimated her delicate appearance. A thought crosses my mind and I look at her neck. She's wearing a silver necklace with its face inside her blouse. I wonder if she is a Crist member. In fact, are all the people working here Crist members? And if they are not, do they know they are working for a gang leader? Suddenly, the questions inundate my mind. My curiosity about Choi Sangwoo intensifies despite the invisible limits I have mentally nailed down. *Does Mayhem have a massive building too? His is probably twice this size to accommodate his huge ego.* My conscience rocks her head to the side.

"Please follow me. I will take you to Mr. Choi's office." Yoojin begins the trek towards the ornate elevators. Her six-inch heels hit the ground in a repetitive manner.

I follow her footsteps only to realize I am getting special treatment for being Sangwoo's scheduled appointment. Briefly, I wonder what Sangwoo has mentioned to his staff. Perhaps I am an important client in a new business venture—which isn't exactly too far removed from the truth. Or maybe he kept things succinct and said I am an important appointment that needs to be escorted to his office the minute I walk into the building. With all considerations aside, Yoojin is all business.

I look at her again through the clouds hovering over my thoughts. Her expression remains impassive.

Yoojin already has one elevator waiting for us. She steps aside and motions for me to enter first. A stranger has never given me such respect and attention before.

"Thank you," I tell her.

"You're very welcome." Yoojin's awfully cheerful. *It has to be fake, just like everything that he is.* My intuition is awake and rubbing her eyes.

The elevator doors close behind Yoojin. The entire interior's made of glass. I can see Yoojin's reflection next to me, multiplied by the four walls. I pretend to focus on my feet while Yoojin stares at the reflection ahead. The elevator whisks us to the top. The speed seems to increase as the lights jump from ground level to the fortieth.

When we arrive on the designated floor, the elevator doors ding open. Yoojin steps out first and motions for me to follow. We are now in another lobby facing a lavish round table adjacent to the door. This floor looks like a glamorous museum complete with intricate paintings and sculptures. The woman sitting behind the grand reception table is older, but her face is a classic beauty. Her hair is pinned against her head, revealing a flawless complexion and intimidating dark almond-shaped eyes. She reminds me of a black feline.

"Good morning. This is Maybelline Lee. Mr. Choi's eight o'clock appointment," Yoojin explains with a smile that doesn't touch any of her other facial features.

Cat Woman rises from behind the chair. A speculative look crosses her face, but Cat Woman is nothing short of professional. "Miss Lee. Please come." She leads me to the gray French doors located to the right of the lobby. "Mr. Choi is waiting for you."

Oh. The gang leader is waiting. My intuition sits down on her couch, quiet for once.

There is definitely no turning back now.

I leave Yoojin and Cat Woman to walk through the door. Immediately when I enter, I am compelled to drop my jaw to the floor in complete awe. The office is grand and vast; white undertones upon a deep red color. The furnishing is modern and elite with a large meeting area in the middle of the room. A CEO office desk wraps around the glass windows with the view of Seoul's skyline. While his penthouse surveys the East of Seoul, Sangwoo's office building surrounds the belly of Seoul.

Sangwoo is on the phone and doesn't notice that I am here. He looks every bit of a CEO and less of a gang leader with his dark suit and tie. Once again, I transport into a different world.

"I want it all completely removed and erased. The documentations need to be shredded immediately. Call me when it is done." Sangwoo's tone is hard and full of irritation. He snaps the instructions into the phone and listens to the reply with a frown across his striking face. "Ren. Get it done."

Did he issue something like a kill order? I swallow apprehensively.

Sangwoo hangs up his phone and turns. He pauses when he sees me. "Good morning." And he is back to his charming self.

"Good morning," I reply. I stand awkwardly in the middle of his office.

Sangwoo glances at the clock above the door. It is an exotic island with small rowboats for the clock hands. "You're late." There is humor in his voice, but the partial truth doesn't escape me. Sangwoo is a man who operates according to time.

"I'm sorry, I took the bus." I wonder why I am so keen to apologize to him.

"I can resolve the problem easily. Once I get you a car, time would be running to catch up to you." The light dances in Sangwoo's eyes. He is in a warm and playful mood this morning. Could it be that he is happy I am taking up his contract? Speaking of which, he hasn't mentioned it yet.

"What time do you have to be at The Trax?" Sangwoo asks. He glances at the clock again, indicating borderline obsessive compulsive.

Taken aback that Sangwoo remembers I have work later on, I tell him, "Four." Is Sangwoo expecting me to start working today? I want to ask him about signing the contract and employee rights, but the look in his eyes defuses me. I am completely intimidated by this man, but not for the more obvious reasons. There's something about him that is slightly alarming. He is too good to be true, yet guessing what lies beneath his façade is proving to be a difficult task.

"Good. I have you for most of the day." Sangwoo heads over to his desk.

It's neatly organized with only a computer monitor and keyboard. A triple stacker houses paperwork and pens. Sangwoo turns the computer screen off and picks up a set of keys from his desk.

"We don't have much time. Come," he tells me with diction.

"Where are we going?" I truly don't know what to expect with this man.

Sangwoo's brown eyes catch mine. In the morning sunlight, he looks foreign and daunting at the same time. He could easily step into the city painting behind him, but instead Sangwoo's standing in front of me with undivided attention.

"We are paying a visit to one of my members," Sangwoo tells me with a guarded tone. "Don't worry. The only service I require from you is to be by my side. Can you do that?"

"Does this mean that I start work today?" I am under the impression we are going to be signing paperwork today and I will be receiving some kind of Crist employee training. Sangwoo's intentions confuse me; what does he want to do with me?

A smile crosses Sangwoo's lips. "We will deal with the paperwork and everything that it encompasses when the time comes. For today, I need to pay a visit to a member of mine and I need for you to come."

I take note that he said, "Need" instead of "Would like." It all boils down to semantics, and it gives me the impression that Sangwoo is no fool at conveying what he wants. *Manipulation skills*, my intuition hisses. This is an essential skill all underground citizens have.

"Is this place in Seoul?" I ask slowly.

"It's not too far from here," Sangwoo answers with a vague undertone.

At the same moment, his phone rings. "Ren," Sangwoo answers without reservation. As he listens to Ren's voice on the other side of the phone line, Sangwoo motions for me to follow him out of the office.

Cat Woman stands from behind her desk at the sight of us. When she sees that Sangwoo is on the phone, she inclines her head respectfully to him and then to me. I hide my surprise by returning her gesture with a short bow.

The elevator is open and waiting.

Sangwoo motions for me to step into the elevator first. When he enters, Sangwoo punches in a code and the elevator drops down. I dare myself to look at our reflections multiplied four times back at us. I appear like a small, lost little girl compared to this larger-than-life gang leader and CEO. How can I possibly be beneficial to him?

Sangwoo remains immersed in his conversation with Ren. His eyebrows come together in agitation. "The acquisition was supposed to happen two days ago. They are stalling and I want to know why. If they want a meeting with me, they'd better have a good reason because I'm not going to waste my time sitting in a board room with a bunch of idiots. I'm not a babysitter Ren, so you can tell the lawyer to draw up something that's worth my time."

I can only imagine Ren on the other side of the phone line doing his best to mitigate not only the client's interests, but also his demanding employer's interests.

The elevator finally descends to its destination. The doors slide open to reveal an underground parking structure. Bright fluorescent hues light the pathway. Various cars park at adjacent angles, giving off the impression of assigned parking.

From inside his pockets, Sangwoo retrieves a key fob that light up a sleek, black Range Rover Evoque. It reminds me of a military car with its hard shell and steel exterior body. I open the passenger door with apprehension. Leather on leather is the best way to describe this exotic car. This is the fourth car I have been in with him. I climb inside the Evoque while Sangwoo glides with ease into the driver's seat.

The conversation switches from a difficult acquisition to the present moment.

"I am headed there now. Clear my schedule for today. Everything else can wait until tomorrow." Sangwoo ends his conversation with a clipped tone. He doesn't wait for Ren to reply before he hangs up the phone and pockets it into the side of the car.

"Are you ready?" He turns to me with a calm demeanor. Sangwoo eyes my seat belt before he starts the car. The engine roars to life, barely making a sound inside the hard leather interior.

"Yes," I answer. *Not that your answer matters*. My intuition shakes her head.

The Evoque cruises out of the intricate underground parking with great agility and torque, nailing every right and left of the elaborate underground maze. The exit is at the end of an incline angled forward like a spiral. The deep colors of the morning light spread over the front windshield as Sangwoo maneuvers to ground level. He straightens out the wheel and the sleek vehicle rounds the back of the building in an unmarked area. In under a minute, the car merges back out to civilization.

"You will be trained to drive automatic and manual transmissions. It is important that you are able to drive any type of car under a short moment's of notice." Sangwoo dishes yet another staple to my job description.

"I'm going to be a driver too?" I am not sure I can even drive one type of car much less a variety of them. If the type of cars he has been driving is any indication at all, Sangwoo is going to be deeply disappointed when he sees me behind a wheel.

"Don't worry. You won't be first pick when it comes to driving, but it is still a necessary skill I want you to have." The corners of his mouth lift into a playful smile. "There are other things I want you to learn first. And I want to know your limits and boundaries as well."

Oh. What have I gotten myself into? I am under the vast impression that I will be stapling paperwork for him. But this gang leader has bigger plans for me to be out on the field with him. He is going to encounter not only surprises, but also regret.

I peek at him from the corner of my eyes. Thank goodness for thought anonymity. Sangwoo focuses on driving and cannot hear my thoughts. Gauging the speed of the oncoming cars, Sangwoo turns the Evoque onto the Gyeongbu Expressway with ease. He guides the car into the merging lane, and the passing cars switch out of its way.

Now that we are on the highway, in a swift movement, Sangwoo touches a small compartment above the driver's seat. The small compartment clicks open at the touch of his fingers to reveal the objects hidden inside.

Sangwoo grabs one and transfers it to me. "Put this on," he tells me with authority.

The designer sunglasses are large and circular; it is the kind I have seen old movie stars wear to hide half of their faces. I examine the letters on one of the legs and the elegant scribble of *Persol* runs along its side. Even the material feels expensive and high-end.

"Why do I have to wear this?" I ask him as I peek over the top of the sunglasses.

"Goes back to the importance of anonymity, May." Sangwoo puts on a similar pair, but aviator style. "There is a lot you need to learn about working for me. You will be doing many things that I ask you to do without questions. Know that I always have a legitimate reason. Trust that I won't guide you wrong."

Here we go again. Gang leader complex. "Even though the questions are innocent enough?" I cannot allow the notion of absolute authority to wane over my free speech rights.

Sangwoo answers my question with an assumption. "You must be thinking I'm a difficult person," he states.

"Not really. Just bossy," I confess. Feeling herded, I push the sunglasses onto my face. The dark tint turns my colorful world to shades of gray and dread. Now I look exactly like how I feel inside.

Sangwoo chuckles as though privy to a private joke. "Just the tip of the iceberg. I am sure if you do a survey on my employees, they would choose other adjectives to describe me."

"Are all of your employees . . . members?" I don't know how else to phrase my curious question.

"Yes," Sangwoo answers with surprising ease. "Except for the custodian and cleaning personnel."

From the corner of my eyes, I can see Sangwoo glancing at me to gauge my reaction. When I don't make another comment, he adds, "Anyone that comes into close proximity with me is always one of my people or affiliated with us in one shape or form. We all understand the rules, responsibilities, and regulations. It is easier that way." There is an airy sense of the cultural elite.

"It doesn't seem like you allow people close proximity. You have your own private entry and exit." My curiosity about this gang leader peaks.

Sangwoo nods his head to commend my observations. "Like I said, I am a private person." He keeps it short. I get the feeling that he doesn't want to make any more comments on his private lifestyle.

My thoughts inadvertently wander back to Mayhem and his loud, obnoxious motorcycle. Not all gang lords choose the reclusive lifestyle like Choi Sangwoo's concrete walls. Apparently, Sangwoo chooses to be a social outcast in both mainstream and underground standards. A voluntary personal choice.

"Power, money, and notoriety are costly. I am quite aggressive about protecting my anonymity and privacy. It is not necessary for people to know where I am, what I am doing, and who I am with. But in my world, people are always willing to trade blood for the whereabouts of a highly sought-after person." Sangwoo is calm and collected with a tint of passive-aggressiveness in his description.

"Are you always so selective about people coming in and out of your life?" It really is somewhat sad to see him so guarded. At this point, I start to wonder if Sangwoo knows what it means to be normal.

"Always," he answers softly. Behind the dark sunglasses, Sangwoo's facial expression remains poker-faced.

"That's no life." My mouth gets away from me.

"Really?" Sangwoo asks, but it is not a question. "How so?" He is more interested in my statement.

I touch the tip of the sunglasses. Suddenly, it is starting to feel heavy on my face. Sangwoo's quiet probing intimidates me. A fear slightly boils in the bottom of my stomach, but I brave it. "If you have to live your life in hiding and in fear of being publicly exposed, shouldn't you rethink everything and do it differently?"

"Easier said than done," Sangwoo mutters. He shoots me down lightly, giving me the impression that he is indifferent to my advice. Sangwoo faces forward as the car speeds down the highway. "Life as a gangster is drastically different from a gang member, gang associate, and indefinitely a gang leader. If I were to break down my walls, step out of the bubble, and be readily available, a hundred thousand of my people will be at risk of danger and death. It is similar to being the president of a country, although the president of this country answers to my Council on the occasion. This world of mine is a game that politicians, lawyers, and gang leaders play. I am one of the many pillars that hold up the revolving axis. Like I said before, I was born into it. I didn't choose this life."

Listening to the somber tenor in his voice, I know that Sangwoo probably questions the existential theory many times over. After three years of studying psychology, I find myself ill informed. If he didn't choose this life, then what about those who do? My thoughts flash to Mayhem and the dark intensity that surrounds him. It takes a certain type of individual to choose the underground world. Mayhem's brain will probably be more difficult to pick at.

"I can't pretend to understand everything about you and your world," I admit as introspection plagues me. "But I do believe that if you keep yourself so guarded and boxed up, you'll die. Not literally, but in a very painful and lonely figurative death."

Simultaneously, the Evoque rounds the bottom of a ramp that exits the freeway. It slowly crawls to the first red light. Sangwoo turns to face me and I see my reflection in his sunglasses. His lips move as though he wants to say something, but slowly resigns. "You sound like someone I used to know." Sangwoo sounds like a broken record.

Goodness, he is too intense. He's going to mention Dead Girl again! My intuition scowls. She's annoyed with him.

I am thankful for the sunglasses to hide behind. The anxiety courses through my blood. There is a subtle tightness around my throat.

"She was close to you?" I brave the question. My insides are coiling with the response.

"She was the only one I allowed to be close to me." Sangwoo's tone is tight. His expression remains guarded. Long, languid fingers adjust the air conditioning button on the car's instrument panel.

"What did you do yesterday?" Dispelling the momentary silence between us, and opting for a more casual topic change, Sangwoo takes control of the conversation again. He doesn't seem muddled or disturbed by the fact that I remind him of Dead Girl. Instead, Sangwoo focuses on getting to his destination.

Thoughts race through my mind about my confrontation with Spyder and the surprise meeting with Mayhem. Part of me wants to tell Sangwoo to garner some third perspective and advice, but the other part of me knows that it's not wise to complicate an already complicated situation. Sangwoo doesn't need to know that Spyder threatened me, and that my random meeting with Mayhem had only intensified the stress I have about this loan situation.

"I had a family dinner," is the only appropriate piece of information I can volunteer. I am still trying to come down from our strained conversation.

"Family dinner," Sangwoo repeats after me with great curiosity. "I thought you said you only live with your stepmother and your father was out of the picture."

"I never . . . mentioned anything about my father." Surprise drenches my outer skin. How does he know that my father is not even in the same country?

"You mentioned you only live with your stepmother, so I imagined it's just the two of you." Sangwoo stands his ground. The tenor in his voice is factual. He gives me a sideways glance as a reminder.

Come on, May. It doesn't take a rocket scientist to understand your family composition. If you only mentioned Eunhye, it isn't hard to deduce your father's nonexistence. I want to hide behind the passenger seat indefinitely.

"I pay attention," Sangwoo says with light humor. The crinkle in his eyes lets me know Sangwoo enjoys my social clumsiness. "So family dinner, you said. Home cooked meal?"

I don't know why I am disclosing more information. "Eunhye cooked salmon and a feast of vegetables. Lina and her parents came over."

"Do you cook?" Sangwoo asks with harbored interest. He keeps his eyes facing forward, but the question feels intrusive and intimate.

"Yes. But I'm better at prepping the food than I am at cooking. I need more time out of the day to learn," I confess. I can't fathom why Sangwoo is interested in my culinary skills.

"What's your favorite meal?" Sangwoo questions further.

"Anything my mom cooks," I reply. My gaze sets on the moving colors outside my window.

"Eunhye or your biological mom?" Sangwoo stuns me with his candor.

I gape at him.

The concrete road runs out at the end of an unknown turn. The car climbs up a higher plateau. A green, ethereal world surrounds us. The air inside the Evoque cools to match the thick forest of trees outside of its tinted windows.

"Are you always so straightforward?" I don't answer Sangwoo's question. Sangwoo has touched a very sensitive nerve of mine and I refuse to let him have the power to shift me.

"Always," Sangwoo answers shortly. So shortly that I get the impression he's testing the waters with me. He wants to know my limits and boundaries.

As though he can read my thoughts, Sangwoo gives me a glance again. The sunlight dances on the lens of his sunglasses. This time, Sangwoo's voice fastens into a lecture. "The first rule of working for me is you have to have a thick armor around your emotions and bars around your thoughts. You'll learn over time, but the rudimentary rule is that you keep calm and undisturbed when people probe and prod at you for answers."

Sangwoo's referral to an imaginary audience is a glimpse into what he has to deal with on a daily basis. I find myself guilty of the same crime. Ever since I met him, I have been asking many intrusive questions but Sangwoo never faltered. He never reveals too much of himself.

"So basically become a human robot," I state.

"Naturally," Sangwoo replies. "We are here."

Still reeling from our conversation, I force myself to look out of the window. We are in some sort of meadow with hues of blue and green. It is breathtakingly beautiful against the mountain terrain. Sangwoo parks the car at the end of a pathway eroded over time by modes of transportation.

Sangwoo places the key fob inside his vest. Then, Sangwoo turns to me with a set expression on his face.

"Once we step out of this car, you will listen to every word I say. If I tell you to run, you will run. If I tell you to leave first, you will leave first. Understand?" Sangwoo's tone of voice is a mixture of impatience and command.

My eyebrows come together in question. What the heck am I getting myself into? My throat is incredibly dry, but it is not something water can simply cure. All I can manage is to nod my head. *Oh God, he's going to kill you and dump you here.* My intuition's whiny voice marches across my mind.

"Good. Let's go." Sangwoo steps out of the car first and I mirror his movements.

My legs feel like noodles when my feet touch the ground. The dirty gravel, mixed with grass and remnants of overgrown weeds, crunches underneath my black sneakers. Sangwoo meets me at the back of the car. He's almost unrecognizable behind those dark aviators, but his distinctive hairstyle and overall look speak volume about his anonymous appearance.

"Follow my lead," he tells me. Sangwoo reaches down and grabs my hand.

Oh hell no. Slap his hand away and run! I force my thoughts to think about thirty thousand as I follow Sangwoo's lead. His grip is strong and commanding. *Don't be a slush,* my intuition groans.

Sangwoo leads the way down the rough terrain and the plateau. We walk through a myriad of tall trees along the inconsistent terrain. There are various birds chirping above, hidden behind thick branches and plush outer layers of the field. Streaks of sunrays cascade the entire clearing. As we continue walking, the voices traveling through the forest become more pronounced.

Finally, we enter a clearing. The beautiful view of the terrain is divided into an anointed area. We are now on an incline where the flat land meets a small hill. There are approximately sixty people gathered in front us, facing the pivotal point of the area. The family members are wearing black from head-to-toe.

Without a word, Sangwoo merges into the crowd and we disappear with the bodies at the bottom of the hill. To the right of us, at the top of the hill stands a priest. He's wearing a black vestment and holding the Holy Bible against his chest. At the center of the scene, right in the middle of the hill is an area for the intimate family members to gather. Next to it, brass and gold bars confine a distinctive coffin. Its lid is closed and a symbol is marked on top of it.

The realization hits me like a rolling train. We are at a funeral. In fact, we are crashing a funeral. *What is going on?*

"He was my best friend." A woman stands facing the coffin. She sniffles over the microphone stand positioned at her forefront. She's dressed in a long, black dress with a large, black floppy hat that covers most of her head. She's crying profusely behind her large sunglasses as she comments, "I know that heaven gained a new Angel, but it breaks my heart that the Lord took him too soon. He was my best friend and my son."

A wave of cries travels through the crowd. An older man grabs the older woman in a tight embrace. She breaks into uncontrollable sobs in his arms.

The priest steps up to the microphone again, signaling the end of the funeral service. Family members bow their heads with grief. The old woman is hysterical now as the man attempts to calm her down.

A million thoughts and questions bombard my mind. I steal a glance at Choi Sangwoo, who has reduced himself to a statue. He doesn't move or breathe; his facial features are expressionless and deadpan.

"It is time for us to say our final goodbyes to our beloved Leon." The priest gestures a hand towards the coffin.

One-by-one, family members approach the coffin. They file in a line, allowing adequate time and space for each individual to say their goodbyes. Some family members place flowers on top of the coffin while others simply place their open palms on top of it as a gesture of farewell.

Sangwoo, who is still holding my hand, takes two steps back as more family members surge forward. Why does he want to be here to see this? Does he know the family members or the person inside the coffin?

"Goodbye, cousin." A familiar figure approaches the coffin next.

I let out an intangible gasp when I see who it is. *Son!*

Son is holding the hands of an older family member. He is dressed in a complete black suit with eyes focused on the closed coffin.

"My cousin was a Crist member . . . . His Boss ordered his execution." The memory of our conversation that day at The Trax floods me.

I feel sick to my stomach as I watch Son place a single rose on top of the coffin. He holds onto the older woman who was crying earlier. Son's eyes are beet red, and according to his facial features, he hasn't slept at all.

I slowly withdraw my hand from Sangwoo's hold. He stiffens next to me, but doesn't react. I watch Son step back from the coffin. He watches the rest of the family members say goodbye. When the goodbyes are over, the process of lowering the coffin into the ground begins. Cables, controlled by a metal bar with levers, lower the coffin slowly.

"Oh god! My son!" The older woman screams again. Grieving family members do their best to hold her back.

My heart hurts as I watch. This is too cruel. I can't watch this anymore. How can watching other people's suffering amount to any empathy or sympathy? I have to get out of here. I don't know what lesson Sangwoo is trying to teach me, but I want to avoid this painful training session.

Without realizing that I will give myself away by doing so, I turn and run back to the clearing. All I know is I want to get out of here as soon as possible. I can no longer stand how taxing it is on my mental, physical, and emotional psyche.

"What's going on?"

"Who are you?!"

I hear the shouts directed at me. I stop dead in my tracks and turn just in time to see sixty pairs of eyes on me. What have I done? Panic sets into me fast and hard. The older woman in Son's arms points at me. Her gaze sets on Sangwoo.

"Gangster!"

"That's the gangster who killed my son!"

Shouts and screams ignite in the clearing as the family members realize Sangwoo's presence. The older woman launches herself in our direction.

Sangwoo faces me. The expression that crosses his face freezes my heart.

"Run!" Sangwoo shouts.

I turn and run, but not before capturing Son's face. *Please don't recognize me,* I pray. I surprise myself at the speed I am running. Maybe I do have what it takes. *Oh don't kid yourself,* my intuition croaks with horror. *Just keep running!*

I hear Sangwoo behind me and before I know it, he catches up.

My chest hurts from the burst of energy. When we reach the car, Sangwoo runs to the passenger side first. His hands are on my waist as he pushes me in the car. Then, Sangwoo rounds the car to the driver's side. The Range Rover Evoque roars to life as Sangwoo releases the brakes and spins the car in the opposite direction.

I am breathless when I look at the review mirror. Some of the younger family members step into the clearing, but they disappear behind the cloud of dust the Evoque leaves behind. Sangwoo speeds away from the clearing with expertise.

"I'm sorry. I panicked." I realize the severity of what I have done as Sangwoo's jaw sets into a fine line. His sunglasses are off and he is less than pleased. "I didn't know you were going to take me a funeral."

It becomes apparent that Choi Sangwoo is the passive-aggressive type. He contains his emotions well, but the dark expression on his face gives way to the temper radiating inside. "You put our safeties at risk," is his tense comment.

My eyebrows come together in anguish. Did he not hear a word I said? He is blaming me for what happened. How could he kill someone and then show to his funeral? Is this who he really is?

I am shaking from head-to-toe. I know I will regret it if I don't ask, so the words stumble out of my mouth with traction. "I know one of the family members. Son, I work with him at The Trax. Did you kill his cousin?"

An obscure look marks Sangwoo's face. The car reduces its speed and comes to a complete stop at the edge of the mountain. In my state of panic, I hadn't noticed that we are now on the other side of the mountain. A beach stretches beneath the plateau the car is on. The view of the baby blue ocean, white sand, and green trees are magnificent. It's all a huge contrast to the atmosphere in the car. I am immune to the moment and the beauty. I have a gang leader to answer to.

Sangwoo leaves the engine running and turns to me. His facial expression is somber. His brown eyes are a fiery tone. "He was my gang member. He died for the gang during a job. I came to pay my respects."

I am beyond conflicted. "Why did you take me here then?"

"Because you will be working for me. This is the reality that you will have to face," Sangwoo answers so simply that it makes me feel as though I should already know the answer. "There is a reason why I have been harping about privacy and anonymity. When I don't take certain measures to protect myself, I will always be the source of anyone's contention. When a member of mine dies, the family will always call me as the executioner. They don't know the truth behind his death. Only I do. But I will not tell them the truth just so that they will like me. I'd rather they blame me than know the true gruesome details of what their son did that caused his death."

I am breathless at Sangwoo's account. How can his explanation be so simple on this side of the coin?

"You didn't kill him," I whisper. My eyes lock his brown eyes into a stare.

Sangwoo lowers those brown eyes away from me. When he looks up, emotions circle them. "I didn't kill him. If I did, as morbid as this may sound, there wouldn't be a funeral for him."

"How can I trust you?" I search Sangwoo's face for the answers. What started out so innocently is now turning into something deeper and darker than I anticipated. How was I to know that Brown Eyes would turn out to be a hardcore gang leader?

"Trust that I will help you repay your debt to Mayhem. That should be your only concern when it comes to trusting me." Sangwoo sits back in his seat. "The rest of the chips will fall into place."

This is the passive-aggressive gang leader complex in action. It is as though Sangwoo is implying he owns me now that I have agreed to be part of his gang. I have yet to sign the initiation contract, but I can already feel the distress.

"I'm not made for this," I confess to Sangwoo. "Maybe there is something else I can do in exchange for the money." *You sound desperate and cheap May,* my intuition taunts. I do my best to ban her. "I can work at your company. I can file and make copies. I'm good with paperwork. I'm not good with being on the field," I continue with my plea.

Sangwoo's jaw line tightens at my alternate suggestion. "We can talk more about it tomorrow. You're shaken up," he concludes.

The tone in Sangwoo's voice makes me reconsider pushing the subject. I cost him his safety, and now I am insisting for a more radical change. I really shouldn't push him more than possible right now. But, where is the justice for me?

"I'll take you to work." Sangwoo starts the car again. The discussion is over.

I resign to my seat. I barely catch a glimpse of the beach beneath us as Sangwoo drives away.

CHAPTER NINE

angwoo is quiet and forgiving during the car ride to The Trax. The equilibrium restores slowly between us. If I can read his thoughts, I am sure Sangwoo is more mindful of what I can stomach. I want to tell him, "I told you so!" but refrain against it. Perhaps Sangwoo will rewrite this whole initiation contract and let me off the hook. I am perfectly fine with stapling and filing in a cubicle at his office. Why can't he understand that? Who am I going to scare out in the underground world? I'm only going to get myself hurt and take people with me in the process.

"We're here." Sangwoo brings me down to reality.

"Thanks." I remove my seat belt slowly. I am still recovering from the funeral incident. I don't want to see Son if he comes into work. I'm not ready to face him so soon.

Sangwoo leans across his seat. "I will call you tomorrow. We can start going over the initiation contract. Any concerns that you have," he pauses, "we can discuss tomorrow."

Give me more time! my conscience shouts. But all I can do is mumble, "Ok. Thank you for the ride."

"Goodbye May." His voice returns to its soft tenor.

I manage a small smile as I step out of the car. I close the door behind me.

Slowly, the Range Rover Evoque pulls away and merges back into the traffic.

My cell phone rings. Absentmindedly, I pick up.

"Where have you been all morning?" Lina demands across the line.

"Lina," I breathe into the phone.

"What's wrong?" Lina is alert to my distress.

"I met up with Sangwoo," I remind my cousin.

She gasps inaudibly into the phone. "To sign the initiation contract?"

"Not exactly." I do my best to dodge all questions until I figure things out for myself first. "I'll tell you more later ok? I have to head into The Trax."

"Ok. Call me when you leave. Spyder's been calling and leaving me messages all day, but it's not to get back together. Something is up. Mayhem's gang is getting more aggressive about the money," Lina says with urgency.

Immediately, I remember the meeting with Mayhem. There wasn't any urgency or aggression in his reminder that the loan is due on Saturday. Maybe his members are taking matters in their own hands. Hundreds of guesses encircle my thoughts.

"I'll call you after work Lina. I'm sure Mayhem's not going to go back on his words about giving us until Saturday," I reassure my cousin.

"I hope so." Lina is breathless on the other side of the phone line. "Have a good day at work."

"Thanks. I'll call you later. Bye."

I hang up the phone and walk to The Trax. *Please don't go to work, Son.* My body is heavy with guilt and shame. I am shocked, confused, anxious, and emotions all rolled up into one. I don't know what to do with the turmoil I am feeling inside. It has been nonstop with Choi Sangwoo and Mayhem. What am I going to do?

When I reach The Trax, the venue is vacant except for employees. Naili closed down The Trax as soon she made the announcement. The public had no time to say their goodbyes.

The first person I see when I enter is Tailor. He is wiping down the bar with white cloths. Bottles of various shapes and sizes are stacked in a robust pattern on the counter. Tailor is clearing all the alcohol content.

"Hey." Tailor flashes his bright smile at me. "You're just in time. We're closing up. Naili wants everything packed and taken down. The new owner will be coming sometime next week with our severance checks."

My stomach sinks slowly. This is all happening too fast. I never realized just how emotionally attached I am to this place until now.

"Are you okay?" Tailor leans forward and waves a hand in my face. He studies my expression.

"I'm fine." I snap out of my trance. "Where's Joolie?"

"She's in the back." Tailor points nonchalantly. "Everyone has an assigned area. Son is out tonight. He's got a family function."

My throat tightens at the mentioning of Son. *I just saw him*, I want to tell Tailor but I keep my mouth closed. Poor Son is grieving over his cousin. Although Sangwoo clarified the role he had in the death, I can't help but feel for Son's pain. Even though he's overbearing when it comes to work, Son is a good soul and doesn't deserve this pain. *All of this is so discombobulated!* For once my intuition's not whining, but reflective.

I look up just in time to see Naili step into the center area. Her red polish and brazen hair, forming a large halo around her distinctive face, is hard to miss. Naili scans the room and when she sees me, she strides over.

"Uh oh," Tailor mumbles under his breath. He withdraws to the bar counter and picks up another glass to clean.

"Hello," Naili's greets me with a whimsical tone. She scans me briefly, seemingly content with my ordinary appearance. "Maybelline, am I correct?"

"Yes. Hi." I take note that Naili has no desire to be friendly with me.

"Son told me that you have been in charge of data input for the past few months, so I am assuming you are familiar with our system." Naili's need for confirmation resonates in her tone.

"Yes," I answer frankly. "I track the inventory system and other paperwork."

"Great." Naili clasps her hands together. The feign smile crosses her lips. "I will need your help in compiling all the forms, data, and other related paperwork for the new owner to survey when he'll come next week."

This is all happening too fast and too soon. "Sure."

"Follow me." Naili motions for me to trail her down the hallway. Just when I think she is going to lead me to the dingy computer, Naili points with a manicured hand towards the meeting room. Inside, on top of the wooden meeting table, is a newly polished laptop with a stack of paperwork.

"This will be your office for today." Naili points to a chair.

Once I settle myself in, Naili hands me the stack of paperwork and shows me how she wants it organized. She is meticulous, detail-oriented, and focused. I develop some respect for Naili's professional demeanor, although occasionally I catch her staring at me in an off-guard way. In all, however, Naili is a businesswoman and she knows exactly how to delegate work.

Fifteen minutes later, by the time Naili leaves me, I have at least ten things to do before my list ends. But as the evening wears on, I am grateful for the amount of work to keep my mind off Sangwoo, Mayhem, Lina, Spyder, Eunhye, and everything else. I get up once for a water break during the shift. Naili comes to check on me before she leaves and is pleased with the progress I make–her business mindset for my professionalism.

When I finish compiling, organizing, stapling, labeling, and printing The Trax is quiet. I turn off the laptop and stretch.

When I return to the main floor, Tailor and Joolie are haunting the bar. The other co-workers have already gone home.

"I have an interview with them tomorrow morning," Joolie is saying when I reach her. She nurses a dark drink in her hand. When she sees me, Joolie pats the stool next to her.

"An interview?" I sit down next to her when Tailor hands me a Bola glass with clear liquid inside.

"It's a Gin and Tonic light." Tailor gives me a wink.

I am not much of a drinker. In fact, I am not particularly partial to the taste of alcohol. I often wonder why people do it to themselves to swallow such a rubber band taste. But after the day I just had, I guess it wouldn't hurt.

I thank Tailor and take a large gulp. The refreshing palate travels down my throat and burns my esophagus. It soothes my rampant thoughts for the time being. Tailor made me a light, fruity version of the real Gin and Tonic.

"The Grove wants me to interview with them. If all goes well, I'll be safe when this place closes down next week," Joolie refers to another underground club not far from here. "What about you, are you looking for a new job?"

More like a job found me, I want to tell her. "I still have my morning job," I tell Joolie the partial truth. I wish for the subject to be more about them and less about me. I turn to Tailor who is always a fresh air of diversion. "What about you?"

"I've been sending in my resume. I think I will try my luck with the major hotels and see." Tailor shrugs with nonchalance. "I still have some money in my savings, so I'm not exactly in a hurry to find one."

Joolie makes a face at him. "Lucky bastard." She finishes her glass and holds it up to Tailor. "Can you pour me another one, dear?"

Absentmindedly, I take another sip of my drink. I am lost in thought as Tailor refills Joolie's glass.

"I'm going to miss this place," Tailor says with sentiment. He hands Joolie her drink, and then folds his face into the palms of his hands. Tailor's eyes are bright and nostalgic. "This place has been good to me for the last three years."

Joolie makes a face at his comment, but she doesn't negate it. Instead, Joolie throws finishes more than half of her newly refilled glass. "Me too. The bastard who bought it seems to want to break it down and rebuild it into three stories."

"Who?" The question escapes my lips before I can help it.

"The new owner. I saw him earlier. Handsome jerk." Joolie has her face in her hands now, mirroring Tailor's body language. "I saw him talking to Naili early in the morning when I was here. He came striding in with executives coming out of his armpits. I basically caught the gist of their conversation about breaking down the halls and building here and there and everywhere." Joolie makes an exaggerated hand motion in the air.

So the new owner is definitely not Choi Sangwoo. He was with me all morning. *Or it could be someone working for him*, my intuition chimes in. I strike her down as fast as I can. I don't need any more reasonable doubts to play with my judgment at this point. I take another sip of my drink and place it back on the counter.

"I'm going to go home. I'll see you guys tomorrow."

"So soon? Stay and have another drink."

"I can't. I'm really tired. Sorry. Next time."

"Ok. Good night." Joolie waves to me. She almost tips over in her barstool. Fortunately, Tailor catches her and winks at me.

"Bye Joolie. Stop drinking." I tap her arm playfully and wave goodbye to Tailor.

"Bye," they reply together in a chorus.

I exit The Trax and the cool summer air greets me. Taking the steps two at a time, I am back on street level in a matter of seconds. I look forward to silence and my bed; nothing but silence and my warm bed. I start digging through my tote bag when I hear the distinctive call.

"Hey."

The voice startles me. I see two men loitering just a couple of feet away near the adjacent abandoned building. The apparent greet is not for me. Instead, it is one of them alerting the other of my presence.

Immediately, I mentally picture myself featured on one of those shows where a deep male voice narrates the dramatization of my abduction. *Maybelline Lee, a 21-year-old college with a bright future, was innocently leaving work when two attackers grabbed her from behind, dragged her to their unmarked car, and drove away in the night . . . .*

My imagination manifests into reality when one of the bigger males walk forcibly towards me.

Shit. Run! My intuition screams and I embrace her, sorry for knocking her down earlier. I swallow hard and tighten my grip around the strap of my tote bag. I tuck my chin into my neck and pick up my pace in the other direction.

"Hey!" Now, the male is addressing me.

"Leave me alone!" I blurt out. I start to run. The blood rushes in my veins and I am all physical at the moment. *Run! Run! Run!*

"Stop!" One of them shouts. The sounds of his shoes thundering after me echo in the abandoned alley.

Before I know it, I am running full speed towards the street. The fight or flight syndrome is kicking in my veins. I am only five feet away from public view. My hands dig frantically into my tote bag for my cell phone. Their footsteps ricochet behind me, increasing in sound and momentum. I turn my head to see the two men running full speed at me. My mind is desperately trying to remember how to disarm attackers.

"Stop!"

"Who are you?! What do you want from me?!"

Before I can run any farther, the two males flank me. They tower over me as though I am merely a simple object. I am no match for their physique and training. The incredible force they use to lift me off the ground knocks my breath away. I attempt to get a good look at them, but the male to my left holds me in a tight grip.

"Let me go!" I start screaming as I thrash my body to the far right.

One of my attacker's places a hand over my mouth to silence me. I snap my jaw at his hand only to realize that I am biting into a hefty white cloth. The powerful chemical permeates from the fabric. When I realize what it is, it is too late. My nostrils have gotten a good whiff and the chloroform travels through my senses.

With quick movements, the two males drag me towards the black car parked on the cross street.

"Hmm! Let me go!" I fight with all my might; my arms are dangling in the air as though I am a rag doll while my legs kick space.

They are too strong. My attackers are wearing strategic black ski masks. *How original*, my intuition cries.

"Nooooo . . . ." I continue struggling. The colors in my eyes fade to black, and my eyelids feel as though a large rock sits on them. All of my extremities fail me. A deep sense of calm washes over me and my limbs numb.

The last thing I see is the back doors to the unmarked car opening. My attackers usher me in. When my body touches the seat, the darkness takes over me.

I sink deeper and deeper into the overwhelming obscurity, into the silent abyss.

THE FIRST SENSATION I FEEL when I regain consciousness is the crick in the left side of my neck. The responsiveness of my arms and legs come next, follow by a dry throat and pounding headache. Fortunately, the heaviness on top of my eyes lift and my facial muscles relax.

The car slows to a stop. The soft hum of the engine reverberates throughout the back seat. It's pitch black outside; a stream of wind leaks between the window and its quarter top.

When I attempt to move from my seat, I realize my wrists are tied together with a plastic wrap in the manner of handcuffs.

"She's waking up," A gruff voice announces. The kidnapper stirs to the right side of me. The male to my left mirrors the same movement.

The colors of my vision focus in a tunnel manner. The smell of the car's leather interior is robust. The leather seat burns against my skin. When I attempt to sit up, I am immediately under the control of my kidnappers. Again, the male to my right places an arm on my shoulder to prevent any range of motion.

Shit! I've been kidnapped! All human concerns and worries flood into my consciousness. Fear, panic, and confusion set in fast and hard. I am dizzy and nauseous. I need to come up with a quick escape plan, or at least call for help.

In a matter of seconds, the car comes to a complete stop. The doors open in a simultaneous manner, and the tap on my shoulder indicates it is time to get out of the car. The kidnapper to my right ushers me out first. Every inch of my body aches. My mind's still trying to catch up with the present. I feel as though I am indefinitely stuck.

With my wrists tied in front of me, my balance is hardly stable as I stumble out of the car. I squint at the unfamiliar territory, even though it is dark outside. The location is very scenic; large overgrown trees and boulders line the aesthetic terrain. I only have a few seconds to take the location in until reality reminds me why I am here.

"Walk." The taller kidnapper pushes on my side.

"Who are you?" I look up at him and ask with a coarse throat. "What do you want from me?" I look at the other kidnapper.

They don't answer. The kidnapper to my left inclines his head as though he wants me to shut up.

"This is a crime. It's a felony to kidnap someone," I snap at the kidnappers. "When I get out of here, I'm going to make sure you spend the rest of your life in prison!"

"Shut up!" I finally get a response from the taller kidnapper. He holds up a hand to slap me.

I flinch and lean to my left.

"Keep your mouth shut before you really do get hurt." The stern voice of the second kidnapper gives me some hope. He sounds as though he wants to correct my stupidity before it gets me in more trouble.

I jerk my arm out of his grip, but oblige. A million escape plans circle my mind. Who would do this to me? What do they plan to do to me? How am I going to get out of this without getting hurt or hurting others in the process? My legs ache to break free from the invisible pull my kidnappers have on my heels. I want to turn around and run in the opposite direction as fast as my leg muscles will let me. But I know that the chances of successfully completing my escape plan will be slim to none.

I tuck my chin into my neck as a defense mechanism. I follow my kidnappers around the bend of the rocky area with blind obedience. Soon, the dirt path fades into patches of grass. The large trees that surround the area give the impression of a park. However, as the pathway elevates, the patches of grass disappear.

Just when I think the hike will never end, at the tip of the elevated plateau stands an abandoned warehouse. Its dark wooden structure looms over the stretch of land we are walking on. Two guards, wearing the same identical ski masks as my kidnappers, flank both sides of the door.

The guards nod at my kidnappers when we approach the threshold. Together, they step aside to reveal a heavily armored door.

"Go in." The kidnapper to my left pushes me forward.

"Don't touch me!" I snap at him. But I force my feet forward into the warehouse. *Oh God, we're going to die.* My conscience is bawling while my intuition holds her. I want to join them.

Dimly lit, the warehouse includes large, towering shelves displaced throughout the vast layout. Boxes, comprised of different shapes and sizes, align in an unidentifiable system. In many ways, the warehouse looks like the stereotypical setup of an illegal business that many movies portray. However, the reality of my situation becomes apparent when I look up at the ceiling. Large dangling chains, fastened with metal spikes, swing from its height. It reminds me of a torture device designed to hang its victim by the arms and possibly neck.

As I continue my trek deeper inside the warehouse, it becomes obvious that this warehouse has dual roles. Not only is it home to illegal transactions, but it also houses a torture chamber. Aside from my footsteps and those of my kidnappers, the echoes of running water surround the warehouse.

"Maybelline Lee. 21-years-old. Born and raised in Seoul, South

Korea. Currently resides with Lee Eunhye at East Point, and studying psychology at Seoul University. Works at Sansachun and The Trax. Daily schedule repetitive and dull as a snail making its trek across the grass."

His voice permeates the silence of the warehouse. It stops me along with my kidnappers. We are now at the center of the warehouse.

I stare at him when he comes into focus. His men flank his right and left side. Today, he is wearing casual blue jeans and a white dress shirt. As usual, his hair slicks back from his face, revealing its marred features.

I am speechless and spellbound. The weight of my involvement with loan sharks, more specifically gangs starts to sink in. It doesn't get more real than this. *Shit, not this guy again!* My intuition gapes at him.

"What is your real relationship with Choi Sangwoo?" Danny asks me. Danny narrows his eyes in the same obtrusive manner when I first met him at Spyder's house. Just like when I first met him, Danny is relentless and merciless.

"Excuse me?" I ask, not bothering to disguise the bewilderment in my voice. They went through such lengths to kidnap me here to verify this question again?

"Answer me!" Danny shouts. The echo of his voice bounces from one end of the warehouse to the next. His fists clenches together with his unforgiving eyes.

"I-I don't know him," I answer, but immediately retract the statement. "Let me rephrase. I do know him. He's my Boss."

"Your Boss? So your Boss picks you up from work, takes you to his hotel, and allows you full access to his company?" Danny questions further. The smirk on his lips lets me know my lie amuses him.

"Are you following me? Who are you?" I blurt out in irritation, forgetting that my life is in the hands of this guy. He's an aggressive stalker.

Danny's jaw clenches together. His face remains frightening underneath the warehouse's lights. "Are you his girlfriend?"

"N-no," I reply. It has only been a few days since I have seen him, but the fear is still there. I don't know how else to calm Danny down. He is clearly upset that I am lying to him. He's convinced I have a relationship with Sangwoo.

"I didn't know you're Choi Sangwoo's type." Danny ignores my answer. With his hands behind his back, Danny begins walking in circles around me.

What's that supposed to mean? I move away from Danny, becoming rapidly aware of what I can do to stop him from harming me. But the odds are not in my favor since my kidnappers are still in close proximity. I realize with a faint glimmer of hope that no matter what, I will not be able to escape so easily.

"Well, if you're so close to your Boss then I am sure he won't have a problem helping you pay back your loan." Danny reaches for my chin suddenly. His hands are cold and sharp.

"Don't touch me!" I move away from him. The hot glare flashes in my eyes. "Mayhem and I agreed that I will be paying the money back on Saturday."

"Is that so?" Danny sneers at me. "You dare mention my Boss?"

"Why wouldn't I? He's more reasonable than you. You were there, fool." I am heated and livid. Perhaps it's the Gin and Tonic fueling my system. Liquid courage is a dangerous weapon.

"Fool? I don't think so little girl." Danny grabs my right arm and pulls me under his control. He narrows his eyes at me as I struggle in his grip. "You have no idea what kind of world you have stepped into, little girl. Promises and dates mean nothing when it comes to people like me who have the power to enforce it."

Danny pushes me away from him. Danny reaches inside his pocket, and for a split second, I think it is for a gun. It turns out to be an unmarked cell phone. Danny thrusts it towards my direction. "Call him."

"What?" My heart picks up another fraction of a beat.

"I am tired of your smart mouth." There is malice in his tone. Danny thrusts the phone into my trembling hands. "Call him. Your Boss. Choi Sangwoo. Tell him to meet you at The Rock with thirty thousand dollars. Now."

The number is already on the screen of the cell phone. All I have to do is press the green button. For a moment, I consider dropping the phone and running for my life.

"Call!" Danny screams, shattering my guarded thoughts. "Fucken call him!"

"Okay, okay." My trembling voice exudes my fear. With shaking hands, I hold up the phone and press the green button. I have no choice but to do this. I have to get out of this.

The phone rings for three intervals before Sangwoo picks up. "Hello."
My heart races at the sound of his voice.

"Sangwoo, it's May." My palms are sweating; my throat is dry.

"May? This isn't your phone number," Sangwoo states with apprehension.

"The Rock," I blurt out. "I'm at The Rock."

"The Rock?" Sangwoo's voice cuts short. Then, the alarm takes over his otherwise calm tone. "How do you know about it? Shit. Are you okay?"

"I–" I attempt to discreetly tell him, but I know nothing I can say will reflect what is really happening. The desperation catches in my throat and I am useless.

"Give me the phone." Danny snatches the phone from me, clearly impatient with my hesitation. "I got your little girlfriend with me here. You will be here in fifteen minutes with thirty thousand dollars, cash."

My heart drops at Danny's statement. His body language, his voice, and his eyes express his semblance–I know I will eventually die. I swallow the dry saliva scratching against my throat.

"If you're not here in fifteen minutes, I think you're creative enough to imagine what will happen to your little girlfriend." Danny shuts off his phone. A sickening smile comes across his lips. "You see, it is a cruel world out here. You probably grew up thinking if you just kept to yourself, go to school, go to work, do the right thing you can make it safely."

My eyebrows come together in question at Danny's rant.

"Little did you know that by making one friend, you could put your whole life in jeopardy." Danny stares me to the ground. Then, he makes a face that claims an epiphany. "Ah, but your luck would have run out anyway because your cousin and her useless boyfriend borrows money from us. Dang, you're screwed either way."

I grind my teeth together. The anger, along with fear, courses through my veins. I feel powerless and am on the verge of doing something truly stupid. If there's one thing this lowlife is right about it, it's that this world is too cruel. I have made myself the victim through and through in this situation. I don't want to be a damsel in distress waiting for the gang prince to come save me. I want to be able to be self-sufficient. But my throat tightens and the overwhelming feeling of my reality tackles my emotions to the ground. I want to cry because of the shock of all this. I want to cry because I know the impending violence that may erupt when Sangwoo arrives. I want to cry because I know no good can come from this.

Suddenly, there is commotion outside of the warehouse and I know Sangwoo is here. A flood of activity, including loud voices and footsteps, can be heard just outside of the warehouse.

"Don't touch me."

His authoritarian voice infiltrates the metal and aluminum walls of the warehouse. Choi Sangwoo enters by himself, holding a black suitcase strapped with a metal casing. The tense facial expression on his face subsides when he sees me. Sangwoo scans me quickly, making sure I am unharmed.

A sense of relief floods through me. *He's here for me. He's really here for me.* It's only been a few hours since I last saw him, but it feels like days. It is such a high-tension moment that everything that occurred earlier means nothing now.

"Choi Sangwoo." Danny turns his attention to the gang leader. "If I knew you would be running here this fast, I would have thought about grabbing your previous girlfriends whenever we want to settle a deal with you." With a wave of his hand, Danny motions for more men behind him. Five more surfaces from the shadows of the warehouse.

My heart races, but Sangwoo doesn't seem affected by their presence.

Instead, Sangwoo narrows his eyes at Danny. Those signature brown eyes hold nothing but menace and rage. His composure is experienced and untouchable. This is not Sangwoo's first time with such a tense confrontation. In fact, this foolish act of Danny's seems to be beneath him.

"This is between your Boss and me. Does Jaewon know you are trying to pull this stunt?" Sangwoo asks Danny coolly.

"Drop the suitcase." Danny ignores Sangwoo's question. He motions to the black case Sangwoo is holding. "Slowly."

Sangwoo drops the suitcase, extending all five fingers out like a fan. The loud thud sends riveting waves across the warehouse.

Danny gestures to one of his men to pick it up. One of the ski masks pops the latch open and examines the money inside. He gives Danny a nod as verification.

"I didn't know Jaewon allows his minions to act on their own accord. Since when does he let you go around settling his loans for him? I'm willing to bet Jaewon has no idea you are engaging in such idiotic behavior." Sangwoo is unaffected by the intimidating demeanor of Mayhem's members.

"Do not say Mayhem's name! You have no right, traitor!" Danny spits in anger. The anger flares in his eyes.

Traitor? My intuition is quick to capture the word.

Sangwoo steps forward. "You have no idea the history your Boss and I have. But, I do know that if you think by obtaining thirty thousand dollars before the Saturday agreement is what he wants, you're deadly wrong."

"You think he will kill me for speeding up the process?" Danny scoffs at Sangwoo's foreword warning. "He doesn't care how transactions are conducted when it comes to you. You're not even on our watch Sangwoo. We are engineering, planning, and executing far greater things than worrying about your next move. This money is rightfully ours. You're just the stepping stone we need to retrieve it faster. This useless girl would have never been able to pay it back without you, so that's why you're involved, my *lord*."

Without another warning, Danny motions for an object. A ski masks steps forward and places a metal baseball bat in Danny's hand. Danny moves towards me with malice.

"Do not touch her." Sangwoo's arctic voice is dire with a warning.

"Oh, you like her?" Danny ignores Sangwoo's warning. He runs a hand through my hair.

I attempt to back away from him.

"I said do not touch her." Sangwoo's voice drops another grave octave.

"Shut up!" Without so much as a warning, Danny grabs a fistful of my hair.

"Ow!" Tears swell in my eyes. As a reaction, I slap him across the face. The anger and pain boil inside of me. I am feeling stupidly brave. *You can't touch me like that!* my conscience growls with angst.

"Bitch!" Danny throws me to the ground.

I land with a thud, hitting the concrete ground elbows first. The nerves spin inside my bones. I don't have time to focus on my pain.

"I said don't touch her!" Sangwoo's growl resonates in the entire warehouse. With a gleam of anger in his eyes, Sangwoo swings at Danny, who retaliates with the baseball bat.

The noise is deafening and haunting. For a moment, I think it is a dream. I think it is all a dream to see Sangwoo fall to his knees as Danny swings the bat again into his chest. Blood spurts recklessly from Sangwoo's mouth in a matter of seconds.

"No!" I finally find my voice. The cry is animalistic and unfamiliar. It is no longer a dream when the color of Sangwoo's face turns a different shade.

"Argh!" With tremendous speed and power, including recovery time, Sangwoo springs back on his feet. He ducks the bat's attempted second swing, grabs the side of its length, and holds it tightly against Danny's chest. With great force, Sangwoo pushes the bat against Danny until he moves five feet across the concrete floor. For a minute, it looks like the two are stuck in a balance of weight and power.

Then, Sangwoo breaks the hold by releasing his right hand and slamming his knuckle hard into Danny's nose. He fights back. He fights back even though blood is everywhere on him. Miraculously, Sangwoo finally gets a grip on the bat.

"Do it and she'll die!" The loud click of a gun loading fills the air. Another Mayhem member intervenes with the weapon.

I freeze. I don't have to turn to know that the gun is pointing at me.

Sangwoo pauses to look at me, and Danny regains his fight for the bat. Sangwoo's distraction is Danny's advantage.

"No!" I scream blindly.

Danny spins the bat around and clubs Sangwoo relentlessly to the ground. As though he shouldn't hesitate for one second to overpower Sangwoo, Danny continues to cycle the bat on top of Sangwoo's flesh as rage takes over him.

"No!" Forgetting that a gun is pointing at my head, I break into a run towards them. With all my might, I push Danny out of the way, causing him to lose his balance. "Stop! Stop it! Please! He's going to die."

Sangwoo sprawls on the ground; there is blood everywhere and he's in a fetal position. With my heart pumping wildly and, I fold my body over Sangwoo's body. It happens too quickly for me to feel the pain as the bat rains on me at odd angles.

"No. May! Get out of the way!" Sangwoo pushes me aside when he realizes what I am doing. His eyes are wide and wild. "Move! Run! This is your chance!"

He is going to die and all he can think about is making sure I am safe, making sure I have a chance to run. This is why he's not fighting back. Sangwoo wants to surrender so I can go.

"Damn you!" Danny lets go of the bat. It clatters to the ground, bouncing in chaos. Extending a hand to one of his men, Danny says coldly, "Give me the gun."

I stare in horror as Danny's fingers curl around the metal body of the gun. Lowering his wrist, Danny points it directly at me. "I ask myself all the time, if the shoe was on the other foot what would you do? And you know what the answer is, don't you Sangwoo? The world isn't big enough for everyone. Sometimes, you just have to take population control into your own hands."

"No! Please!"

Boom.

Darkness consumes me. A flurry of activity ensues. Shouts. Footsteps. Clatter. Commotion.

People. More people are coming.

CHAPTER TEN

ound travels faster than light. The loud shot reaches my ears first before my sight zooms in on the oddly shaped bullet whizzing out its socket straight at me.

I am indefinitely frozen and paralyzed. Everyone knows that feeling when you are well aware of something coming at you, but you feel powerless to react quickly. During gym time, there have been countless occasions when I see the ball coming to my face, but I don't move. I don't even raise my hands to block it because I am paralyzed from the inevitable. Nine out of ten times, I just let the ball whirl through the air, drop low, and slam me in the face.

The same paralyzing notion occurs with the bullet. I see it. I see it clearly with my twenty-twenty vision, but I don't move until Choi Sangwoo pushes me hard onto the ground. My body slams against the rough concrete, and it brings me out of my trance in time to see Sangwoo cover his body over mine.

"Move!" With a spurt of energy, Sangwoo angles his body and the bullet silences when it pierces through his flesh . . . .

My last memory is Danny flees the scene as groups of men invade the warehouse. Ren. Ren and his distinctive facial tattoo. Ren shouts orders as some men rush to Sangwoo's aid while others hoist me to my feet . . . .

"PLEASE LET HIM BE OKAY." I close my eyes tightly and then open them again to look up at the bright lights. The ambient bustle of the hospital brings me back to reality, pulling me away from replaying the scene in my mind again. I look down at the large gauze wrapped around my right arm. Images of Danny's metal bat flash in my mind's eye.

I am sitting on the bench just outside of Sangwoo's private hospital room. In fact, the entire floor is on reserve for him. Although not lethal, the gunshot wound still calls for an operation. Sangwoo's private doctor is still in his room for the last thirty minutes. As time goes by, I am growing more and more anxious.

Presently, there are thirty Crist members loitering at the clandestine hospital. All dressed in identical dark suits they roam the hallway like phantoms, haunt the entire floor like ghosts, and hover outside of his hospital door like vampires. When they first arrived at the hospital, surprise rippled from one to the next. It becomes quickly apparent that when they are not gawking at me, they are gaping. I do my best to ignore them and focus on the seemingly translucent walls. The desire unfolds through my entire being to shut down the memories and block out the stares so I can withdraw into my own thoughts.

Coarse footsteps round the side of the building.

Ren returns from wherever he was. Three Crist members stop him, and a hushed conversation ensues. They glance at Sangwoo's door before throwing a look my way. Ren makes one final comment and they retreat into the shadows.

"Hi," Ren says when he finally approaches me. "How are you doing?" The intricate, embroidered tattoos on the left side of his face are stark underneath the lucent hospital lights. I am too busy staring at Ren to notice he's holding something.

"This is your bag." Ren hands me my tote bag. I thought it was lost in all the chaos.

"Thank you." A sense of relief floods me. "I'm doing ok." I look up into those brooding eyes, feeling judged and analyzed.

"He will be fine," Ren volunteers the information to my surprise. There is kindness in his eyes, but it is the dangerous kind that shouldn't be underestimated. "Being shot at is part of the business."

I can only gape at him. *Is he joking? Weird gangster,* my intuition scoffs. The last thing I want to hear right now is the necessary staples that come with a gangster's world. Fortunately, I don't have to comment on Ren's foreboding statement.

The door to Sangwoo's hospital room opens. A doctor, looking as though he belongs to the Mafia family with his black slacks and white lab coat, steps out with a nurse who has blue scrubs on. For a moment, the doctor examines the men outside of Sangwoo's room with a startled expression. Evidently, he wasn't expecting the turnout. The doctor scans the hallway; when his eyes land on Ren there is recognition in them.

"Ren," the doctor addresses Ren. His eyes are large and round, fixed together on top of a slightly crooked nose. When he speaks, there is a foreign accent to his tongue.

"How is he?" Ren asks with an even tone.

"The bullet was safely removed. It was only a fraction of an inch away from the old wound, but fortunately it got his flesh instead of the bone. His vital statuses are regular and undisturbed. It feels like a large bug bite for him right now. He should be able to leave by the end of today." The doctor glances at me.

Old wound? The word swirls in my mind. Gathering the notation of the doctor and Ren's casual attitude about Sangwoo's wound, I am way out of my league. I was raised to be afraid of violence and pain, but now those who embrace it surrounds me.

"Can we see him?" Ren asks with speculation.

"Of course." The doctor nods sharply. "If there is no need for me here, I will be on my way. My flight for Japan leaves in forty-five minutes." It becomes clear he's here specifically for Sangwoo.

Ren bows to him.

The doctor returns Ren's bow and then to me. His eyes dart furtively at me before he turns down the opposite hallway. The nurse retreats to the nurse station near the elaborate elevators.

"I want to see him," I tell Ren.

He gives me a taciturn look, but doesn't protest when I follow his heels to Sangwoo's room. As we walk by the other Crist members, some dart apprehensive glances at me while others murmur in whispers.

" . . . Looks just like her."

"Same eyes . . ."

"Skin tone."

I do my best to force their cryptic mumbles away from my ears. I focus on entering Sangwoo's room. It is faintly lit and spacious with white furnishing.

"He's not even trying to hide Boss." A rapid-fire, ardent voice is complaining in anger.

"Han, calm down," Sangwoo replies, his voice is hoarse and impatient.

"Calm down? If we don't do anything to retaliate, our reputation, Crist's reputation, will be mocked! I will take care of it," the male exclaims with earnest.

"Han, I have my reasons. Jaewon doesn't know. I am sure of it," Sangwoo continues in the same defensive manner.

"It doesn't matter!" The protests grow angrier by the second.

"I don't want to talk about this anymore. You are not to take matters into your own hands. End of discussion." It is the first time I hear the dangerous sharpness in Sangwoo's voice. Now, he is starting to sound like the gang leader everyone regards him as.

"As you wish, Boss." The male bites down on his last word and turns on his heels.

Ren and I are still standing by the door. Han stalks towards us; he is dressed in black from top to bottom with half of his face covered by the jacket he is wearing. When he sees Ren, Han stops short and bows to Sangwoo's right-hand man. He glances at me briefly; his eyes narrow slightly, but in a matter of seconds he is gone.

"Who is it?" Sangwoo asks from his bed.

I walk into the room with Ren.

Sangwoo lies on large pillows in his hospital bed. There is a gray patch on his left arm to cover the gunshot wound. The IV tube remains attached to his right arm. There is no need to monitor Sangwoo's status, so the hospital machines are silent.

"May." Sangwoo breaks into a small smile when he sees me. For someone who was just shot, Sangwoo doesn't seem disconcert or jaded. In fact, Sangwoo looks healthier with color on his cheeks.

"Hi," is all I can manage.

"Boss." Ren bows his head.

Sangwoo acknowledges Ren first. "Tell everyone to disband. There's no point in gathering at the hospital and making a scene. I don't want any publicity for this."

"Everyone is just all worried about you," Ren states. "Han has a point."

"Why don't you go outside Ren?" Sangwoo cuts him off with a dark look. "The last thing I need right now is for you two to tell me what to do."

Ren looks hurt and rejected. Ren opens his mouth as though he wants to say something, but he simply bows in respect and retreats.

"Are you okay?" Sangwoo asks me after Ren is gone. His eyes survey my face. When he sees the gauze around my left arm, Sangwoo points to himself. "Look. We're twins," he jokes.

"You're the one that got shot and you're asking me if I'm ok?" I ride along with the humor. I don't even want to address the twins comment.

"It's not the first time I've been shot," Sangwoo says casually. "It's part of . . . my world, May."

I grimace at his confession. Only in a gangster's world would they boast about getting shot and surviving it.

"Why did you do it?" My question comes out as a whisper.

"What?" Sangwoo asks as though he doesn't know.

"Why did you jump in front of me?" I press on further. All the hours of waiting has resulted in a lot of angst and questions.

Sangwoo's eyes narrow in a pervasive manner. "May," he says simply.

"You could've been killed." I don't know what I am expecting him to say or what I want him to say. All I know is I am scared and frightened beyond reprieve.

"Because I care about you," Sangwoo retorts finally. The hard look softens in his eyes.

Oh no. I am not ready for this. I am immobilized, not because I am thinking of a smart comeback, but because I don't expect such a sensitive answer from him. How can I tell Sangwoo that seeing him take that bullet for me was horrifying? More important, how can I confess to him that it brings back some of my darkest memories? The memories that I carefully boxed and shelved away in the restricted sections of my mind?

"Thank you," is the only thing I can say. I take a step back, feeling defeated and helpless.

Sangwoo stares at me with an impassive look, giving me the impression that he is wracking his brain on how to deal with me. In the end, he beckons me to come closer. Every step I take to him is a conscious effort. I am well aware there is no going back now.

When I am by his side, Sangwoo reaches for my wrist. His warm hand wraps around my skin. I make no move to take my arm back. I already know that the moment he jumped in front of me, something in the cosmic universe seals us. I already know that no matter what, Choi Sangwoo will be in my life as long as he wants me. *This mysterious, lonely gang leader wants me.* The thought shakes me just like the first time. *He wants you because you remind him of Dead Girl. There, I said it!* Sticking her tongue out at me, my intuition attempts to butcher the mood.

"Can I ask you for a favor?" Sangwoo's voice is soft and dreary.

"Yes," I agree, willing to do anything to reduce the guilty feelings I have. "Whatever you need."

"You . . . ," Sangwoo replies slowly. His eyes capture me at first, and then his gaze takes me in.

Oh no. The feeling starts in the middle of my heart and travels down to the depths of my stomach. Butterflies bloom in a manner I never thought possible. I am falling for him. I am falling for Choi Sangwoo even though I do not know who he is. I am falling for him even when the darkest part of me knows I shouldn't. *Me. He wants me?*

"Can you get me some water? I'm dying of thirst." There is a short twinkle in his eyes.

It snaps me out of my thoughts, and I free fall from the great precipice I am on. I don't know what the appropriate response is. Do I laugh or call him out on the play? "I'll be right back," I tell him with resignation.

"Thank you, May," Sangwoo calls after me as I exit his hospital room. How can he change emotions and the course of a moment so quickly? He is playing with me, I finally decide. He wants to leave me in the dark about how he truly feels. Sangwoo knows that by saving me from the near fatal bullet, I am mentally and emotionally at his mercy. He has me right where he wants me. Now, it is my job to figure out if my feelings for Sangwoo are genuine or gratefulness. *This is not the time to talk and think about feelings. You just feel bad for him. There's a difference between actually liking someone and feeling bad for him*, my intuition warns.

I walk out of Sangwoo's room and around the hoard of Crist members. Ren is on his phone; he looks up at me when I pass him. Two nurses occupy the nurse's station. They are in a deep conversation when I approach. The nurses are older in age and they remind me in a homesick way of Eunhye. When I ask for water, the nurse who has a long scar across her forehead hands me ice chips too. Her kind smile lets me know that she is aware of who Sangwoo is.

On my way back to Sangwoo's room, the silent elevator opens suddenly. Its steel doors slide apart to reveal the uninvited guest inside.

A dark figure exits. Today, he is wearing a casual black baseball hat pulled low over his distinctive, prominent features. He's wearing his signature bomber jacket and accompanying black ensemble. On his hands are brass knuckles. At first glance, the brass knuckles look like fancy jewelry. But the violent nature of their purpose is clearly daunting.

I feel his presence as if I am tuned to him. *Why is he here?* My intuition sits higher on her chair; she has her undivided attention on him. She wants to clap at his presence, but holds back for the moment.

"Jaewon," I call his name before I can help it. Even the simple act of saying his name sends chills wracking down my body.

Mayhem lifts his head, gracing me the arresting view of his jaw line. The shadow under his hat doesn't allow light to reach his eyes, but I can feel their intensity on me.

"Mayhem," he corrects me with a voice that is similar to liquid, if liquid sounds just as flawless. He is correcting me with brute humor.

"What are you doing here?" My voice reflects the intimidation I feel. The courage I have inside struggles to surface.

Mayhem studies my face. His tenor and tone clips. "I think you should ask yourself the very same question."

"What?" I don't know how else to respond to the crass question.

Mayhem's demeanor is cool and calm, emanating unbridled

composure. "You don't know what you are getting yourself into."

"You should leave," I tell him boldly. "Crist members are everywhere here. You won't stand a chance."

Mayhem lifts up the baseball hat. Light hits those dark eyes of his and I feel like disappearing neatly into the floor. "You have a lot to learn about our world May. Sangwoo's men won't touch me even if I strangle their Boss in his hospital bed."

"How can you be so cruel?" His motive for being here confuses me. I've always pegged him to be heartless, but Mayhem is turning out to be crueler than I imagined. "First, you send your men to kidnap me and demand the money a day ahead of the agreement we made. Now, you're here as though nothing happened and telling me I don't know what I am getting myself into. I don't know much about your world, but keeping your word is something that all organizations should adhere to am I correct?"

Mayhem's jaw locks together. He's not rattled by my complaints—a direct result from a severe heightened gang lord complex greater than Choi Sangwoo's. Without warning, Mayhem grabs the front my sweatshirt; he does so in such a sleek manner that he's barely touching me. Mayhem draws me to him and the distinct smell of his cologne permeates my nostrils. "I'm going to let you in on a little secret. In our world, we only keep our word as a personal favor. We never keep our word just because we gave it to you. Your cousin and her useless boyfriend will be happy to know that their debt's paid in full. And thanks to you, I was also able to take some blood from Choi Sangwoo too."

"Let me go." I reach up to pry his fingers off me. My heart thuds wildly behind my ribcage, but not for the obvious reason of provoking a gang lord past his composure. I'm shaking because of the emotions he induces. It's wrong to feel this way about this dangerous and violent man. How can someone from such a dark world be so alluring even when he is cold-blooded?

"I will be seeing you soon." Mayhem relinquishes his grip. His lips part as those dark eyes scan my face. He steps back from me, from my space, and leaves me feeling dejected.

Holy crap. What does he mean he will be seeing me soon? My intuition gives Mayhem a soft wave.

With a casual stride, Mayhem begins his journey down the hospital hallway. I am motionless as I watch his silent and deadly gait. Sangwoo's men stand guard. They stop pacing as Mayhem comes closer. Surprise and trepidation taint their facial expressions.

Ren hangs up his cell phone in the middle of the conversation. The tattoos on his face scrunch together.

"Mayhem," Ren addresses him. He squares his shoulders as though bracing for a fight. "What are you doing here?"

There is amusement in Mayhem's tone of voice. "You don't want to play this game with me, Ren. Step aside." As if he is reading Ren's mind, Mayhem adds in that signature liquid tone of his, "I am not about to kill your Boss with his men outside. There is still a code of conduct in our twisted world."

Ren appears as though he is about to die from the tough decision any second. In the end, he relents.

No! Panic sweeps me as I watch Ren step aside for Mayhem to come through. Even the rest of Sangwoo's gang seems intimidated by the rival gang lord to respond.

Mayhem touches Ren's right shoulder. "Good man. It is always a regret of mine that I didn't keep you close by my side."

Ren lowers his head and keeps silent.

The height of Mayhem's power ripples through everyone in the hallway. Even the nurses have ceased their conversation. We watch with bated breath as Mayhem saunters down the remaining length of the hallway and enters Sangwoo's hospital room.

I am gripping Sangwoo's glass of water and ice chips so tightly my hands start to sting from the cold. *What I would give to be a fly on the wall in Sangwoo's hospital room right now,* my intuition sighs. She's enamored with Mayhem and can't stop dreaming about their first date.

Minutes tick by. The hospital room remains silent. Sangwoo's men begin to show their anxiousness. Ren's facial expression is closed and tense. The air is palpable with strain.

Then, just as quickly as it started, the wait and tension dispels.

The door to the hospital room opens and Mayhem comes striding out. His dark eyes acknowledge the fact that we are like frozen statues. With one last glance at me, Mayhem retreats into the awaiting elevator. The steel doors depart to reveal that Mayhem didn't come alone. Six men are waiting inside for his departure. Seconds after Mayhem steps inside, the elevator doors whisk to a close.

Silence fills the doorway again.

Ren hurriedly enters Sangwoo's hospital room. A moment later, he returns relieved. "His water. Boss wants his water," Ren tells me.

What? I enter Sangwoo's hospital room with my heart in my throat. To my surprise, Sangwoo has his eyes closed. There are no traces of tension from Mayhem's visitation.

I settle Sangwoo's water on the table stand to his right. I turn to watch him sleep. Sangwoo doesn't have the most angelic sleeping face. For one, his forehead creases in an obscure manner and his lips lock tightly together. He looks better awake than unconscious, but he is still far from unattractive.

I walk quietly over to him and in my haste, trip over the wire of his IV tube. I land squarely across his chest and Sangwoo's eyes pop open.

"I'm so sorry!" My clumsiness stuns me. "Uh . . . I got your drink," I tell him quickly to make a hasty cover.

Sangwoo's in shock too. Our faces are inches apart. He can just lean in . . . . What am I thinking? *Snap out of it May. Ew!* My intuition makes a face.

"May, can I . . . ask you something?" Sangwoo murmurs.

I nod. Is he going to ask what I think he's going to ask? Where did this growth spurt of feelings come from? Am I really moved that he saved my life? "Anything."

"Can you . . . get off my arm? I think you killed my circulation." Sangwoo lets out a groan.

"Oh god! I'm so sorry!" I quickly remove myself from his body.

Sangwoo laughs with good humor. The blood rushes to my cheeks again. "I see that you're fine now. I have to get going before Eunhye calls the Swat team to come looking for me." I run a nervous hand through my hair.

Sangwoo clears his throat and he's back to his gang leader mannerisms. "I'll have Ren take you home."

I frown. "I can take the bus. I don't want to bother him."

An unforgiving look marks Sangwoo's face. "He will take you home. It's not a bother. I am not going to take any more chances of you slipping through my fingers like last night."

Whoa. Possessive much? "I don't owe anyone else money." I try to make light of the situation.

Sangwoo doesn't find my comment amusing. Slowly, he sits up and starts to take the wires out of his left arm.

"What are you doing?" I reach out to stop him. He's truly similar to an errant adolescent who chooses drastic measures to obtain what he wants. My touch causes Sangwoo to freeze. "Why are you taking them off?"

"If you don't want Ren to take you home, I will," is Sangwoo's stubborn justification.

"Don't be foolish." I take my hand back from him. So this is the passive-aggressive trek Sangwoo wants to cross with me. "Fine. Ren can take me home."

Sangwoo lies back on the hospital bed. I hand him his cup of water. Sangwoo thanks me with a boyish grin. For the first time since I have met him, Sangwoo looks youthful and mischievous after getting his way.

Taking advantage of his good humor, I attempt to satisfy my curiosity. "What did Jaewon want?" The question is casual, but the ominous feeling plagues me.

"Oh? Since when does he let you call him by his name?" Sangwoo takes a large gulp of the water.

"He wasn't too pleased with that," I admit.

"No one's allowed to call him by his real name." Sangwoo finishes his water and sets the cup at the edge of the hospital bed.

I give him a speculative look, waiting for the answer.

Sangwoo finally divulges a piece of the puzzle with, "Let's just put it this way, Mayhem and I go way back. Our histories are heavily intertwined. As much as we want to get rid of one another, we are entangled in a paradox. He can't live with me, and I can't live without him. But the rivalry and competition is real. There may come one day when one of us has to die at the hand of the other, but we are stuck in an infinite loop for now."

My breath steals away with Sangwoo's account of his relationship with Mayhem. For a moment, Sangwoo is lost in a trance. He breaks out of it quickly. "Were you afraid when Danny attacked you?"

"Yes," I answer softly. My eyebrows come together at the memory. "Why couldn't he wait until Saturday for the money?"

Sangwoo stares at me with an indescribable facial expression. His brown eyes are soft and caring, gentle and sensitive. But there is something much more. "Danny has always been the black sheep, even in this world. As a child, he had many socio-emotional problems. Mayhem is the only gang lord he listens to. Even so, sometimes Danny loses his way. Last night was the perfect example."

"So did Mayhem come here to apologize on his behalf?" I have an impending desire to know the truth.

"No," Sangwoo answers clearly. The look in his eyes tells me that Sangwoo is not going to disclose any more information about their meeting. I have one more stipulation to add to the initiation contract." Sangwoo changing the subject of the conversation is an indication that the topic of Mayhem is over.

"Oh?" *Sheesh. He's really not going to let you live it down*, my intuition grumbles.

"Since you will be released from The Trax soon, I think it would be best for you to quit Sansachun too. I need you to work full time with me when you start." Sangwoo lays the ground rules. He gauges my facial expression carefully. "Will that be a problem?"

I don't want to push Sangwoo any further. Besides, quitting the minimum wage job is not something I will fight with him about. "Ok."

"I'll call you." Sangwoo's tone is firm. He's surprised that I am not putting up a fight about keeping my first job.

"I hope you get better soon." I reach for Sangwoo's hand. My gratitude causes Sangwoo to freeze. "Thank you." It is the right thing to do in order to show my appreciation.

The smile doesn't touch his brown eyes. "Ren will take you home." Sangwoo's hands are cold and unresponsive.

NO MATTER HOW HARD I want to put it into words, I cannot describe why I'm drawn Choi Sangwoo. In many cases, girls go through phases of being head-over-heels for bad boys, but this bad boy is different. This bad boy is a lonely, complicated, and mysterious gang leader. In most of the stories I have read, my literary heroines meet their significant other through friends and family with the occasional landmark exceptions such as at school, work, and a romantic public place like the library. Usually, the situation introduces people. In my particular case, the circumstances introduced me to Sangwoo's world.

My relationship with Sangwoo is far from a love story or something like good-girl-falls-for-bad-boy. It's rather complicated about how I feel about him and the entire situation. Sangwoo wants me by his side, but the reasons dance on the fine line of business and romance.

I resign to this fate and I bury the nagging feelings that I've met Sangwoo before in a box at the base of my heart. I don't know how to feel that he almost died for me. Is this normal in the underground world? People get shot, recover, and make feigned amends with their enemies? I have a lot to learn if this normal protocol. Moreover, the relationship between Sangwoo and Mayhem is intricately complex. From the way Sangwoo described it, it's the type of relationship where one cannot live without the other despite the rivalry. There must be more pieces to the puzzle, but Sangwoo is not going to give up any details soon.

These are the thoughts that encircle me during the car ride home.

Ren ends up taking me home, even though I tell him I am fine with taking the bus. He gives me the same offended look Sangwoo does. Unlike Sangwoo, however, Ren has more faith in my ability to walk to my apartment. I thank him graciously before I leave the car. Ren returns my goodbye with a simple nod. He's lost in thought about the current events. I don't blame him. In fact, I'm thankful for the silent car ride. I had time to absorb the chaos and control the emotions it riled up inside me.

When I let myself in my apartment, I find a note on the back of the door. Eunhye's neat handwriting lets me know that she is doing a forty-eight hour shift at the hospital. This means that my mother has no idea I have been gone for the past twenty-four hours. Part of me feels fortunate that Eunhye's not here to see me in this state, but the other rational part misses my mother. I'm grounded by the innocence and simplicity that Eunhye represents. I quickly call Eunhye and leave her a message.

Then, I return the missed calls from Lina. My cousin answers on the second ring.

"Where have you been?" Her voice is worried and stressed. "I got a call from one of Mayhem's guys saying that our debt is paid off. I thought it wasn't until Saturday."

I debate clearly whether I should tell Lina what happened, but I figure telling her in person is better. "Choi Sangwoo was able to take care of it." *By nearly having his arm shot off.* My thoughts travel back to my confrontation with Mayhem at the hospital; he could have cared less about upholding the Saturday agreement. I had high hopes for Mayhem to be reasonable, but instead he supported Danny's arbitrary approach to collecting the loan.

"Really?" Surprise resonates in Lina's voice. She brings me out of my musings again. "That's so crazy May. It makes sense now. Spyder been blowing up my phone. I don't know if he knows that our debt's clear. But I'm at the point where I don't even want to talk to him about it. Let him brew over it."

I am quiet as I listen to Lina's rapid voice. Slightly dizzy from everything that has happened, I slowly melt into a mindless puddle.

"Is something wrong?" Lina's attune to my silence.

"No. I'm just really tired," I confess to my cousin. "I don't think I can work at Sansachun anymore. Sangwoo wants me to start working for him full time."

"Is that a condition of the contract?"

"Something like that. I'll tell you more in person."

"I see." Lina's voice is soft and understanding. She's still reeling from the news that her thirty thousand debt has been cleared overnight. "Are you stopping by to tell Mr. Chun soon?"

"I think I'll just call him. I'm actually scared of confrontation with him," I confess as Mr. Chun's angry face comes into my mind's eye. "I have to make up an excuse or something."

"I have your back," Lina offers eagerly. She wants to help me as much as she can. "I'll add a word in that you're busy with a family issue. Which is true."

"Thanks cousin."

"No. I should be the one thanking you."

"Lina," I start to say, but hesitate.

"What is it May?" She holds her breath.

"Nothing," I mumble. I blow out a batch of fresh air. There's no point in starting the spiel now. "I have to go, Lina. I'll talk to you later, okay?"

"That's fine. Bye May. Thank you."

"Bye."

I hang up the phone. A deep feeling of dread comes over me. I am exhausted. A warm shower, some hot food, and sleep sound heavenly.

HER DARK EYES HAVE ME in a hold. I am the prey locked in the gaze of the predator. She opens her mouth to speak. There's disdain in her voice and body language. The dark halo that forms around her angelic face twists and turns like snakes. There is horror in my voice, but I cannot make a sound. She comes closer, reaching out for me . . . . The memories and the pain intensify. "No!" It finally escapes my lips. "May!" she hisses my name before the cloud of smoke and kaleidoscope of colors consume her. "Misun," is my choked sob.

MY ALARM GOES OFF IN a rhythmic pattern. Another nightmare. It's the fourth nightmare since the shooting and hospital incident. My heart is racing. The sweat clings without mercy to my pores. I turn in bed and stretch, kicking off my warm bed cover. My body aches, especially my arm. I feel a hundred pounds heavier and an impending headache unfolds on the right side of my head. One glance at my alarm clock and I realize I have slept late into the evening.

Today is my last day at The Trax. It is finally time to face the reality of a chapter ending. The vague memory of calling Mr. Chun to let him know I can no longer work sweeps into my mind like a fan. He was less than happy with me, but Lina's assistance in helping me lie lessened the blow.

It's been exactly two days since my kidnapping incident, and approximately forty-eight hours since I last saw Choi Sangwoo. He's been sending me short text messages, asking how I am doing, but other than that, he's made no plans to see me. Even through the phone, it's apparent that Choi Sangwoo is too busy for the girl he took a bullet for. But I am fortunate enough to avoid the initiation contract for now. Nonetheless, I know better. For someone like Choi Sangwoo, his silence is much like the calm before the storm.

I drag myself out bed and head to the kitchen for a drink of water. On my way, I realize Eunhye is home. The door to her bedroom is ajar and I can see my exhausted mother underneath her bed covers.

"Mom," I whisper by the door. "Hi."

"May." Eunhye struggles with sleepy eyes. "Are you going to work?"

"Yes. Last day."

"Call me when you get off work tonight."

"I will. Go back to sleep."

"Bye honey."

I close her bedroom door quietly and continue my journey to the kitchen. Even the simple act of pouring myself a cup of water causes my muscles to ache. I have to fight through the fatigue and headache. I rally my last drop of energy and get ready for work. It is the last day at The Trax, so uniforms are unnecessary. I dress in casual black jeans and a long-sleeved black shirt. I study myself in the mirror and realize how much I've changed in the last three weeks. The girl staring back at me is thin, gaunt, and dressing like the gangsters around her now–black-on-black.

I think about wearing something brighter to lift up the mood, but I am already five minutes behind the usual bus schedule when I leave the apartment. As I turn down the last step of the apartment complex, I stop abruptly. *What is he doing here?* My conscience cannot contain herself.

Ren stands five feet away from me against an illegally parked car. He waves to me with a weary smile when we make eye contact. How long has he been waiting for me?

"Hi," Ren greets me when I reach him. The tattoos on his face are stark in the evening light.

"Hi," I answer warily. I notice the gray, unmarked sedan he is leaning on. "What's going on?" Maybe Ren's here to tell me news about Sangwoo.

"I've been assigned to be your security." Ren dispels my worries about Sangwoo and transitions me to the next concern.

"Oh no." I shake my head at his revelation. I don't need a babysitter. "I'm fine. I don't need security."

Ren looks crestfallen. At the same moment his phone rings. A look of relief comes across his face when he sees who it is. "Boss. Yes. I am outside right now. Yes." Ren hands me the phone. "He wants to speak with you."

How apt of Choi Sangwoo to be readily available on the other side of the phone line. "Hello?" I take Ren's phone.

"May." Sangwoo's signature voice is smooth over the phone line. "I've assigned Ren to watch over you. I had a feeling you were going to go to work tonight."

I glance at Ren, who is waiting with bated breath. "Sangwoo, I don't need security. I'll be fine. It's my last day at The Trax anyway."

"You are fearless, aren't you? A rival gang member kidnaps you and nearly takes your life, yet you go on as though nothing's happened." Sangwoo takes the liberty of recapping the past forty-eight hours.

"What am I supposed to do?" The words escape in a whisper. "I have to go on with my life." Their debt has been paid in full and some more.

"You need security. I will explain to you later. It will do my conscience a great deal if you'd just let Ren take you to work. If you are going to sign on to be an employee of mine, this is one of the constituents. I will see you after work. Have a good last day." Sangwoo hangs up the phone promptly, leaving me hanging.

I pull the phone away from my ears and stare at it. *Who does he think he is to give me instructions?* My intuition sashays back into the picture; she's had enough rest. Granted Sangwoo is my future Boss, this still crosses the invisible boundaries of individual freedom. I didn't even get to ask Sangwoo about his arm and if he's discharged from the hospital. I suppose I will just have to wait until I see him. Again, even the details of that possibility are vague. I never know when these gang lords are coming or going.

"Here's your phone." I hand Ren back his mode of communication. It's not Ren's fault that I am all flustered now. The thought of thirty thousand dollars and Sangwoo getting shot for me crosses my mind. *Shit.* I really can't fight him on this.

"Do you know the way to The Trax?" I ask Ren tentatively. The kinks are working in my mind. How do I retain my independence while trying to balance a gang leader's desire to control every aspect of my life?

"I am instructed to take you wherever you wish to go," Ren responds with a passive tone. The tattoos on his face remind me that his call of duty is beyond chauffeur, so I should be treating him with care. I cannot see myself getting used to Ren driving me around.

"Ok." I awkwardly stand back to let Run lead the way to the gray car.

Ren opens the back car door for me. Already, he is establishing a hierarchy. I don't want to fight him on it. I know now that it is not my place too. Besides, it would be awkward sitting next to Ren. What kind of conversation can I possibly have with a gang leader's right-hand man? I settle in the back seat while Ren starts up the car. Ren switches on the radio and the world news blasts the silence away. Perhaps he's feeling the same awkwardness and wants to ease it. Regardless of the reason, I am grateful for Ren's tact. I am able to disappear into my thoughts about Choi Sangwoo.

I conclude that Sangwoo haunts me in a very myriad, complex way. I suppose this is the tricky part of a new relationship attempting to establish itself. In essence, Sangwoo's exact intentions with me are debatable. He is out thirty thousand dollars and a pint of pride. Yet, Choi Sangwoo is willing to shower me with his security and employment offer. I don't know if I should be afraid of his ulterior motive or his friendship. What does he want with me? *That's the million dollar question,* my conscience mumbles in a whisper.

Sangwoo doesn't want a relationship with me. We have established that in a vague manner. Sure, the hint of attraction exists, but the topic of conversation keeps coming back to that damn initiation contract. It doesn't make sense that Sangwoo truly thinks I'm gangster material. *He just wants you by his side.* My conscience kicks in again. *Don't forget Dead Girl May.* Damn it all.

"We're here," Ren announces, pulling me away from my dark thoughts. His tone is clear and precise, raining over the voices of the radio. Reality drowns out my conscience.

The familiar streets that lead to The Trax unfold. Just two days ago, I was kidnapped here. The morbid memory is like a sour thought. Now, I return like royalty with my personal armor and guard.

"Are you going to wait here?" I ask Ren with a guarded tone. He doesn't need to guess that I am having second thoughts about returning to The Trax.

"Yes," Ren answers with an air of discretion.

"I don't get off work until twelve." It's only polite that I let him know the wait time.

"I will wait." Ren inclines his head in a manner that lets me know I have no idea how patient he can be.

I remove my seat belt and leave the car feeling, for the first time, an ominous and nail-biting sensation. I know I am slightly crazy and neurotic to return to The Trax days after my kidnapping incident. For all I know, Mayhem's gang members are lurking in the shadows waiting for a second strike. Perhaps Choi Sangwoo does have a point about my sanity. What's more alarming is no one at The Trax knows of the incident. Since the closing announcement, the venue's security cameras have remained disabled. I argue with myself that because it is my last day of work, I have every right to be here. Besides, Mayhem has the money. There is no need for him or his minions to come after me anymore. The pillow of thought gives me comfort and courage to go to work.

"I'll see you later," I tell Ren as he gives me an inexplicable look. He inclines his head towards me again, and I know Ren's surprised I am not kicking and screaming about this ordeal. Little does he know I plan to give his Boss a piece of my mind later.

I turn to The Trax, committing the steps and walkway to memory. This will probably be the last time I cross this distinctive threshold again. I make my way through the doors to find the skeleton of a once lively and cluttered venue. The walls are stripped bare to its bleak wooden tones. A vast, open area is cold and empty where muddles of tables and booths once were. Even the lights above are dim and forgetful. Only footsteps and soft conversations circle the desolate venue.

It takes me all but three seconds to see Son. He is in the opposite corner of the room chatting with Naili. Son's intense eyes follow Naili's rapid lips. As usual, Naili adorns her distinctive dress and demeanor. She waves her arms in the air, stringing invisible words and exaggerated examples. Naili stops abruptly when she catches my eyes. Son follows her gaze with dull eyes that become bright and attentive.

Oh no. I hope he didn't recognize me at his cousin's funeral.

I steady my pace as I walk awkwardly to them. From my peripheral view, I can see Joolie, Tailor, and some of the other co-workers working on the massive bar. Sans alcohol and other additions to the bar, the entire l-shaped island is now bleak and uninhabited. It appears as though Joolie and Tailor are in charge of breaking down the furnishing.

"May," Naili's drawl of my name brings me back to reality. Her eyes are twinkling with earnest as though she has a secret she can't wait to share with me.

"Hello," I greet her courteously. Behind her, Tailor makes eye contact with me. He waves while Joolie rolls her eyes in exasperation at Naili's back. I do my best to suppress the smile that threatens my lips.

"I'm going to need you to compile some more data today." Naili inclines her head forward, occupying my vision. This time around, unlike the fervent stares she usually shoots at me, her eyes are soft. I wonder if Naili knows about my recent kidnapping. There's no trace of information behind her black eyes.

"Sure." I am highly suspicious of this data-compiling quest she has going on, but there's nothing underground in the paperwork.

"Son will help you with the organizational process today. We want every document compiled into a binder and labeled," Naili continues to instruct me. "Also, the new owner will be here later in the week to hand out severance checks."

The thought hits me with interest. I will finally get to see who the new owner of The Trax is. I attempt to hide my curiosity.

"Naili, phone call." One of her people, an older man wearing a complete dark blue three-piece suit, steps out of the hallway. He holds out a black cell phone for her to take.

"Excuse me." Naili quickly excuses herself. She hurries to the man, takes the phone, and disappears out of sight.

Son and I are now alone. "Hey." I offer him a smile to reduce the awkwardness. I want to make small talk to distract any thoughts or notions, but Son doesn't give me much.

"Hey," is Son's remark. His eyes are still too bright and attentive. "How are you?"

"I'm good." *Shit.* Does he know something? Inadvertently, I bite my lower lip to stop the anxiety from reaching my face.

"Let's get to work." Son takes on his assistant manager persona and produces a nonchalant gait down the hallway.

I feel my stomach drop as I follow him.

We make our way to the meeting room where the laptop is next to three piles of paperwork. I take my usual seat in front of the laptop while Son opts for the seat to my right. I glance quickly at the pile of paperwork to my right and it's mostly computation data. More specifically, the data reflect the most recent revenue. I roll up my shirtsleeves and get to work. I am desperate to dive in and reduce the invisible tension in the room. Son follows my lead and does the same. While I calculate and compute, Son organizes the physical evidence comprised of receipts ranging from checks to photocopies of other payment types.

"I feel like I haven't seen you in a while." Son makes the first casual attempt at a conversation.

"I think it's been about a week." I am careful with my choice of words. I am grateful for the light and casual conversation.

"I missed work last week because of my cousin's funeral." Son doesn't miss a beat. His fingers flip through the pile of paperwork indiscriminately, but the emotions that radiate from him are palpable.

I pretend to be having trouble with the excel spread on the computer, mumbling a few, "What is going on with this?" and "This doesn't make sense," and finally, "I'm sorry about your cousin Son."

I can feel the power of his stare at my profile, but Son buys my nonchalant response. "It was a quiet gathering," he tells me softly. Son's fingers flick through the paperwork at a rapid pace. "We're all heartbroken. It was supposed to be a day for family until he ruined it."

I am in the middle of organizing the spreadsheets by numerical order when I hesitate. The better part of me asks Son, "Who ruined it?" My voice is coarse and airy, giving away too much. But I am a victim to Son's despair at this point.

Son holds the stack of paperwork in his hands with a sign of defeat on his face. "The gang Boss. He was there. He infiltrated our most private moment. Of course, like the coward he is, he ran away when we spotted him."

I wait with bated breath for Son to mention the Boss's female counterpart that day, but he doesn't. Instead, Son has a faraway look on his face. I can see the sorrow in his eyes and the anger in his heart.

"How did your cousin die, Son?" I ask with apprehension. The sentence is a string of whispers.

Son lowers his head. He releases the stack of paper in his hands. "I told you, the gang leader ordered his death."

"Because of what?" I feel terrible for pushing the topic further, but the need to know overpowers my better judgment. I want to know even though Choi Sangwoo said he'd rather the family believed it was his fault than have them know the truth.

Son looks up at me. The dark, defensive bar crosses the light in his eyes. "Does it matter? My cousin is dead. The gang leader could have protected him, but he chose to turn his back on him. The gang leader regarded my cousin as another expendable ant in his pathetic army. Then, he had the audacity to show up at my cousin's funeral as if he was mourning. He was wearing dark sunglasses. I never got a chance to see his face."

I can feel the anger and spite rising in Son's throat. The mix of hate and trepidation spills onto the table and over our paperwork.

"I'm sorry," is all I can say. I don't know how else to express my sentiments without angering Son. I know it is not my place to give any opinion, but I can't help myself. Son doesn't know the truth of the matter any more than I do. I want to tell Son that he's not the only one in the dark.

"He brought someone with him too." Son looks up at me, bombarding me with the information. The anger doesn't subside in his eyes. "He didn't bring his entourage. He brought a woman instead. He was trying to soften the blow. That manipulative bastard."

I focus on the set of documents in front of me, but my stomach's having trouble keeping all this information down. I can feel the intense emotions boiling inside of me. The look in Son's eyes tells me he doesn't suspect it was me, but the tone of his voice is accusing.

"I would like all of these to be exported by the end of today." Naili is at the meeting room's threshold; she successfully sneaked up on us. Naili's eyes are murky as she gazes at Son. Naili holds another stack of paperwork in her hands as she moves into the room. Naili throws the paperwork on the table; it lands in front of Son. The soft gust of wind reminds us of our workload.

The intense vibe of employer and employee ripples between the two of them. I can feel my scalp prickling from the anticipation of what is going on. If she had overheard the conversation, Naili doesn't show it. Instead, Naili lowers her gaze from Son and shoots it over to me. "Today is your last day. Make it count please." Naili's lips press in a hard line as she reminds us.

Son and I remain silent. Without another word, Naili exits the meeting room.

"There is something underground about that woman too," Son snarls. The look of disapproval taints his facial expression. He gives me an apologetic look, surprising me with his regret. "Sorry May. I didn't mean to start talking about my cousin's funeral. I just feel like out of everyone here at work, you understand me the most."

Son's confession colors me with astonishment. "Really?" This is the last thing I expect Son to communicate to me. He was one sentence away from accusing me with fraternizing with the enemy. Now, he says I'm the only person he can vent to here.

I give Son a weary smile. "I understand Son."

He gives me a subtle acknowledgment in return.

"Do you have a job lined up after?" I change the subject, hoping for an ounce of subtlety.

Son shrugs, grateful for the change of subject as well. "My family owns a store in Busan. They would like me to help, so I might be packing my bags and heading there by the end of the week."

This is news to me. Son has been morbidly private about his family, especially their affluence. In fact, I don't know much about Son in the first place. But maybe a change of pace and environment is good for him. "What about you? Anything lined up?" Son turns the table on me.

I pause shortly from the laptop. "I'm still working my first job," I lie to Son, feeling my face changing different shades of embarrassment. "I'll find something else hopefully." Choi Sangwoo's face parades across my thoughts.

"I'm sure you will May. It's weird seeing this place crumble within a week," Son mumbles in response. "There's some powerful money behind all this."

"You think?" I ask him with renewed interest.

Son shrugs again. This time his tone is guarded and he glances at the door to make sure Naili's not standing there. "The new owner must have black money on his hands. An obscene of black money. He's making Naili pack everything up in a week *and* giving him all the data about this place. We all know The Trax was doing well. We were gaining momentum. I talk to Naili at least once a day when she calls, but I never saw this coming."

"You didn't know The Trax was going to close?" I join Son in his whispering.

"I found out the same day as everyone else," Son hisses back. "Now, who would have the kind of money that sends people packing in a week?"

The answer is on the tip of my tongue, but I refuse to admit to it. Son has a point. Who has the kind of money to buy this place and reinvent it all within a matter of weeks? Son and I both understand that there is a powerful gang involved. I don't know why it never crossed my mind before. Mayhem and Crist are not the only two gangs in this country. Perhaps there are more, and I have only met the tips of the iceberg. Choi Sangwoo did mention he has a Boss above him. I shudder to think just how deep this underground world is.

"I just hope the severance check will be worth it." Son grounds me back to reality from my reverie. "If I'm coming back to pick up a check, it better be worth it."

"How much do you think it is?" I am curious about this new owner's affordability.

"Rumor has it the checks will be five digit numbers." Son's eyes twinkle with dollar signs. He's clearly holding out on the rest of us.

"What?" Hope blooms in my heart. Suddenly, my thoughts race off to the finish lines. *More college money!* My conscience claps.

No. Use it to pay Sangwoo back and be free of his damn initiation contract, my intuition snarls. That's right. Maybe with the severance check, I can put it towards paying Choi Sangwoo back. Maybe he will take it and I don't have to sign any initiation contract. Why haven't I thought about it before? Sangwoo's more reasonable than Mayhem and will be lenient with the money deadline. The only reason why I agree to the initiation contract is to pay Sangwoo back thirty thousand dollars through labor. But what if I can bypass the contract and the labor by simply paying Sangwoo back thirty thousand on a payment plan? I am sure I can work something out with him.

Bingo! My *intuition carries out an early victory dance.*

"You find the severance check funny?" Son leans closer to grapple with the ridiculous expression on my face.

Little does Son know, I am having an epiphany. "You're a genius Son. You know that?"

Son gives me a look that lets me know I am foolish, but joins me with a smile. Absentmindedly, Son passes me the next piece of paper and we bury ourselves in work. The tried tension between us slowly recedes into the air.

"WE SHOULD GO TO FOX."

Six hours, thirty minutes, and ten seconds later Son, Tailor, Joolie, and I stand five feet away from the closed doors of The Trax in a quandary. We are deciding where to go to celebrate our last night as co-workers. Tailor and Joolie vote for Fox, a relatively unknown bar just a block from The Trax. Son and I are too exhausted from our data compiling to veto the decision.

"I'll buy everyone the first round," Tailor offers first. His eyes are excited and brimming with the thought of drinking tonight. For once, he will not be the bartender responsible for everyone's intoxicated state-of-mind.

"You should buy every round," Joolie jokes with Tailor. "Bet you're excited to be on the other side of the bar instead of always serving people." She slips her arms around Tailor and motions for us to follow them. Joolie has grown not only closer, but also fonder of Tailor this past week. Perhaps all that time working together has solidified Tailor and Joolie's otherwise murky relationship.

Son gives me a small nudge to tell me he thinks the same. I return his look with a grin. Together, we set off after Joolie and Tailor who are holding onto one another tightly. We leave the comforts and the confines of The Trax. We do not want to linger around it any longer. Everyone else has already left for the night. Some of the other co-workers opted to leave for the comforts of their homes while others are too upset to celebrate. Our immediate group is left to tend to ourselves. Tailor and Joolie are not particularly upset at the way it's working out. Son and I, on the other hand, have too many heavy thoughts on our minds to work at it.

As I walk in the shadows of the looming buildings with my co-workers, I am hyper aware of Ren. I expect to see him lurking in the shadows, stalking me, but there is no sign of him. Although I look for the distinctive gray car, I know Ren probably has a different vehicle by now. By the time we enter Fox, I am entirely convinced that Ren is gone.

Fox is a nifty little sports bar westernized in the true sense. The walls are complete with a kaleidoscope of banners and ribbons of sport memorabilia. It is crowded and deafening tonight. A sports game is on and the entire bar is packed with fans wearing their favorite colors. Tailor leads the way through the throng of people. He acknowledges one of the bartenders and skips the line.

"Let Tailor work his magic." Joolie is giggling already. She hooks an arm around my neck. "I'm going to miss working with you Maybelline."

I don't know where the burst of emotions comes from, but I go along with it. Joolie appears to be in a happy and celebratory mood.

"Please don't say my full name," I joke with good humor.

"It's beautiful. Maybelline."

"What about me?" Son chimes in. "You're going to miss me Joolie?"

Joolie extends her arm and brings Son under her hold. "You too control freak!"

"Hey!" Son makes a playful jab at her.

"Drinks first. Hugs later!" Tailor returns with four shot glasses. The pristine liquid dances under the lighting of the bar. "Patron." Tailor hands each of us a shot glass, including a slightly larger glass filled with a chaser.

I make a face. I am not much of a drinker, but for the cause of tonight, I hold my shot glass in my right hand and my Sprite chaser in the other.

"Fuck The Trax!" Joolie suggests the toast.

Tailor bursts out laughing while Son and I exchange amused, incredulous looks.

"Fuck The Trax!" I find myself joining my co-workers. We shove our glasses together and toss the liquids to the back of our throats. I swallow the Sprite chaser as soon as the Patron shot goes down.

Suddenly, I am alive. The sharp shooting sensation of the alcohol brings me to life. My blood is hot in a matter of seconds and my head is light in a matter of minutes. I am a lightweight. Son and Joolie laugh at the facial expression I make.

"Come on, May. It was just one." Joolie points to the colors dancing on my cheeks.

"All it takes is one," I complain to her.

"Come on." Tailor leads the way through the crowded bar towards a table. Fortunately, the people there are leaving. Joolie plops down into a chair, laughing loudly. Tailor touches her cheeks while Son swats at his hand. I have never seen my co-workers so relaxed and carefree. I feel a stab of guilt that I never took the time to hang out with them often.

I take the seat next to Joolie. As my co-workers launch into conversation, I scan the bar quickly, feeling watched, but realize quickly the alcohol contributes to my paranoia. I check my phone as Son orders another round of shots. Joolie wants Patron while Son argues Grey Goose will do the trick. I do my best to block out their bickering and see that I have one missed call from Choi Sangwoo and another one from an unknown number. I stow my phone back in my pockets. I don't want to see Choi Sangwoo tonight; I make up my mind. The mixed thoughts and feelings I have towards him are starting to show their confused and ugly heads–especially under the influence of alcohol. I need time away from him, away from his power and influence.

Son ends up buying us Grey Goose for the second round. Before I know it, we are reminiscing about ex-customers by the fourth round.

"Number Nine girl. I can't believe after all this time, we never got her name!" Tailor finishes his fourth shot of Grey Goose and wears the Asian Flush on his cheeks with pride.

Son is a giggling mess as he adds, "I told you she's a hard egg to crack." He runs his hand through his messy air.

"Oh boys." Joolie shakes her head at them. "Who was your most memorable customer?" Joolie urges me when she notices my silence.

Choi Sangwoo's name flashes in my mind. Of course he's turning out to be more than just a memorable customer, but I bite down on my tongue. "I don't think I have one. If anything, it is Number Nine girl too."

I am on my third glass of water in hopes of diluting all the alcohol before I throw up.

"Aww, you're no fun. I think for me it was that night when that gangster guy was throwing up at our bar." Joolie makes a face at the memory. "Super-Gorgeous-Sexy is my name for him!"

"You weren't even there." Tailor unknowingly makes the situation lighter for Son, who freezes at the verbal mentioning of Choi Sangwoo. It's Tailor's jealousy talking too.

"I was there when he first came in! Table Twelve, I still remember. What a good-looking son-of-a-bitch." Joolie licks her lips as though she is reliving a fond memory.

The last thing I want to do right now is talk about Choi Sangwoo. It is completely uncharacteristic of me, but I am on my feet and shouting, "Who's ready for round five?!"

"Yes!" Tailor shouts while Joolie and Son groan.

BY THE END OF THE night, Joolie is outside of Fox vomiting stylishly in the bushes. Tailor has her hair in his hands, fighting off the bouncers who are telling us to leave. They are stereotypical in black ensembles complete with leather gloves and trench coats.

"I'm going to take her home," Tailor is telling the shorter bouncer.

"I'm taking both of them home," Son corrects him. "Sorry man."

"We'll be fine. I can handle my alcohol. Bartender, remember?" Tailor makes his point. "You need a ride home May?"

I scan the street. Alcohol is coursing through my system, but I feel sobriety returning to my head. The cool summer weather, along with Joolie's vomit, is setting the picture straight for me.

"No. I'm having someone pick me up," I lie. I want to be by myself for a moment. I need time to think and let things settle. Alcohol makes me antisocial for all the wrong reasons.

Son eyes me warily. His eyes twinkle as though he is about to say otherwise, but decides against it. "Ok. We'll see you next week at the severance check party," he jokes instead.

"Ok." I turn to Joolie who is borderline unconscious. "I'll see you next week Joolie."

She lifts up a hand to wave to me. The bouncers are making a face at her. Joolie gives them the middle finger. Son lowers her hand and makes a motion to apologize to the now irate bouncers on her behalf.

Tailor gives me a sheepish smile while he wraps Joolie's arm around his neck. "You sure you don't want a ride?"

I shake my head. "I'll be fine Tailor."

Son gives me a tentative smile. "Alright. Bye May."

"Bye."

"Get home safe."

"Have a good night."

I step back to watch my co-workers head down the opposite side of the road. The bouncers eye me with anticipation. *Don't worry, I'm not going back inside the bar.* My conscience sticks her tongue out at them.

I expect a peaceful bus ride home, but before I take another step, my name ricochets off the empty street. The shrill echo sends the back of my neck prickling. I stuff my hands inside my sweatshirt and pick up my feet.

"May!" I recognize his voice before I even see him. "May, honey!"

Everyone on the street, including the few who are lingering outside of Fox focus their attention on me. I freeze and turn to see that Bryan is running towards me. A large, permanent grin plasters on his face. Two figures follow closely behind him.

"May, baby." Bryan wraps an arm around my shoulders, forcing me into a hug. I imagine him with a leash around his neck, eager and loyal like a canine. But if I had a collar for him, I would tie him around the tree and leave him there for the next sucker. Alcohol is really a truth serum. *Leave him alone, he's adorable.* My conscience and her soft spot for Bryan intervene every time.

"What are you doing here May?" Bryan glances at Fox with an anxious expression. "You don't go to these places." Behind him, two of his friends grin at me. I have met them before–Dumb and Dumber.

"I don't. I went out with my co-workers." I don't know why I am entertaining Bryan with the reason. "What are you doing here?" Curiosity strikes my better judgment.

Bryan looks for my co-workers. A smile crosses his lips as though he can see my imaginary colleagues. "Just got some drinks with my friends." He nods to the two other goons, making a point that they are real. Bryan grins sheepishly at me. His fabricated crush on me gets under my skin in a very strange way.

"Good for you Bryan. Bye. Have a good night." Of all the people I can run into, it has to be him. *And I don't even know that many people. It's bad luck through and through lately.* I turn towards the bus stop.

"Wait. Where are you going?" Bryan follows me eagerly. "Bye guys. I'll talk to you tomorrow." He waves to his friends who gape at his audacity to ditch them.

"Bryan!" Dumb and Dumber shout after him, but Bryan makes a gesture for them to hastily retreat.

"I have to meet my boyfriend." The alcohol gives me courage. I pick up my pace and continue my fervent gait down the street. Thoughts of regret bombard me. I should have gone home with Son and them.

"Wha-what?" Bryan lips tremble. He stops walking, causing me to slow my pace too. Bryan's eyes meet at the bridge of his nose.

Choi Sangwoo and I are far from being girlfriend and boyfriend, but the words slip out of my mouth before I can myself. Although I say it to discourage Bryan, I can't help but feel that the declaration brings with it the same power that makes people cower when I tell them I am associated with Crist.

"I'm going to meet my boyfriend Bryan." I try the words out again, feeling a sense of empowerment and liberation with it.

"I don't believe it! You don't have a boyfriend May!" Bryan counters me. He grabs onto my arm with a hasty motion. The reaction is more intense than I expect.

"Let go of my arm Bryan! What are you doing you freak?" He is crossing the invisible boundaries I draw for him.

Bryan is really starting to tick me off. He is just a little high school boy, flirting with me harmlessly, so why is he getting all worked up?

"Bryan! Stop!"

"I want to meet your boyfriend."

We are too engrossed in our bickering to realize we have reached the end of the main street. The layout makes way for a labyrinth of alleys. Bryan is still in my ear, yapping away as we round the corner of the side street. This street is infamous as a dead end because major roads, streets, and pedestrian access are restricted. The only way out is in.

Shadowy figures are ahead of us. They tower and loom over one figure in particular. The conversations are varied and incoherent, but there is one command that stands out.

"Get up."

I grab Bryan's hand quickly and drag him behind the wall of the last turn. Bryan and I take our places behind the wall to peek out.

There are four men standing in the middle of the deserted alley. To the right of them, leaning listlessly against the gray brick wall, is a woman with blackened eyes, reddened lips, and trodden facial features. Her eyes turn down, staring at the male lying in a crumpled heap next to her towering heels. The male, completely unidentifiable in the darkness, is too unconscious to know that his misery is their triumph.

"Get up." The more dominant figure of the four steps forward. He extends the heel of his right boot towards his victim's head. When his victim doesn't respond, the man looks at the expecting woman. From the depths of his breast jacket, the man extracts an envelope to transfer to the woman.

The dim light from the main street makes his distinctive gait and demeanor all the more recognizable. The chill starts from the back of my neck and spreads down my neck.

Ren. Sangwoo's Ren. Sangwoo's gang. *So this is where he's been! He stopped following me to beat someone up.* My intuition has her I-told-you-Choi-Sangwoo-is-shady hat on.

"Come on Ren. You can do better than that," says the woman. She gives him a speculative look, but shoves the envelope into her purse.

"Your work here is done," Ren tells her coolly.

The woman hesitates, but decides it is better for her survival to walk away while she can. She tosses her long hair back and fixes the front of her jacket. Without another word, the woman heads toward our direction.

I grip Bryan's arm and pull him deeper into the shadows of our shelter. I motion for Bryan to keep quiet as the woman makes her way past us. Her high heels click in a repetitive manner.

"Take care of him." Meanwhile, Ren turns back to the gang members.

"What's going on?" Bryan whispers beside me.

I shake my head and hold a finger to my lips. Who is that man on the ground? *Oh no. Just when I think I have Choi Sangwoo figured out.*

There is a flurry of activity as two gang members approach the victim on the ground. Together, they grab a handful of his hair and drag him in an upwards motion. Before I can help myself, I gasp loudly when I see who it is.

Danny. Danny unconscious, helpless, and beyond lucidity.

"Do it." Ren is cold and heartless.

"Shit!" Bryan hisses beside me.

I cringe in silence.

Bryan and I watch in horror as Crist members jump on Danny. Calculated moves, combined with merciless punches, rain on Danny's body. His eyes are hinges; bruises mark his flesh. Reminiscent of a soulless corpse, Danny is unconscious through the beat down. Blood seeps from his forehead down to his cheeks. His flesh starts to bruise, changing shades with each violent blow.

"Ugh!" Danny's eyes barely flick open when another vicious blow ensues. Instinctively, he tries to fight back. It becomes apparent Danny's been drugged; his equilibrium and balance offset by his insufficiency.

Where is Mayhem? The desperate thought hits me. Images of the overpowering and dangerous gang lord who has the power to protect Danny grip me.

"Bryan, we have to do something or he'll be killed!" I turn away, not wanting to look anymore.

"You're kidding. These are gangsters, May."

"They've drugged him. It's not a fair fight!"

"Fine. We'll leave."

"No! Bryan! We have to do something."

"Hell no!"

"You go distract them. I'll get him out of here and we'll meet around the back corner."

"Hell no! Rule number one as a responsible citizen, never ever get involved with gang business!"

"Bryan! You want to say you witnessed a murder?"

"I don't, but this is dangerous May."

"Bryan, we don't have time. Go!" The blood is running thin in my veins. I shove Bryan out of our hiding place with haste.

Bryan gives me a death glare as he stands in the middle of the alley. Bryan takes a deep breath before he shouts, "Hey! What are you doing there? I'm calling the cops!"

Heads turn to look in Bryan's direction.

"Who the fuck are you?" Ren's thundering voice echoes down the alley.

"I'm calling the police!"

"Bring him to me." Ren inclines his head.

The gang members drop Danny at Ren's command. They unleash their full attention on Bryan.

"Shit!" Bryan whimpers as he runs down the opposite direction of the alley.

What have you done to him? my conscience shouts. There is no time to battle with her. I lean into the wall as the Crist members' race after Bryan. Meanwhile, Ren faces a whimpering Danny. A small chuckle escapes from his lips.

Ren crouches down to Danny's height. "If that's one of your minions, he will meet the same fate." Ren kicks Danny in the stomach before he straightens up and stalks out of the alley.

I hold my breath as Ren rushes by me. When I am sure he is out of sight and ear, I leave my hiding spot. The stretch of gravel and cement twists like a snake under my feet. My heart is beating a mile a minute and my palms are sweaty.

"Oh gosh." As I approach Danny, the extent of his injuries becomes strikingly apparent. "Are you okay?"

He's in a fetal position with bruises, cuts, and blood. Gang or no gang, he needs my help. I swallow hard and look around the desolate alley. Suddenly, the cool summer weather is cold and biting.

"Come on." I stoop down for Danny's right arm and hook it over my shoulder. I collect him in a careful manner, mindful of his injuries. When I straighten up, I stumble under his weight. He is heavier than I anticipated. Danny's head drops onto my side. He clings to me in his unconscious state.

"Slowly," I mutter as I support his body. Danny moans in pain, exuding the stress of drugs in his system. How can I forget what Danny did to me a couple days ago; how can I forget that he shot Sangwoo? The reality ripples through me. Yet here I am, blindly helping Danny without consequence again. I am too engrossed in my thoughts to hear the footsteps return to the alley.

"May?" Ren addresses me. The tremor in his voice marks a shocking recognition.

With Danny still dangling at my side, I meet Ren's gaze. Three other Crist members are gaping at me in shock.

"May!" From the mouth of the alley, I see Bryan rounding around the corner. The fourth gang member has Bryan in his hold.

"Please." Ren extends a hand to me.

I move away from his gesture. My heart beats soundly in my chest. I don't disguise the puzzled look on my face. "What are you doing to him?" *Revenge.* I already know the answer, but I don't want to face the reality of this world. Ren is not acting on his own accord. This is Sangwoo's orders.

Ren lowers his gaze. His voice is gruff and contained. "Please let him go."

"Are you going to kill him?" I ignore Ren's passive request. I survey the other members.

They don't answer me. They keep absolute silence, throwing tentative glances at Danny. Bryan is stuck in a state of shock. The gravity of the situation is all over his face. The understanding that my involvement is beyond a simple good Samaritan act dawns on Bryan.

Meanwhile, Ren's cell phone interrupts the implicit stare I have going with him. Ren answers the call with lightning speed. He doesn't take his eyes away from me when he states clearly, "Boss, there's been a compromise."

Ren holds his phone away from his ears as though in pain. "Miss Lee is with us," he answers through gritted teeth. Ren closes his eyes as he listens to Sangwoo's words on the other line. Without another word, Ren hangs up the phone. His eyes are a murky, indescribable color.

"Please release him," Ren repeats again. This time, there's stress in his voice. His eyes are wide and large, almost pleading.

"What are you going to do with him?" My voice is heavy from pressure.

Ren ignores my question again. He instructs one of the Crist members. "Take him. Put him in the other car."

One of the gang members approaches me with apprehension. I don't miss the fact that he is gaping at me, staring at every feature on my face. He gives me a respectful bow before he lifts Danny out of my arms.

The Crist member holding Bryan releases him at Ren's command next. Together, the four Crist members make a hasty retreat out of the alleyway. They disappear into the shadows of the night, blending into the silhouettes of the building and using the darkness of the night to escape into their underworld.

Meanwhile, Ren and I are at a standstill. Bryan rounds out our formation of a triangle. I realize I am shaking. "I want to see Sangwoo. Take me to him," I manage to utter.

Dark expressions color Ren's face. "As you wish." He is too formal with me. This is the true gangster in him.

Ren's body language changes along with a daunting demeanor. For the first time since I have met him, Ren intimidates me. I see him for who he is and not just Choi Sangwoo's right-hand man.

"Come on Bryan." I don't break eye contact with Ren. If I am going to get into the car with Ren, after what I just witnessed, I am going to take Bryan with me.

Ren looks like he wants to object, but he holds his tongue. "Follow me."

"What's going on May? How do you know gangsters?" Bryan leans in and whispers desperately to me. "Do you trust him? Where are we going? Are they going to kill us?"

I shake my head furiously to shut Bryan up. I am in no position to explain anything to Bryan nor is he to hear it. My mind is in a rapid, roller coaster state. Bryan and I follow Ren out of the alleyway towards the direction of the main street.

There is a dark, unmarked car parked on the side of the curb. The emblems on the car are nonexistent and the windows are a blackout tint. Ren reaches the car first and opens the door to the passenger seat for me. He glances at Bryan again and I know Ren is trying to pin a label on us. There is no need for me to explain. I want to talk to Sangwoo and only Sangwoo.

I slip into the passenger seat while Bryan gets in the back. The look on Ren's face subsides. He is satisfied with the marked distance between Bryan and me. He closes the passenger door and makes his way around the car. Instead of breaching the driver's side, Ren stops in front of the car. His cell phone is against his ears.

"May." Bryan taps my shoulder, but I quickly brush his hand away.

"Shh. He's talking." I motion for Bryan to quiet down. I want to hear the conversation.

"Yes, I have her with me. She has a boy with her. I'm not sure." Ren's voice is low and rough. He has his back to the car, but I know he is speaking with Sangwoo.

"Yes. We will be on our way." Ren hangs up the phone promptly. He glances nervously at me, but I pretend to look out of the side window.

I am in a bleak and downtrodden mood. The anticipation of seeing Choi Sangwoo rolls over me in waves. It has been two days. This dark gang leader's motive with me is on a crossword path. What does he want with me? Is he good or bad? Or is he both?

As Ren takes the unmarked car down an unknown turnpike, I am well aware that we are disappearing into a darker and bleaker world. Misaligned globes replace the normal city lights. Buildings are square giants made out of towering brick walls. The streets become desolate and deserted, empty and abandoned.

Bryan is silent in the back seat until the distinct area comes into view. "Wow," he mutters loudly when the building becomes more prominent. Towards the back of a desolate street, a simple sign displaying the club comes into sight.

"Limelight Lounge." Bryan scoots forward in the back seat and taps my shoulder. "There's a waiting list to get in here. We don't have to pay to get in, do we?"

"We own the place. You're covered." There is sarcastic humor in Ren's response to Bryan's awe.

"What?!" is Bryan's incredulous reaction.

I feel my feet going cold. Choi Sangwoo lied to me. He told me it was beneath him to invest in any type of nightclub or bar. Yet, he owns one of the most exclusive venues in the country. What else is he hiding from me?

What did I tell you? My intuition has her brown detective trench coat on again. This time, she has a gigantic magnifying glass with her.

"May. You hear that? Crist owns Limelight!" Bryan's awe is dripping onto the back seat of the car.

"Shut up," I mutter to him. Maybe bringing Bryan along was a mistake.

Ren pulls the unmarked car to the curb. Four bouncers are outside of the wooden front door. Ren steps out of the car first with Bryan and me in tow. Ren nods his head in acknowledgement at the bouncers; in return, they incline their heads with respect. The bouncers eye Bryan, but their gaze linger on me the longest. Just like the other Crist members, these bouncers are curious about me.

Inside the dark club, Ren leads us to a grand and winding staircase draped in decadence. Long, plush curtains weave throughout the rails. The loud cacophony of music, emanating from the first floor, intensifies in stretched echoes on the second floor. Stray, flashing neon lights roam the second floor landing where private partitions and booth stretch for miles. Through the darkness and chaos, Ren manages to lead us to Choi Sangwoo's reserved seating.

"Boss," Ren addresses the gang leader when we reach the secluded and secured section.

Poles wrap around the dome-like partition complete with its own plush seats. In the middle of it all, dark suited men surround Choi Sangwoo. Open bottles and empty glasses are strewn everywhere on the granite table, indicating the duration of time. When he looks up at us with those distinctive brown eyes, complete with gloss and vitality in them, it is difficult to believe Sangwoo had a bullet in his arm two days ago. Here he is, sitting nonchalantly with alcohol and the sins of society at the tip of his fingers.

Yep, I am not ready for Sangwoo's offer and his world. *Disgusting.* My intuition disapproves of his lavish lifestyle that can feed a third world country.

Sangwoo breaks into a smile when his eyes meet my gaze. "May."

I don't answer him. I am staring at him like a deer caught in the headlights. Sangwoo does a quick survey of his table and his men. He motions with one hand for them to leave. At his command, all ten of them rise. I don't miss the fact that they are gaping at me with the same intrusive stares. They file away from the partition and leave the area.

"How could you be so cruel?" I ask Sangwoo. I find my voice and my courage.

"What?" Sangwoo's brown eyes flick over to Ren.

Ren cringes slightly as he braces for the confrontation.

"I don't know how this gang business works, but to beat someone who's been drugged in the street is not only cruel, but unusual." I can no longer hold back my train of thought.

Sangwoo looks at Ren, who remains quiet. For the first time, I notice the muscles in his lower jaw clench together. "You drugged him?"

"Well, it was the only way we could get our hands on him. You know how violent Danny is," Ren explains with contempt. He throws a furtive glance at me. Suddenly, I feel like a snitch. I did not anticipate for this information to be new to Sangwoo. Apparently, Ren has improvised a piece of the puzzle. *Damn you and your assumptions.* My conscience shakes her head.

Sangwoo picks up his drink. Casually, he dismisses Ren. "We'll talk later Ren. You can go enjoy the night."

"Boss—" Ren starts to argue, but is immediately silenced by the look on Sangwoo's face. Ren bows to Sangwoo and retreats.

For a long second, Sangwoo stares after Ren before he turns to me. "I can explain. Please, sit down."

I am a sucker for those brown eyes. I know it's against my better judgment to be sensitive to this gang leader, but I cannot help myself. I sit across from Sangwoo, marveling at the softness of the plush club chairs. Meanwhile, Bryan takes the seat next to me in complete astonishment. We are out of our element and way over our heads. I stare at Sangwoo, convinced more than ever that I truly have no idea who he is.

Sangwoo acknowledges Bryan with a calm tone. "You are?"

"Spyder's brother," I introduce him. I want to spare Bryan the gang leader's wrath. I am suddenly conscious that Sangwoo thinks I have a romantic connection with this puppy dog.

"Spyder's brother and May's boyfriend." What the hell is he up to now? Bryan stretches his arm across my shoulders suddenly. Now, he has the galls to speak. If only Bryan knows who is sitting across from him.

Slyly, I reach under the table and pinch his knee. Bryan jumps, but keeps his arm on my shoulder.

"Boyfriend?" Sangwoo narrows his eyes at me. He doesn't look comfortable with the thought. "I didn't know you have a boyfriend."

"He's not my boyfriend." I take Bryan's arm off me. I want to kill him right now. *Now is not the time to proclaim your love for me,* I want to tell him.

Bryan looks hurt that I am brushing him aside. "May," he calls softly.

Perhaps he is conjuring a master plan of some sort.

"Tell you what, Bryan. Why don't you go downstairs and grab yourself a drink. Anything you want, it's on the house. One of my men will help you." Sangwoo motions towards the staircase where two guards are looming in the shadows. The look in Sangwoo's eyes is hard and cold. His jaw locks tight. It becomes intensely evident he does not want to entertain Bryan right now.

"I'm not going anywhere." Bryan crosses his arms over his chest. "I'm here to protect May."

"Believe me, she is well protected." Sangwoo picks up his drink. He tosses it back and tells Bryan again with a dire tone. "Go on and enjoy yourself a drink. We will still be here. I need to talk to May."

Sensing the impending turmoil, I have no other choice but to shoo Bryan away. "Go. I'll be fine." I nudge his shoulder gently.

Bryan looks at me with a desperate look in his eyes. "May, I can't leave you."

"Bryan. Please. Just give us a minute." Now I have to work on getting him off my back.

Bryan fights with me through our eye contact, but decides he's better off letting me win. "Fine. I'm only going because May is asking me, okay?" Bryan asks Sangwoo before he gets up. Bryan gives me a longing look before he leaves the table.

Sangwoo waits until his men escort Bryan downstairs. Then, Sangwoo faces me next. His eyes are burning with an indescribable intensity. "Are you dating that boy?" There is possessiveness and jealousy in his voice.

Excuse me! "No." My eyebrows come together in question. Why would Sangwoo ask me such a thing? It is pretty clear Bryan and I do not match.

Sangwoo studies my face. "Why is he with you tonight?"

There is no reason why I should be explaining myself to Choi Sangwoo, but before I can help it, I want to justify myself. "I was having drinks with my co-workers after work. I bumped into Bryan after I left the bar. Of course, you would know all of this if Ren did his job as my security guard instead of seeking revenge."

Even though the nightclub is dark, it's still easy to see the colors creep up on Sangwoo's face. It is difficult to decipher if it's the alcohol he's consumed or my biting words.

What Sangwoo says next spins me on my head. "Danny was found loitering in front of The Trax, while Ren was waiting for you to complete your shift. Apparently, he is not done harassing you even after I paid the thirty thousand dollars, complete with a bullet wound to my arm." As if this is a regular conversation, the corner of Sangwoo's mouth twists into a subtle smile.

I stiffen in my chair. *Whoa.* This is not the reason I am expecting to hear. Once again, Sangwoo is one step ahead of me.

"I know what you are thinking, and I can assure you I'm not that kind of person." Sangwoo's eyes are pulling me in, deeper into this dark and vast world of his. "I just don't want him to hurt you. You are a valuable asset to me May. I'm sorry you had to see it. I'm sorry you had to see my men defending you, protecting you."

I swallow hard. Everything in my body feels numb. I want to apologize for being a fool, but at the same time showing Sangwoo my weakness will not get me very far. Even though Sangwoo may have ulterior motives that benefit me, I am still not convinced he is entirely honest with me. I am weary of Sangwoo. Time has passed since that very first meeting at The Trax. The feelings and emotions that I had for Sangwoo are subsiding and waning. It is not the same anymore. It may never be the same anymore.

"You're dumbfounded," Sangwoo concludes. He reaches over the table for the dark bottle of alcohol. Sangwoo pours himself another glass and motions to me.

I shake my head. I am one drink away from losing my sanity. I can't risk my rationale at this point in the conversation.

"I want to pay you back the thirty thousand dollars." I brave the notion. I force myself to look into the deep surprise treading in Sangwoo's brown eyes.

"Pay me back?" Sangwoo tests the words out. His eyebrows come together. He places his drink back on the table. "Why would you want to do that?" Sangwoo asks clearly, despite the loud music thudding in the background.

I am suddenly uncomfortable under his stare. "I don't want to sign the initiation contract. This life, your life, is not for me." I secretly wish he could see the hesitation in my eyes and the fear in my voice. "Please."

Sangwoo sits back against his seat. Out of habit, Sangwoo puts his hands together in a prayer position. Sangwoo's brooding brown eyes harden. "I think you are missing the point May. I don't need you to repay me thirty thousand dollars. I am not asking you to sign the initiation contract in place of thirty thousand dollars."

"I thought when you said we could work something out this was the bargain-for-exchange? Thirty thousand dollars for the initiation contract? So instead of an initiation contract, I am willing to pay you back the money for the contract to be retracted." I desperately want to make this clear. The anxiety returns with a vengeance inside of me.

The crestfallen look on Sangwoo's face becomes deceptive. "I don't want thirty thousand dollars from you, May." This time, his statement is unforgiving.

I don't know how else to tell Sangwoo I want nothing to do with his world. "Sangwoo, please. Let me pay you back. I can't do what you want me to. I can't sign an initiation contract. I can't be part of your world."

"Is this why you have been so distant with me?" Sangwoo asks. His voice is tough and soft, a dangerous combination. "You're having doubts. You don't have faith that I can teach you and support you . . . and be with you?"

My heart skips at his last words. He wants to be with me? What? I am helpless with this man. This gang leader has sugar dripping from his tongue. How do I fight such a demon under this package of a man?

"I can give you time." Sangwoo offers simply. "You don't need to sign or participate in anything anytime soon. I will give you time."

"Sangwoo, I made my decision," I insist. An overwhelming sense of discomfort grips me. "There's no point in making you wait for something I have my heart set on. You said so yourself that you were helping me out with the thirty thousand dollars as a repayment for helping you that Saturday night when you were drunk."

Despite my reminder, Sangwoo remains silent. Our environment takes over. The club music roars over us. The loud cadence encloses our reserved area. The flashing lights continue to spark behind us.

"I can give you the world," Sangwoo speaks up and continues the point of ignoring me. He leans in, reducing the distance between us. Sangwoo's mere presence renders me helpless. "Anything you want, anything you desire will be at your feet. Your stepmother won't have to work such long hours just to make ends meet. You won't have to juggle two jobs and go through the last two years of college with uncertainty. I can guarantee you the world. Take my hand and join me, May."

I am speechless at Sangwoo's words. Along with his melancholy and suave, I feel like putty in his hands. "Sangwoo," is all I can make out.

"Trust me May. I won't let you down. When you join me, everything you do will be a hundred percent legal. I will not ask you to do anything you are uncomfortable with. I need someone like you on my team. I need your tenacity, loyalty, and shrewdness," Sangwoo counts my traits.

"I don't have any of those qualities that you are speaking of," I tell him. *Don't speak so lowly of yourself. You're a catch! But I get it, you're trying to sell yourself short to be less appealing to the gang leader.* My intuition is eating a bag of popcorn as she waits for the cinematic climax of this melodrama.

"Tenacity. By insisting that you refuse to sign my initiation contract is a mark of tenacity. I don't like to talk about myself often, but do you know how many people would be willing to give up family members, donate their pride, and leave behind their fears to be in your position?" Sangwoo asks. He doesn't wait for me to answer. "Loyalty is what you showed to your cousin. I know you would do the same for me. And shrewdness is the passive-aggressive intelligence I know you have in you."

"Sangwoo," I protest.

Sangwoo holds up a hand to stop me. "I will give you time. You don't have to say yes or no right now. Not tonight."

I swallow hard, biting down on my bottom lip. The look in his eyes is hard to decipher.

Sangwoo reaches forward for the glass of alcohol he has for me. Sangwoo hands it to me and without thinking, I take it from him this time. *What the hell, I might as well.* I close my eyes as I swallow the cool and hard liquid. Where do we go from here? *Don't give it!* My intuition pushes for more.

Suddenly, a voice replaces the loud music overhead. My eyes scale down the balcony to see Bryan gracing the stage. *Oh no, what is he doing now?* On the other end of the stage, Sangwoo's men are loitering at a leisurely pace. The entire dance club houses Sangwoo's men and only a few, selected outsiders. The thought dawns on me that Sangwoo has reserved the venue exclusively for tonight.

"You told me you don't invest in nightclubs and bars," I tell Sangwoo quickly.

"I don't." Sangwoo sits back in his seat. He has his eyes on the stage. "I inherited this place."

I catch my jaw before it falls to the floor. I don't have time to dwell on Sangwoo's confession.

"Ladies and gentleman, may I have your attention?" A booming voice resonates across the nightclub.

Meanwhile, Bryan heads straight to the DJ to retrieve a microphone. The DJ's booming voice announces the special event. "Good evening ladies and gentlemen. We are hosting a karaoke event tonight. And a guest here is about to sing a ballad for someone special."

"This is for you baby!" Bryan shouts. He points up to the balcony where Sangwoo and I are sitting.

I lower myself in my seat. *What is he doing?* I eye Sangwoo to see the corners of his mouth twist in amusement. Sangwoo is clearly thinking about Bryan.

"Let the beat drop yo!" Bryan suddenly warps into his other personality.

The resident DJ begins to play a smooth hip-hop beat, whining and turning with echoes of bass and treble. Everyone in the club stops dancing, talking, and even drinking to turn their attention to the stage. Smirks and entertained smiles pass from one person to the next. Bryan turns the microphone in his hand and makes his home on the stage. Grinning with confidence, he starts the first verse. *What can he possibly sing? Please don't rap, is all I can think.*

"When a man lovesss a woman!" Bryan hollers over the microphone. His voice, melodic and falsetto in tenor, rings through the venue.

"Wow!" The crowd claps loudly at Bryan's first verse.

Oh wow. Who knew the kid can sing! Bryan's melodic and heartwarming voice would have done the song justice if he didn't overact.

"When a man loves a woman, he can't keep his mind on nothing else. He'll trade the world for the good thing he's found!" Bryan serenades the microphone.

I stare shell-shocked at Bryan's angelic voice. In the year and a half that I have known him, I didn't know Bryan sings so well. I look up in time to see Sangwoo staring at me. There is a ruminating look in his eyes.

"If she's bad, he can't see it. She can do no wrong. Turn his back on his best friend if he put her down. When a man loves a woman," Bryan croons in the background.

Sangwoo brings his drink to his lips. He turns back to face the stage. The light cascades his handsome profile. There is darkness to Sangwoo that, for the first time, I feel scared. His good-and-evil complex confuses me.

I force myself to focus on Bryan, fighting the tears that threaten to grace my eyes. I lose myself in the melodic hum of the music and the harmony of Bryan's voice. The crowd circles the stage that Bryan stands on, crooning and pointing up to me. I don't see them. I don't see Bryan. They are a sea of people and I recede, like a faceless entity, back into the darkness with a dark demon sitting by my side.

BRYAN IS SICK AND THROWING up. Choi Sangwoo's gang bought Bryan ten shots of alcohol after his rendition of Percy Sledge's *When a Man Loves a Woman*. It was all fun and games when Bryan was drinking with them, but when he started dry heaving they all dispersed. It became my duty to help him vomit outside of Limelight half an hour later. It is almost three in the morning. I am exhausted.

"Ready to go?" Bryan hunches over the sidewalk, sliding in and out of consciousness. He shakes his head at me, motioning for another second of equilibrium. "Why did you drink so much?" I scold him. Poor kid. Seasonal gangsters take alcohol seriously.

"You shouldn't have taken all those drinks from them," I nag him.

"The drinks were free. Damn, gangsters will screw you up."

"Oh Bryan."

"How do you know gangsters anyway? Damn May, I always knew you were legit."

"Hahahaha."

I enjoy talking to Bryan when he is drunk off his butt. I pat his back in a rhythmic pattern.

"Good night, Boss."

I look up to see Choi Sangwoo stepping out of Limelight. He is pulling on his jacket, but stops halfway when he sees my arms around Bryan. Sangwoo eyes narrow and I instinctively withdraw my arms from Bryan.

Sangwoo's expression is hard to read. "Are you ready? I'll take you both home."

"You got shotgun May. I don't want to sit next to him," Bryan slurs in his drunken state.

Sangwoo and I exchange glances. "You have to excuse him, he's really drunk."

Sangwoo gives me a tight-lipped smile. "Don't worry. The feeling is mutual." Leaving me to conclude what I will from that statement, Sangwoo comes up to Bryan.

"What are you doing?" Bryan whips around, but Sangwoo's sharp reflex catches him.

"Taking you home." To his credit, Sangwoo is a good sport for dealing with Bryan. I am sure any other guy would have left Bryan's drunken butt on the streets. Despite the fact that Choi Sangwoo is full of surprises, there is one thing I am sure about him—he doesn't act without rationale. Maybe that is what it takes to be in the gang leader's chair.

A sleek, marble gray car pulls up to the curb. The valet, undoubtedly part of Sangwoo's gang, steps out and hands him the key. The valet is careful not to make eye contact and bows his head. The valet takes Bryan from Sangwoo's arms and puts him in the back seat. Sangwoo opens the door to the passenger seat for me expectantly. I slide in easily.

I have my seat belt on by the time Sangwoo slips into the driver's seat. All is quiet inside the car. The emblem on the steering wheel lets me know I am in a Bentley. This is car number five or six since I have known him. The quiet engine gives nothing away as Sangwoo pulls from the curb. He does not ask me where Bryan lives. His limitless, stalker knowledge never fails to amaze me.

"How is your mom doing?" Sangwoo surprises me with his question.

"She's doing fine," I answer.

"Why are you asking about my mother-in-law?" Bryan snaps from the back seat.

I turn back and throw Bryan a dirty look. He blows me a kiss. *I'm starting to really like this kid*, my intuition laughs.

I catch Sangwoo glancing in the rearview mirror at Bryan. Sangwoo continues driving without a word; he turns on the radio. Music flows through the speakers and fills the car. Soon, Bryan slouches over in the back seat. I keep glancing at Sangwoo, curious of what he's thinking. Again, Sangwoo keeps his eyes on the road with one hand on the steering wheel. The cool, calm, and collected way he appears in front of me is what drew me to Choi Sangwoo in the first place. I realize it is not his striking features, but it is Sangwoo's presence and aura. *Mayhem's is on a different level too,* my intuition croons.

Soon enough, the Bentley comes to a slow stop in front of the familiar terrain that marks Spyder's house.

"Stay here," Sangwoo commands to me. He gets out of the car and opens the back seat.

I watch as Sangwoo drags an unconscious Bryan out of the back seat with superhuman strength. He wraps Bryan neatly around him and stalks up to the house. Sangwoo goes through the gate and is at the front door in no time. When the door opens, Spyder sticks his head out. His jaw drops at the sight of Sangwoo. He bows deeply and listens with impeccable concentration as Sangwoo briefly explains the situation.

"Come in. Come in please." Spyder steps back for Sangwoo to bring Bryan in. Then, Spyder stares at the car with no sign of recognition on his face. He doesn't see me. The windows are too dark. With one last lingering glance, Spyder closes the door behind him.

The minutes tick by. I sit in the warm car. I want to kill Spyder because if it wasn't for him, I would never be in the situation that I am now. The irony of being outside of his house strikes me as mocking. I try not to think about what Spyder has done to Lina. What can I do now? I cannot kill Spyder because that would be illegal. *You can get Sangwoo to kill Spyder.* My intuition is dark and brooding.

Sangwoo finally emerges from the house. He opens the driver's door and languidly slides in.

"What did Spyder say?" I cannot contain my curiosity.

"Nothing important." Sangwoo keeps his face closed. He starts the car again. "Do you have time to talk?"

Oh no. He wants to talk more about the initiation contract. Sangwoo really is persistent. "It's late," is all I can manage.

"Just thirty minutes of your time." Even his way of pleading is classy.

I give in like the fool I am. "Ok. Thirty minutes."

A smile rides on his lips. "You won't regret it." Sangwoo turns the car down the steep hill and guns down the road.

THE W SEOUL HOTEL IS bathed in decadence despite the fact that it is four in the morning. Early birds and late birds are sitting in the restaurant and bar area. Sangwoo and I are in a private booth towards the very back of the venue away from the public eye. Sangwoo orders me a cup of coffee and Spanish tea for himself. Both orders come with the hotel's specialized pudding.

"Would you like to try some?" I look into the specks of light lingering in his eyes. Sangwoo offers me a cup of pudding with a small smile on his face. He's at ease with lasting alcohol in his system.

"Pudding," I repeat in my zombie state. It seems so trivial to eat pudding with him. I am exhausted and wired from the alcohol coursing through my system.

"Yes." Sangwoo doesn't open his container though. He takes a sip out of his tea, combating the alcohol he consumed earlier.

"I've never known a guy who has a sweet tooth," I say. I drink my coffee, but I don't open the pudding either.

"I don't. That's why I'm not eating mine. You?"

"Me neither."

I am stuck with the ominous thoughts I reserve for him. I thought that after the little escapade with Bryan, Sangwoo would call it a night. Yet, here we are, back at his current haunt drinking tea and coffee. What a combination. *Does this man ever sleep?*

"So, are the feelings mutual between you and Bryan? You like him as much as he loves you?" It takes me a moment to realize Sangwoo is teasing me.

"Are you kidding me?" I blurt out in disbelief. "No way. He thinks he has a crush on me, but it's nothing more than a game."

"He is clearly in love with you." Sangwoo settles against his seat. His eyes are studying me beyond reproach.

"He thinks he is." I make a face. "He doesn't know what love is."

"Do you?" Sangwoo stops me in my tracks.

At a loss for words I stare out of the window just in time to catch a plane flying against the breathtaking backdrop of the night's sky. I don't answer him.

"What's bothering you?" Sangwoo finally asks. "May."

"I am still stuck on what happened to Danny today," I admit, intertwining my thumbs on my lap.

Sangwoo's eyes frost. "Why did you help him?" Sangwoo gives me the impression this is one of his burning questions.

"How could I not?" I blurt out. "He was hurt and in pain."

"But he was willing to kill you last time," Sangwoo justifies.

"I'm not that type of person." I lower my eyes away from our intense eye contact. "That's why I keep telling you I can't do what you want me to. Maybe you're used to such violence, but this is foreign to me. Gang or no gang, I couldn't stand by and watch him get killed." I hope my sincerity is getting across.

Sangwoo goes silent; he's trying to read my mind. "He could have hurt you again if Ren hadn't intervened," is Sangwoo's cold response.

"Why do you want to justify this?" I question with confusion.

"This is how it is in our world—constant reminding and reinforcement. Like I told you before, Yoon Jaewon and I will be forever intertwined in this underground world until one day the final straw will break. Danny shot me in the arm, so he pays a hefty price for it. Jaewon will come to me, but we both know it is a fair trade for him damaging my flesh." Sangwoo's stone words warrant a warning. His face closes with an unforgiving expression. "Besides, he owes me beyond reprieve for what he has done."

Once again, I am seduced into Choi Sangwoo's world. "What did he do to you?"

I don't expect Sangwoo to answer me, but he does. Sangwoo's jaw clenches together. "Yoon Jaewon did something to me that I will never forgive."

"What is it?" What could Mayhem have possibly done to Sangwoo? This is it. I am finally getting an answer to their complicated relationship.

"Our rivalry isn't as simple as it's perceived. To my last breath, I will avenge his death. I am just taking my time, waiting for the right timing to serve Jaewon the pain he has inflicted on me." The look in Sangwoo's eyes is frosty. He is all over the place and cryptic.

"Sangwoo, what happened?" I ask slowly. The anticipation is taking me through different levels.

"H-he shot my little brother. He was shooting at me, but he accidently pulled the trigger on my brother." Sangwoo's voice is heavy with emotion.

A jolt shocks my body. I stare at Sangwoo with the oddest sensation ever. Words may not hurt, but they do make a significant impact. I feel as though something cold goes through me as I absorb Sangwoo's confession.

"It is one of the most emotionally painful experiences in my entire life. I think I cried more than I'll ever cry. That little kid meant everything to me. I wanted to kill Jaewon afterwards, but I wasn't in the right mind state. And even now, I haven't had my revenge." Sangwoo looks away, becoming cold and distant in a matter of seconds. "Jaewon and I work for the same Boss, but we are still rivals. If the ties in this industry didn't bind us, I would have killed him. He is the only person I cannot directly hurt, but if one of his men comes after what I care about I will return the favor."

"I'm so sorry Sangwoo." My condolences are fair and meek.

My words have no time to soak in before Sangwoo continues on, "I care about you May. I don't want this life for you either, trust me. But because of circumstances, because of what Lina and Spyder did to you, I am your only lifeboat. Even if I let you walk away, this dark world of mine is not finished with you yet."

I am speechless. What does Sangwoo mean that this dark world of his is not finished with me? The bottom of my stomach drops and I feel terrible. I mentally kick myself for taking Sangwoo here emotionally and mentally. If I had just shut up, he wouldn't have to repeat such a horrific past and solidify his reason for the initiation contract. I feel sick to my stomach.

The wistful look in Sangwoo's eyes attacks my cluttered thoughts. "Have you ever lost someone?" He returns the question to me.

It is an inevitable question in a conversation like this one, but my darkest nightmares resurface. "No." The selfish part of me speaks up first.

Sangwoo's brown eyes fixate on me. "I've lost two people that I've loved. My brother and the love of my life, my first girlfriend."

Dead Girl. "I'm so sorry." I am dumbfounded at Sangwoo's revelation. I keep my facial expression taut.

Sangwoo stares out of the window to watch a car zoom by as his brown eyes fade and his eyebrows burrow together in thought. Without thinking, without realizing the emotions I bring along with it, I gently extend my palm and settle it on Sangwoo's right cheek. His soft skin melts into the palm of my hands. If Sangwoo is surprised, he doesn't show it. His eyes glaze over as they trail from my arm to the hand that is now on his cheek.

I don't know why I am doing this, why I am so forward, why I am making such a move. Is it his story about his brother or is it my own pain? I am a slave to my emotions–to the look of sorrow in Sangwoo's eyes.

"May," my name escapes his lips. It is tantalizing and encompassing. Without another word, another moment of hesitation, Sangwoo leans forward and kisses me. His proximity is intoxicating and my train of thoughts halts.

Oh shit. He's kissing me. Choi Sangwoo is kissing me. I am a puddle of feelings. *No! Get away from him!* My intuition is kicking her shoes off in a fit.

Sangwoo's fingers dance across my chin as his lips, soft and controlling, press against my own. It is my first kiss. I have no idea what I am doing. All I can do is part my lips and let him take over. I am lost in Sangwoo's embrace and the moment. He smells dangerous and mysterious. He is dangerous and dark. He is everything I need to stay away from. At the moment, I forget everything that's happened and all the reservations I have for him.

I fight the tears that are forming in my eyes. The conversation will haunt me tonight. His simple question, "Have you ever lost someone?" will plague me to the world's end. I wish I could tell Sangwoo the truth. I have lost someone. But no matter how I picture myself doing so, I am not ready to confide in him. It is too twisted and complicated. Most of all, I'm afraid that the reason why he is pursuing me is the same reason why I'm holding back my tongue.

Sangwoo doesn't know I struggle with an internal secret behind the walls I've built over the years. It is nothing more than a mere memory, but deep down I am desperately running away from it all. It is my darkness. And when it's time, when I'm ready, I'll tell Sangwoo about it.

He and I share the same agonizing pain. So I close my eyes and let him kiss me, letting the moment fool us.

CHAPTER ELEVEN

F alling head-over-heels for someone is a complicated concept. The challenge heightens when your potential sweetheart is a gang leader with a deep, dark past and therapeutic issue. I am not ignorant of this world that involves violence, turmoil, and disorder. I know that I am completely at a loss of what truly occurs in the treacherous world of Sangwoo and Mayhem. No ounce of creativity or imagination can conjure up the far-reaching reality. I am done with the guesses.

Sangwoo drives me back to my apartment. Dawn is breaking the horizon by the time I step out of the car. Shades of light orange and red streaks light the apartment complexes, providing a dreamy hue of colors. Sangwoo's dark car is a stark contrast to the light.

"I'll see you later May." His tone is tight and arctic. Traces of the sensitive Sangwoo, the man I succumbed to just an hour earlier, are gone. The gang leader returns with his emotionless bearings and mysterious interest in me. There is a prickling light in his eyes as if we share a secret. If Sangwoo considers our kiss a tentative secret, it might as well be. We speak no more of any initiation contract or kiss.

"Bye." I wave lightly to him. Sangwoo nods his head before the dark window consumes him.

I know I have gone off on the deep end far too soon. I watch the car disappear around the bend feeling a slight sense of abandonment. Emotions and speculations riddle my entire being. I don't know where we are going to go with what has manifested. I am weak. I went there to talk to Sangwoo about abolishing the initiation contract and ended up kissing him. My intuition has called it a night after using Lina's term of slush for me. I am too stubborn for her to reason with.

I trudge into the apartment feeling empty and confused. The lingering sensation of Sangwoo's kiss is on my lips. Although romantic and heart stopping, there was something missing in his embrace. As harsh as it sounds, it felt as though Choi Sangwoo was not kissing me. He was kissing Dead Girl. Even though it was my first kiss, ever, I know it wasn't right. Sangwoo was kissing someone in the past, from his memory. The familiar prickling sensation fires in my eyes as the realization hits me. I refuse to cry. I don't want him. I don't want him the way I thought I would want him.

Eunhye is sleeping when I make my way down the hallway. By the time I reach my room, I surrender to the harsh emotions. Pressing my face into my pillow, I let it out. All the frustration and hard emotions unleash from the depths of my soul. I cry and cry. I am a bundle of nerves and foreign emotions. I cry until the deep lulls of sleep consume me. I toss and turn, feeling warm one minute and cold the next. The exhaustion and restlessness catch up to me and before I know it, I drift into the darkness with pools of tears.

THE LOUD CHATTER IN THE living room wakes me. The cadences of laughter ring between the walls. The early morning sunlight beams yellow and orange rays into my bedroom. I am warm and comfortable in my bed, nestled in with my pillows and blanket. I want to be in this state of limbo forever, but as my thoughts start to run from me I know I cannot lie in bed forever. I have things to do, decisions to make.

I force myself out of bed with tousled hair. Bypassing the kitchen for now, I opt for the bathroom to brush my teeth and a thorough rinse of my face. The girl in the mirror is too gaunt and pale; her eyes are puffy and red. *You definitely fit in now.* My conscience tosses her tresses from her face. For the first time in a long time, I apply some light makeup to conceal my puffy red eyes. The miracle of Maybelline products masks my feelings of darkness and hopelessness for now. It is one more thing to keep my hands busy and thoughts away from Choi Sangwoo.

Absentmindedly, I travel into the living room to see Eunhye engaging in a rapid conversation with her best friend.

"Well, look who's finally awake." My mother looks up from her cup of coffee. Eunhye's hair sweeps out of her face in the usual dramatic manner. Her eyes are shining with excitement. "You got in very late last night."

"It was the last day of work, so we celebrated afterwards." I want to keep some type of partial truth going with my mother. I glance at the individual sitting to her right with his rightful cup of coffee. His kind eyes, hidden under heavy eyebrows, are smiling at me. Im Dongwan, or Mr. Im, is Eunhye's childhood friend.

"A phone call or text message would have been nice," Eunhye reminds me with a stiff tone.

"Good morning, May." Mr. Im saves me. He is always dressed in some of the finest ensembles. In many ways, Mr. Im is a fashionista in his own right. Today is no different. He is in signature black slacks and a gray dress shirt. Mr. Im has dark black hair that he slicks back to reveal a prominent facial structure complete with a widow's peak.

"Good morning Mr. Im," I return his warm greeting. It's been a month since I have seen Mr. Im, but he looks just as youthful. The man doesn't age. "How are you?"

"I'm doing very well. Join us for coffee?" Mr. Im motions toward the coffee filter and my favorite coffee cup is already waiting.

"Sure." I grin at him, wary of Eunhye's speculative eyes. I know her motherly instinct is kicking in. I make my way through the living room and into the kitchen. The fear of Eunhye's probing questions causes me to smile like a mindless zombie, feigning paper hearts and happiness. It's better than having to explain the type of chaos I have conjured.

"Your mother tells me you've been quite the workaholic this summer." Mr. Im doesn't spare me a dull moment. We pick up where we left off last time. In many ways, I consider Mr. Im an uncle from another mother–literally.

"I'm just doing the best I can. I like keeping busy." I pick up the coffee filter and pour myself a cup of coffee. The blatant smell stirs my senses, and for a fabricated minute, I am in a temporary moment of content.

"What I would give to be young again with that determination and energy." Mr. Im flashes me that charming smile of his. "I see my nephew in her," he tells Eunhye.

Nephew? All of Mr. Im's relatives are in the United States. He rarely talks about his family, so the mentioning of a nephew sparks my curiosity. Apparently, I am not the only one surprised by Mr. Im's revelation.

Eunhye's breath hitches with enthusiasm. "I can't believe you have been hiding him from me. This nephew of yours is such an enigma. Where has he been?" The context of the conversation lets me know that this is the topic of the day.

Mr. Im faces Eunhye again. A quiet and subtle transition occurs. Now, I am the fly on the wall as the two of them engage in conversation. I hover to listen in on their conversation, half-conscious half-daydreaming.

"He is a world traveler or a nomad, whichever way you look at it. There isn't anyone or anywhere that he's particularly attached to. He's been shuffling back and forth from Busan to Seoul for the past month. We keep in touch throughout the years, and whenever he's back in town, he makes it a point to spend time with me." Proud parades Mr. Im's tone of voice.

"So he doesn't have a place to call home?" Eunhye does little to hide her piqued interest.

"In America," Mr. Im replies with a tentative facial expression as though he isn't sure himself.

"And why haven't we heard about this nephew of yours?" Eunhye gives her childhood friend the full inquisition.

He rewards her with an apologetic smile. "I don't talk about that side of my family, you know that. They're not the black sheep of the family. They're actually the black herd."

Eunhye lets out a laugh complete with head tossing and hand slapping. Mr. Im brings out the adolescent in her. "Since I have the afternoon off, I'll make lunch and you can invite him over. I'd like to meet him."

"Oh no. I don't want to bother you," Mr. Im protests. He catches my gaze and gives me a wink. We both know there is no such thing as refusing Eunhye.

"Nonsense! How long have we've known each other Dongwan? Bring him over. Besides, it's just us today. We can have a late lunch," Eunhye persists with her invitation. Her facial expression riddles with the threat of disappointment if Mr. Im turns her down.

"You sure it won't be a bother?"

"I'm sure. Invite him over!"

I listen to the latter half of their dialogue with a desolation. I watch Eunhye engage Mr. Im in another conversation, feeling a bout of overwhelming sadness and nostalgia. I rarely get the opportunity to see Eunhye laugh so freely since my father left. It is only with Mr. Im does Eunhye express such free emotions and language. The feelings I have worked so hard to keep a lid on surfaces. Suddenly, emotions whisk me away and my thoughts run from me. I find myself thinking about my father and his painful absence. My heart struggles to breathe and the tears prick at my eyes. In less than forty-eight hours, I have become such a crybaby.

I have to find something to do to keep my mind and body busy. Leaving Eunhye and Mr. Im to their lunch plans, I make my way out of the kitchen to the bathroom again. By the time I emerge, I am freshly showered and wearing a black camisole over gray sweatpants. My hair piles away from my face. I pack the laundry basket to its max, hitch it to my side, and make my trek to the laundry room. Although it is a painful chore, I am especially happy to do it today. I am desperate to keep my mind focused on something other than gang lords and the dark underground world they inhabit. I resign to the notion that if I keep my hands and mind busy, I will unravel all the complexities that Choi Sangwoo brings me. I am sure he doesn't do laundry to exercise mind over matter with his problems. *I don't think he even uses the bathroom,* my intuition adds with sarcasm.

Eunhye and Mr. Im are still conversing when I enter the living room.

"Laundry?" Eunhye's right eyebrow lifts in a delicate manner.

Eunhye finds it surprising I am doing laundry on the day I have off. This only lets me know she's aware of a bigger issue plaguing me. A mother's intuition is no joke. I don't want to give anything else away since I am already an open book. I simply give her a nod and a smile to Mr. Im.

"We're having lunch soon. I will call you." Eunhye lets me know my afternoon plans.

"Ok mom," is my subdued response. "I'll see you later Mr. Im."

"Don't have too much fun," Mr. Im teases.

With great humor, I promise Mr. Im my inhibition to have fun before I close the door behind me. East Point apartment complexes are divided into various sections based upon the number of units. Fortunately for my unit we have our own laundry room with an arcade included. Usually, numerous children and adults occupy the laundry room. Today, the day I wish for the loud and crowded distraction, the apartment complex is eerily quiet and vacant. Not even a single load of laundry pounds in any of the washing machines.

I make my way to the nearest washing machine. There are six of them facing the dryers on the approaching adjacent side. I take my time putting in the laundry. Each piece of fabric gets time and attention from me. By the time I'm done with the laundry detergent and setting the machine to the pre-wash cycle, I realize I have two hours to waste. I decide to call Lina.

"May." Her familiar voice brings equilibrium to my chaotic mind state. "How are you?"

"I'm ok." My answer is as far and distant as I am.

"Is something wrong?" Lina takes notice of my tone. "I haven't seen you in a few days. You've been distant." My cousin does me the favor of not mentioning my negligence of her text messages.

"A lot's going on, Lina." I swallow hard. I am on the brink of a nervous breakdown.

She sighs across the phone line. "Is something going on with you and Choi Sangwoo? You never told me how he was able to take care of our debt."

I hesitate, not sure how to answer her question. I know it will open a can of worms, including some insects. How do I even begin to tell Lina that Sangwoo got shot because of me? Where do I even explain the complicated feelings I have for Sangwoo? The lingering sensation of his lips is still fresh.

"Oh no," Lina gasps and another breath of air dances across the phone line. "Don't tell me you signed the initiation contract!"

"No, no. Nothing like that," I reply to lay my cousin's worries to rest.

Lina grows silent over the phone line. I know Lina is contemplating whether it is a battle she wants to get into with me.

"Everything's going to be ok," I tell my cousin softly. It is more for my state of mind than for hers.

"You know whatever it is, I'm here," Lina replies. She changes the topic, offering a lighter topic of conversation. "What are you doing today?"

"I'm doing laundry. I'm also having lunch with Eunhye and Mr. Im this afternoon." I am glad for the change in subject.

"Mr. Im? Haven't seen him for a while. Are you doing anything afterwards? Maybe we can meet at the park for a run. I know you don't like exercise, but we can catch up and get some sun."

"A run actually sounds good right now."

"You serious? You'd run with me?"

"Why not?"

Little does Lina know I am delighted with her offer. They always say keeping busy is the best remedy for unwanted thoughts, painful heartache, and errant emotions. As we continue talking, Lina fills me in with the details of her life. She's set to quit Sansachun in a week and already has a job interview lined up with an accounting company. It is a receptionist position, but according to Lina it is a much needed graduation from working at a convenience store. Aunt Yuna and uncle Dom are particularly happy about her decision to move on to better things. Lina surprises me with the contemplation that she might return to school in the fall. My cousin doesn't let me absorb the news before she tells me that Spyder is bothering her again, adamant about a reconciliation. In just a few days, my cousin's life has drastically changed. I feel guilty for being so neglectful lately.

After finalizing our park plans, I am in better spirits when I hang up with Lina. I even play a couple of games in the arcade room, hoping to ease my boredom and keep my thoughts of Choi Sangwoo at bay. By the time I fold the last pair of clothes, my cell phone rings. It's Eunhye sounding anxious and happy.

"Are you done?" My mother has her I-am-cooking voice on.

"Just finished."

"Lunch is ready."

"Ok. I'll come right up."

I **DRAG THE LAUNDRY BASKET** up to our apartment. When I reach the door, the delicious and mouth-watering smell of lunch permeates my senses. I set the laundry basket in the living room and enter the kitchen. Eunhye is bustling about, setting up last minute dishes. Mr. Im is sitting at the kitchen table immersed in conversation with another male. They really did invite Mr. Im's nephew over. He was just a topic of conversation moments ago; now, he is sitting at my kitchen table. The elders really do make things happen.

"May. Come sit with us." Eunhye places the final dish on the table. She's gone all out. There are grilled vegetable wraps with hummus, spicy beef stir-fry noodles, and salad with burnt almonds.

"Looks really good mom." My stomach rumbles at the sight of food. Eunhye beams at the compliment. She motions for me to sit down again. I round the kitchen table just as Mr. Im faces me. I catch his kind smile before my eyes land on his nephew.

"May, this is my nephew. Yoon Jaewon. Jaewon, this is May. Eunhye's daughter," Mr. Im introduces us.

Before I even make eye contact with Mr. Im's relative, his presence marks my senses. *Oh no. This cannot be happening. Only in the movies, only in the books, only in the romantic fantasies. This cannot happen in real life. In fact, this cannot happen in my life. Oh shit!* My intuition springs to her feet with her undivided attention on him; her jaw hits the floor with a deafening ping.

Yoon Jaewon.

He really does look like a Yoon Jaewon–rich, aloof, dark, and handsome. How did he go from Mayhem to Yoon Jaewon? It's a night-and-day, black-and-white contrast.

I am screwed. I find myself locked in the eyes of none other than Mayhem. The dark, smoldering man sitting in my bland kitchen table paralyzes me. The contrast is striking. His per usual arresting, handsome features are extraordinary. He is lighter skin than I remember in the afternoon sunlight. Thick lashes surround his dark, intense brown eyes. The strong nose and accented lips, framed by a chiseled facial structure, reminds me of just how attractive Mayhem truly is. He wears a black t-shirt, black jeans, and black rugged outdoor boots. *As dark and dangerous as they can make them.* Something resembling sparks, along with surprise and butterflies, course through my system. I am the prey locked in the red gaze of the snake's glare.

Say something. I am gaping at Mayhem, or Yoon Jaewon, as Mr. Im's eyebrows twist in question. Little does Mr. Im know his looks-could-kill nephew not only mesmerizes me, but I am actually petrified to my very last bone. Does Mr. Im know that his dear nephew is the leader of a dangerous and violent gang? One look into those kind eyes and I know Mr. Im is clueless. Another glance at Yoon Jaewon's eyes and I know he will have my throat in his hands if I tell his uncle about his true profession.

"Nice to meet you." A stretch of that signature smile crosses his lips. He notices my shock. Mayhem doesn't allow surprise or amusement to color his feigned facial expression. He's calm and cool, reserved and reticent. Mayhem could almost pass as a normal male.

"May." Eunhye places a small hand on my back. I am like a child again, scared and frightened of strangers. The desire to run and hide behind Eunhye's back is like a siren calling to me.

"Hi," is all I manage to squeak. My voice sounds like I accidentally hit my big toe on the side of the bed. *Keep calm*, I mentally tell myself. *This is going to be quite the difficult task*, my intuition mumbles.

Mayhem. The notorious Mayhem is sitting at my dingy kitchen table. But his name is not Mayhem now. It is Yoon Jaewon. The stunning and striking Yoon Jaewon has that signature smirk on his face as if he secretly enjoys the word *shock* and *dead surprise* tattooed on my forehead.

Breathe May. Breathe. Keep cool. I sit down next to Eunhye, feeling her intense gaze against my cheek.

"Are you ok?" Eunhye is in my ear. This is the first time she has ever seen me this way.

"I-I am hungry." I blink several times, trying to drive away the amazement. My thoughts are screaming at me to hold it together.

Yoon Jaewon is the picture of peace and content.

"Let's eat." Eunhye beams at Mr. Im as though they are sharing some telekinetic thoughts. She hands me a vegetable wrap. Then, she gestures towards Mayhem. "Make yourself at home Jaewon."

"Thank you so much for your kindness Eunhye." Mayhem's voice is passionately smooth. He is all hands and fingers on Eunhye's food; Mayhem picks up two vegetable wraps and a handful of the stir-fry noodles. His mannerisms, including his uninhibited demeanor in serving himself, are a clear indication of his underground tendencies. There is confidence exuding in the way he serves himself, the way he chews his food, and even in the way he sits in the chair. I don't miss the fact that Mayhem calls my mother Eunhye instead of the proper greeting of Mrs. Lee.

I quickly note that Mayhem believes he owns the ground he walks on. Oh my. The gang lord complex might be even more severe in his case than Choi Sangwoo's. *Shit. Sangwoo.* How would he react if he knows Mayhem is sitting in my kitchen right now? For some reason I cannot explain, I know Choi Sangwoo and Yoon Jaewon are on a different playing field. Mayhem intimidates me more—maybe because I am sure this gang lord parades the lower levels of the underground world frequently. There is something about Mayhem that's the concoction of danger, darkness, and obscurity.

"Jaewon is from the United States, but divides his time between Busan and Seoul. He owns his own business and is quite the entrepreneur." I snap out of my reverie to realize Eunhye's talking to me. The look in her eyes lets me know that Eunhye is too far gone for me to save her. She's already succumbed to his gang lord's charms.

"Own business?" My cheeky tongue gets the best of me. I am sure Mayhem didn't divulge what his true business dealings are.

"Yes. I do financial consulting for big companies. My firm works with clients from both private and public sectors," is Mayhem's cool response. His voice is a milky tenor. His dark eyes are just as penetrating as ever. I feel the bottom of my stomach dropping slowly. *Holy moly.* He is even more intimidating than Choi Sangwoo. How is it possible that he can stop me in my tracks with just one stare?

Of all the people he can be related to, why does it have to be Eunhye's childhood friend? *Fate? Destiny? Freak coincidence?* My intuition starts counting them off.

"He owns several firms actually." Mr. Im places a hand on Mayhem's shoulders. Mr. Im looks at his nephew with a proud facial expression. There is a profound amount of emotions emanating from him.

"You're so young and handsome too. Are you dating anyone?" Eunhye flashes Mayhem an endearing smile. She has a fork stabbed into her forgotten salad.

Oh no. I hope this is not a setup. Shit. Is this a setup? Panic ripples through every cell in my body. There is no way Eunhye and Mr. Im could have cooked this idea up within the couple of hours I was doing laundry. Damn it. Why didn't I pay more attention this morning? Mentally, I kick myself for being a victim yet again.

"No." Mayhem's confirmation is strong. There's a wicked gleam in his eyes.

I feel the blush sweeping my entire face. Mayhem's eyes are unwavering and concentrating. The butterflies inside my stomach catch flight and flutter. I am almost dizzy from the amount of thoughts and feelings bursting inside of me. Choi Sangwoo doesn't come close to making me feel this way. I lower my gaze from Mayhem and bite into my vegetable wrap. I can't even taste it. I am all mind and no physical feelings.

"He's an eligible bachelor, but extremely picky." Mr. Im grins. He takes a bite into his own vegetable wrap. "The only girl I can think that might meet his standards is May."

Shit. This is a setup! The horror grips my throat. I casually dip the remaining vegetable wrap into the marinated sauce. "I don't think I'm Jaewon's type." *Did I just really say that aloud?*

"How so?" Mr. Im is surprised by my answer.

Because he probably like leggy brunettes who ride shotgun in his many cars and can keep up with his volatile lifestyle. If only thoughts can be heard without judgment and censorship. But all that comes out of my mouth is, "Um." This is an epic fail on my part.

Mayhem watches with the same passionate and haughty stare. It is electrifying. I have his absolute attention with my answer. Even Eunhye and Mr. Im appear to be completely oblivious to Mayhem's attention on me.

"Uncle, she's still in school and painfully shy. Let's not put any more pressure on the kettle. We just met." Mayhem steps in just like a knight in shining armor wouldn't. His eyes are twinkling with humor. He finds this hilarious.

Still in school and painfully shy? Yep. That would describe you. My intuition has no shame in shaking her pom-poms for Team Mayhem.

"Right." Mr. Im gives me an apologetic look.

"That doesn't mean you can't be friends," Eunhye offers. She is trying to salvage my awkwardness.

"Of course," Mayhem adds quickly out of courtesy.

Eunhye laughs at his smart comment. She's finally eating her salad. "You've managed to make my May speechless."

Because he's a powerful gang lord mother, I want to tell her. I suffocate a sigh in my throat. Annoyance and frustration slowly replace the shock. This is wrong. This isn't right. Mayhem has no right to invade my life and involve the people who care about me in his game. *She's still in school and painfully shy?* He is trying to add more wood to the already burning fire of emotions I have for him. I cannot let him get to me like this. One gang leader is enough to deal with, but now I have a gang lord at my kitchen table. What do they want with me?

I watch Mayhem pick up a pair of chopsticks and start his eradication of the stir-fry noodles. *Gosh.* How can someone look so attractive just eating? Every single frame Mayhem moves in can be a picture.

"Eat May." Eunhye places more grilled vegetable wraps on my plate.

I mumble thanks to my mother and nibble on my food. She gives me a fishy look. Eunhye knows that I am not normally shy. Perhaps my behavior signals to her that this blind date plan is not working out.

"So, what are your plans now that you are in Seoul?" Eunhye turns back to Mayhem with renewed interest.

He is chewing his food casually, holding his fingers around the chopsticks like an expert. I don't miss the fact that he has gold knuckle braces on. I wonder briefly what they are for, but I know I am better off not knowing. I also ponder if Eunhye's too blinded by Mayhem's charm to see the knuckle braces. I want to ask more questions, but I force myself to focus on Mayhem's business answers.

"I am working with a couple of businesses at the moment. They are both mergers and acquisitions. I draw up a financial plan first and then help them execute it when they are ready." Again, his tenor is cool and confident.

I also kill them if they don't pay back my ridiculous interest rates, the thought percolates in my mind. I peek at Mayhem to see his eyes are set on me again. The corners of his lips lift into a smile as though he can hear my thoughts. *That's right, I know who you are.*

I lower my eyes back to my plate. My cheeks are probably tomato status. I don't know how much I have eaten. I've lost my gauge.

"You must be quite an asset to the companies," Eunhye remarks in awe. "Have you always been in finance?"

I want to roll my eyes so badly.

"Yes. I have always had an affinity for numbers," Mayhem replies casually. "This is quite a remarkable meal, by the way. Thank you for not only cooking lunch, but inviting me over. I haven't had a home cooked meal in a long time."

I can see Eunhye falling in love with Jaewon right then and there. While he is eating her food, Eunhye is eating up his words. She beams and her cheeks flush. Even Mr. Im is impressed with his nephew. What is up with these gang lords not having home cooked meals? I am sure with the amount of money he has, Jaewon can easily hire someone to cook for his convenience.

"Believe me, it is my pleasure," Eunhye gushes at Mayhem's response. She playfully pushes at Mr. Im's shoulder. "Dongwan, I am so impressed with your nephew. Where has he been all this time?"

"In America," Mr. Im answers truthfully. "Someone with his talent belongs in a society where he can benefit from all the opportunities."

Eunhye and Mr. Im's chatter fade into the background. I bravely glance at Mayhem again. He has a piece of chicken between his chopsticks. Mayhem pops it into his mouth and casually chews. His eyes never deviate from our eye contact. I swallow hard, feeling my palms moistening. I am officially out of my element here. *I want to be that pair of chopsticks!* My intuition swoons over him. I quickly slap her down. She has no shame.

"I am sure I am not the only one with ambition." True to the gang lord style, Mayhem chimes in the conversation that Eunhye and Mr. Im are having.

Eunhye glances at me. The motherly instinct in her activates. "Well, my May is certainly making her path in life. She's a junior in college, and she works two jobs."

Please mom. I want to remain as anonymous as I can. But I am sure Mayhem probably has information about me in a file somewhere. I have been around Choi Sangwoo long enough to know that these gang lords have access to information that presidents struggle to obtain.

"College and two jobs?" Mayhem asks as though this is news to him. "What do you plan to do after college?"

Join your rival gang, my intuition snickers. "I don't know yet," is the boring answer I come up with.

Mayhem doesn't look disappointed with my boring answer. "You can work for me." He staggers us all.

"Oh!" Eunhye gasps with delight. She drops the fork in her hand. "That would be wonderful. May!" My mother slaps my shoulder as though we hit the jackpot. She is beside herself at the prospect.

What the hell am I going to do at his financial company? This has to be a joke. I already have one gang leader who is trying to recruit me. I mentally and physically cannot handle another one. I quickly come up with a bevy of excuses. "I don't think my psychology degree will be beneficial to Jaewon's company. My field of study focuses on human development and perception, not finance and loans."

"We give our clients a psychological assessment when it comes to the larger loans. I usually employ in-house psychologists. You never know what kind of people you're going to get when it comes to money." Mayhem's tone clips at the end of his sentence. The look in his eyes smolder at the prospect as if he's really entertaining the idea.

I feel an extraordinary sense of self-consciousness. This is worse than sitting in front of a mirror or looking at a photograph. Being put under the microscope by such an attractive and powerful man is nerve-wracking in every sense of the word. I am tongue-tied and a nervous wreck.

"That sounds like a wonderful idea," Mr. Im chimes in. His eyes sparkle with eagerness. "Why wait until graduation. I'm sure Jaewon has an internship program right now."

"I do," Mayhem replies shortly. The glint in his eyes deepens.

Oh hell no. I am not doing this. This is worse than peer pressure. This is gang and elder pressure. "I don't think—" is my feeble attempt to speak my mind.

"Don't be shy May," Eunhye admonishes me. "This is the perfect opportunity." My mother faces Mr. Im and does me the embarrassing favor of explaining my employment history and situation. I am helpless. I want to stop her from going on about it, but Eunhye is like a speeding train when she talks. In the grand scheme of things, this is a great opportunity for me if Mayhem wasn't a gang lord. But Mr. Im and Eunhye don't know the truth.

"May, this is a great opportunity to get your foot into the workforce. Jaewon's companies are some of the most reputable in the world." Mr. Im burns me with his stare.

How can someone so young own several companies? Not that I remotely entertain the idea of working for him. I simply recall Sangwoo's words that Mayhem is one of the wealthiest gang lords the world has ever seen.

He's probably a billionaire, my intuition sighs. I glance at Mayhem who has a guarded facial expression on. His mouth presses into a hard line. He's done eating. From the hooded look in his eyes, I know Mayhem is assessing me. I am not going to play into the palm of his hands. I will not do anything in front of Eunhye and Mr. Im without careful calculation.

"I'll think about it." I want to make Eunhye happy and Mr. Im feel like he's making a difference. Little does Mr. Im know, his nephew's suggestion deploys a death trap for me.

"That's my girl!" Eunhye wraps her arms around me.

"Excellent." Mr. Im flashes me a grin.

"We can exchange information after. You can call me when you are ready." Mayhem's tone comprises of a heavy bluff and amusement. The murky look in his eyes is daunting to the very last blink.

I'm not going to! I want to snap at him. Instead, I take the high road because Mr. Im is sitting here and my mother will be more than happy to set me in my place if I act up.

"Thank you." I pick up my glass of water and proceed to drink. I notice that Mayhem is drinking coffee—one of Eunhye's most potent dark coffee. I am a coffee lover, but the death coffee he is drinking had my nerves tweaking for hours on end the first time I tried it. One glance at Mayhem's cup and I know he is close to finishing it off. Maybe gang lords have a very different stamina from us little people. They probably don't have inhibitions or fears like us mortals. *Like I said, they probably don't need to use the bathroom either,* my intuition taunts.

"So tell me more about yourself Eunhye. Have you always been a nurse?" This time around, Mayhem turns the table on Eunhye.

My mother blushes at his concern. She is enamored with him. "Well, I started working at this particular hospital when my husband, May's father, decided to move to Seoul. We—"

"Mom, I don't think we should talk about that right now." I have to intervene. The mentioning of my father hovers like dark clouds over my head. Quite frankly, I don't think it is any of Mayhem's business to know personal details about us. If anything, I am protecting the Lee women from the gang lord's wrath.

My remark stings her, and Eunhye gapes at me. My mother is not in on the Yoon-Jaewon-is-a-gang-lord secret. "May—" She looks hurt that I am objecting to her disclosure.

Shit. I need to get out of here before I turn into a mess. "Excuse me for a minute." I stand from the table and make a quick exit down the hallway. The last image I see is Eunhye's flustered facial expression along with Mr. Im's confused grimace. I avoid Mayhem's eyes altogether. My heart pounds in my ribcage. My head is dizzy. *What the hell is going on?* Who does Mayhem think he is coming into my home and getting my mother not only to like him, but to also disclose our personal information? I am beyond disturbed.

I rush into the bathroom and throw water on my face. I don't even know if the water is cold or warm. My hands are shaking. I cannot handle the pressure of sitting across from Mayhem anymore and listening to him lie through his teeth about being a legitimate CEO for the sake of Eunhye and Mr. Im. The irony and the lies strike me as something wicked and cruel. I have to do something. Will calling the police help? I am sure he is on their most-wanted list. *He's probably in with them too.* My conscience takes the opportunity to remind me.

I wipe my face with a fresh towel and resign to going into my room. I can lie that I am not feeling well. I turn off the light in the bathroom and make my way out to the hallway.

"Wait." Strong, powerful hands grip my wrist. He reaches for me like a shadow embedded in the wall.

"What are you doing?" My back is against the wall as Yoon Jaewon, or as the dark underground world knows him as, Mayhem, leans into me. Casually, he invades my space. Mayhem's hands extend against the wall on both sides of my shoulders. He has me trapped and locked in his hold. Mayhem's familiar and seductive cologne pervades my senses. I close my eyes, believing that it will reduce the dark attraction I have for him.

There have been moments before when I wanted to get a good look at Mayhem, but I couldn't. Even at the hospital, he was hiding underneath the dark hat. Now that Mayhem is right in front of me, up close and personal, I feel an alarming sense of being enraptured in his presence. The darkest eyes I have ever seen are gazing at me with scrutiny and something else. The knot inside my stomach twists, leaking butterflies and something else.

"Very cozy life you have here. I am sure that Choi Sangwoo would be able to afford a better home for you and your lovely mother." Mayhem's voice is cool and guarded. There is dark sarcasm in every inch of his words.

"That's none of your business," I snap.

"It's very much so my business," Mayhem offers simply. He changes the subject. "I wasn't looking forward to this lunch, but seeing Choi Sangwoo's associate is a pleasant surprise."

Gah, my intuition gasps loudly. "Surprise? It was a shock for me."

"You were happy to see me." Mayhem lifts up a dangerous, overly confident eyebrow.

Oh you have no clue, my intuition drawls. "Please leave my house," I tell him curtly. The emotional loop Mayhem's throwing at me is uncomfortable.

Mayhem's lips curl into a smile. "Is this how you treat your all your guests? Because if you don't, it isn't fair you're treating me like a pariah when I'm here trying to spend some time with my uncle."

"Does your uncle know that his beloved nephew isn't just a simple CEO of a finance company? That his nephew is actually a violent, malicious, vindictive, and crass gang lord who knows no bounds when it comes to morals and the order of life?" I am a spitfire, emotional and slightly disgusted with myself for being fascinated with this man.

"You will keep your mouth shut." Mayhem presses forward and for once our eyes are at the same level. "You breathe a word to my uncle and I will show you what a true crime lord can do." The threat behind his voice is real. "Choi Sangwoo is child's play compared to me."

My breath hitches in my throat. Every aspect of my body coils at his dangerous tone and robust threat. "So you do have emotions," I marvel. This is Mayhem protecting one of the closest people to him.

Mayhem's eyes run along my face. "You have no idea who I am. Don't try to guess." There is a touch of evasion on his part.

"You've killed?" I ignore him and ask with vigor.

"Maimed," Mayhem responds.

"You've been in jail?"

"Prison."

"You disregard the world and its rules?"

"I'm all sorts of bad."

"Who are you then?" I feel the courage racing through my veins.

Mayhem angles his face to accentuate his jaw. Those penetrating eyes cut deep into the depth of my soul. "You're not ready for the truth." He takes a step back from me. He is taller than I remembered. It is wrong for me to feel the electric current running through my body. I want to slap my hands for wanting to touch his face—if only for a few seconds. In that instant, I realize there must be more to Mayhem than the petulant rumors.

"It seems like you and I are meant to meet either way," I tell him with a bittersweet notion.

Mayhem's eyes narrow in a speculative manner. I am not imagining it. Mayhem lowers his voice another octave as he agrees softly, "I guess we are."

A sense of bewilderment slips through me.

"How did you really get involved with Choi Sangwoo?" Mayhem asks. His tone indicates this is a pressing question. "I doubt he picked you out of the dreadful litter he has. I also highly doubt that he put you through his many initiation rituals."

The ominous feeling spreads in my heart. "Why do you want to know?" The stubbornness in me riddles with contempt.

"Because I can help you escape his wrath before it's too late." The darkness in Mayhem's eyes gives way to something much softer.

My eyebrows come together in question. "Escape his wrath?" It is an interesting choice of words. He transports me back to our moment at the hospital. Mayhem is pushier and more forward than Sangwoo; his cryptic messages are untouchable.

"You don't listen to warnings and threats very well do you?" Mayhem asks with harsh conviction. Gold armor replaces the elasticity of the conversation. "It's a shame that you don't know anything about my world. You need a healthy dose of fear injected into you."

"Danny tried," I snap.

"He was never going to really shoot you." Mayhem stuns me with his confession.

"What?"

"If you're expecting an apology, you're not going to get one. You were unharmed. It was Choi Sangwoo who got shot."

"You really do live in your own world of rationale and logic." I shake my head at him.

Mayhem ignores my statement. Instead, there is light humor dancing in his eyes. *Oh goodness.* He is super attractive like that. My breath catches in my throat and I am speechless for the moment. "Let me make this clear to you. I can either make your life or ruin it. The choice hangs in the balance," Mayhem warns with a biting tone.

"What is that supposed to mean?"

"It means that you are my means to Choi Sangwoo."

And the true snake reveals its motive.

I am at his mercy. Mayhem cannot play me like this. I refuse to let him. I swallow hard. "I am not some helpless person you can utilize."

"We'll see about that."

"There's nothing about me that you can take advantage of."

"I beg to differ."

I can only gawk at him. "What is it about me that you gang leaders want?!" I exclaim. The burning question finally gushes out.

"There's nothing more valuable in a person than her ignorance," Mayhem answers with a low growl.

Alright, time to pack the bags and move. My intuition withdraws first.

Mayhem lifts an eyebrow at my speechlessness. He is the dark Angel disguised as a human; his features are not only physically attractive, but also emotionally manipulative. It's as though Mayhem was designed and engineered to execute the female species.

"You have five seconds to get out of my way." I stare him dead in the eyes while my heart thumps like crazy in my chest. How is it that I am feeling all these *feelings* for him when I don't even have any for Choi Sangwoo? The emotions I harbor for Sangwoo doesn't come close to this.

"Or what?" Mayhem breathes.

I bite my lower lip, staring at the pretty face with the personality of a jerk to back it up. "Or this!" I pick up my left foot. I kick Mayhem in the shin while shoving my hands at his chest. Causing him to stumble, I take my chance and run out of the apartment door. I am all impulse and avoidance like a small child running away from her problem. *Very mature, May.* My intuition stifles her mocking laughter.

Mayhem recovers quickly, but doesn't chase after me. He doesn't even make a sound. I don't know if he's laughing or planning to kill me.

I don't want to stay and find out. Eunhye and Mr. Im turn from the kitchen when I sprint out of the apartment.

"May!" Eunhye calls after me, but it is too late.

I slam the door behind me and run like hell.

"MAYHEM IS MR. IM'S NEPHEW?!" Lina stops midway through her jog and nearly causes several people to collide behind her. "What the hot fudge on a Sunday?!"

"Lina." I grab a fistful of my cousin's shirt and pull her to the side of the trail. True to my promise, I am jogging with Lina. A two-mile trail snakes through this city park. Towering trees loom over the running trail and slant in opposite directions. We are lost in the thick forest of the trail, but the memories still haunt me.

Lina has her hair tied out of her face while mine is under the hold of a ponytail. The hot summer air feels nice against my skin. The run has definitely kept my mind off Choi Sangwoo, but now my thoughts and concerns focus on Mayhem—Yoon Jaewon. It is too funny how the tables are turning.

"Can you believe the odds of that?" I keep my breath controlled as I bend down to touch my knees.

"He's after you," Lina concludes. She is breathing hard, wiping her damp forehead with the back of her hand. "You have to be careful May. For all you know, he could chop you into little pieces, bury you under wooden floorboards, and then go after us. Oh my gosh, it's never going to end. This is all my fault."

"Please don't be paranoid Lina," I rebuke my cousin. It is also for my piece of mind. "He's just Mr. Im's nephew. If anything, now Eunhye and Mr. Im know him."

"How is he?" Lina asks for the notorious gang lord's personality.

"Crass, controlling, aggressive, overly confident. Basically, he is the works. He has this severe gang lord complex. Or more specifically, King syndrome."

"He should tell Sangwoo." Lina is serious.

"Why?" I ask.

"So he can protect you," Lina urges. "He's going to be your Boss."

"Sure. Choi Sangwoo is going to take out his guns and knives to kill Jaewon for that," I tell her. "Lina, it's not going to happen that way. We're not starring in a drama."

"Hmm." Lina scrunches up her nose. "Maybe he likes you."

"Sangwoo?"

"No. Jaewon."

I roll my eyes and burst out laughing. "I'm sure he likes me when he told me he could ruin my life."

Lina shakes her head. "Think about it, he said he was pleased to see you in the kitchen."

"Well, he wasn't shocked." The memory plagues me. I am suddenly uncomfortable with the notion that Mayhem might've known all along the connection between the two of us. But what if he was just as surprised? If that's true, Mayhem should win an award for his immaculate reaction.

"May, you are an attractive young woman. Gorgeous slushes probably surround these gang lords. It's not rocket science that maybe they want someone who is more grounded and girl-next-door." Lina has it down to a science. I don't miss the fact that my cousin used her term of slushes for sluts. It is easy to see that Lina's theory derives from the plethora of Korean dramas influenced by American romantic-comedy themes.

I highly doubt this theory. Choi Sangwoo wants me because I remind him of Dead Girl. Yoon Jaewon sees me as a means to get to Choi Sangwoo. I am different shades of reasons for these gang lords.

"I don't think it's about attraction with these guys Lina." My voice is soft.

"Look, if you don't want to sign that initiation contract with Choi Sangwoo then don't. I will help you as much as I can to repay him back.

As for Yoon Jaewon, just stay clear of him and hopefully there won't be any trouble." Lina places a hand on my shoulder as though she wants to ease my anxiety. This sounds great in theory, but I am going to fail miserably. I am not the only active agent in this course of my life. If only Lina can understand the depth of Choi Sangwoo's persistence.

"Ok. Let's just keep jogging." I resign to letting this go for now. I pick up my pace and step back onto the trail.

"May, you can't just stuff this all under the rug!" Lina groans behind me, but the sound of her sneakers lets me know she's giving in.

"Last one back buys snack!" I shout. My sneakers thud on the ground as I push my body to the limit. I don't want to hear my cousin's advice. I need time and distance to think everything through. I need to let the whirlwind die down.

AFTER OUR JOG LINA AND I grab a snack at the local bistro. We spend the rest of the afternoon talking about topics that do not include gangsters, gang leaders, or money. Hanging out with Lina brings a fresh batch of air. For once, my mind's not convoluted with dark thoughts. It actually feels good to people-watch and be in the moment. However, in the course of the afternoon, Eunhye leaves me two angry messages. She wants to know why I ran out and when I am coming home. Choi Sangwoo calls once and leaves me a text message to call him back. By the time I part ways with Lina, the feelings of dread come back. *At the rate you're going, an anxiety attack is only another event away,* my conscience mumbles out of pity.

Mayhem clouds my thoughts on the way home. The impression he's left on me is marred with rumors and his true identity. I am plagued with the notions that Mayhem lives up to his reputation, but at the same time there is more to him than the status and repertoire. Every single time we meet, Mayhem warns me about Choi Sangwoo, yet he falls short in giving me a reason or a shred of evidence. If I didn't know better, I would think he actually cares.

Maybe he does. My intuition shrugs. Yoon Jaewon and Choi Sangwoo are complete opposites. While Sangwoo is cold and kind, Jaewon is mysterious and provocative. Sangwoo is reserved and careful while Jaewon is reserved and aloof. Sangwoo hides his true intentions while Jaewon wears his instincts on his sleeve. Two different men—two very different gang lords.

Why are you thinking so much about this? Absentmindedly, I sigh. I have to stop going down this spiral. All these questions lead to no answers. I am back to square one. *Gotta keep busy. Gotta keep moving.*

My apartment comes into view. With one last spurt of energy, I finish off my water bottle and round the last bend. When the towering gate comes into view, I spy a sleek, midnight blue coupe to the right of the intercom. The 320i BMW is as glossy and extravagant as ever.

I pause in the middle of the sidewalk. Without warning, my heart thumps in a rhythmic manner. Memories of last night spread like wildfire through me. He is here. Choi Sangwoo is waiting for me. *You should turn and run down the opposite street,* my intuition snaps. But if I run, I have to keep running. If I get away today, there's nothing to guarantee I will get away tomorrow.

I gather up my mental barriers and approach the car. "Sangwoo?"

The Crist gang leader is sitting in the driver's seat dressed down in dark gray. His unwavering gaze is muted. As the evening light, a rich combination of orange and yellow dye, reaches his eyes; I notice how tired and indifferent Sangwoo looks. "Hi May."

"What are you doing here?" I do my best to keep my voice steady. I hesitate when I smell the alcohol radiating from the car. I don't miss the fact that an open bottle nestles in one of the cup holders.

"Why didn't you pick up your cell phone?" Sangwoo's tone is arctic and distant, perhaps even accusing and aggressive.

Damn. He's mad that I've been ignoring his phone calls all day. "I was out with my cousin." It is slightly annoying having to report to him. "I'm sorry," I add out of courtesy.

Sangwoo doesn't answer me. My eyes travel back to the partially empty bottle of Vodka in the cup holder. Was he drinking while waiting for me? Choi Sangwoo has an indefinite sad side to him. It is dark and lonely, cancerous and decaying. Why is he drinking already? In the short time that I have known him, Sangwoo's affinity for alcohol seems to have skyrocketed. *Alcoholic!* my intuition chortles.

"Sangwoo, how much did you drink?" I am wary.

"Hmm. This many." He extends ten fingers. There is a glossy look in his eyes. If anything, it is an indication of a weakness.

I have never seen Sangwoo so childlike. I briefly conclude that only when he is drinking does the gang leader demeanor deteriorate.

"Get in the car May. I want to talk to you." Sangwoo motions with his head towards the passenger seat.

"Sangwoo, you're drunk." It doesn't escape the both of us that my tone hints frustration.

"No. I'm not." His brown eyes dilate. This strange, erratic behavior is a flaw of Sangwoo's. "I want to talk. I'm usually a patient person May, but you are testing my limits today. You ignore my phone calls and now you don't want to talk to me. What did I do wrong?" There is sorrow in his voice. Sangwoo is at the very edge.

A gentle, prickling sensation attacks my eyes. I swallow hard. My palms are clammy and my heart is heavy. How do I tell Sangwoo I need time and space away from him? What can I say to put into words all the things I am *not* feeling about him? I know I cannot run from him and avoid the necessary conversation, but at the present moment I am desperate to avoid it all.

"May," Sangwoo calls to me again. This time his tone changes. It is heavy with judgment and contrite.

"Five minutes." My intuition shakes her head at me over her black rimmed glasses. I ignore her and make my way to the passenger side of the 320i. There is no point in turning back now.

Sangwoo leans toward me once I am in the seat. His brown eyes glaze over, murky and lost. "I am a very patient man May. But with you, I think I am starting to lose my discipline."

My blood freezes at his conviction. Discipline? What is Sangwoo talking about? He cannot insinuate that I am wearing his patience thin when he expects not only loyalty from me, but also absolute submission. Last time I checked, I didn't sign an initiation contract.

"May," he calls to me. His voice becomes so soft that it distracts me. "I like you. I really like you." He leans forward and his hands are around my back. The smell of alcohol coils around my senses.

Emotions sweep me away. My heart pounds a mile a minute. *Shit.* He knocks my breath away with the confession. Without any qualms or reservations, Choi Sangwoo tells me that he likes me. Memories of last night's kiss grip my mind. I let Sangwoo hold me, hoping I'd feel something, hoping that I'd say, "I like you too." But my lips won't move. The forlorn realization slips over me. I don't have the feelings that I should for this man. Maybe it is because I know Sangwoo is under the influence of alcohol. Or maybe I know that his feelings for me are marred and tainted. It's not me he wants; it's the girl I remind him of. Why won't he come out and say it?

Sangwoo reaches for my hand. He intertwines his fingers in mine roughly. I can't let this go on any longer. I pull back from him. "Sangwoo, I think you should go home."

"Do you know how worried I was when I couldn't reach you today?"

Sangwoo ignores my suggestion. His brown eyes are tracking beams. "You're distancing yourself from me. Why?"

I lower my gaze. My hands rest in my lap. How can I explain to Sangwoo that I cannot return his feelings for me? He is pursuing a relationship with no future. "I think we're better off as friends. I don't ha-have the same feelings for you Sangwoo. I'm sorry."

The hurt sears across his composed facial expression. The alcohol has already lowered his first line of defense. Now, I am tearing through the concrete walls of this poor soul.

Sangwoo withdraws from me and sits back in his seat. No longer making eye contact, he stares out of the front windshield. "Why not?"

Why not? A million thoughts explode like a supernova in my mind. How do I even begin to explain the turmoil and confusion I have? "I just don't think we're compatible," is my feeble attempt to save feelings and cap pain.

"Compatible," Sangwoo repeats the word as though he is trying it out. He faces me now. "You're right. We're not compatible. I'm a gang leader revered in my world for not only what I do, but also who I am. You are just a citizen in the mainstream world scraping by under a law and a government you don't understand. I have access to all the riches the global sphere can offer while you barely make minimum wage. I am knowledgeable and skillful at things you cannot even fathom while you struggle with everyday mortal problems. So you are right. We are incompatible to the last fault. But the feelings I have for you, my persistent chase after you, is sincere and true. It has nothing to do with compatibility. It has to do with the emotions that govern us all. This is my weakness—my feelings for you."

Don't cry May. You are stronger than this! I bite down on my bottom lip. I want to unleash the brutal truth that is on a tight leash around my heart. But I am quiet as I listen to Sangwoo's rage. I have never been much of a fighter. I am weak and passive in adulthood due to my upbringing and circumstances.

"Did you know the end of the month is coming May?" There is deep pain traveling through Sangwoo's tone.

"Sangwoo, please." I find my voice. I don't want to talk about anything remotely relevant to that subject. This game of I-know-that-you-know is causing me great grief. *He knows*, my intuition hisses.

Sangwoo closes his eyes. The silence tears through us. He is coping with a headache and indifferent emotions. Little does Sangwoo know I am afraid for him. I'm petrified of the consequences of our actions. I must put a stop to it. "I'll drive you back to your hotel." I glance anxiously outside of the window.

Sangwoo turns to me. Surprise colors his pale facial expression. It is clear the alcohol is moments away from consuming him. All it takes is one phone call and his members will be here. But I know that is not what he wants.

"You will?"

"Yes. It's the least I can do."

"Yes, it's the least you can do for breaking my heart."

Without another word, Sangwoo opens the driver's door. He stumbles and rounds the car. I step out of the passenger side and wait for him. Once he is in the passenger seat, I make my way to the driver's side.

Do I have the mindset to drive right now? Yes. I'm determined to take him home and get us out of this situation. *Drop him off for good!* My intuition rolls her eyes. She is over him.

"You're going to have to give me instructions." The driver's seat is too low for me. I play with the side buttons until the seat's incline matches my length. Thank goodness for the automatic transmission on the 320i. I can drive without worrying about shifting gears.

"I have a GPS system." Sangwoo points to the screen above the middle instrument panel. "Talk to it." His cell phone rings, but Sangwoo ignores it.

I have never driven such a powerful and lustrous car before. Its advanced technology is beyond me. I fish for the keys in the ignition and turn the engine on. The car hums smoothly. I fiddle with buttons on the GPS panel until a female voice speaks. "Good evening Mr. Choi. Where would you like to go?" Even the car adheres to the needs of the gang leader. What is money not able to buy? *You.* My intuition has a smug smile on her face. I wave her aside to focus on the directions.

"The Aston House at the W Seoul Walkerhill Hotel." I still remember the first time I was there with Sangwoo. At the time, he was alert and earnest to speak with me. Now, the alcohol has consumed his consciousness. Sangwoo's eyes are closed and his heavy breathing takes over.

"One moment please. I am calculating the fastest route to the Aston House at the W Seoul Walkerhill Hotel." The GPS acknowledges my command. The screen blackens as a red bar streams across it. Then, a majestic map pops up on the screen. "Please make a U-turn onto the main road."

"Here we go," I mumble. I release the brakes on the 320i and feel the smooth engine roar to life. Although I received my driver's license at the age of nineteen, I haven't driven a car in a year. But the car's familiarity ignites my beginner's skills. Although the 320i was built for speed and agility, I drive slow. I follow the instructions of the GPS system for the thirty-five minute car ride. The drive to the W Seoul Hotel is quiet and eerily tense. I do my best to shun my thoughts. I need to concentrate. The sooner I drop him off, the sooner this will all be over with. Sangwoo remains sound asleep in the passenger seat.

When I pull into the familiar Aston Walkerhill curb, the gorgeous view stuns me just as it did the first time. The familiar incandescent lights lead to the hotel's broad entrance. I follow the winding curb until it stops in front of the entrance. A valet approaches my driver's side. He peers in and immediately recognizes Sangwoo in the passenger seat.

"Good evening." Confusion lives in the valet's eyes.

"Good evening," I answer him shortly. From my side, I see three men approaching the car. From their dark suits to the signature chains peeking from their necks, I know they are Crist members. One of them takes the valet by the arm and moves him away from the car. The other members flank the car on both sides. One Crist member reaches for Sangwoo while another ushers me out of the driver's seat.

"Leave me alone." Sangwoo wakes with great effort. He is sluggish and disorderly. Sangwoo bats one of his members away. In a direct manner, Sangwoo points to me. "She's with me."

In the meantime, I look for the familiar tattooed man. But Ren is nowhere to be seen. It becomes apparent that Ren must be on a special mission or absence of leave. I turn my attention back to Sangwoo and his men. They are bowing to me in such a way that I don't know what else to do but bow back.

"Let's go." Sangwoo points to the revolving doors of the entrance. He stumbles forward and hands are ready to catch him. Sangwoo slaps them all away except for mine. He lets me hold his right side. Just like the night when I took him home, Sangwoo leans against me in his drunken state.

We make our way into the grand hotel with his members in tow. A Crist member is already holding an elevator for us. Hotel guests in the elaborate, golden lobby are staring at us with muddled facial expressions. I keep my eyes focused on the ground away from the speculations and judgment.

Inside the baroque elevator, Sangwoo leans against the glass walls with his eyes closed. His men are darting fervent glances at us. The worried expression on their faces becomes paramount when the elevator doors ding open. Sangwoo stumbles back into my arms and orders for his men to fall back.

The grand foyer of his state-of-the-art penthouse suite is just as extravagant as I remember. The similar décor of white and royal blue furnishing sweep the entire grand area. The fireplace, adjacent to the grand windows is dark and portentous. Silence, dancing with loneliness, pervades the air. Although elite and rich in its texture and design, the suite is forlorn. Great power and anonymity requires an intense price of solitude.

As we pass by the living room expanse, I realize I don't know which hallway leads to his bedroom.

"Where is your room Sangwoo?"

He mumbles an incoherent response. Staggering towards the left hole of darkness, Sangwoo moves down what turns out to be a hallway. I follow him, taking note of the paintings that line the walls. Most of the paintings are accounts of nature–sunsets, sunrises, mountains, and oceans. It strikes me that Sangwoo probably didn't choose these paintings.

At the very end of the hallway are large French doors. The doors lead to a master bedroom that's larger than my apartment. Two magnificent windows display the extensive view of downtown Seoul. Bright, shimmering lights glitter through the window. Varying degrees of color dance richly in the room.

Sangwoo stumbles onto the oversized bed positioned in the middle of the room. His room is empty except for the bed and a large circular office desk. To the right side of the room is the bathroom. Directly across from it is another door to a walk-in closet. There is nothing in Sangwoo's bedroom that reveals the dark underground world he rules. In all honesty, it is a simple bedroom of a very sad man.

"Sangwoo," I call to him softly.

He is unconscious on the bed in a deep sleep. I approach the bottom of the bed. My heartstrings tug in various directions. I let out a deep breath, bracing myself. Slowly, I reach down and take off his shoes. Tough black boots clatter loudly to the floor. I reach for the comforter and cover it over Sangwoo.

I watch him for a few seconds. Sangwoo's eyebrows are together in a frown. I swallow hard. I feel a sense of sorrow wash over me. Choi Sangwoo's addiction to alcohol is escalating.

Taking a glance around the room, I note the amount of pills on the bed stand nearby. More specifically, a stack of photographs catches my

The blood freezes in my veins.

Younger versions of Choi Sangwoo are smiling, smirking, and grinning at me. But he is not alone behind the exotic backdrops. In all of the photographs, there is a girl with Sangwoo in various intimate poses. Her large, dark eyes accentuate the halo of hair around her youthful face. Her smile is stunning and vibrant. She is easy to fall in love with.

Dead Girl.

My heavy heart realizes that Dead Girl looks like me.

Misun.

CHAPTER TWELVE

I am shaking all over when I rush by the Crist members. They gape when I make the hasty exit out of Sangwoo's suite. I look like I have seen a ghost. The last thing I care about is what they are thinking. I abandon all of my senses and better judgment as I run from the Ashton Walkerhill.

My heart is heavy and my mind slips into a chaotic daze. No matter how hard I try, the images of Choi Sangwoo and Dead Girl replay in my mind like the photographic memories I inadvertently thumbed through. How was I to know I was picking up Sangwoo's past? I want to cry and let all of the emotional discrepancies out. I am weak with jealousy and betrayal. Those photographs confirm everything that I have been suspicious of. I am beyond hurt by the revelation. The potential of having feelings for Sangwoo, of having any type of relationship with him— friendship or romantic—is over and done. The true reason why Sangwoo pursues me is too bitter to take.

By the time I reach the end of the road, I am a puddle of tears. Breathing hard, I do my best to gather my composure. My cell phone rings in my tote bag. Dreading who the caller is, I retrieve my phone and answer the call. To my dismay, it's an unknown number.

"Hello?"

"My shin stills hurts."

I swallow hard at the sound of his voice. My throat becomes rigid. Slowly, I look across the street. A dark figure perches on his expensive and fine-tuned motorcycle. The distinctive sleek body of the bike contrasts with the setting sun's cascade of colors. Mayhem has his helmet on and he's dressed entirely in black leather. At a distance, he looks like an enigma and is the epitome of a shadowy figure from the underground world. *Oh em gee!* My intuition dances on her tiptoes.

"Are you stalking me?" My tears stall for the moment. I am in too much shock. How did he get my phone number? How does he know that I am here? Is there nothing that these gang lords don't know about me?

"Don't flatter yourself, sweetheart. Did it ever occur to you that the world is round?" Mayhem drawls. His black helmet glares at me. I cannot see his face, especially those dark eyes of his. Even though his face is covered, Mayhem is still strikingly attractive.

"You live in the same hotel as Sangwoo?" I ask shortly.

"He lives in the same area as me," Mayhem corrects me. "Judging from your tears, the meeting with Sangwoo didn't go so well did it?"

"Why do you care?" I cannot digest this coincidental meeting fast enough. My stubborn streak rears its ugly head.

"I don't." Mayhem's tone changes to arctic ice. "Call your mother back. My uncle wants to know what happened too. I don't want them thinking you ran out because of me."

"No, we wouldn't want that." I hold my cell phone close to my ears, keeping my eyes steady on him. Even from across the street, Mayhem is still disarming behind his massive helmet.

"I warned you about Choi Sangwoo. Sometimes, the bad guy is actually the one you should listen to. We're the pariahs for a reason." Mayhem's voice remains calm and undisturbed.

"Why don't you just tell me what you want to say?" I am hot-tempered. I don't have time to decipher his cryptic messages.

"I don't want to suck all the fun out for you." Mayhem tilts his helmet. "I suggest you head home before Sangwoo stumbles out here in his drunken state."

I bite my lower lip, reeling in haste. Why does he care?

"I don't care about the melodrama you have going on, but I would hate to see something unnecessary occur because Sangwoo is out of his mind right now." As though he can read my thoughts, Mayhem tosses out a sound advice.

I am speechless as I clutch my phone to my ear.

"If you want a ride home you can ask me," Mayhem adds as if he's testing me.

"I can find my way home," I reply. *Can't you see I need your help?* My intuition pouts.

"Suit yourself." Mayhem hangs up.

I listen to the dead phone line as he kicks the motorcycle stand. Mayhem settles onto the motorcycle and starts the engine. Its fierce roar pierces through the silent street. Without another moment to waste, Mayhem leans on the steel body and races down the dangerous slope. At the same moment, a taxi crawls around the bend.

Mayhem's called a taxi for me.

BY THE TIME I REACH the apartment, I run for the comforts of my bedroom. I want to be alone with my thoughts. I am in too much of a hurry to notice that Eunhye is pacing back and forth in her room.

"I will try, but I'm not making promises. Remember, you promised me that you'd let me handle the situation. She's not ready. If only you could see her now. She's active. She's working and making friends. I don't want to disrupt what she has going now. Now is not a good time." Eunhye's hands are in her hair. Although my mother's back is facing me, I can hear the anxiety and exasperation in her voice.

Eunhye lets out a deep sigh as she listens to the response on the other side of the phone line. "Sure, I can make the arrangements for you. I will do my best this year to make sure she comes. Yes." Eunhye pauses yet again to continue packing her overnight hospital bag.

I stand in the gap of the door listening to her conversation. A chill comes over me when I recognize the tone–the only kind of tone Eunhye has when she is speaking to *him*.

"Eunhye, who are you talking to?" I never call Eunhye by her first name–at least not to her face. I am still reeling from what just happened and this puts the icing on the cake. *I don't care anymore. Throw everything you have at me karma!* My intuition is wearing her safety helmet. My conscience is swinging her bat.

"Oh, you're home!" Forgetting that she is on the phone, Eunhye quickly hangs up. Eunhye places a hand over her chest in surprise, but she forces a smile. "Where have you been? You took off right after lunch. Actually, you ran off."

"I forgot I had to do something with Lina," I lie. My eyes scan her face as though I can catch the deception.

"You could've said goodbye. Jaewon was quite hurt." Eunhye is doing her best to deflect from the actual topic. She frowns at my facial expression.

"I'm sure he'll live." I am cold and unreasonable right now.

Eunhye places a hand on her hips. "What is going on with you? You were very rude at lunch. Then you took off and ignored my phone calls. Are you okay?"

"I should be asking you. Who were you talking to?" I casually ask. I ignore Eunhye's sensitive question.

"Someone from work," Eunhye lies. Through her teeth, she is lying to me.

"Oh." If Eunhye wants to lie to me, I will let her. From now on, if anyone wants to lie to me, they can. I don't care anymore. I don't want the truth to disappoint me anymore.

"May." Eunhye closes her eyes and sighs in frustration. "The end of the month is coming–you know that right? You know what that date means for our family."

Stunned by Eunhye's reminder, I feel hurt and on the verge of bawling from the stress. First Sangwoo, Mayhem, and now her. "Eunhye, I don't want to talk about that." I do my best to keep my voice from shaking.

Eunhye remains motionless at my disapproval. Slowly, her shock displays itself. "May, it's something that we need to talk about."

"Can we talk about it later?" I do my best to keep the anguish in my voice controlled. I don't want to talk about it. I want to avoid it as long as I can. I cannot handle another blow right now.

The crestfallen look on Eunhye's face evokes guilt in me. "May," Eunhye starts to say.

"I'm not feeling very well." I have to pull out the sick card. Perhaps my gaunt facial expression is the decision maker.

Eunhye looks as though she wants to say something else, but her cell phone rings again.

He's calling her back, my intuition says sadly. I don't need to hear his voice; I remember it clearly. I give Eunhye one last look before I head to my bedroom. A wave of emotion comes over me. The heavy feeling in my heart is difficult to overcome. Eunhye and I have a relationship that is not easy to explain. Our relationship is usually not this tense, but whenever it comes to this time of year the space between us is very clear. How can I not remember?

I allow for the darkness of my room to consume me. No dinner. No human needs. Nothing and no one. For the second night in a row, I cry myself to sleep. I let my emotions ride on my tear ducts. I cry for all the memories and the pain. It is metaphysical at this point.

SHE COMES TOWARDS ME SLOWLY. I reach out to her and let out an animalistic cry. "Shh, don't cry." She wraps me tightly in her arms. Her hands run through my hair in an endearing manner. I continue to sob, weeping uncontrollably for the sister that I never got a chance to know. Misun.

MY EYES ARE HEAVY. I open them for a fraction of a second to see Eunhye kissing my forehead softly. "I love you baby. I wish I can make things right for you." The darkness and the heavy lull of sleep consume me. The pain rolls in another set of waves.

MONDAY MORNING IS BLEAK AND gloomy. I wake up under a cloud of darkness and morbid thoughts. I toss and turn in bed buying time and trading senseless thoughts.

The first thing I think about is–because of circumstances, I am no longer waitressing at The Trax. Because of coercion, I am no longer working at Sansachun either. I am jobless and am an emotional wreck. I conduct a mental countdown only to realize I have two months left before school starts again. Thoughts about my responsibilities and school distract the reality of Choi Sangwoo, Dead Girl, and Mayhem. I think about my savings, my goals, and my possible future. I want to graduate and help others. But this can only happen if I abandon the dangerous and treacherous path these gang leaders are luring me down.

Choi Sangwoo's pursuit seems innocent on the outside, but his true intentions are malevolent. It is no longer sweet and innocent. Slowly, it is becoming dark and tainted. Sangwoo wants to shape me into someone I can never be. Especially after last night, I don't know if I can trust him. I am the flesh and bone of the person in his memories. To him, I am Dead Girl. Nothing is more painful than that realization. Now that I know why he's chasing me, I don't know whether to feel relieved or restrained.

I listen to Eunhye bustling outside of my bedroom as she gets ready for work. Before she leaves, Eunhye checks up on me. I close my eyes and pretend to be sleeping. She lingers in the doorway for a few seconds before leaving.

I lay in bed for another hour before I have the strength to force myself out of bed. I take a long, drowning shower. I am heavy and intoxicated with emotions, but life must go on. I cannot be a victim of someone's ill intentions. I resolve to be strong and resilient.

After I am dressed and done with my morning coffee, I check my phone to see the missed calls and messages. I have been avoiding the machine in hopes of a speedy recovery.

"Come out with me." I stare at Lina's simple text message. Next to Lina's text message bubble is Choi Sangwoo's number. I have six missed calls from him, including a handful of text messages. *I want to see you,* he says. *It's important,* he writes.

MULA IS A POPULAR PLACE not only because it serves just about a million different types of milk tea, but also because it houses a large flat screen in the center of its main room. Large windows line every wall, creating a bright atmosphere. Every other weekend, Mula has a movie day where they show the latest blockbuster movie. This attracts a lot of business, a genius-marketing move. This weekend's movie theme is horror. Large crowds of people are already here for the presentation. Tables and chairs are scarce, so people made sofas with cushioned pillows on the floor.

When I first arrive, it takes me a while to find my cousin in the crowd. Lina is sitting with a number of friends on the packed floor. She's in a blue beanbag near the center of the room.

"Lina," I call to my cousin.

"Yah. Shut up. He's about to chop that guy's head off," nags a person in the audience.

"I'm sorry." I do my best to duck under the screen.

"Come on." Lina jumps out of her seat and takes my hand.

Momentarily, I look back at the movie. The music is starting to escalate, noting the suspenseful part is coming up.

"Grrr . . . I'm going to find you," the murderer taunts. He is walking down the dark, narrow hallway looking for his victim. He stops in front of a bland door. The camera pans into the next room to reveal the frightened little girl. She hears him breathing outside, but she still doesn't move.

"Run!"

"You're going to die!"

"Don't be stupid!"

"Run!"

Various shouts and encouragements bombard the screen. A few people laugh. Horror movies are so predictable. There's always someone foolish enough to investigate the unknown noises.

Lina tugs at my arm and we head away from the crowd. Instead of going to the counter for a drink, we duck into the hallway where the soda machines are.

"What's going on?" Lina asks me. Her eyes are perplexed. I don't know how else to tell my cousin what is going on. My responding text message has alerted Lina.

"I can't do this with him." The truth rushes from my mouth. I need to vent and ruminate. "Choi Sangwoo. I can't continue to see him."

Lina stares at me with confusion and shock. "What are you talking about May? What happened?"

"Misun," her name slips out of my mouth. "Lina. He . . . Sangwoo has pictures of her with him. They were together." The words are stuck in my throat. I am not sure if I am shaking from the painful memory or the confession.

Lina's eyes enlarge. She places a hand on her mouth. Tugging at my arm, my cousin pulls me against the wall. Her voice trembles. "Are you sure?"

I nod my head. "It makes so much sense now why he's chasing me."

My cousin can hardly believe it. "Okay. We'll figure something out." Lina reels from the news. She examines my face. "You do look like her . . . when she was this age."

I close my eyes; I refuse to listen to Lina reminisce. "I didn't come here for that Lina. I need you to help me figure out how to get rid of him. I really need to do this."

Lina nods her head slowly. "We'll talk about this later." Then, she changes her mind. "Actually, give me a second while I let my friends know I'm leaving."

I nod in return. Good. I will have her by my side to digest all this. *They always say breakups are hard to do and you can't do it alone.* My intuition purses her lips.

Waiting anxiously, I watch Lina retreat to the main room. I'm too engrossed to notice that I am not alone. Suddenly, I feel his presence.

"I hear the new Pepsi Vanilla is good." Leaning against the wall as though he owns the building, Choi Sangwoo's smoldering gaze renders me just as speechless as his surprise appearance. He is dressed down in a navy blue sweatshirt over dark jeans. The conventional CEO gang leader is currently replaced by this down-to-earth man.

Stalker! my intuition hisses. She recoils from his intense gaze.

"Sangwoo." Surprise colors my tone. How did he know I was going to be here? "What are you doing here?"

"Just catching the movie." Sangwoo nonchalantly leans against the soda machine. He surveys my facial expression with great interest. When I don't relent, Sangwoo admits, "I called you several times and left you messages. I was worried something happened to you last night. I had Ren track you down. I'm sorry if I'm being overwhelming. I just worry about your safety."

I am breathless at his admittance. Not only is he keeping a close tab on me, but Sangwoo also has the ability to turn it into something of good intentions. I am dealing with a very dangerous man. Admitting defeat, I turn back to the soda machine to avoid his intense eyes. I extract some change out of my pocket and make a scene of putting them into the coin slot.

Sangwoo watches me with a guarded expression. "I'm sorry about last night. I shouldn't have drunk so much. Thank you for taking care of me, again."

"It's okay," I assure him shortly. I busy myself with selecting the new Pepsi Vanilla can. When the can clatters down the machine, Sangwoo retrieves it for me. "Thank you," I mumble.

"If I said anything that wasn't right, I'm sorry." Sangwoo watches my every move. "I'm an idiot when I drink. Of course you already know this."

I flush at the thought of how we met. I hold the cold soda in my hands as I try to smile naturally at him. "It's ok. You're going through a lot. Besides, I forgot most of the stuff you said anyway," I lie to him.

"Really? Well, I hope you didn't forget what I said about liking you," Sangwoo replies, leaning closer. "Because I remember clearly saying that."

I can only stare at Choi Sangwoo. No boy has ever outwardly confessed to me. It is the strangest sensation ever. And it scares me half-to-death. "You really mean that?"

Sangwoo smiles. He enjoys the drained look on my face. "What are you surprised for?"

Because you're obsessed with Misun and you want me to replace her, my intuition snaps. I attempt to play it off with a laugh. We both know the true reason why he's attracted to me, but we are playing this constant game of guesses. "Are you sure you got all that alcohol out of your system?" I attempt to ease my passive-aggressiveness with him.

"I have." He gives me an intense look. Sangwoo shifts on his own two feet and composes himself. "What are your plans for the rest of the day?"

I glance back at Mula. My search for Lina is useless. My cousin is lost in the sea of people.

"Spend some time with my cousin," I tell Sangwoo.

"I thought you spent some time with her yesterday already." Sangwoo's gang leader complex is evident in his tone. "Can I borrow you for the afternoon?"

What world did he come from? Who says things like that? "Sangwoo," I begin to articulate myself. How do I tell him I need some time and distance from his intense concentration on me? I don't want to spend more time with him. How do I tell him I know the truth? One look into Sangwoo's intense stare and I know I can't yet. I need one final confirmation.

I must look like a lost puppy because Sangwoo stares at me with apprehension. I hope it's not another funeral crashing moment. I want to ask him if it is, but I am well aware of the fact that I don't know

Sangwoo's personality the way I should.

"I can spare a couple of hours." It feels like I am admitting defeat. I don't know how else to communicate with this gang leader. *No! You need to get away from him!* my intuition snarls. *He's trying to salvage this non-existent relationship and garner your pity! This is his last ditch effort!*

"I'll only take a few hours of your time." Sangwoo reaches down for my hand.

The simple impact of his palm against mine causes me to gasp. His name, his face, and his actions transport me to my memories. All over again, I hear the voice, *"His name is Choi Sangwoo! I'm in love."* I launch into a vortex of memories, spinning until I am dizzy.

I open my eyes to see Choi Sangwoo's eyes peering inquisitively into mine. "May?"

"Sorry?" I stare up at him.

"Are you okay?"

"Y-yes."

"Ok. Let's go." Sangwoo motions toward the door. Sangwoo has a complex look on his face as if he is deciding what to do with me. Making up his mind, Sangwoo places an arm around me, drawing me closer to him. His touch makes me forget my senses. "We're going to have a good day today. Trust me."

I trust you like I would trust playing Russian Roulette. My intuition is bitter. I've betrayed her.

There is an internal war going on in me. Maybe it is because I am convinced that no matter what kind of fairytale day Sangwoo has up his sleeve I will not fall for it. Maybe it is because I want to see who Choi Sangwoo is. Maybe it is because of an unspoken reason that draws me to him . . . .

I stop by the front entrance to tell Lina I have to go. She is speechless when she sees who is in my company. Her gaze lingers on Sangwoo, guarded and suspicious. "Are you sure?" My cousin asks me in a whisper.

I nod my head. From our distance, I glance back to see Sangwoo staring at us with an impenetrable gaze. I promise to call Lina later. My cousin holds onto my arm a little too long before she finally relents. She makes me promise again before she finally lets me go. Lina disapproves, I know.

I follow Sangwoo out of Mula to the awaiting car—yet another black-on-black Mercedes E-class. *What are you doing May?* My intuition is not happy when I get into the car. Sangwoo starts the engine and an energetic trance beat invades the quiet space. The dark windows are up, but a gentle mist paces the car.

"Where are we going?" I hold my breath at his answer.

"A place for you to get to know me," is Sangwoo's short reply.

I stiffen in my seat at his unexpected response. I wonder where this place could be. I have to remind myself that I am not sitting in this car as Sangwoo's girlfriend. Maybe it's because I've never had a real boyfriend, so maybe I'm all wrong for thinking his intentions are romantic. Sangwoo's mentioned before that he wants me by his side, but he never said anything about a girlfriend. Now, I am all discombobulated.

Maybe I don't know what to do when someone is showing interest in me. Sure, you can count Jun in the fourth grade when he knocked that dodge ball into my head to ask me out. Then, there was Bon in the fifth grade who cut a lock of my hair as a courtship ritual followed by the men in his household. But none of them have wanted me, pursued me, and chased me the way Choi Sangwoo does.

"WE'RE HERE," SANGWOO ANNOUNCES AFTER the half-an-hour drive. The car slows down in the parking lot of Bae Scenic Park, a private park with its own-gated entrance. Sangwoo turns off the engine of the car. We sit in the car for a moment, staring at the scenery. Bae is Seoul's most popular park because it's reminiscent of a portrait. Deep brown mountains surround the area along with a lively lake—mild slopes drop into massive areas of green grass.

"We're having a picnic here?" I ask as Sangwoo when we get out of the car.

"Yes," Sangwoo replies. He reaches down and nonchalantly intertwines his fingers into mine.

I jump slightly. Sangwoo rewards me with a look that lets me know he wants to hold my hand. I do not understand his motives, but I don't have the heart to take my hand back. I hurt for him. This poor soul thinks I am someone else. I just want to hear him out today, and he is getting the wrong message. *Be a bitch and tell him to get lost.* My intuition yawns. I do my best to ignore her. She is impulsive.

I expect us to get onto the trail and walk, but Sangwoo leads me off the trail and down the hills towards the quad area of the park. As we get closer, I hear the spontaneous commotion. When we finally descend the grassy knolls, large white tents hanging like canopies above various picnic tables come into view. Crowds of people scatter in and around the tents.

It is a barbecue party; loud chatter, laughter, and commotion surround a large, modern grill. Dance music is playing above the tents. I was not expecting this big of a production.

When we get closer to the crowd, Sangwoo's simple presence stops everyone in their tracks. Even those who are busy eating and chattering pause. "Boss."

It is easy to see the impact of Sangwoo's presence on his members. His relaxed demeanor eases them, however. It all happens very fast. Sangwoo secures the hold he has on my hand. *Oh no. He's introducing you to everyone and their moms*, my intuition groans. Sangwoo pulls me deeper into the crowd.

"Let me introduce you to some of my most trusted men. David, Shawn, Kevin, Phillip, James, and you already know Ren over there." Sangwoo points out a particular group of men standing to the far left. They are faces–one facial expression blending into the next. Some of the men look vaguely familiar; some of them I recognize from The Trax–the very first Saturday I met Choi Sangwoo. All of them, except for Ren, stare intently at me during Sangwoo's introduction. I can feel the spotlight on me.

"Oh my god."

"She looks–"

"Is this possible?"

Whispers break out in different directions. *Even his gang members notice the resemblance between Dead Girl and me. Why won't he just give up?* The thought saddens me.

"Hey! Hey! This is May," Sangwoo introduces me to silence the whispers.

"Hi," I say meekly. I have no heart to end Sangwoo's youthful excitement. I entertain him with a question. "Why do they all have American names?" I whisper to Sangwoo.

He laughs. "Nicknames make it easier on the international platform."

"What's your English name then?" I ask.

"Crist–pronounced as Christ," Sangwoo replies.

"Of course," I respond, letting out an awkward laugh.

The Crist members find this humorous as well. Slowly, the tension fades away. For a top gang in South Korea, they are less intimidating. Maybe Mayhem's gang is the one I should watch out for. *Why are you thinking about him?* My intuition is pouting at me under her big speckled glasses. *Can you imagine having a picnic with Danny? Can you imagine hanging out with Mayhem?*

"Let's get some food." Sangwoo brings me back to reality. He steers me over to a table. We barely sit down when plates of food are in front of us.

Ren and his girlfriend are sitting across from the table. Instead of his usual reserved personality, Ren smiles when his girlfriend whispers in his ear. The two of them create quite an arresting sight. They remind me of a love story far too uncommon for someone like me to understand. But I barely have time to marvel at them before I am distracted by other events.

"Have some food." Sangwoo notices my hesitation.

"Thanks." I pick up my fork.

Sangwoo leans into me. "Piggy is one of my best chefs. What do you think?"

"Piggy?" I ask, turning around to see the grill. Through the crowd of people I see Piggy. He is the short, meaty man wearing a white apron complete with a chef's hat. He makes eye contact and bows. I force a tentative smile on my lips.

Sangwoo places an arm around my shoulder again. "Have some more to eat."

"Sure." I am slightly uncomfortable at the attention he's showering me with. We are acting, does he know?

Soon enough, other Crist members swarm our table. Ren is in full swing, dishing jokes about everything imaginable. I didn't expect him to have such a great sense of humor, but his well-versed renditions cause laughter to erupt around the table. I see Ren in a new light, but I know it is short-lived. When it is Sangwoo's turn, the tone of the conversation shifts to a more serious note. Sangwoo elaborates on some of his men's backgrounds. Sangwoo discloses some of the reasons why his men joined him. As Sangwoo tells me the stories, I realize the depth of his heart for them. They are more than just members to him, they are his family and blood. Sangwoo isn't their intimidating leader; he is their friend, brother, and even mentor. Sangwoo knows each of his men personally. I watch him share inside jokes and stories. In many ways, Sangwoo's men are not the stereotypical gang enforcing street terrorism and black market trafficking. They are people who chose an unconventional lifestyle.

This is the first time I see Sangwoo relaxed and in the moment. I do my best to remain unbiased until the very end of the event. When the day starts to fade away, a swarm of mosquitoes gathers around the tents. Some Crist members depart, seeking shelter near the hills and down by the vast lake. Sangwoo and Ren, including some other members, take a hike up the hills. Soon enough, Ren's girlfriend and I are the only ones sitting at the table.

Grace smiles at me—a heartwarming smile that I don't expect from her. Because of the large group dynamic, I haven't had a chance to talk to her. Now that we are alone, Grace doesn't hold back.

"So how long have you and Sangwoo been going out?" Grace asks. She is finishing her plate of vegetables—a healthy mix of celery and spinach.

"Oh. We're not going out." Immediately, I am defensive.

Grace gives me a knowing smile. She is very pretty with a round face and short jet-black hair. In that very moment, I realize why Ren's relaxed and mellow today. Grace is his rock.

"I think you and Sangwoo make a good couple." Her large brown eyes glimmer with romanticism.

I can only bite my tongue. *She's lying,* my intuition critiques.

Grace picks up her drink and I notice the pink sapphire ring. "Congratulations," I tell her. I am breathless by the sight of the ring. The wealth of these gang members will never cease to amaze me.

Grace pulls back her hand to admire the ring. "Ren proposed to me a month ago during our seventh anniversary."

"Wow." I marvel at Grace's revelation. Seven years together.

Grace inclines her head. "I thought he was never going to propose. When he finally did, it was some sort of relief." Grace pauses as she studies my confused facial expression. "Relief that we are on the same path after all this time."

"What do you mean?" It is astounding to me that someone like her can have such doubts. Grace seems so sure of herself now. Looks can truly be deceiving.

"I always joke that I am Ren's mistress." There is humor dancing in Grace's eyes. "Ren is married to Crist. This . . . business will always be his first priority. His devotion and loyalty to Sangwoo is something that drove me crazy with jealousy in the beginning. Over time, as I got to know Sangwoo, the feelings of jealousy subsided. Now, I think I am just as bad as Ren," Grace explains.

Grace's disclosure shakes me up. It's a glimpse into what Sangwoo means to them. Taking my silence as a cue to continue, Grace glances at me with an appraisal. "Sangwoo is a very lonely and private man. It's quite a surprise to us that he brought you here today. I'm sure you noticed the stares and whispers. It's only because we are so used to seeing him alone. Today, he is smiling and recounting memories. It is a rare sight for all of us."

I swallow hard. I don't want to be responsible for Choi Sangwoo's temporary happiness. He is under the impression that I will be joining his family soon. Even the Crist members are contemplating my role in their Boss's life now. I am deeply disturbed by what this all means.

"Would you like a drink?" Grace gestures towards the bottle of alcohol across the table. She reaches for the darkest bottle and proceeds to pour herself a glass.

I decline politely. "No thank you. I don't really drink." Actually, I prefer to stay sober. *Everyone's an alcoholic here,* my intuition mumbles.

"Oh–" Grace starts to say, but loud laughter interrupts us. "They're at it again." Grace rises from her seat and motions for me to follow.

"What's going on?" I follow her suit. I slap discretely at my arm. The mosquitoes are starting to get more aggressive under the summer heat.

"If we hurry, we can get in on the bet!" Grace grins at me. She races towards the hill. I follow her. Who am I kidding? I'm not made for their world in the vaguest sense. I am too uncoordinated and unfit by any standards.

By the time Grace and I ascend the slope I am the only one breathing hard. She saunters over to the crowd that has gathered in the middle of the hill.

In the intermediate grassy area, there is a large blue mat where the rest of the gang has assembled to watch the two individuals. Both shirtless and dripping with sweat, the men are exchanging various punches with their boxing gloves.

Grace giggles at the sight. "Go honey!"

Ren and Sangwoo stop exchanging warm-up punches long enough to look at us. Ren blows a kiss at Grace as Sangwoo winks at me.

I want to react, but I only freeze. A gust of wind blows, whipping my hair into my face, but I still can't take my eyes off Sangwoo's body. *Still a girl after all,* my intuition grumbles. She eyes the ripples of Sangwoo's body warily. His abs compact together in a toned physique. Sangwoo turns around to reveal the all-around tan he has. *God, the Devil in an Angel's disguise.*

"They do this all the time, sparing to show who's Boss." Grace giggles as though it is an inside joke. Other Crist members are smirking at the sight. No one has dared to bet against Sangwoo yet.

I can barely make a comment because I am busy watching Sangwoo duck just as Ren makes a swipe at his head. Sangwoo retracts on the mat, but comes charging at Ren with a combination of left-right-one-two-left-right punches. Ren is knocked down at the last punch; he quickly scrambles to his feet. Sangwoo dives for Ren's stomach.

"Oh! Get him!" Some Crist members cheer, clapping and whistling loudly.

"Not fair! Ya'll root for me!" Ren shouts as he ducks again. Everyone laughs when Ren stops, drops, and rolls just to get away from Sangwoo.

Sangwoo stops going after Ren because he's laughing too hard too. He breathes heavily as beads of sweat rain down his forehead.

My cell phone rings at the same moment. Distracted, I reach inside my tote bag. I stare at it with hesitation when I see Eunhye's number flashing on the caller ID. Why is she calling me? An uneasy feeling comes over me. She wants to talk about the end of the month and my father. I choose to ignore the call.

"Right, May?" I look up to see Sangwoo approaching me. He flashes me a smile as he wraps an arm around my shoulder. Surprised, I look at him only to have Sangwoo's eyes draw me in deeper. I feel like I am falling and losing control. I have to keep it together until tonight is over.

The last leg of the event involves social conversation and activities. Sangwoo keeps his arm around my shoulder the rest of the time we stand talking to Crist members. We laugh at Ren's story of how he proposed to Grace; we playfully argue over the details of some popular movie; we laugh some more when a handful of Crist members plays a popular game that involves throwing a small golf-like ball into cups. Well, I mostly watch with good humor, doing my best to mask what I am really feeling inside. My laugh is fake and my mood is a façade. I cannot wait to leave here.

It takes a good fifteen minutes to get out of Bae park once the skies grow dark. Crist members take their time saying goodbye, making more plans and promises. Ren lingers to speak with Sangwoo, throwing careful glances at me while Grace keeps me company.

"It was really nice meeting you." For a second, I think she is going to hug me but she holds her distance. I suppose gangsters don't give away hugs so easily.

Once the last car pulls out of the parking lot, Sangwoo takes me home in a dark Honda Prelude. The Mercedes E-Class we arrived in is long gone.

"Did you have fun?" Sangwoo slows down at a red light. He glances at me with an expectant expression.

"It was great." I stare out of the dark window. Under this window tint, the sky is a murky black color with ominous darts for stars. Little does Sangwoo know I am deeply sadden by the amount of emotions I am feeling. It is hard for me to come to terms with all these unwarranted sentiments.

Sangwoo smiles with confidence. The light turns green. "I knew you would."

I am quiet by his assumption. There is something like fire boiling deep inside of me. I know what he is doing, but I am powerless at his suggestion. The car comes to a complete stop in front of my apartment complex. Sangwoo cuts the engine off. Darkness and silence usher themselves into the cool car.

"I'm going to be honest with you May. Things are not turning out the way I am anticipating." In the darkness, his facial expression is tentative. Sangwoo's statement reminds me of self-containment. "I don't want to force you into doing something that you don't want to. I still need an answer from you although I already know your answer."

Realization dawns on me that Sangwoo is talking about the initiation contract again. I am a bundle of nerves, but I refuse to let him bully me into something I know I don't want part of.

"Sangwoo," I begin to say.

"My feelings for you are very strong May," Sangwoo cuts me off. There is tentative aggravation in his tone. "The last time we talked about the initiation contract, you mentioned you wanted to pay your way out of it. That was not the point. How can I convince you otherwise? This has been the source of my contention with you these past weeks."

"Sangwoo, I would be useless for you." It is my turn to cut him off. The gang leader is having a hard time understanding what I want to convey. "The people who surround you today possess a certain talent that I can never compare to. What is it about me that is valuable to you?"

I am pushing at him to admit to Dead Girl–to Misun. I know I am pushing for an assortment of problems to open up, but if he wants to go to war I have to defend myself.

Sangwoo sighs. "I really do wish that you'd consider my offer May."

I am slightly hurt and confused by this man. How can Sangwoo do this to me? This isn't fair at all. "I'm sorry Sangwoo. I'm not going to sign your contract. In fact, I think we should stop seeing each other."

There is stillness in the air that is indescribable. I cannot explain the emotion that tears through the car. I can feel my heart ramming into my chest. I finally said it. *Yes! Tell him girl!* my intuition shouts.

"You want to stop seeing me," Sangwoo repeats. His voice is bitter. Like a statue, he is cold and unforgiving. He appears as though he wants to say something else, but Sangwoo cuts himself short. He surprises me as he responds concisely, "You're right. I'm not good for you. Everything about my world is dangerous."

I bite down on my bottom lip, feeling lost now that he's agreeing. How can he say such things to me? This man can turn so cold in a manner of seconds. A sense of emptiness strikes down on me. I feel a deep void protruding in my chest. After all the time we've spent together, Choi Sangwoo is letting me go so easily. I realize then that I am expendable in his world. This is it. This is really the end. And I am responsible for it in all of its entirety.

"I'm sorry Sangwoo." I am well aware that it doesn't mean anything to him at this point.

"There's no need to be sorry if you've already made up your mind." He doesn't look at me. "If you don't want to see me anymore, then this is the end. I don't want to beg you if you are adamant about your decision."

"I just can't be who you want me to be."

"That's fine."

My throat feels tight. I don't know what I want from him. *You want him to admit to Misun,* my intuition mumbles with sorrow. *He's not going to give you that satisfaction. If you are not going to give him what he wants, he's just going to walk away. Gang leaders have no heart and no mercy. It's your fault for expecting anything more.*

"I guess this is goodbye then, May." Sangwoo eyes are deep and penetrating, relentless and unforgiving. I expect him to shoo me out of his car, but he waits patiently.

He's not going to chase me and I will not turn. This is it. After weeks of speculation of what could possibly be, this is the end. I am dumbfounded that is all my undoing. Why does this feel like a breakup? I wait for Sangwoo to say more, but the gang leader remains silent. He is brooding with intensity that wavers between tension and anger.

"Goodbye Sangwoo." I remove the seat belt. I avoid eye contact with him, committed to making a hasty retreat.

Sangwoo remains as still as a statue. He waits until I am out of the car before he guns it. The Honda Prelude squeals down the street, whipping its tail around the bend. The race car leaves a cloud of smoke in its wake.

CHAPTER THIRTEEN

I am torn and lost. I cannot articulate the emotions trampling on my constricted heart. I want to cry and desperately cling to something that is tangible. My knees feel like noodles as I walk to the apartment. However, with every step, I am unraveling. As I flee, foreboding and ominous feelings course through my system.

Don't cry May. Hold it together. You are stronger than this! It cannot be this easy and simple to leave a gang leader. This cannot be the conclusion to the past two months. Why am I feeling this way when I am the one who said goodbye first? I realize with absolved hope that I want more out of Choi Sangwoo. I want him to fight for these feelings. If he is so willing to let me walk out of his life, then there is nothing more we can do for each other. Sangwoo said so himself–he doesn't want a relationship with me. Inexplicably, Sangwoo has always seen me as Misun. By turning down his initiation contract, I am rebelling against everything that Sangwoo wants me to be.

By the time I reach the apartment door, the tears are a mess against my hot skin. I close the door behind me, anxious and exhausted. Fortunately, Eunhye is not home from the hospital yet. It is dark, but I manage to stumble into my bedroom. My cold and welcoming bed greets me. A lump of emotion is in my throat. I want to cry, but the tears constrict in my tear ducts. I am out of tears.

The walls feel as though they are caving in. With resolution, I allow the darkness to swallow me up. This is the third night in a row.

MONDAY MORNING IS BETTER AND worse. By the time Tuesday comes around, Lina is less than happy with my decision to cut Choi Sangwoo out of my life. My cousin predicts karma will come back and bite me where it counts. Lina warns me that no one can run away from a gang leader unless he wants them to. Ironically, I am doing a better job than my cousin predicts.

On Wednesday, I begin the hunt for my next job. I consider school as I look for a part-time job. Working two full-time jobs this summer has taught me to prioritize and focus on my goals. I want to graduate early and start my career. I regard it as my self-improvement goals. I scour the local paper looking for part-time waitressing jobs. I end up scheduling an interview at a small restaurant downtown. It is less shady than The Trax, so Eunhye will be happy about that.

On Thursday, I clean the entire house and even manage to squeeze in some time for a jog. Eunhye is amazed by my change of attitude and determination. Things are still tense between us, but Eunhye is too busy working double shifts at the hospital to reconcile with me.

By Friday night, I am slightly stir-crazy. I am surviving post-Sangwoo. The anger, resentment, and bitterness I have for him slowly recede. I realize I *can* go on because Sangwoo brought more misery than joy. Now that I am free from the constant apprehension, I feel liberated and vindicated.

Lina and I make plans to go out. My cousin wants to go dancing. It's been months since I have gone out with her, so I agree. I am in a blissful mood anticipating a night of dancing and drinks until I receive the phone call. The call belongs to an unknown number. "I want to see you. I need to see you," he slurs into the phone line—a clear indication that he's been drinking.

I don't know what else to do. I should answer him, but I don't. Choi Sangwoo was so strong in letting me go, so why is he relenting now? By Sangwoo's own omission, he was determined to end the beginning of us. He likes the idea of us, but the reality can never compare. In the end, I delete Sangwoo's call and put my phone away. *Out of sight, out of mind.* My intuition already has her dancing shoes on. Choi Sangwoo who?

I **GET BUSY PREPARING FOR** the night out with Lina. I own very few dresses, so I pick a simple black number with a boat neck and sleeveless arms. I have a hard time deciding what to do with my hair, so I let it hang in long tresses. I choose to go with the all black theme and wear dark, liquid eyeliner. When I am done with myself, my outside mirrors my dark, murky insides.

I am hunting for shoes when Eunhye makes her way into the apartment. My mother is still in her blue scrubs. The look on Eunhye's face is a mixture of surprise and interest.

"How is the job hunt going?" Eunhye's tone is subdued.

"I have a couple more interviews lined up." Since our blowout, Eunhye continues to be short with me.

"Where are you going?" Eunhye finally addresses the elephant in the room.

"I'm going out with Lina," I reply quickly.

"I would like for you to stay home May." Eunhye's tone is slightly harsh.

I close my eyes. I don't want to fight. "I promised Lina I'd go."

"May, we need to talk. You can't avoid this conversation." The hurt in Eunhye's eyes resurface. "Have you forgotten your own father? Have you forgotten who I am to you? Have you forgotten what you should do?" I can't say I don't expect it, but it takes me a few seconds to realize what she is talking about.

"Why? What for?" It is disrespectful to talk to Eunhye like this, but I cannot help myself. "I thought you promised I would never have to do anything I didn't want to do."

"It would just be nice for us to all be reunited. Ever since–" Eunhye starts. Her eyes are wide as if she's looking for the May underneath all the makeup I have on.

"I don't want to reunite," I cut her off. "Can you not bring this up anymore? Do what you want."

"You better lower your voice, young lady," Eunhye warns me.

But I am overdue. I am tired of being hustled and pushed into doing people want. "Just leave me alone Eunhye. I don't want to talk about the end of the month. I don't want to talk about *her*."

"I have been leaving you alone! I let you go do whatever it is you want to do. I want you to be happy! But I also just want you to remember–" Eunhye stares at me in disbelief when my cell phone rings.

I cannot do this right now. I am not in the right mindset. I am too angry and hurt. If I don't stop, I might say something I will regret later. So I answer my phone as a form of distraction. It is Lina on the line. "Hello? Yeah, I'm leaving soon. Give me ten minutes."

"May . . . don't leave. Not now." Eunhye tries to stop me. Her voice is broken. "I was hoping we could spend some time together. You can't keep avoiding the situation and me. You can't keep denying it every single year. Sometimes, we have to face the pain and hurt. It's the only way we can move on."

"I'm sorry, but you're right mom. I'm too selfish. After all these years, I'm still too upset. The therapy didn't work for me." Without another word, I leave the apartment.

After all this time, it still hurts and is an overwhelming memory.

"LET'S GET OUR FREAK ON!" Bryan is shouting at the top of his lungs. He is too embarrassing to be out with. The flamboyant outfit he is wearing doesn't exactly help either. Why did I decide to do this to myself?

"You lied to me!" I scream into Lina's ear. My cousin is too lost in her own world to respond. She is busy making make-out eyes with a guy across the dance floor. Lina invited me out, but conveniently forgot to mention that Bryan is tagging along too. Even though Lina and Spyder are over, my cousin still keeps in touch with Bryan. Now, I am stuck on the crowded dance floor with him. In no way, shape, or form am I ever a club girl. It's just one of those nights where it's better to be out than to be at home wallowing in misery. It is part of Lina's idea to get me out of the house, away from Eunhye and Sangwoo. It sounded like a good idea, but now that I am being herded on the dance floor, I am rethinking everything.

Club Groove is a new dance club that opened a few weeks ago. Bodies pack every nook and cranny of the venue. It also doesn't help that it smells like fresh paint and old money. The venue is extensively designed with a grand dance floor, three fully loaded bars, and scattered seating areas throughout the club. The theme tonight is white and purple.

"Lina, I need to get away from Bryan." I tug at my cousin's arm, making gestures at Bryan who is gyrating inappropriately on the dance floor.

Lina doesn't hear me clearly through the loud hip-hop music in the background. My cousin nods her head and replies, "Yeah. That guy over there wears sneakers and he's at the bar."

Huh? I don't have time to gape at my cousin. Bryan yanks at my arm roughly. "May! Let's dance!" He has a large, mouthy grin. Fortunately, Bryan hasn't brought up what happened last time we hung out. The club only buys me time from his inquisition. Right now, Bryan is in full swing and nothing can stop him.

"Lina! Help!" I scream over the loud music when Bryan drags me deeper into the crowd. The sea of people quickly swallows Lina. Before I know it, I am in the middle of the dance floor. Flashing lights of white, purple, and yellow wash over the bodies around me.

"Come on May." Bryan puts his hand down the small of my back. I quickly swat his hand away. The club is deafening loud. The bass of the music hits my chest every time it drops with the whining techno beat.

"What are you doing?!" I squeal at Bryan who starts dancing. The spinning disco ball jerks wildly above the dance floor, showering us with glittery light. Bryan places his right arm on his hip and starts wiggling a finger at me.

Despite all the troubled thoughts I have been having, and the rude-awakening of the conversation with Eunhye earlier, I let out a laugh. It is just a simple laugh, but it does the trick.

The girls who are dancing around us stop to watch Bryan in amusement. Bryan has his attention to me. As foolish as he is, Bryan knows something is bothering me so he goes all out to make me laugh.

"Come on, May. Dance with me!" Bryan places both hands on my shoulders and pushes me side-to-side.

"I'll show you how you dance!" Forgetting that I am a social turtle, I crawl out of my shell for the first time in a long time.

I am not one of those girls who know their hands from their feet. I am more of an awkward turtle who chooses to bob her head in a simultaneous manner. So there I am on the dance floor causing a scene with silly Bryan. I rock my body to the beat of the music. Bryan comes closer and I turn with him. Our backs press together as we pump our arms up and down. Bryan's laughing in my ears; he thinks it's hilarious.

"I'm doing a turn!" I announce over the loud music. As I spin, I catch sight of someone standing near the bar. He is dressed in all black, sticking out blatantly in the club. He is drinking from a black mug in his hands. I can't tell if he is watching me or not, but the familiarity of his presence is unnerving.

"May!" Bryan bumps into me. I nearly stumble on the dance floor, but catch myself just in time. *Bryan!* I want to shout at him, but I quickly turn back to the bar.

The individual is gone.

My dancing mood vanishes. My heart thuds against my rib cage, seeking release. *Who the hell was that?* My intuition wipes the sweat off her forehead.

"I'm thirsty." I tap Bryan on the shoulder. Leaving him behind, I push through the crowd of people to find a way out. The girls who have been watching us take the opportunity to pounce on Bryan.

I make it out of the dance floor and scan the area. Lina is occupying a table nearby with make-out boy. He is dressed in a sleeveless white linen shirt, casual blue jeans, and dark sneakers. He's definitely different from Spyder. I'm not sure if he's an upgrade yet.

"You feel better now? Letting loose after all that drama?" Lina asks. She offers me a glass of water and then settles back in her new friend's arms. "This is Kim. Kim, this is my cousin May."

Kim smiles at me and I notice the dimples in his cheeks. Judging from the alcohol bottle on the table, he and Lina are reaching their limit. *Isn't Kim a girl name?* I resign to biting on my tongue. I don't trust my judgment, especially since I am under the influence. My heart thumps wildly and my face is sweaty from the heat and the dancing.

I gulp the shockingly cold water down my dry, desiccated throat.

"What drama?" Kim asks Lina. He's a nosy body.

Lina gives Kim a look that lets him know she is not about to get into it. "Let's dance. I wanna dance now."

I leave Lina and her boy toy to their own accord. I have a pressing need to use the bathroom now. As I walk by the poolroom's entrance, it is crowded with people watching a billiards game in action. The line to the bathroom is short, surprisingly. My head spins in a strange, unwavering way. When I am done, I make my way back to the bar to get more water.

The bar is overcrowded. Bodies wrap around its obscure shape. I attempt to get the bartender's attention, but fail miserably. The flashing lights in the background are not helping either.

A dark figure stands next to me. Without any effort at all, he waves to the bartender. "One glass of water." Without a word, the bartender scurries to get the order.

My eyebrows crease together. Only one person in this club has such power. A thrill shoots down my spine. "What are you doing here?" I blurt out. Aside from being shocked that the dark crime lord is here, I am also pleasantly surprised. It is a strange mix.

Mayhem—Yoon Jaewon—narrows his dark eyes at me. He's dressed in a black, Executive two-button wool suit complete with a silk tie and black slacks. On his left wrist is a signature black diamond watch to complete the CEO look. The deliberate tousled hair frames Mayhem's handsomely stunning features. Mayhem's in his element here in the dark club with the loud, disturb-the-peace music.

As though he is just another face in the crowd, Mayhem casually takes a drink from the black mug he's holding. "Does it occur to you that this is a public venue? I should be asking you the same question."

"I'm here to dance," I answer without thinking. Suddenly, I hate Mayhem for making me answer such an obvious question. I scowl at him. I don't even thank the bartender when he hands me a glass of water.

"That's what you were doing on the dance floor?" Mayhem makes me feel like a complete fool. He remains cool and undisturbed. It's quite unnerving. Why did I choose to look so 'girly' today? I feel very self-conscious when Mayhem looks at me like that. I am not ready for the intense inspection of my features.

"You're stalking me again." I want to remind him of our recent meeting—at my apartment and then near Sangwoo's hotel.

"Or you're stalking me," Mayhem remarks with a biting attitude. "I invest in this club. I have every right to be here."

I gape at him. Mayhem invests in this club? Jeez. How much money does this man have? This is another bone chilling coincidence.

"So you were watching me." My head is spinning. This conversation doesn't even need to make sense. I peer up at him. I feel Mayhem's eyes gazing at me. I am so close to him that I can see his perfect, sexy jaw line. He's so good-looking it should be illegal. Actually, he isn't legal. I want to laugh, but I arch my face higher to meet his eyes that are shadowed by the black hat he's wearing. *Damn. He's good-looking.* My intuition sashays into the conversation.

Mayhem throws his head back as though I breech ridiculous. "Who said I was watching you?"

"Well, you–" I try to coolly recover from Mayhem's denial. I jerk the mug out of his hand. "What are you drinking?" *Nice way to change the subject,* my conscience states sarcastically.

One whiff and I recognize the distinctive smell. Coffee. Black coffee. "There is something wrong with you." I make a face at him. *Who drinks coffee at a club?* Damn, this dizziness won't go away. I am partial to it, nonetheless. It gives me courage to speak to him.

"Everything's right with me." Humor sparks in Mayhem's eyes.

He always has a comeback at the tip of his tongue. "So what are you doing here?" I give Mayhem back his mug. "I can't imagine black coffee being your choice of drink at a club." I am sarcastic and bold.

"Unlike people who come here to get drunk, I have a different purpose," Mayhem responds. His dark eyes scan the bar area, meticulously scouring for something I am not privy to.

"You make no sense." I shake my head at him. *He's so freaking good-looking, he doesn't have to!* My intuition knows no shame.

"I don't have to, do I?" Mayhem echoes my thoughts. "I hope that fool on the dance floor isn't your boyfriend because I'm sure Eunhye will never approve."

I follow Mayhem's unwavering gaze to the dance floor where Bryan is gyrating tastelessly with some girls. I didn't dance like that with him, did I? Bryan's crush on me is nothing but innocent. If anything, Bryan knows our relationship is more like brother-sister. The alcohol makes it easier to like Bryan.

"He's not my boyfriend," I scoff at the ridiculous notion. I take another sip of my water. "He's Spyder's brother. You remember Spyder, don't you?"

Mayhem turns back to me. The smoldering look in his eyes causes my breath to hitch. "I do." I don't understand it. If I didn't know any better, it seems like I answered a question he's been longing to know the answer to.

"Something tells me you're not here to club." I am interested in his motive for being here. Maybe Mayhem's here for some dark, underground work. After all, a gang lord's office is the world. Mayhem did admit he invests in it.

"No. I'm not here to club," Mayhem answers shortly. The corners of lips curl into a secretive smirk. He doesn't elaborate any further. Mayhem doesn't readily invite me into his dark underworld.

I am well aware that in the feigned darkness of the club, Mayhem blends in seamlessly. Yet, groups of girls and women eye him from the bar. The gang lord remains oblivious. Mayhem is so obscure that it's hard to determine if he's oblivious or really good at ignoring it. Whatever the case may be, Mayhem is retrieving a sleek wallet from inside his Executive suit. I catch a glimpse of a picture inside it.

"Who's that?" I ask without censorship. Although the club is dark and the music continues to throb mercilessly, I can still see the picture vividly. The photograph is old and ripped around the edges. Mayhem, young and boyish, is standing next to a little boy who is the mirror image of him. They are wearing identical shirts with dirt on their faces, leaning against two motorcycles.

"My little brother," Mayhem mumbles. He's uncomfortable that I have seen him. Mayhem quickly snaps his wallet shut.

He shot my brother . . . . Sangwoo's forlorn voice invades my memory. A chill wracks my body. "Where's your brother now?" I lean into Mayhem, reducing the space between us. I want to hear his answer.

"He's dead." Mayhem's response is cold and unrelenting.

My eyebrows crinkle together. "And Sangwoo's brother?" My insides feel muddled. I brace for the impending answer. A gloomy, foreboding mood grips me.

Mayhem narrows his eyes at me. The easygoing attitude dissipates; the intimidating, enthralling, and precarious gang lord emerges. "He doesn't have a brother. He shot mine to death." Although his tone of voice is torrid, Mayhem's tortured expression makes me cave in.

I gape at him. The club floor shatters beneath me. I am speechless and reeling from Mayhem's candor. "He said you shot his brother," I mumble. I don't know how Mayhem hears me, but he does. *I told you. I told you Sangwoo's shady. Now we have confirmation he's also a liar,* my intuition states quietly.

The realization dawns in Mayhem's eyes. The smile doesn't reach his eyes when he tells me softly, "Sangwoo fed you some bullshit story about how I shot his brother right?" Mayhem pauses, but continues at the distressed expression on my face. "He never had a brother, sweetheart. I warned you to stay away from him. And now that I know he had to lie to you—to get close to you—I would suggest you stay away from me too. Our world will tear you apart. You're not built for this. Spare yourself the heartbreak."

I feel as though I am spinning on a revolving axis. I am dizzy and emotional. For a moment, I forget I am in a dark and loud club. Instead, I feel as if I am standing on a platform with a bright spotlight on my face. I am powerless to the emotions I feel.

"Until we meet again." Without another word, Mayhem turns from the bar and disappears into the dark crowd. True to his mystifying style, Mayhem does little to clarify the misconceptions about him. This man allows rumors to fuel his reputation. Only those who are directly involved have access to his truth. Perhaps this is Mayhem's secret to his throne in the underground world. Unlike Sangwoo who displays it all under the guise of anonymity, Mayhem's path to his throne relies on what others say about him. Who is the true Mayhem then? The true Yoon Jaewon?

"Wait! You can't just walk away!" I shout after Mayhem. Panic grips me. I want to know more, but Mayhem is long gone.

The club music, though alive and pulsating, sounds distant in my ears now. Although the lights continue to wan above the dance bar, I am blind to it all. How can Mayhem brush me off like that? How can he walk away without explaining more? The torn expression on Mayhem's face—when I mentioned his brother's death—is more ingenuous than anything Sangwoo has ever told me. Without a doubt, I believe Mayhem. Choi Sangwoo lied to me. I was under his hold for so long that the truth remains beyond distortion. But why? Why would he make up such a horrible lie? Did Sangwoo want me to sympathize with him? Did he think that would draw me to him even more? *Well, it did, didn't it? He got you to kiss him out of pity.* My intuition purses her lips.

I gulp down the rest of the water and wave for the bartender. Through the loud music, I order a drink known for its potent alcohol content. Then, I lean against the bar and guzzle down the acidic taste. He lied to me. Why did he lie to me?

I start to fall apart here. Everything that has plagued me since Choi Sangwoo's appearance in my life starts to unravel. Like an origami, the dark corners of my mind fold in. All the intangible things I've tried to hide under false pretenses come crashing down around me.

I feel like crap as the alcohol rips through my veins. I can no longer hide my impulses.

"I can do it. Calling him . . . ." I whip my cell phone out and dial the last known number.

My head starts to spin. I feel lightheaded and more importantly, I am not thinking.

"Hey! Excuse you!"

"What the hell is wrong with you?!"

"Excuse you!"

Here and there, I bump into people. The club is getting darker and darker, making it hard for me to see where I am going. I don't care. I have to get out of here. I want to stop the spinning.

"Oof!" I happen to walk right into someone's chest.

"May?"

"Oh shit!"

Just as I fall, Choi Sangwoo catches me.

SEOUL MUSICAL THEATRE SITS ON fifty flights of cold, hard concrete. I don't know why Choi Sangwoo has brought me here, but we are standing on the very top flight near the largest pillar. The entrance to the building is only twenty steps away. For a Friday night, the venue is strangely vacant. Below us, people are strolling against the nightlife backdrop. Cars race through the busy intersection, adding white noise and life to the otherwise quiet city. The view is spectacular, but reality paints a darker picture.

"Why did you drink so much?" Sangwoo scolds me. His voice brings me to the present moment.

"Says the alcoholic." My inhibitions are long gone.

Sangwoo narrows his eyes. He is less than pleased with me. However, Sangwoo refrains from nagging further. He's already given me an earful in the car. I can't recall a single word he's said because my intuition keeps chanting, "Liar, liar!" every single time Sangwoo speaks.

Tell him May . . . tell him what you want to tell him, my intuition urges. I cannot get the words out fast enough. I am dizzy and nauseous. I am under the influence of alcohol and frankly, I don't care if I am being a friend to him or not.

"You're different from what I assumed you would be." Sangwoo's words are cold, accusing, and isolating.

"So are you," I rebut quickly. The alcohol spins in my head. The thudding in my heart makes the situation more precarious.

Sangwoo stares ahead as though he is deciding what to do with me. There is evidence of stress in him. I don't know how else to tell Sangwoo that I am in pain too. I want to ask him why he is here, why he is still pursuing me, but I cannot find the right words. I am worried that Sangwoo's answer will deter me from making the final decision to walk away from him. Mayhem's dark warning comes into my mind. I cannot believe *that* gang lord told me the truth about his brother and ditched me to make the connection on my own.

"Have you ever loved anyone?" Sangwoo asks, slicing through the tension with the sharp, introspective question. There is an ulterior motive to his question, but Sangwoo masks it well.

I am used to his mood swings and randomization. I slyly answer, "Why are you asking me this?"

"Because I was thinking about my first love today," Sangwoo says with nonchalance. "The end of the month is approaching and I cannot stop thinking of her." Sangwoo is directly talking about Dead Girl now.

My heart constricts at his slow revelations. The conversation suddenly takes a twisted turn. Sangwoo wants to go to war with me. Ok, we'll go to war.

"So you drink to forget her," I mumble in disbelief.

Sangwoo attempts to redeem himself. "Only when I have a lot on my mind. Everything that I do takes a toll on me." There is sadness in his tone. Sangwoo stares up at the night sky again. "Will you dance with me?"

"Now?" I stare at him in disbelief.

"Yes." Sangwoo leans forward. From inside his black blazer, Sangwoo pulls out a small, black iPod. I am amazed to see that ear buds are connected to it. Music pours into my ears when Sangwoo places an ear bud in. Brian McKnight is singing about not remembering why it all fell apart.

"What are they doing?"

"Aww, that's so cute."

I pull out of my daze. People have stopped walking on the street to stare at us. "Sangwoo, stop. Please." I step back from Sangwoo. I extract the ear bud. I know what he's doing.

"I like you May. I know I haven't been exactly honest with you. But my feelings are true," Sangwoo mutters as he buries his face in my hair.

I stop struggling in Sangwoo's arms, letting the words seep into me.

Dead Girl. Misun. I can feel Sangwoo's emotions surging through his entire being for the love of his life. If seeing me hurts him so much–reminds him of her so much–why can't he stay away from me? *Because he just can't help himself. The pain she left him can only be relieved when Sangwoo finds a suitable replacement.* My conscience has her box of tissue out. My intuition is long gone. She doesn't want to witness this.

He's the perfect one for me. I love him so much! Nothing will ever separate us. I found love, May. Her passionate voice and beautiful face surges through my mind. I am falling down a great precipice as the memories threaten to take over my entire being.

"May. Are you okay?" There is alarm in Sangwoo's voice.

I nod as I feel the cool night air against my skin.

"I was going to call you," I mutter. Before I can help it, the burning tears start to form. Damn it! I press my fingers on top of my eyelids to stop the burn. But the tears continue to flow effortlessly.

"May." Sangwoo wraps an arm around me. "Why are you crying?" Sangwoo asks softly.

"I-I–" I shake my head at a loss for words. I begin to sob. "I didn't want her to die. I just wanted to forget her. After all these years, I wanted to let her go. I forced myself to believe that you wanted me for me, but all along you only wanted me because I reminded you of her. Why do you keep stringing me along, keeping me in the dark, and lying to the both of us?"

Sangwoo freezes. Slowly, he unhooks his arm around me.

Whether I am alcohol driven or not, I don't care. Anguish and betrayal pound in my chest. I cannot control it anymore or I will lose the rest of my sanity. Ever since I met Choi Sangwoo, I have known this day would come. Denial can remove anyone from the truth, further than they can imagine. It is time that we should stop lying to one another.

"You want me to take you home?" Sangwoo offers. He wants to run. He wants to deny the impending truth.

"No! I have to tell you now." I cling to his arms.   Tears are dampening my cheeks.

Sangwoo's own eyes widen. "May, you don't have to do this."

I hold onto the sleeve of his shirt desperately. "I have to. Please, let me. I can't keep pretending that I don't know. I can't keep having you lie to me. I'm tired of it. I deserve better than this. You don't like me for me, and you know it. I remind you of her. Everything about me reminds you of her–my face, my physique, even my voice."

Sangwoo's jaw locks tight. His brown eyes become hooded and

guarded. "May," he starts again.

"You knew Lee Misun . . . didn't you? Do you remember her the way I do?" I am desperate for him to understand this dark past of mine. "Lee Misun was my stepsister. She was Eunhye's biological daughter."

I tell Sangwoo my truth.

MY EARLIEST MEMORIES REVOLVE AROUND the death of my mother. The living room was adorned in brown and black furnishing. The sobs circulated the house like musical notes rising and falling in a rhythmic pattern.

I was only nine-years-old at the time, lonely and scared. I was unresponsive to the hugs and kisses of the adults coming in and out of my home. Occasionally, I looked up at the large picture frame propped in the middle of the room. My mother's glamorous and smiling face beamed down at me. Even though I was young, I knew about death. I knew that when a person dies, they don't come back.

"Daddy, are you going to live with me now?" I asked him through teary eyes. There was an uncomfortable feeling in my throat from crying too much.

My father shook his head as he stooped down to my level. "No, honey. You're going to live with me." He pulled me into his arms, held me tightly and started to cry all over again. It was the first and last time I would ever see him with so much emotion. I was too young to understand the magnitude of the situation.

The first time I met his *other* family, his wife on legal papers and their daughter was when I officially moved in. I was standing in the middle of the large, lavishly decorated living room lit with fluorescent lighting and the smell of Jasmine tea.

Lee Eunhye, my father's first and only wife, hunched over to look at me. Her kind eyes matched her soft caress on my burning cheeks. "She looks exactly like Misun."

"Eunhye." My father touched her shoulders. The recent events have caused him great strain and stress. "I'm all she has." He took Eunhye's hands into his palms and said, "We're all she has."

Eunhye stared at my father with an indescribable look. "Of course." Right from the beginning, Eunhye was never a heartless or a cold woman toward me. Eunhye kissed the top of my head and hugged me tightly.

Eunhye spoke softly to my father. "You hid everything for all these years, and now you bring home a little girl."

My father didn't answer her. Instead, he pressed Eunhye's palm onto his lips. It was a sign of remorse and apologies rolled up into one gesture.

Eunhye bit her lower lip as her eyes welled up. "What should I do Hyun?"

"Please." My father was anguished.

Eunhye had her eyes pinned to me. "Maybelline, you're my daughter now." Eunhye tightened her embrace around me.

Now that I'm older, I know the reason behind the strained meeting. My father was pleading with his wife to take me in—to adopt me as her own. At the time, I hated Eunhye. Most of all, I hated my father. I hated everything that had to do with his home. All of a sudden, I was now living with him. For nine years, I lived with my biological mother in a little apartment that my father paid for. At a young age, I didn't realize that my biological mother was my father's mistress. She was his best-kept secret for nine years until she died. The little family with my mother was all I had ever known. I always thought that fathers didn't live with mothers and daughters. But after my biological mother's death, I understood I was the *other* woman's child—the half-sister of Lee Misun.

I first met Misun two days after my mother's funeral. Eunhye took the necessary steps to introduce me to my cold half-sister. Misun recently returned from boarding school and was seven years older than me.

"Misun, why don't you say hi to Maybelline?" Eunhye introduced us. Misun stared at me with dark eyes and pursed lips. We could have passed as twins. At the time, dressed in her school uniform, Misun was already a tall and mature seventeen-year-old. Misun's hair was always dark, long and layered. The halo formed around her face accentuated its oval shape, light brown eyes, and heart-shaped lips. She was beautiful beyond measure.

"Who is she?" Misun addressed our father.

"Your sister." My father narrowed his eyes at her. "May will be living with us from now on."

Misun stared at me for the longest time. Instead of a warm and welcoming smile, she turned on her heels and stalked upstairs.

I looked at my father hoping for an explanation, but the fallen look on his face told me I was not going to get one. I assumed that Misun's cold and isolating behavior would result in her ignoring me entirely. However, I got a good dose of reality when Misun approached me that night. I was climbing into bed when she turned up in the bedroom we shared.

"So, you're the whore's daughter."

I turned and made eye contact with my half-sister. Misun watched me with an intense facial expression. She had cold, arctic eyes for such a beautiful girl.

"What did you say?" I asked. At the age of nine, I wasn't sure what the word whore even meant. But when its intonation was coupled with Misun's disgusted facial expression, I just knew it was a bad word.

"Your mother is a whore," Misun repeated with disdain. "You know— a woman who opens her legs for men. A home-wrecker. A mistress."

I could only stare at Misun in shock. How could someone be so cruel and hateful towards me? I wanted to fire something back, but I was too young and overpowered by her.

"You girls aren't asleep yet?" On cue, my father showed up at the bedroom door.

"Yes." Misun flashed a forced smile at him. "Good night daddy."

Taking my chance to escape her, I crawled into my bed and pulled the covers over my head. I held my breath when I heard the bedroom door close and Misun's footsteps. I was always a quiet and mousy child. I was no match for my older half-sister who had a fiery personality and behavior.

"Get up!" She yanked the covers off me.

"Wha–?" I sat up in bed and stared at her. "Leave me alone!"

Without warning, Misun threw my pillows onto the floor. "You're sleeping on the ground."

"There are two beds. You get your own bed, I get mine." I pointed out.

"You're sleeping on the ground!" Misun narrowed her eyes at me. Her beautiful face contorted into harrowing features. With one more swipe, Misun successfully threw my blanket on the ground. I growled at her, refusing to let her bully me. "Give me back my pillow and blanket."

"You're sleeping on the ground!" Misun grabbed me roughly, tossed me on the ground, and threw the covers on me. She slapped a pillow against my head, strong enough for me to twist to the side. "You're not wanted here and you'll never be wanted here. What gives you the right to come into my house and take my things?" Misun leered in front of my face.

I sniffled, not wanting to her to see me cry. "Why are you doing this to me? What have I done? I hate you!"

Misun narrowed her eyes at me. She bit down on her bottom lip in disgust. "You're not going to be living here long, so I don't care if you like me or not."

At age nine, after losing my biological mother and having my entire world turned upside down, I cried myself to sleep that night. I felt helpless, scared, and hopeless. I just couldn't understand why Misun hated me. Although it was hard for me to adjust to it, I was desperate to make some sense. Days passed, weeks went by, and months accumulated. I cried myself to sleep every night because I missed my biological mother so much that it hurt. Nothing from that point on ever felt the same. Nothing felt worth it. Although my father took me in, he never attempted to develop a relationship with me other than being my disciplinarian. Eunhye, on the other hand, opened her heart and treated me as though I was her own. But Eunhye became blind and deaf when it came to how Misun treated me. How could I compete with her biological daughter?

Misun came home one afternoon with a basket of two kittens. My father bought it as an early birthday present for her. Misun was over the moon about the precious kittens.

"Mother, look, aren't they beautiful?" Misun showed Eunhye.

"Oh my god, aren't they a sight?" Eunhye cooed at the small, white kittens. "They're sisters?"

"Yes, but you see this one is darker and this one is lighter. They have the same mother, but different daddies." Misun gave me a look.

"May, why don't you come look at them?" Eunhye motioned for me to join.

Before I could lean across the table Misun interrupted me. "Daddy, look!"

"Honey, we're eating. Why don't you put them in the living room?" My father put down his newspaper long enough to redirect Misun.

"We should get more animals. This house feels so empty with just the four of us," Eunhye suggested.

"Come on kitties. Get down from the table." Misun ushered the kittens down the table.

At the same, I was reaching for a spoon. Without warning, Misun pushed one of the kittens into my hand. It happened too quickly for me to register.

"Ow!" I jerked my hand back when I felt its tiny claws digging into my hand.

"Meow!" The kitten screeched as it landed on the floor with a thud.

"Are you okay May?!" Misun reached for my hand to examine the scratch.

I pushed her away from me. I hated how Misun pretended to care about me in front of our parents. I didn't understand her reasons for being so fake.

"May," My father warned. "Your sister is only trying to help.

"I hate her!" The nine-year-old in me vehemently remarked.

As soon as I said it, I appeared to be the defiant and dangerous daughter. Eunhye had a terrified look on her face while Misun's lips pursed together. My father ordered me to finish my food in my room. I was not welcomed at the table with that type of behavior. I went to sleep hungry that night.

At the same time, Misun started the pattern of sneaking out of the house. Around one in the morning, she would tap on the bedroom window to wake me. My job was to open the window for her to climb through. One night, I overslept and left her outside for thirty minutes before I heard her knocking.

"You stupid kid! I reminded you so many times!" Misun grabbed a handful of my hair when she made it through the window.

"I didn't hear you!" I whimpered.

"Do you have any idea how cold I am?! I could get sick and die!" Misun threw me onto the floor. I hit the carpet with a thud; the pain shot down my back. "Ow!" I rolled and knocked into the basket where the two kittens were resting.

They both screeched and jumped. I landed on one of them and heard the body of the small creature crush under me. "No!" I gasped in horror.

"Oh my god! You killed it! You killed it!" Misun was screeching at the top of her lungs. Misun screamed loud enough to wake our parents.

"What happened? What's going on?" The bedroom door opened and light flooded into the room.

"May!"

"Oh my god! What have you done?!"

Blood. Blood was everywhere. From my bed to my own hands, I was covered in blood. The kitten I had accidentally fallen on was flattened to death. It was a traumatic sight—one I don't wish to describe.

Misun was sobbing in our parents' arms. No matter how I tried explaining that it was an accident, my parents didn't listen. Misun told them that I had done it on purpose. She told them I deliberately sat on the kitten during our argument. It was a measure of how much power Misun had over me that I didn't tell them she had been sneaking out at night.

From then on, I was considered the passive-aggressive and

dangerous child. My parents sent me to therapy after that. I had to spend countless hours discussing why I was angry and upset inside. The therapist concluded that along with the terrible shock of my mother's death, I was very distressed about the new environment as well. Everything was correct, except for the fact that I did not intend to harm the kitten. After that, I looked at Misun in a completely different light. I became scared of her. I was terrified of my half-sister and her ability to deceive and manipulate.

My father and Eunhye grew distant. I rarely left my room and rarely spoke to them. That's why they believed Misun and viewed me as the perpetual liar. However, Misun stopped making my life a living hell when she started dating. On her good days, it was as though we were best friends.

"He is the love of my life." Misun swooned over her first boyfriend one afternoon. Whenever she got ready for date night with him, I had to endure her recollections. "You see, he belongs to a group named Crist. I think I really like him. Choi Sangwoo!" Misun gushed about him right from the beginning.

Misun lowered herself in front me so that we were eye-to-eye at one point. "I'm going out with him tonight. Remember to let me in okay?"

Pretty soon, Misun got heavily involved with her boyfriend. She snuck out every night with him and didn't return home until dawn. I kept her little secret until one night where it all fell apart.

"Do you know how to kiss May?" Misun was applying her make-up, drawing dark lines underneath her eyes. It was six months into the relationship and Misun was into deep. Misun wanted to run away with this Choi Sangwoo.

I was in the middle of brushing my hair before bed so I didn't answer her. I learned not to talk to Misun.

"Of course you don't," Misun went on, running her hands through her long tresses. "Sangwoo and I kissed last night. It was the most beautiful thing! His lips are incredibly soft. I love him so much. He's the perfect gentleman. I think he's the one. I want to marry him one day."

I was shocked by the way she talked. "You're dirty going around letting boys kiss you." I couldn't keep my elementary mouth shut. I blurted out my feelings without a second thought.

Misun whirled around to face me. "I'm dirty? I'm not the one who came from a whore."

My jaw dropped open. Anger sparked inside of me like fireworks.

"Girls?" My father knocked on the door.

"Shit. I can't let him see me like this!" Misun quickly ran into the closet.

"May?" My father entered the bedroom. "Where's Misun?"

I was so angry at Misun's comment. Completely forgetting what kind of person Misun was and what she was capable of, I didn't lie for her. Instead, I pointed to the closet. "She's hiding in the there."

"What? Why?" My father opened the closet door.

I could see Misun eyes sending daggers at me. Thinking she was going to get a good spanking, I smiled genuinely for the first time. She deserved it. I was tired of listening to her degrade my mother. For once, I wanted my father to see his oldest daughter for who she really was.

"Eunhye, come in here and see your daughter!" My father called for his wife.

When Eunhye entered the room, she was beside herself. "Misun, what are you wearing?"

"She sneaks out every night to see her boyfriend!" I volunteered the information. I was on a high and never coming down from it.

"Boyfriend? Misun!"

"What is going on? What are you doing?!"

I watched with glee as our parents lectured her. They shouted at Misun and ultimately grounded her. A sense of satisfaction rushed through me as I watched our parents berate her. I felt a sense of justice and liberation.

"Go to sleep. We'll continue this in the morning." My father walked out of the bedroom in frustration. Eunhye, upset and on the brink of tears, left in disappointment too.

As soon as the door closed, Misun turned to me. She had been crying. All of her makeup smeared black across her beautiful features. "Why did you do that?" she asked through gritted teeth as she advanced towards me. "Why did you do that? Answer me, you whore's daughter." And that was the last straw.

I stood up. "My mother is not a whore!" I jumped.

"I'm glad she's dead! But why did she leave you? Get out of my house! You don't belong in my family!" Misun's words shocked me. As if someone had stunned me with a gun, I froze at her cruel words. Up until then I endured all I could, but Misun's words seared through my heart.

"How can you say something like that?" I asked her, my eyes brimmed with tears. My heart started to race and I felt like I couldn't breathe. "What have I ever done to you?!"

Misun glared at me. "Do you have any idea how much I hate the fact that all of a sudden you exist? You're just a stupid kid. You don't know how many fights my parents have had over you! They almost broke up because of your whorish mother and you!" Misun's accusing eyes pinned me. "Get out of my house!"

I was stunned by Misun's revelation. But I refused to back down. "I'm not going anywhere. It's about time I stand up to you. You think you run this place? You think you're so bad? Does that boyfriend of yours know who you are?!" I screamed.

"Don't you dare talk about Sangwoo!" Misun snapped back at me. "Daughter of a whore!"

"I hate you!" All hell broke loose as I ran at her. All the anger and hate unleashed. The fury inside of me lashed out at Misun. The first thing I did when I got to Misun was slap her across the face. The sting felt cathartic.

"Ahh!" Misun's arms intensely tightened on my shoulder blade. She dug her nails into my skin. The pain exploded and blinded me for a split second.

"I hate you!" I screamed as we both fell to the ground. I pinned her down to the floor and with all my might pressed my hands against her face. I scratched it as hard as I could and saw the slashes thicken with redness . . . blood . . . .

Misun struggled as she screamed. Our bodies became rigid, but somehow Misun managed to slip out from under me. Before I knew it, I was the one on the floor. I braced myself for her fingers to claw at me, but I heard the crash of something breaking.

Glass . . . Misun smashed the glass pencil holder she kept under the bed. She held it up to my face as she breathed heavily.

"I hate the fact you look like me. I'll ruin that face of yours tonight!" Misun lowered it near my cheek.

"What is going on in there?!" Voices ring outside of our bedroom.

Quickly, Misun got off me. She crawled five inches away to bring the glass against her own face. With a clean swipe, she braced for the pain before she cut herself. Blood seeped through her skin, and Misun bawled like a little child when she tossed the glass fragments near me. I watched in horror as I realized Misun had done it to herself.

"What is going on?!" Our parents entered the bedroom.

"Sh-she attacked me! The glass! She—" Misun screamed in pain as tears ran down her cheeks.

"No I didn't! She did it herself!" I got up from the floor, watching my father's facial expression with panic. My insides were screaming, tearing apart.

Misun cried at the top of her lungs. Her body shook violently as she emphasized the blood on her face. "First the kitten and now me? Why can't you stop May! Can't we just get along? Why do you hate me so much?"

"Daddy, you're not falling for her act, are you? I didn't do it daddy! Don't believe her please! She's been nothing but mean to me!" I screamed, searching his face desperately.

"Misun! Your beautiful face!" Eunhye rushed over and gathered Misun in her arms. Eunhye started to rock Misun back and forth in her arms. Eunhye stared at me with a horrified expression. I was nothing more than a wild animal to her.

"May . . . let's go." My father grabbed my arm, jerking me forward.

"Daddy, you don't believe her, do you? Daddy! Where are you taking me? Daddy! Please! You have to believe me!" I screamed as he dragged me out of the bedroom. I clung to him as much as I could– trying to make him understand, trying to make him believe me, trying to make him be on my side.

I could hear Misun wailing in Eunhye's arms.

"Stop struggling May!" My father barked at me.

"Please! Listen to me! It's Misun! Daddy, please believe me!" I started choking with tears. My eyes got extremely blurry and I felt so weak I couldn't struggle anymore . . . .

They sent me away in the end. No more therapy and no more medication. They sent me straight to Seoul's Psychiatric Center. There, I was placed in a room until an analyst came for me. The doctors evaluated me as a child-in-need. The term was used to describe a child who needed to be carefully evaluated and treated. I was considered abnormal and reckless.

They tried to visit me regularly, but the last time I saw Misun was the day she came with our parents. I had no choice but to see her.

"Don't hate me May," my father told me. He sat across from me with his hands clasped together. The small hospital room felt too big for him.

I looked away from my father. Why are my insides so twisted? I didn't want to look at him. How could I look at my father when he didn't believe me? He chose Misun over me. Wasn't I his daughter too? Didn't he love me too?

My father sighed and got up, no longer patient with my silent treatment. "Misun's waiting outside. She wants to come in and talk to you. I just wish for you two to get along. Why can't you just get along?"

For the first time, I saw my father's tired face. I wanted to express my emotions to him, but I couldn't. After all this time, I came to be this type of person. I wanted to talk, but the words could never meet my voice. Daddy waited for me to say something, but when I didn't, he walked out of the door without another glance at me.

Misun entered the room next. She was different from the last time I had seen her. Her face still had a bandage on it, but she had cut her hair and dyed it a light brownish color. Lee Misun and Lee Maybelline did not look alike anymore . . . .

She walked slowly into the room, almost dragging her feet. "How is it here?" Misun finally asked; her voice soft and different. She looked around my desolate hospital room.

I scoffed, but didn't reply. How is it supposed to be in here? She got what she wanted. I am out of the house and no longer competing for our parents' attention anymore.

"My boyfriend and I are going on a trip soon," Misun divulged brightly, as if we were having a normal conversation. Misun seemed to have forgotten who sent me here.

I stared out of the window. Why do I care about where she's going with her boyfriend? Misun was also very egocentric. She only cared for herself. Her wicked ways knew no bounds.

"Oh, my boyfriend is such a badass!" Misun said as she leaned forward in her seat. "Did you know he just shot his rival's little brother?"

I closed my eyes. I didn't want to pay any attention to the rubbish Misun talked about. Why was she always pushing the topic of boyfriend on me?"

"I like the way he holds me May . . . his hugs are always nice," Misun sighed. "And you know what else he told me? He says he would never love another girl the way he loves me. No one can ever take my place. He wants to marry me later on–"

"Shut up!" Surprised at my own voice for coming out so strong and clear, I locked eyes with Lee Misun. "Shut up. I-I don't want to hear about you and your boyfriend. Will you please shut up? You shouldn't have come here. I don't want to see you. I hate you. I want you to die a painful death because that's what you deserve!"

For the first time, Misun saw how angry I was. She got up quickly from her chair. Misun's expression rapidly changed from soft to anger. Even if it surprised her to see me being aggressive, Misun never faltered. "I'm just trying to be nice."

"Nice?" I sneered at her face, suddenly feeling the urge to call her every dirty name I knew. "You don't think it's a little too late?! Look where you've sent me to! They treat me like I'm crazy! But you're the crazy one. I hate you!"

"I don't hate you May." Her voice changed once again. "You might think I hate you, but all I wanted is for you to get out of the house. And now that you're out, we can be friends."

I couldn't believe it. Why isn't she screaming back at me? Why isn't she the Misun who sent me here? The Misun who mutilated herself to get me here? "You're sicker than I am," I concluded. "You're the one who should be in here."

Misun reached out to cup my chin in her hand. Studying my face, Misun said softly, "We look so much alike. With this face, we're always going to be reminded of each other."

"Let me go." I pushed Misun's hand away roughly.

Misun stumbled. "May, you are–"

"Get out! Get out!" I screamed.

"I'm trying to talk to you."

"Get out!"

"Fine! Don't ever expect me to come back here to visit you! I'll make sure you stay in here, you little brat!"

"I just hope you die! Get the hell out of my life! Go!"

After she left the room, I could hear Misun telling daddy that she tried to patch things up but I refused. I fell back into bed, crying all over again, falling apart.

Little did I know that the cosmic universe listened to my words, even though I didn't mean it in the literal sense.

Misun did die.

For the next three months, no one came to visit me. It was like I didn't have any family at all. Misun was a monster and I was glad my parents spared me the agony. But when the days went by without a word, I started to worry.

"I am so sorry for your lost."

"We know . . . Thank you. It's why we haven't been able to visit May sooner. Is she sleeping?"

"Yes. May I ask, when is Misun's funeral?"

"T-tomorrow. The end of this month. "

"How did it happen? If you don't mind me asking. "

"A drunk driver hit the car she was in. Apparently she snuck out of the house while we were sleeping to go see her boyfriend." Eunhye's voice was tense. "She was running away with him."

I gripped the bed sheets as I listened to my father, Eunhye, and the nurse outside of my room talking. The impact of the news hit my chest like a ton of bricks. I only started breathing normally when it hurt.

Misun died at eighteen-years-old, just a couple months after her birthday.

For the longest time, I refused to believe it. She was still alive. Misun would be waiting for me to get out of the hospital so she could plan to ruin my life. But Misun died. I confirmed it myself. My father took me out of the center to attend Misun's funeral at the end of the month. Only when I saw her lying in the casket did I really believe it. But I never learned to accept it. I refused to believe that Misun was gone. Just like that, she was gone. After all the pain and misery Misun brought me, she left without warning. Everything felt like it was all in vain. Even though her death came abruptly and in such a disturbing way, I never cried once.

"SO YOU COULD SAY I blamed myself for her death. I stayed in the institution for six months. That's why I've never known much of anything. The psychologist on my case labeled me as socially inept and emotionally deficient. My obscure and traumatic childhood became repressed memories."

Choi Sangwoo's head remains lowered, listening to the sound of my voice. The gang leader seems drained after hearing my confession. His silence parades the steps of the musical theatre that we are standing on.

I look at Sangwoo with an internal battle brewing inside of me. With great deliberation, I wipe away the last traces of my tears. "I guess you could say I knew you before I even met you. I forgot that her first boyfriend, the only boy she's ever loved, goes by the name Choi Sangwoo."

Again, Sangwoo keeps his lips pressed into a firm line.

"That's why we can only be friends. That's why I'm freaking out because the end of the month is coming. The anniversary of Misun's death. Every year, my parents and I visit her grave. In the past few weeks that I've known you, I was always careful about never letting myself like you because I know you see her in me. No matter how nice you are, I didn't let it go any further," I continue with the full-blown confession. "I realized something. You two are the same type of people. Misun was a violent, vicious, and scheming person who was out for herself. She liked to play with people, pushing them to their limits without a care for the consequences. Misun loved to twist things. She was a bully. And you're just the same . . . . When you told me your brother was shot to death, I kissed you out of pity and sympathy. But I knew all along you're a liar. It was the other way around, wasn't it? You shot Yoon Jaewon's brother didn't?"

Sangwoo finally looks at me. The color is gone from his face. The brown eyes that once mesmerized me is now dark and pained. When he doesn't answer me, I go on.

"Why did you lie to me?" I press on; completely shaken from my confession, I tell myself to hold on a little longer. "What else are you lying about?"

He doesn't answer for the longest time. When Choi Sangwoo finally does, chills come over me. "When I saw you for the first time at The Trax, I couldn't believe it. I almost grabbed you. I stared at you for the longest time, wondering how you could look so much like her. You are more like her than you can ever imagine May. I see a piece of her in you."

"But I'm not her." I step away from him slowly. It feels liberating to have Sangwoo finally confirm and confess. After all this time, Choi Sangwoo is still stuck on the sister who put a black hole in my childhood. "I'll never understand your twisted mind. You had me fooled. I thought you really . . . just liked *me*." *Don't make it easier on him. You know your feelings weren't genuine either,* my intuition rationalizes.

Without another word, I walk away from Sangwoo, feeling the tears welling up in my eyes again. I can feel Sangwoo watching my retreating back. I can almost hear him telling me not to go. Why am I becoming a crybaby all of a sudden? Why did I let the memory of Misun make me cry once again? *No, you're crying because you reached an epiphany.* It is my conscience's turn to speak up. She's been awfully quiet, battling right and wrong.

I wipe my tears with the back of my hand. The memories I have tried to lock in the back of my mind have unraveled. I am losing my senses fast. I should go home, sleep through this, and tell Eunhye what has happened to me . . . . I want to clear the air with my stepmother too. If I can be honest with Sangwoo, then I can be honest with Eunhye.

Without warning, Sangwoo grabs me into an embrace. He's chased after me. "May. Please. I want to talk." Sangwoo's grip on my wrist tightens.

"Sangwoo, please." It is my turn to plead with him. I attempt to pry his hands off me.

"I was wrong. I was wrong to see you as Misun, but I couldn't help it. You are your own person, I understand. My feelings for you are genuine." Sangwoo encloses his body around me.

I don't want to hear it. I refuse to answer him.

"I like you," Sangwoo repeats.

"Stop." I plug my ears like a child.

"I like you!" he shouts.

"Stop, please!" I refuse to hear it.

"Maybelline Lee!" Sangwoo forces me to unplug my ears.

"You only like me because I look like her!" I cannot hold it anymore; my heart starts to beat so fast it hurts. I blink uncontrollably to stop myself from crying, although the tears are dying to come out. The sudden emotional impact is too much for me to handle. I am faint and nauseous.

"May, it's not about Misun. Think about us," Sangwoo encourages me. His brown eyes jump all over my facial features.

"Why are you doing this to me? Please don't force it," I implore him. Any minute now, I am going to double over and throw up.

"Don't you like me?" Sangwoo's demeanor and simple question stop me in my tracks. "Don't you have any feelings for me?"

Before I can make another move, I feel Sangwoo's strong arms slip around my waist and settle themselves across my stomach. The cartilage of his left ear slightly touches my forehead at an angle. My back nestles inside his warm chest.

I close my eyes and feel the salty tears spurt down my cheeks.

I love the way he holds me May. His hugs are always nice. He said he would never love another girl the way he loves me. No one can ever take my place.

How vividly I remember her exact words . . . .

"Even if you remind me of her, I have fallen for you May," Sangwoo breathes.

I don't have time to let his words absorb before his lips settle on mine. Sangwoo holds me in his embrace for what feels like a lifetime. I feel my grip slipping as I settle on top of a cloud—a cloud of robust and rudimentary emotions. I push him away quickly, creating a stark distance between us.

Then, all the pressure inside my throat erupts.

CHAPTER FOURTEEN

Memories of how I get home are scattered fragments. Hot flashes of Choi Sangwoo stumbling with me in his arms, cold chills of sweat, and a spinning sphere of dizziness tamper with my memory. Doors opening and closing, along with spontaneous commotion erupts in a pattern. Eunhye's concerned facial expression transitions into my blurred vision. I am cold and aching, a melting pot of emotions and dilapidated control.

Eunhye's voice hushes with traces of fear. She asks Sangwoo a slew of incoherent questions.

"Mrs. Lee, I'm sorry. May's had a little too much to drink," Sangwoo responds in his rebuffing style.

The bubbles of colors that are obstructing my vision finally fade to black. I am traveling down a spinning vortex. It is comforting to give in to the exhaustion and darkness.

WHEN I WAKE UP THE next morning, I am sick and pale over the toilet. Eunhye stands over me with a hot compress. She is beyond upset. "I don't understand why you are on such a self-destructive path," Eunhye rebukes me with motherly care. I don't have the heart to confess to Eunhye that my self-destructive behavior has to do with Misun. How do I tell my stepmother that Choi Sangwoo, the man she met a couple of months earlier, is actually her dead daughter's boyfriend? How do I explain Sangwoo was the one Misun was running away with the night that she died? Even more so, how do I tell Eunhye that Choi Sangwoo is pursuing me because of my resemblance to Misun? I realize the magnitude of this ridiculousness and resign to being sick.

I feel terrible for making Eunhye worry. I'm supposed to be an adult, one who can legally drink and hold her alcohol. Instead, I am causing Eunhye such worry and grief like an errant child.

By the time night falls, I am sick with fever and cold symptoms. It is near dinnertime when Lina and her parents visit. Aunt Yuna brings her special concoction of lime juice proven to chase away common cold symptoms. Uncle Dom offers some warm chicken soup. They discuss about me in hushed whispers; I catch minced words like drinking, depression, and therapy. Eunhye realizes I am conscious and listening, so she ushers them out of my bedroom within five minutes. Only Lina stays with a solemn expression.

"Do you know how worried I was when I realized you left the club?" My cousin's tone hitches with anticipation. She sits to my right and runs her fingers through my hair. "What did he do to you?"

"Nothing," I whisper back. My world is dark and bleak. Memories of the painful confession swirl like poison. I don't want to tell Lina that Choi Sangwoo confirmed Lee Misun is the reason why he pursued me. In fact, I don't want to talk about him at all.

"Don't lie to me May. I know something bad happened. You don't ever drink like this and now you're sick to your stomach. Tell me. I might be able to help you," Lina pleas with me. She is probably wondering why I am pushing her away.

"It's nothing Lina."

"You are so stubborn."

I roll over to face the wall so Lina cannot see the tears falling. I need time to be alone, to digest the situation. After two minutes of silence, Lina gives my shoulder a squeeze and she bids me good night.

I travel in and out of sleep, uncomfortable and shivering from an invisible cold. I am content with my gloomy world. I want to wallow in misery without company. I want to let the pain ride itself out until I am stripped down to the bare minimum. That is what they taught me in therapy. Only after am I raw will I be able to recover.

In the middle of the night, fervent voices wake me. I listen carefully and realize that Choi Sangwoo is outside of my bedroom.

Eunhye tells him I am sick and turns Sangwoo away. I hear them talking in hushed whispers outside of my bedroom. Sangwoo insists on seeing me, but Eunhye's motherly instinct of protecting her young cub kicks in. I can hear Sangwoo's persistence being drowned out by Eunhye's harsh tone. In the end, Eunhye wins; Sangwoo's passionate voice fades into the darkness . . . .

———————————————

MY CELL PHONE WAKES ME on the fourth morning of my purgatory. I have been in bed for two days, out for the count. All I do is eat, sleep, read, and repeat. By the end of the week, I am restless and my cold symptoms are almost gone. I am grateful to see that my phone is capable of receiving messages from someone other than Choi Sangwoo and Lina.

There is a short message from Naili that my severance check is available for pick-up at The Trax. If I am not there by two in the afternoon, Naili will mail it home in a week. I spend five minutes debating whether I should go out or not. Eunhye has given me strict orders to stay home until I fully recover. But I need to get out. I need to do something. My back aches from the sleeping position and I am anxious to get some fresh air. For the past couple of months, I occupied myself with endless hope and possibilities. Now that I have finally come to my senses that it was all illusions, I need a good dose of reality.

I shower, dress, and head outside for the first time in days. The cool summer air is refreshing. It is humid outside–an indication of summer rain. I take the bus to The Trax with great anticipation. I keep my thoughts occupied with plans for the remaining summer and school.

When I arrive at The Trax, a barrage of spontaneous noise and commotion greet me. There is construction of the main entrance; the incline leading down to the front doors is being elevated to street level. The entire brown and red building is now a bare gray color. More than a dozen construction workers parade the building; some are carrying ladders while others are attaching lengthy chutes against the side of the building. It is chaos and routine here. I am witnessing the power of money moving tangible objects.

"Hello, how can I help you?" A whimsical voice greets me near the side of the building. A newly installed door poses as a temporary entrance. A man in his early fifties, dressed in a black suit, is holding a brown clipboard by his side. He looks like a guard of some sort.

"I'm here to pick up a check." I am careful with the curiosity brimming in my eyes.

He regards me with a kind smile. "Yes, please come in." Stepping aside, the guard points me to the entrance.

I thank him and step inside. The strong smell greets me first; fresh paint and wood pervade my senses. The entire interior is also bare; just a vast open space exists in a hollow shell. Even the signature bar of The Trax no longer exists. My eyes sweep the area with nostalgia. Although it is different here, I am not sure I am against it. The place feels renewed and refreshed. I am sure the new owner is on his way to creating his dream building.

"May." Joolie is the first person I see. She is standing next to Tailor who flashes me an identical smile. There are a handful of ex-Trax employees around the open floor. We exchange smiles, but I gravitate towards Joolie and Tailor.

"Hi." I magic a smile on my face. So far, it feels doable to put on a façade that everything is fine.

"You lost weight!" Wearing her long tresses in a ponytail, Joolie pulls me into a hug. A Cheshire grin spreads across her face. Before I can respond to Joolie's comment, she launches into an inquisition. "What have you been doing? Have you found a job yet? The place I'm working at is actually looking for new people if you're interested."

My mouth goes dry at Joolie's rapid-fire questions. "I've been busy with family stuff," I answer vaguely.

Joolie's lips form a perfect circle as though she understands. "So is Son. He's opting to have his check mailed to Busan. Apparently he's helping his family run business. That makes a lot of sense about his bossiness huh?"

A smile spreads across my lips at Joolie's statement. Suddenly, a feeling of nostalgia comes across me. I miss working here. I miss The Trax distracting me from my mundane life. I don't have to think about Choi Sangwoo and Misun when I am taking down orders and serving people. I miss the chaos of the restaurant and bar world. I took the distraction for granted. Seeing Tailor and Joolie reminds me that my worries, concerns, and memories can reduce with a busy work schedule.

"We should all make plans to hang out some time," Tailor speaks up, pulling me out of my reverie. He places a gentle hand on Joolie's shoulder. My eyes sweep over to Tailor who is dressed down in a gray sweatshirt and corduroy pants. It is clear something has developed between Tailor and Joolie. Joolie is especially attentive to Tailor; there is an undeniable spark in her eyes when she looks at him.

"Hi Tailor."

"Hi May. How are you?"

"Doing well. You two?" I eye them warily, grateful for the fact that the conversation is shifting. I don't want to ask bluntly if they are dating, but I do want to know.

"We're good." The light flickers in Joolie's eyes again. She wraps an arm around Tailor and leans into him. Joolie is answering my question with her body language.

"Congratulations," I tell them. A surge of emotions comes over me. They are finally together after months of flirting.

Tailor looks slyly at me. "Thank you. We're trying it out. If it doesn't work, I can always return her."

"Hey!" Joolie punches Tailor's arm in a playful manner. They are still in their honeymoon stage. Joolie seems like a different person now that they are official. I suppose a relationship has the power to morph you into a different person.

Tailor faces me with a goofy grin. "We're waiting for Naili. She's probably going to show up with the new owner."

That sounds like Naili's style. Turning my head, I survey the vast open space once more. The other ex-Trax employees are engaged in hushed conversations; some scan the room in the process while others glance anxiously at their cell phones. No one likes to play the waiting game.

"We definitely think it's one of the best options out there, but we are still open to other possibilities." Naili's signature voice permeates the air as she enters the room. Her shockingly red heels click with every step that she takes. Signature red nails, paired with a black jumpsuit, mark Naili's immaculate appearance. She is engaged in conversation with a man walking beside her. Naili's black lacquered eyes sweep the entire area until they land squarely on me.

Oh shit, my conscience curses. _Yes!_ My intuition fist pumps into the air. My eyes travel from Naili's gaze to the man standing next to her. _Heart attack._ I find myself locked in the stare of the blindingly handsome, enigmatic, and mysterious gang lord–Mayhem. My breath snags in my throat. The revelation hits me out of left field. The new owner of this venue is Mayhem–Yoon Jaewon. All along I have been mentally accusing Choi Sangwoo, but in actuality it is none other than the other elusive and brazen gang lord.

A tint of a smile crosses Mayhem's lips. Effortlessly, I lock in his dark, smoldering gaze. There are no traces of surprise on his model-like face. He is dressed in an all-black Executive suit today. The only thing that stands out about Mayhem is the expensive wristwatch on his arm. His black, tousled hair marks his tall, dark and handsome package.

"May I have your attention, please?" Naili clears her throat and calls for the chatter to lower. She really doesn't have to. Everyone in the room is already quiet and stationary. Expressions of disbelief and apt attention travels from one face to the next. They focus on Mayhem, obviously surprised at his youthful and inexplicable appearance.

Joolie nudges me and murmurs, "He's hot!"

Tailor flashes Joolie a disapproving look. I am too stunned to speak. Joolie and Tailor have no idea that the man standing in front of them is responsible for instilling fear and tyranny in people. Memories of my last meeting with Mayhem creep slowly into my mind.

Naili clasps her hands together and begins her short address. "Thank you for taking the time out to come today. As you all know, I am forevermore grateful for your service at The Trax. We've had a number of great years. But like all good things, it must come to an end. I always prefer to walk away from something when it is at the height of its success rather than its low point." Naili pauses momentarily to look at Mayhem.

It is clear from Naili's passive facial expression that the brooding gang lord affects her. Mayhem, on the other hand, is closed from public discussion. How does he manage to appear so elusive in front of more than a dozen people? *They teach those skills in gang-lord-training-one-oh-one,* my intuitions teases me.

Meanwhile, Naili takes a deep breath as she finishes her speech. "The new owner of this building was kind enough to write everyone a severance check as a parting gift." She extends a dramatic hand to introduce Mayhem. The blush on Naili's face says it all how she feels for him.

Without feeding into Naili's fawning, Mayhem steps forward. His hands clasp together in a business-like manner. Those brooding eyes scan the room. When he speaks, Mayhem's tone is clear and professional. "First off, I want to thank you for your superior service to The Trax. Naili and I both know the sacrifices and hard work you all have contributed to this venue. I know some of you are still looking for jobs and rearranging your situations, so hopefully these checks can support you in your endeavor." Such an arrogant gang lord, isn't it he? The pity smile Mayhem adorns us with accompanies the set of thin, white envelopes he has in his hands.

Naili leads Mayhem onto the floor with us little people. She knows everyone's names and helps Mayhem hand out the envelopes. Everyone's eyes are glued to Naili and Mayhem. Some appear to be fascinated while others are less than amused.

"Joolie." Naili gestures towards Joolie who can hardly stand on her own two feet at this point.

"Tailor." Naili quickly points another finger to Tailor.

Tailor takes the envelope from Mayhem with a guarded facial expression. Judging from Tailor's reaction, I don't know if he recognizes Mayhem or if he's jealous that his girlfriend is outwardly gaping at Mayhem.

"And the last envelope." Naili doesn't say my name when she points to me.

Mayhem hands me my envelope and speaks clearly, "I would like to speak to you after."

"Oh!" Joolie lets out an inaudible gasp next to me. Her jaw is on the floor. Tailor rolls his eyes at her.

Naili's eyes narrow at me like daggers.

I take the white envelope from Mayhem slowly. Instinctively, I bite my lower lip. What could he possibly want with me? The morbid thoughts seep in. For some reason, I think Yoon Jaewon might have bought The Trax to force me out of a job. But then again, he is a very busy man. Why would he take the time out to pursue a personal vendetta against me? My biggest crime against him was helping my cousin pay back her debt. Mayhem got to draw blood from Sangwoo in the process too. What more could he want from me? *He's probably still mad at what happened at the club. You made him talk about his brother getting shot by his rival.* My intuition shrugs as she looks up from her wheel of guesses.

"You know him?" Joolie turns to me when Mayhem and Naili make their way back to the front.

With careful discretion, I shake my head. Back towards the middle of the room, Naili excuses us. "Thank you everyone. Have a good day." She turns quickly to capture Mayhem's attention. They exchange a few words before it becomes apparent that Mayhem dismisses her. Naili throws me a short look before she walks out of the room first.

Slowly, people file out of The Trax. Some are already ripping through the envelopes. Joolie doesn't want to leave me, but Tailor pulls her to her senses.

"Keep in touch May." Tailor places a hand on my shoulder.

"Good luck. Call me please," are Joolie's last words before Tailor pulls her towards the exit.

As though a dark cloud hovers over me, I look up to catch the penetrating gaze of Mayhem. He is breathtakingly handsome–dark, smoldering, and mystifying. This gang lord always has me in a flurry. No one else makes me feel this way, not even Choi Sangwoo. Is this what attraction feels like?

"There's a bar down the strip. We can talk there." Mayhem snaps me out of my reverie.

I AM LONELY AND SAD. These are reasons enough for why I decided to follow Mayhem to the bar across the street. It is different with him right away. Unlike Choi Sangwoo, Mayhem doesn't hide from society and the general public. Instead, he blends in with the shadows created by the light. I am wary of Mayhem's intent on putting himself out there. Someone who parades out in the open, given his background and title, is not only demonstrating recklessness but also an absence of fear. I am constantly reminding myself that Mayhem is the more violent and unpredictable gang lord. What could he possibly want to talk to me about?

The bar Mayhem chooses, Sine, is an exclusive venue tucked at the very end of the strip. It is a sleepy Wednesday afternoon. The bar is scattered with customers under its dim lustrous lights. Instead of playing loud dance music, Sine displays its sophisticated side with a chorus of classical music gliding through the atmosphere. The décor is white and black furnishing.

Mayhem strides straight to the bar. I follow him like a lost puppy. Why am I so intrigued with what he has to say?

"What would you like?" The bartender is all over Mayhem like a moth to the flame. He is a big, bald man wearing a white T-shirt that is a little too tight for his body frame. I wonder indolently if he is gay. The gaze he has on Mayhem is suspicious enough.

"Cognac and tonic on ice," Mayhem orders with authority. He doesn't look at me, but implies to the waiter that I am with him.

"And for the lady?" The bartender peels away from Mayhem long enough to acknowledge me.

"Water," I mumble.

"Water?" Mayhem inclines his head toward me. He lifts an eyebrow. I don't know if he is interested or curious at my choice. "Just so you know, I can afford to buy you a drink."

I grimace at his arrogance. "I don't drink during the day."

Mayhem's face darkens shortly, becoming more angular. He holds his tongue as he settles with grace onto the barstool. Very few people in the world have his refinement, yet Mayhem chooses to be a gang lord. I think about the irony for a second.

"Your drinks are on the house." The bartender smiles brightly at Mayhem before making a hasty retreat.

"I think he likes you." I am bold and unforgettable.

"I have that effect on men and women," comes the conceited and shallow response only a gang lord is capable of.

I have the irresistible urge to stick my tongue out at Mayhem. He brings out strange impulses in me. It is bad enough that my head is swimming with thoughts about what Mayhem wants to talk about. Coolly, I slump back on the stool with hunched shoulders. I feel like I am fraternizing with the enemy. The alarming thing is I am not sure that I am. A compelling notion tells me I should confess to Mayhem. I want to tell him that Choi Sangwoo confirmed the truth about shooting his brother. But I am not sure I want to open up that can of worms. I am sure there are probably other misconceptions about him. I am not ready to find out just yet.

"How long has my uncle and Eunhye known each other?" His question grounds me back to reality.

I look back to see the remarkable gang lord gazing at me. Mayhem has his head cocked to the side as he surveys my facial expression. It takes my breath away. *You're so damn handsome,* my intuition swoons. She doesn't care about his profession or mercurial personality. All my intuition cares about is Mayhem's features and appealing presence. He makes her squirm.

"They are childhood friends," I answer him simply. Slightly surprised that he doesn't know this, I want to ask Mayhem but hold my tongue.

"Eunhye is not your biological mother," Mayhem concludes the obvious. "I met your half-sister years ago. It must have been before you came into the family." The reason behind Mayhem's question comes to light. When he notices my facial expression, Mayhem states, "You don't like talking about your family."

"I don't like talking about my family with you," I correct him. The animosity is unattractive, so I add, "There's nothing to talk about anyway."

"You're sad," Mayhem states. "You're an innocent, sad, lonely girl."

"I would like to think about myself as being content and choosing to be a loner, thank you very much," I refute.

"What about the innocent part?"

"I have an edge to me."

The corners of Mayhem's lips curl in amusement. "And what kind of edge are we talking about?"

"I go out . . . clubbing, like you saw that night." *Yeah, very hardcore May.*

"Yeah, you're a badass." Mayhem rolls his eyes in the way that only hot and attractive gang lords do. *No, only the way Mayhem does.* My intuition corrects me.

Suddenly, I feel uncomfortable and exposed. "What do you want to talk to me about? The last time I checked, I don't owe you any more money."

A sly smile twists across his lips. Mayhem muses at my frank approach. "You think all I care about is money."

"Don't you?"

"Well, being one of the richest gang lord's in the world certainly doesn't make me casual about monetary funds."

I am speechless about the size of his ego. Before I can make a comeback, Mayhem continues, "From the shocked look on your face, you didn't expect that I bought The Trax or had any ties to it."

Of course. I've never seen you step foot inside of it. "Your point, please." I am tongue and cheek. If I want to keep this stone façade going, I have to let every single Mayhem charm bounce back as soon as it hits me. I square my shoulders and hunch forward. "Actually, I'm surprised that someone like you with all the money in the world would spend it on such a small venue to uphold your master-of-the-universe plan." I make it a point to stress the last word.

Light dances in those dark eyes of his. "My master-of-the-universe plan hardly has anything to do with venue investment. It actually has to do with collecting little shrewd girls like you and whipping you into shape."

Shit. Did he really say that? My jaw drops into my stomach, but I hold my ground.

"Your drinks." The bartender is back. He places Mayhem's carefully concocted drink in front of him before my glass of water.

"Can I have a Gin and Tonic over ice too, please?" I need alcohol if I want to keep up with this gang lord. Who cares that I am barely getting over my sickness.

The bartender flashes Mayhem a look as he waits for approval. After Mayhem's quick nod, the bartender scurries back to the bar.

Mayhem takes a drink from his glass. He watches me, and the feeling deep inside my stomach rumbles. I think Mayhem's mouth moves in amusement. His eyes shimmer in the oddest way.

"Is this how you chase after girls?" I'm subjective and curious about him. What does he mean whipping girls like me into shape? Is he some kind of sadomasochist or into some handcuffs, chains, and whips lifestyle? Gang lords must have illegal preferences just like their lifestyles.

Mayhem's contemplative look says it all. "First of all, I don't chase after girls. Second, I'm not a girlfriend or wife kind of guy. When I mean whipping little girls like you into shape, I am not going to elaborate. I will let your imagination take you where it needs to go."

My eyes enlarge without subtlety. I don't hide the surprise I am experiencing. Mayhem really is too bold for his own good.

"The reason why you are here, sitting with me, is I am going to offer you a job. I will be opening up a store in place of that poor excuse. I need waitresses for the restaurant section."

Mayhem is offering me a job? What is going on with these gang lords going after me for my service?

"I'm not interested." *Wow.* I feel powerful turning down the King.

"Your drink." The bartender is back. He settles a moon glass in front of me and quickly disappears.

Mayhem waits as I take my first sip of the alcohol. The cool drink refreshes my dry throat. The taste, however, reminds me of that night at Club Groove. Throwing up will probably be more embarrassing in front of Mayhem himself.

"I figured you wouldn't know how to grasp an opportunity when it is served on a silver platter to you." Meanwhile, Mayhem casually finishes his drink. He waves the bartender over. In a matter of seconds, the bartender produces a replacement drink.

"I don't want an opportunity from someone like you," comes my shrewd reply. To prove my point, I take another mouthful of my drink. Instant courage is what alcohol offers. "You gang lords have an astronomical complex mixture of jerk, control freak, and obsessive compulsive in you. I don't want anything to do with that." The pent-up annoyance is freely flowing through me.

A low, alluring chuckle escapes his lips. "Oh, someone is bitter." Mayhem's implied reference to Choi Sangwoo stirs something inside of me. He cocks his head to the side, leveling his penetrating gaze on me. "Played with a wolf and got bitten by his lies, didn't you?"

I swallow the anger that has absorbed. I don't want Mayhem to know that he is right, but then again I don't want to refute the truth. It is a double conundrum with this man. So I do the only thing I can; I finish off my drink. The momentary sting of the alcohol makes me forget it all.

Mayhem lets out a low chuckle as he observes me. Enjoying the fact that he is under my skin, Mayhem leans forward. His voice becomes husky as he asks me, "Let me guess, he promised you the whole world, but wants you to play by his rules only. You believed until you found out that his true interest in you is based on fabrication."

There is a knot in my throat. I don't know how long I can handle this type of scrutiny. Gang lord and mind reader?

"I warned you about him, didn't I?" There is a drawl to his voice. If I didn't know better, I would think Mayhem actually cares.

"I didn't come here for you to tell me what I did wrong," I hiss with disapproval. Who does he think he is?

"Then why are you here?" Mayhem asks softly.

Oh shit. My breath is stuck in my throat. *He's giving me that panties-off look!* My intuition doesn't know what to do. I finally squeak, "For the free alcohol."

"Of course." He finds me hilarious. Casually, Mayhem takes another sip of his drink. He motions to the bartender. "Another round of Gin and Tonic." Mayhem's voice is domineering. "Let me give you some advice. When a gang lord pursues you, you should always be careful of his ulterior motive. When gang lord two warns you about gang lord one, you should think twice before walking away from gang lord one. I'm not telling you what you did wrong. I'm doing you a favor by giving you a forewarning about the world you are walking into."

My heart slams into my ribcage. What world am I walking into? "What are you talking about?"

Mayhem replies tersely, "A world where money powers morals, lies strike fear, and the pursuit of happiness is based on individual revolutions." Mayhem leans forward, closing the gap between the two of us. "Everything that you think gangsters represent, and what our world encompasses, is the direct result of social media fabrications. Choi Sangwoo has sugarcoated everything he's shown you. I am talking about a world so dark and overbearing that even fallen government and ex-army shrivel up in fear and choose suicide rather than face the likes of me."

He is just trying to freak you out May. Don't let him. "Why?" I sound like a mouse with her tail trapped.

Mayhem leans on his stool. The corners of his lips curl into that smile again. "Your ignorance protects you from fear."

"I'm not afraid of you." I am not about to be bullied.

Mayhem acknowledges my bold comment. "Good. Don't be. I'm only one of many. If anything, I'm the dark Angel you'll be calling on when this world comes for you."

"No one's coming for me," I reply.

Mayhem scowls. "Let me just tell you this. When someone betrays me, I prefer to hold the gun to their heads. When someone betrays Choi Sangwoo, like the coward that he is, he stabs you in the back. So, you don't know how he does it or where he does it. I think you are forgetting that when someone comes for you, there's nothing you can do to stop them. All you can do is defend yourself."

All the research I've done on gangsters and the underground world appears to be useless now. I am petrified of what reality brings. Mayhem is not making the situation any better.

Mayhem studies the look on my face. "You have no idea, do you?"

I swallow hard. Fear slowly seeps into my bones. I don't even notice that the bartender already has our third round of drinks. With haste, I drink the remains of my second glass.

Mayhem smiles without teeth as he watches me.

"YOU REALLY ARE ONE OF a kind. What zoo did you escape from, and are you planning to go back?" I ask, slurring my words. We are on our sixth, seventh, or eighth round of drinks–I don't remember. The colors of the bar are dancing in front of my eyes. All this talk about the deep and dark underground world has gotten me faded. I am no longer feeling stressed, fear, or anxiety. I am just a bubble of happiness bantering with this hot gang lord who is reminding me every minute I am out of my element with him.

"You have a strange sense of humor," states Yoon Jaewon–as my drunken state prefers to call him as. My intuition adores his name as well. "May I remind you who you are talking to?"

I let out a laugh. I lean against him; he is all rock body and muscularly defined. "You think I'm afraid of you, but I'm not. I know who your uncle is. You're not as intimidating as they say you are."

"Then why did you run from me that night?" Jaewon smiles crookedly at me. He's got me right where he wants me to be.

I frown at him. The memory of meeting Jaewon at my apartment unravels. "Because you said, 'there's nothing more valuable in a person than their ignorance' and I took offense to that."

Jaewon's eyes harden. "Then what makes a person valuable?"

I scrunch up my nose. "Their heart."

Jaewon scoffs. He looks away, shaking his head at me, clearly amused by my innocent answer. "You're so legal it's humbling."

I gape at him. "And you're so cruel."

"You really have no clue, do you?" Jaewon's voice is steady and taut. "I'm supposed to?"

"You need a good dose of fear."

I feel a thrill shoot down my spine. "You really do look down on us little people." I marvel at the gigantic size of his ego.

The light in his dark and attractive eyes thins. "Once you experience the world the way I have, it's hard to understand and relate to things like college and a nine-to-five job."

I shake my head at Jaewon, letting out a disbelieving laugh. "I can't believe this. Your ego is suffocating. College and a nine-to-five job is how we regular people live. You wouldn't know what to do if your power was stripped away from you. I bet you don't even know how to be poor."

Jaewon's calm and collected look suits his impressionable features. "I don't. I inherited my throne." The alcohol slurs in his tone.

What? I gawk at Jaewon. Our banter comes to standstill. The alarming truth knocks my alcoholic state down another notch. At this point, I have to keep drinking or I will snap back into sobriety–vomit and all.

"You inherited your gang lord position? Your throne?" I ask him meekly. *Choi Sangwoo said you worked your way up.*

Realization causes Jaewon to look down at the granite bar top with a chuckle. Jaewon's stunning profile disarms me. "Let me guess, Choi Sangwoo said he was the one blessed-in. He also told you I shot his brother. He said I'm blah blah blah."

I squirm on the bar stool, slightly uncomfortable as I realize the height of Sangwoo's lies.

"Everything is the other way, sweetie. I was blessed-in the gang after my father was killed. My uncle, Mr. Im to you, took me in and sent me to America in hopes of keeping me away from my father's business. Instead of following my uncle's instructions, I followed my father's footsteps anyway. Long story short, Choi Sangwoo was ordered by his Boss to kill me as his initiation requirement. Being the idiot that he is, Sangwoo mistook my younger brother for me, and you get the gist of the history."

I blink uncontrollably, swallowing hard. I am numb and astounded. Without thinking, I wave to the bartender again.

"*I* THINK YOU SHOULD STOP drinking." Yoon Jaewon reaches for my glass, officially separating me from my companion. He's nursing a black cup of coffee now.

"I'm fine. Last one." I hold a finger to my lips. Breaking into a large smile, I start to giggle. "I'm really drunk." *More like beyond intoxicated. Don't be so sloppy.* My intuition has that motherly nag going on.

"You act like you've been locked in a cage and only now do you get to run." Jaewon's voice barely registers over the ringing in my ears.

"You have no idea," I slur as my eyes droop. I can hardly keep them open. "How can you? You're a dark, tall, handsome, and attractive gang lord with issues. How can you possibly understand someone like me?"

"You think I'm dark, tall, handsome, and attractive?" Deep humor travels in Jaewon's response. His expression is unsurprising and just as haughty.

"No." I shake my head. "Nope. No. Never."

Jaewon laughs. He throws his head back and laughs freely. I never knew he had such a straight, bright white smile.

"WHATEVER, GET OFF MY PLANET," I mumble. The lights behind the bar are starting to appear as hanging rainbow icicles. I am beyond intoxicated. I don't know what we are bickering about. In fact, I don't know how long we've been here. Many things were said, including facial features being compared to zoo animals.

"And what planet would that be?" How can Jaewon make this strange banter so interesting?

"This one." I point to my drink's murky liquid.

Mayhem leans in. He smells yummy–a dangerous concoction night, charm, and allure. "You're right. I see planet Mayhem."

Why is he so full of himself? "You know, I'm half expecting you to introduce yourselves to me."

"Well, there's me and then there's myself, and then there's I," Jaewon replies with a snicker.

"Wow. And explain to me how do you live with yourselves?" I ask with a fresh, entertained grin.

"I have people who tend to my every needs." There goes that King complex again.

"Wow. And where are they?" I point around the bar, showing Mayhem that he is here alone. "If you're so popular, why are you sitting here on a Wednesday afternoon getting drunk with me?"

"Because I am a businessman and right now, there's a deal Mayhem wants to close with you." *Oh em gee.* Jaewon's eyes smolder in that hot way as he watches me. By now, my eyes are seeing stars dance around him. His lips are moving, but I cannot hear him. *Snap out of it May!*

Jaewon's voice comes back into my ears. "It is better to have people know you than to be nameless until your very last breath," Jaewon offers his perceptive advice. He points to himself. "I am Mayhem. You are–" he pauses. His eyebrows come together in question. Realization dawns on me that Jaewon has no idea who I am.

I gape at him, pausing in my drunken world. "You don't know my name?"

"How am I supposed to remember? You don't matter," Jaewon answers casually with a fresh boyish smile on his lips.

"You're kidding." I'm hurt in a strange way. In my alcoholic state, I feel neglected and rejected.

"Everyone knows my name. I don't need to know theirs."

"Guess Yoon Jaewon. I am sure in your drunken state, you can recall something."

"Don't say my name."

"I think I'm allowed to since you don't know mine."

"You can leave now." His jaw clenches together. How does he get the galls to be mad at me when he's the one who doesn't know my name? Besides, what's so special about his birth name that I can't say? Mercurial gang lord.

"Fine. I'm leaving." I don't have to put up with this shit. Why should I talk to someone who doesn't even remember my name? I deserve better than this. I get up too quickly and end up tripping on my . . . feet? "Shit!"

Mayhem catches me seconds away from eating the floor. I lock eyes with him once again. *God, he really is good-looking.* I am a mix bag of emotions as I look at him. "Thank you," I mumble. I break out of Jaewon's hold and head for the entrance dramatically.

The wind hits my hot skin as I run from the bar. The air smells humid, but the fresh air feels refreshing. There are dark clouds hanging above, a clear indication that summer rain is imminent. I continue my gait down the desolate streets. I make my way back towards The Trax's direction to the bus stop.

With alcohol in my system, I am fearless. I spin around to see if the infamous Mayhem has followed me, but he is nowhere in sight. All the streetlights blend and I stumble again. Maybe I really am breeching the fine line between drunk and blackout. I cannot hear my intuition anymore. Where's that crazy girl when I need her? I need to figure out how to get home fast.

"Hey!"

"Shit!"

Just as I turn again, Yoon Jaewon coalesces in front me like a ghost. Where did he come from? He didn't run after me when I left the club. *Or did he?* My conscience surfaces with a scarf covering the bottom half of her face.

I look at Jaewon as he looms over me. "Come on. I'll take you home." He's completely sober, I think.

"No, thank you. I can take care of myself." Why is he trying to be such a gentleman?

"You either let me take you home or I will carry you," he threatens me quickly. The firmness in Jaewon's voice is indicative of his persona.

Surprise grips me. Talk about bossiness. Before I can respond, Jaewon's shoulders hunch over the lower half of my body and he lifts me off the ground.

"What are you doing?!" I squeal as my feet dangle.

Jaewon lets out a rare, genuine laugh. Through blurry eyes, I like the gentle crease his mouth forms just before his perfect white teeth reveal themselves; his dark eyes finally light up like gems. Even though I am drunk, my attraction for him spikes tenfold. Regardless of his infamous reputation, there is a truth to Yoon Jaewon. Behind the mystifying exterior and rampant misconceptions, an intriguing man exists at the core.

"I know I'm beautiful, but could you please stop looking at me like that," he says, bringing me back into reality. Jaewon sets me back down on the ground.

"You're so full of yourself!" I stick my tongue out at him. Somehow being drunk justifies it. I feel free and silly, caught up in the moment. "You are a terrible flirt."

"I'm not flirting with you. You are not immune to my charms. You're blushing even in the dark." Slowly, Jaewon draws himself to me and wraps an arm over my shoulder. I try to push away his sudden need to be my best friend, but Jaewon has his hand firmly around me. He is forward and pushy, daring and attractive. A thrill shoots through my entire being.

There is something wanton about him. The effect Yoon Jaewon has on me is telling; it all comes naturally with him. With Choi Sangwoo, everything was forced and formal. With Yoon Jaewon, the emotions ringing inside of me are different. Alcohol really is the miracle substance.

"So you're telling me pickup lines don't work on you?"

"What lines are you talking about?"

Jaewon leans in close. His voice becomes husky and intoxicating with temptation. "So, you want to go back to my place?"

I smirk, rolling my eyes in the dark. "I don't know. Can two people fit in a box?"

"Yes. The box I live in is equivalent to twenty thousand square feet, actually." The gang lord's ego comes into play. "So you can join me in the dream. I always thought you existed in the dreams for a reason."

What is he talking about? "And I always thought you existed in my nightmares. I guess we're both wrong."

Jaewon's lips curl into a bemused smile. "You're right, you're not much of a flirt."

"Gang lords aren't my type," I snap smartly.

Jaewon cocks his head to the side. "Well, we'll have to change that." He continues walking.

Ohhhh. My intuition swoons. I am speechless at his self-confidence and worship. All I can do is follow Jaewon like a lost puppy. The alcohol continues to dance in my head.

We walk down the dark street, eventually crossing the end of the strip back to The Trax. The cool night air caresses my face, propelling the alcohol in my system. I should be afraid of him, but I feel protected instead. His presence sends sparks through my veins.

"If you think you can take advantage of me because I'm drunk, think again." I find myself making a stand.

Jaewon leans in real close, so close that I can smell that distinctive cologne of his. His voice becomes husky and tantalizing. "I can't take advantage of you unless you don't want me to."

What? Really? Instinctively, I reach out to touch him. I don't have a plan, but I do it because I want to make sure he is real.

Even in his intoxicated state, Jaewon sees my attempt five seconds faster. He quickly removes his arm from me. *Oh, the King doesn't like to be touched?* Jaewon frowns and we lock in another stare.

Suddenly, the air coalesces around us and the rain begins to pour overhead. Massive droplets bombard us, hitting the cold ground at thundering speed. I feel as though we are being attacked.

"Shit!"

"No!"

Jaewon and I throw hands above our heads and run under the overhang of The Trax. The construction site is down for the night; the entire area is isolated. In the darkness and shattering racket of the rain, Jaewon pulls out the keys to the building from his vest. When the doors open, Jaewon leads the way. Once inside, we follow the side wall of the building to the main vacant area.

Jaewon tosses the keys on what's left of the old bar. He takes off his Executive jacket to reveal a black linen shirt. His hair remains matted against his chiseled facial structure—highlighting his dark, shimmering eyes. His black linen shirt is damp, but Jaewon disregards it for now. The gang lord scans the empty room and spots an assortment of different colored spray bottles in front of an empty wall.

"That's illegal!" I hiss when Jaewon takes two black and red spray bottle, shakes them up in each hand, and squirts the wall. I forget that I am also wet from the rain. I am too caught up in the moment.

"Don't worry. I own the building, literally." Jaewon steps back and begins to work.

I am entertained, amused, and afraid all at the same time. I can only watch him. He's an artist too? Gang lord, mind reader, and artist. Jaewon continues to spray the wall at arm's length. With great dexterity, Jaewon is aiming the bottles at an angle intricate loops and spirals. Mesmerized, I watch Jaewon's blazing concentration. He's perfect just like this.

Damn May, you are drunk! My conscience's cheeks are red too.

"Mayhem," I mumble when Yoon Jaewon steps back from his work. Right in the middle of the wall, in large black and yellow colors is the word *MAYHEM*. The font is italicized and bold with obscure coils and rings.

"That looks good," I say breathlessly as my eyes jump excitedly to take in the color and texture. My pupils dilate because of my excessive alcohol intake. This is the most artistic thing I have ever seen in person. What Jaewon created is what abstract artists do—a graphic voice that resonates through the creative font.

Jaewon smirks as he looks over his shoulder at me. He's not modest at all. Jaewon gestures at one of the spray bottles. "Your turn."

"I can't." I back away, shaking my head.

"Alright, I'll write your name for you," Jaewon offers. This gang lord is not the type to beg. Jaewon raises his hand to the wall, but asks shortly, "Uh . . . What is it?"

"You really don't know my name?" I gape at Jaewon. I thought he was just being a jerk at the bar, but I guess his bluff is really the truth.

Jaewon stares at me, perhaps knowing I am hurt. "It-it has something to do with the month right? Um . . . April."

He's got to be kidding me. April? "If you're known for the fear you strike in people, I am sure you can remember my name."

"April is more suiting for you." Like the nuisance that he is, Jaewon proceeds to add to the tagging of his own name.

"What are you writing?" I walk closer to him. "April loves Black Coffee," I read when Jaewon's done with the tagging.

That's some crazy stuff. My intuition is gaping at the majestic art in front of her. *This guy's spontaneous, creative, artistic, dangerous, hot, and everything else under the sun.*

"My name isn't April."

"It is now." The silent room rings with his laughter. It is so unlike the

Mayhem I am used to seeing that I take it all with humor. His laugh is . . . nice. It is smooth and just deep enough to please the ears. *Oh, the miracle of alcohol.* I am April and he has paired me with his affinity for black coffee. *Well, you do drink a shit ton of coffee too.* My intuition parades the tagging with a dramatic walk.

"Hey, you're the freak who likes black coffee so you should be writing Mayhem love black coffee." I turn to rebuke Jaewon for his crass humor, but my eyes nearly jump out of their sockets.

He's taking off his shirt. Mayhem—Yoon Jaewon—is taking off his wet black linen shirt.

The bands of muscles wrap around his incredibly disciplined body. Yoon Jaewon is extremely fit, a direct reflection of a remarkable workout regimen. I don't have enough seconds to count how many abs his stomach packs, but on his tan body the muscles make their marks. He has incredibly broad sculpted shoulders that lead to chiseled arms and biceps. Jaewon's stamina for speed, sweat, and pain must know no bounds according to his physique. There are tattoos on his back, but Yoon Jaewon keeps them hidden with his body angle.

"You were saying?" Jaewon holds his wet shirt casually.

"Put your shirt on." I turn my back towards him.

I can hear the smile in his voice. "From the look on your face, I take it you've never seen the male physique."

"I've seen plenty and better." I am lying through my teeth.

"I'm sure April."

"My name is not April."

I wait for his smart response, but his silence compels me to turn around.

"Hello?" Jaewon has abandoned our conversation. His cell phone is against his ear. "I'm at the new site. When it stops raining. One second."

Alas, I am reminded that Yoon Jaewon isn't just a simple man who can spare an excess amount of time. He is, after all, Mayhem and gang lord to the masses. *His profession will always be his wife.* My intuition reminds me of Grace's words.

Yoon Jaewon faces me, wary that I am listening to his important conversation. "It's raining pretty hard. We'll leave when it stops. Make yourself at home."

"I want to leave now," I tell him. "I—"

"Shh." Jaewon places a finger on my lips. Everything stops for the moment. To Jaewon, it is a simple motion to shut me up, but it does more than shut me up. My heart skips several beats when his finger slides from my bottom lip to my chin and then away.

Without another word to me, Jaewon addresses his phone. "Danny." Just like that, Jaewon reverts to the cold and distant Mayhem. He leaves the room hastily, eager to finish his conversation. I hear Jaewon's faint footsteps down the hallway.

Oh em gee. Did he really just put his finger against my mouth? A thrill shoots through me for some reason. A part of me is now comforted–Jaewon is not the murderer Choi Sangwoo made him out to be. He is not as cold as his reputation makes him to be, but Yoon Jaewon is mercurial and unpredictable. *He made me laugh tonight; he's like a pain eraser.* The thoughts swim in my head. *He's far from a pain eraser and you know it! More like a pleasure bringer,* my intuition snickers.

Drunk and exhausted, I sit against the wall and close my eyes. I am well aware that I am resting under the tagging of *APRIL LOVES BLACK COFFEE* . . . . I drift off into sleep wondering why Mayhem is so obsessed with black coffee and when will he come back . . . .

*H*MM. THAT FEELS REALLY NICE. "Five minutes." I hear him say through my heavy slumber. His hands cup the side of my face gently, guiding my head onto his comfortable and sturdy shoulders. Yoon Jaewon wraps something heavy around my body and the cold disappears. "Sleep," he tells me. *I like him. I really like him.*

A VOICE STARTLES ME AWAKE.

"Wake up. Wake up."

I open my eyes to see figures slowly forming together. Bubbles of light and streaks of color come together. *Shit. Where am I?* It takes my memory a couple of seconds to form. Every inch of my body aches. My head pounds like a hammer. My limbs feel numb.

I move to see Yoon Jaewon stirring besides me. His large, Executive black vest falls off me. I have no recollection of even sleeping next to Jaewon, but here I am lifting my head off his sturdy shoulders. The early morning look really does suit him. The rain has stopped and the large, main room is cool. We fell asleep on the floor like homeless people right underneath the *APRIL LOVES BLACK COFFEE* tagging.

"May," he calls my name.

I blink several more times to realize that it's not Jaewon calling my name. It is a figure standing a couple of feet away from me. He is angry and impatient for my consciousness to return.

When I realize who he is, I scramble to my feet. "Sangwoo," I say barely above a whisper. *Stalker!* My intuition releases Jaewon from her hold.

Choi Sangwoo's brown eyes are dark and hooded. Ren stands behind Sangwoo with the same marred facial expression. "May. What are you doing here with him?" Sangwoo's voice is horrified and angry. He's dressed in a gray suit with the front buttons undone; the dark dress shoes he's wearing contrasts invariably with his ensemble.

What is he doing here? How did he get into the building? I feel my breath leaving my senses behind. "Sangwoo," is all I can muster up. I haven't done anything wrong, so why does he make me feel so guilty?

From beside me, Yoon Jaewon stands up. He lets out a yawn and casually stretches. Thank goodness Jaewon has his shirt on. I vaguely remember him taking it off last night. At the moment Jaewon narrows his dark eyes at Sangwoo as he seethes with antagonism and disapproval.

"Breaking and entering is not something I take lightly Sangwoo." Jaewon drapes an arm around me and pulls me close.

What is he doing? My intuition is giddy as soon as Jaewon touches her.

Anger flashes in Sangwoo's eyes. "So this is what you do now, Jaewon? You steal my assets and treat them like trash on the streets?" Sangwoo sneers at him. There is a no-holds bar to his attack.

Jaewon stiffens at Sangwoo's remark. "She is not your asset or property to own. And what I choose to do with my potential member is up to me."

Potential member? Oh no, if this is Jaewon's plan to thwart Sangwoo's intentions with me I am beyond screwed.

Sangwoo doesn't entertain Jaewon's comment. He steps forward without regard. Jaewon slips a hand into his back pocket. A gun? How has Jaewon managed to hide a gun from me all this time?

Sangwoo stops all movement. His light brown eyes rove over to me. "May, are you okay?"

Jaewon bites his lower lip in anger. I can tell he doesn't like being ignored. "Of course she's okay. She's with me."

"That's my concern," Sangwoo snaps. "I never touched any of your girls, why are you all over mine?"

"Yours?" Jaewon and I retort in unison. At least I am on track with one of the gang lord's.

This is unbelievable. Choi Sangwoo continues to consider me

buyable property. I am wary that Jaewon still has his arms around me.

"She's not your girl," Jaewon replies with a firm tone. "She's my girl."

"Your girl?" Sangwoo sneers with great disdain. Sangwoo is riveting in his presence; the scorn across his face reflects a dangerous and dishonest man. A man who will tear, rip, and destroy others' lives to get what he wants.

"You have nothing to claim her. She's not an asset or a bitch we can fight about," Jaewon presses on, obviously not intimidated. As though this is a casual confrontation Jaewon continues in that signature unruffled demeanor.

I have the sudden urge to kick Jaewon in the shins. Who does he think he is to call me that? I don't like being claimed as anybody's girl nor will I ever like being labeled as someone's bitch. But in a twisted way, I understand what Jaewon is doing. He enjoys pushing people's buttons, and he's working overtime on Sangwoo's. Jaewon doesn't mind getting into a fight with Sangwoo, just as long as physical combat is involved.

"I'm going to pretend," Sangwoo replies through gritted teeth, "that I didn't hear that. Stay away from her. Come May."

I stay rooted to my spot. I am hungover and sick. I want nothing to do with Sangwoo–especially since learning the truth about Misun and the lies about Jaewon. Sangwoo probably lied about the death of Son's cousin too.

"No." My voice is a strained whisper. My gaze renders him helpless. "I'm nobody's girl. I don't belong to any of you. I'm my own person." I've officially snapped. There is so much more I want to say to Sangwoo, but I am too emotional right now. I am not in the right mind state.

Jaewon's lips purse together in an I-told-you-so fashion at Sangwoo. The hurt that comes across Sangwoo's face is difficult for me to watch.

"May, I didn't mean it that way. You know where your loyalties are. Come to me." Sangwoo extends his hand. He remains persistent.

Loyalties? Is that what he is about? "No. Sangwoo, I'm not going with you. We . . . we ended it, remember?"

"No!" Sangwoo snaps, causing me to jump. He closes his eyes, anguish spreading across his face. When he opens them, those light brown eyes of his plead with me.

"No, May. Let's talk about this privately."

"Sangwoo–"

"Listen to me!"

"Let the lady speak, Sangwoo." Jaewon shifts slightly. He reaches into his pocket and extracts a pack of cigarettes. I watch in disgust as Jaewon places it in his mouth and magically summons a lighter. Jaewon inhales deeply and soon a cloud of smoke surrounds us. I want to take the cigarette and jam it down his throat. I don't appreciate the cloud of cancer. *We're going to have to work on this nasty habit of his.* My intuition is willing to for life.

Sangwoo's jaw clenches. At the same moment, he holds up a hand to stop Ren who makes a movement to advance towards Jaewon.

Sangwoo's eyes dart from Jaewon to me. "How long have you been talking to him? You two are friends now? How could you do this to me?" Sangwoo demands; his voice no longer controlled. "You're supposed to be mine."

It is the gang leader complex. He wants instant gratification. "Sangwoo, I'm not property you can own. How many times do I have to say it? I can be friends with anyone I want." I look at Jaewon too. "I'm not doing anything to you Sangwoo. This is not a betrayal because I was never yours."

"Then why are you with him?!" Sangwoo shouts, pointing at Jaewon as though he is the shred of evidence. "You know what he's done to me."

"He's done nothing to you." My eyebrows come together. "Other than gang-related things, he's done nothing personal to you. You're the liar. You didn't inherit any throne. You're the one who killed, maimed, and robbed for your position. Mayhem inherited his position. You killed his brother, not the other way around. You're just like Misun. You twist and lie about everything!" The truth comes pouring out of my mouth.

Jaewon scoffs beside me, clearly amused at the unfolding of events. "Tell him, April." He continues to inhale his cancer stick.

I shoot him a death glare. Surprisingly, Jaewon relents. Perhaps having a citizen argue with his rival puts Jaewon in a great mood. He shrugs and motions for me to continue. It is very unlike of the infamous Mayhem to concede.

Meanwhile, Sangwoo remains poker-faced. His eyes become guarded and dark, angry, and violent. "May, don't do this. Come to me." Sangwoo levels his voice.

Jaewon rolls his eyes back to Sangwoo. Lazily, Jaewon blows the cloud of smoke at Sangwoo. It is a pacified warning for Sangwoo to keep his persistence at bay.

The hurt in Sangwoo's eyes is taxing. I know exactly how he feels. He sincerely feels like I have betrayed him. Sangwoo is feeling as though I had gone behind his back to make alliances with his enemy. "Sangwoo, please. There's nothing else to talk about." I want this to all end.

Sangwoo ignores my request. "It's him, isn't it?" Light dawns on Sangwoo's eyes with his assumption. "If you're talking to him, why didn't you tell me? Why can't you be truthful?"

Truthful. The word stings me more than he'll ever know. "And you were so truthful when all along you pursued me because of Misun. You don't want me Sangwoo. You want someone who is long dead." All of a sudden, I turn into a weakling. I feel the tears welling up in my eyes. My heart is hurting inside my chest begging for some type of release.

Sangwoo takes another step forward. Suddenly, Jaewon steps in and closes the gap. Their height, physique, and danger rival one another. "I wouldn't come any closer Sangwoo." The humor is lost in Jaewon's demeanor.

"Step aside Jaewon," Sangwoo says through gritted teeth.

"You should learn how to handle rejection better," Jaewon states simply. "In our world, we're used to having things our way, but with Martyrs we use the hands-off policy remember?" Jaewon launches into gang jargon that shuns me from the conversation. "You don't want the Boss to hear about this."

Sangwoo ignores him with blatant disregard. "May, come with me." Sangwoo extends his hand again as if I am a child in need of guidance.

I shake my head at him. *No. I'm not going back to you. I'm not going to let you lie to me and hurt me anymore.*

"May, don't be stupid. You don't want to be on the other side of me. Be a good girl and listen to my words." Sangwoo unleashes the power of his contention. "Come."

"No," I tell him. I hold my stand. "Please, leave me alone." I am not a child. He cannot speak to me this way. I refuse to give into his obsession of Misun.

"Go Sangwoo. You are starting to become an itch no one wants," Jaewon says indolently.

Sangwoo steps back. The last breath exits sharply out of him. "Fine." Those mesmerizing, light brown eyes are now cold and unforgiving.

"If you do not stand next to me, then you will perish with the rest of them," Sangwoo speaks clearly to me, enunciating every syllable.

Then, he's gone.

I spin on a revolving axis, reeling from the emotions and fighting the impending tears. My feet stick to the ground and I cannot move.

Yoon Jaewon leans in from behind me. His masculine and protective physique envelops me. His voice is an alluring tone as he whispers, "Don't worry. I'm the dark Angel you summoned. If Choi Sangwoo declares war on you, I'm your first line of defense, April."

For the first time, as Yoon Jaewon lowers his eyes, I see kindness in them.

READ MORE IN THE
APRIL LOVES BLACK COFFEE SERIES
BY T.B. SOLANGEL

Book I: First Impressions

Book II: Last Conversations

Under the pseudonym Solangel, her other online stories include: Banana Pancakes, The Joy of Being Happy, The Ardors Series, and Love Bugged.

These stories will be published by T.B. Solangel.

Made in the USA
San Bernardino, CA
24 July 2014